The Troubled Mind Of
Mary Shelley

The Troubled Mind of Mary Shelley

Wendy L. Bardsley

Methuen

THE TROUBLED MIND OF
MARY SHELLEY

First published by Methuen in 2021

1

Methuen
Orchard House
Railway Street
Slingsby
York YO62 4AN

A CIP catalogue record for this book is available from
the British Library

ISBN: 978 0 413 77831 4

Typeset by SX Composing DTP, Rayleigh, Essex
Printed and bound in Great Britain by CPI Group (UK) Ltd, Croydon, CR0 4YY

www.methuen.co.uk

For those who hold themselves
together in times of despair.

Acknowledgements

Books I have found particularly helpful in discovering the life of Mary Shelley and which have helped me give voice to the characters in this novel are named below. I also thank friends and family who have encouraged me during difficult parts of the work (they know who they are). I am also grateful for the countless valuable portrayals and histories on the Internet of Mary's life and of the people she knew and loved. To have explored the creative intelligence of a woman who breached the rules of society, like her mother, Mary Wollstonecraft before her, and even ventured into writing about the supernatural through story when questions about life and the hereafter were on everyone's lips, has been deeply inspiring.

Frankenstein, Mary Shelley, Penguin Classics, August 2003, *The Diary of Dr. John William Polidori – 1816 – Relating to Byron, Shelley Etc.*, Giniger Press, January 2017, *Mary Shelley*, Miranda Seymour, Simon & Schuster UK, February 2018, *Romantic Outlaws: The Extraordinary Lives of Mary Wollstonecraft and Mary Shelley*, Charlotte Gordon, Windmill Books, February 2016, *Romanticism: An Anthology* (Blackwell Anthologies) Duncan Wu, August 2005, *Mary Shelley Collection: Frankenstein, The Last Man, Selected Tales & Stories*, Independently published, April, 2020, *Dracula*, Bram Stoker, Penguin Classics, September 2004, *Mary Shelley, A Biography*, Muriel Spark, Constable, 1988, *Death & The Maidens*, Janet Todd, Counterpoint, 2007, *The Vampyre and Other Tales of the Macabre*

(Oxford World's Classics) John Polidori (Author) Robert Morrison (Editor) & one more. *Byron, Life and Legend*, John Murray, October, 2014.

"Learn from me, if not by my precepts, at least by my example, how dangerous is the acquirement of knowledge, and how much happier that man is who believes his native town to be his world, than he who aspires to become greater than his nature will allow."

Frankenstein (1818)
by Mary Wollstonecraft Shelley

1

London 1814

Young Mary Godwin awoke with a start as the coach jolted and slowed. Through the open window, the familiar scent of spring breezed in from the fields. At last she was almost in London! Soon she would be in Somers Town. Here the birdsong was light and easy, not harsh and clamorous like the call of the gulls in Dundee. The last few months in Scotland had been frustrating, she had longed for something familiar; a tree, a house she knew, but mostly the voice of her father.

It was almost April, a warm and soft afternoon. She braced herself, struggling from a troublesome dream. Her dreams sometimes disturbed her, though she found them interesting too for were they not part of her own mysterious self, her imagination at liberty delivering stories of its own accord. The fact that she remembered them so well, made William Godwin, her father gaze at her with wonder. She should always make notes about her dreams, he said, for it was quite a gift and would help with her writing. Writing was one of her passions and her father would snap his fingers before her eyes if he found her lost in a daydream; she was always a dreamer. She had also made notes about whaling in Dundee, which intrigued him, and she intended to write about it properly once she was home. Men spent months sailing in cold Arctic waters and ships often sank or were lost in snowstorms and mists. She had often wondered how the captains disciplined their crew when confronted by icebergs, sharp as an army of swords and just as formidable.

The church bells of St Pancras chimed out the hour. It was 4 p.m. She wondered about her father's business, had the juvenile bookshop experienced much trade? And how was her half sister Fanny? There hadn't been many letters of late. Fanny was three years older, and according to their father an astute young woman with a wise head on her shoulders. Her placid temperament and flashes of insight charmed everyone who came to the house. As for herself, people said she was emotional and far too imaginative, which was probably true. But the fears and fantasies that haunted the mind and could terrify the soul – oh how she loved them! Was there really a God, she asked herself, a supreme being, a transcendental deity powerful and strange, as was often discussed at the Baxter's. It was such a wonderful idea. Did ghosts and demons actually exist; were there people with supernatural powers?

As the coach clattered on her mind flooded with questions. She longed to talk with Shelley. Had he visited Skinner Street lately? If he had, would he visit again? Percy Bysshe Shelley was clever and handsome and she knew he found her attractive. She was sixteen years old and full breasted, with a delicate powdery skin and what the Baxters called 'flaming hair'. Might Percy think her quite grown up since last they'd met? Her father liked Percy's company and claimed he was filled with enlightened ideas akin to his own. Percy would quote from her father's well-known book, *An Enquiry Concerning Political Justice*, a daring critique of the government urging ordinary people to think independently and not be led by their noses. It had impressed Shelley no end and Mary was proud of it. What could be more important than that people should think for themselves about how they should live? William Godwin, her father, was a distinguished literary figure and many learned people respected him. Shelley saw him as a leader, a warrior, a man who understood things and wrote about how life might be better. But she'd heard her father call Shelley an aristocratic young ass who still had a lot to learn.

She changed her position in the coach. It had been a long journey and her limbs were stiff. Regaining her place in her family back home wouldn't be easy. Her stepmother, Mary Jane, was difficult.

They were bound to have words. Well, she was Mary Wollstonecraft Godwin, shrewd and intelligent, and ever since early childhood wont to speak out, even amongst her father's guests who were often illustrious figures; she'd had a governess and a tutor and had studied from her father's library, always having him close at hand to help her. She wouldn't be ignored. And she wouldn't placate. Learning with her father had been one of her greatest joys. But she cringed on recalling the boarding school in Ramsgate where six months had felt more like a year, for the girl she would be and the girl they had struggled to form had fought within her, and according to how girls should develop in *A Vindication of the Rights of Woman*, her mother's celebrated book, she had absolutely wasted her time.

Just now though none of that mattered, her heart belonged here in Somers Town and she thrilled at closing on London! Her two year stay in Scotland with the Baxters, friends of her father, had been a deeply rewarding experience; they were clever and accomplished people and Dundee was a flourishing city; there, she had come to know the sea with its great expanse of water and dark resolute strength. But it wasn't only for the sake of her health that her father had sent her to Scotland. Oh no, she wasn't deceived in the least. There were bitter jealousies at the house in Skinner Street and Mary felt resentful that she did not feel particularly welcome in what had now become Mary Jane's home. Her own daughter, Claire, was constantly put on a pedestal. – She had been to a very good boarding school. – Her French was excellent. – "Tout le monde devrait parler francaism!" Mary sighed. Mary Jane would continue to set her up against Claire and there were bound to be the usual quarrels. But Mary knew she answered her father's questions quicker and more thoroughly than Claire did, and she was also brighter and prettier. But it hurt her dignity that her stepmother should treat her so high-handedly. A passage from her mother's book entered her mind

> "*It is time to effect a revolution in female manners – time to restore them their lost dignity – and make them, as a part of the human species, labour by reforming themselves to reform the world . . .*"

"Dignity"? – The word bothered her. Had women lost their dignity? If they had, how had it happened, and when? Did life take dignity from anyone who didn't have power – those with disabilities, the poor, the elderly, not just women, but all those people who could not fight for their rights? She thought of what she'd learned in the past 16 years of her life. She was well schooled in literature, history and the Bible; she'd learned some French and a little Latin and Greek, and she did not suffer boredom for she always had lots of ideas. She thought of how it had been at home in Somers Town, that little cosmos of thought and behaviour that had helped form her character. Oddly, she felt she didn't belong there now. Or she didn't belong in the house on Skinner Street. There was such disharmony in the household. Mary Jane was so competitive. Charles, her son, was three years older than Mary, and Claire was six months younger, they were both bold and confident, always praised and generally feted whilst Mary must suffer her stepmother's ire over mere trivialities. And what was the point? She would always be her father's favourite. Was she not his "pretty little Mary", the one true daughter of him and Mary Wollstonecraft whose portrait hung on the wall? She smiled to herself and relaxed. No matter how often Mary Jane scowled at the portrait, William Godwin ignored her.

She felt pensive. She had missed her dear Papa and her half sister Fanny. Though they had different fathers, they were both Mary Wollstonecraft's daughters and the bond was strong. Fanny though sometimes grew morose if they talked about their mother and the way Fanny's father, an American entrepreneur, had deserted her. Gilbert Imlay had seduced their mother in France at the time of the French revolution. Mary wondered how much Fanny remembered from the days of her childhood when she'd gone with their mother to search for a ship carrying silver for Imlay, a business venture he'd said, or that was the story, but the ship was never recovered and Imlay too had disappeared. William Godwin in London had fallen in love with their mother and in an extraordinary turn of fate, for her father had despised marriage, had married her thinking he had found an angel. He had then raised Fanny as his own, developing, it seemed, a strange fascination for the quiet and self-possessed girl.

Mary touched her long strong fingers. Did she have her mother's fingers? Might the shape of their fingers be the same? She would never have asked her father; her mother's name was rarely mentioned. But her father's heart was generous and open and his second wife had found her way in. Now they had a child of their own, little William Godwin, who was often hard work and could cause his mother to shriek with despair, though without doubt she adored him.

The coach turned a bend and sped down a hill, the horses slowing as the road levelled out. The place looked different, she thought. Somers Town was undergoing change. A new road had been built in the time of her mother as a bypass from London and her home was north of the toll road. They were building houses on the fields, the skyline was changing and the light embraced the land in ways she found unfamiliar. Somers Town was metamorphosing. Her few visits home in the last two years had been brief, and she had so much to tell them it was hard to keep up with her thinking. She'd have such conversations with Fanny! Claire and Mary Jane had little if any interest in what she'd been doing in Dundee and her stepbrother Charles more often than not sat reading. But her father and Fanny were always eager for news. Her father would ask what was happening up there, how it had changed, how the poor fared against the rich. Cities might differ greatly from each other in nature and mood, he said, especially if close to the sea. She had much to say about Dundee and might even make him laugh, or he might draw back in dismay. Sailors told tales about their cargoes, boxes holding bodies of the dead! She and the Baxter girls had cringed on hearing that but they had half wanted to believe it. Financially though Dundee, it seemed, was on the up. The wool industry there had prospered through the building of three storey mills and men had arrived in droves to find work. Her father would be glad about that. It was important to him that men could find work and he would want to know about their pay. Some days Mary had gone to the docks with her friends to talk to the sailors, asking them where their ships were headed and what they held in their cargoes, how long it took them to reach their destination and what hazards they might encounter. Their tales amazed her. Ships often carried treasure, which might easily be lost or stolen as had happened with Imlay's ship. Piracy was a constant menace and sailors were ready for anything.

She glanced at the bag at her feet. *"Letters Written during a Short Residence in Sweden, Norway, and Denmark"*, the wonderful account of her mother's travels, was safely packed away. That was a treasure in itself and she didn't dare lose it. Her mother had shown immense courage, travelling alone with her baby, and earlier when crossing the channel to see France in the time of revolution. France was now a Republic, but many had died for that. She recalled one of her mother's lonely passages

" . . . I dreaded the solitariness of my apartment, and wished for night to hide the starting tears, or to shed them on my pillow, and close my eyes on a world where I was destined to wander alone . . .'

How she would love to have embraced her in her sadness. But William Godwin had finally made her happy. Yes, he was a good man and Mary was proud to be his daughter. Her parents had understood each other and her mother had thrown aside her cares and started living.

Mary glanced at the elderly couple opposite. They had been on the road many hours but they hadn't had much to say and she herself had spent much of the time sleeping. She looked through the window. The day was cold, but this was London and not half as cold as Dundee. The afternoon light fell on the couple. The old woman's eyes glistened in the growing dusk. The elderly rarely rested when travelling in coaches, the roads were muddy and uneven and coaches might even turn over, a good coachman was a godsend and usually got something substantial to put in his pocket.

'Have we arrived?' the woman said sleepily.

'I think so,' said her husband, yawning. 'We're in London. But I think my legs have gone dead!'

'Oh, my dear,' she said, patting his thigh. 'Do stretch them out.'

'I think we die little by little,' he said wryly, 'until we are totally deceased. Yes, that is exactly what happens. Emmanuel Swedenborg knew all about that, you know. About being deceased, I mean. They say he could talk to the dead.'

'I cannot believe it,' Mary said quietly.

The elderly couple looked at her and waited.

'If only it were true,' Mary said hopefully. Emmanuel Swedenborg, an anatomist, had also been a scientist and philosopher, but he'd believed some extraordinary things. When she was at home she would visit her mother's grave in St Pancras churchyard and lay fresh flowers . . . Oh if only you could talk to the dead . . . 'There is no proof of it, you see,' she said softly.

'As a matter of fact, I don't believe it either,' said the woman with a laugh. She pushed on her gloves and feigned a shiver. 'Best not talk to the dead, even if you could. I can scarce put up with the living let alone the dead.'

'What a privilege though,' chuckled the man. 'Think of the things you would ask them.'

For a moment or two they were silent. Then the woman spoke again. 'They say he could talk to angels.' She turned to her husband. 'Emmanuel Swedenborg, I mean. Now what would you say to an angel, my dear, do tell me?' She smiled at Mary and Mary smiled back. Her mother had believed in angels and claimed she'd seen them in the woods as a child, but only the once. Why had she only seen them once? Did angels torment you so you only half believed in them, like half believing in love? To believe in anything fully was troubling; it sort of ate you away with its own energy. She believed fully in her love for her father though she feared its loss.

She thought again of Shelley. Percy Bysshe Shelley didn't fear anything, he questioned constantly and answered only to himself; he didn't fear demons and he didn't worship gods. And strangely he proclaimed he actually looked forward to dying and saw it as a kind of adventure. But what if it wasn't, what if it wasn't like anything at all, what if it was absolutely nothing. She would talk with him about that if she saw him. The new age of science craved certainty. Scientists were trying out new ideas constantly and the Baxter's dinner parties had buzzed with stirring conversations. "Body snatching" was a popular conversational topic and the practise had become ubiquitous. People both laughed and grimaced about it. She thought again about the tales she had heard from the sailors. Might it be true that they held dead bodies in their cargoes? In order to be licensed surgeons, medical students needed to do dissections, and acceptable cadavers were hard to come by so they were often stolen from graveyards or even from coffins. She'd heard some terrible tales and had built up gruesome fantasies of what might be happening. – *Men with torch lights and spades digging into graves to prise open coffins and drag out the fresh new dead.* Body snatching was a very lucrative business; there were those who would even commit murder to get what they wanted.

She scratched at her arm, it was itching insufferably today, perhaps the excitement of coming back home had caused it to blister. Her father would be disappointed that the Scottish air hadn't healed it. He'd thought she might benefit from the better air of Dundee, but the problem remained. She winced; the urge to scratch was compelling. What an awful burden it was, like the burden of living with Mary Jane and her children.

She bent her head and entered her darkest thoughts. She felt she had somehow killed her mother simply by being born. How ridiculous to think like that, but she could not help it. Until he'd married Mary Jane, her father had been a tortured soul. Life was at least more bearable for him now, but he rarely seemed happy. He had loved her mother as an absolute equal and it seemed the time they'd been together, even though brief had been bliss. Mary had basked in the pleasure of their sublime union and vowed she too would be equal to any man she met – even Percy! Ah, her beloved Shelley. He was twenty one years old and very learned, but she had seen the look in his eye that said he was listening when she talked. She talked and he heard. But was she not the daughter of Wollstonecraft and Godwin? Of course he would listen. She straightened and pulled down her sleeve, covering the weeping blisters. Would Mary Jane be unpleasant when she arrived? Most likely. If Shelley were there, Claire would be flirting and resent her having come home. But Shelley was *hers*, not Claire's, at least in her dreams. Shelley was a poet, a fantasist, and believed in free love, which made Claire childish and silly. He might love anyone he wished, he said, not just Harriet his wife. But the thought made Mary anxious. Her mother had believed in free love, or at lease she had tried to. In reality though emotions got in the way and her mother had succumbed at last to a life deemed respectable. London wasn't France and life could be miserable when your fellow creatures rejected you.

A familiar unpleasant feeling sped through her blood. Oh, the biography! If only her father hadn't written her mother's biography and exposed all her secrets, what pain it had caused him. Now everyone knew that her mother and Imlay had never been married and that Fanny was illegitimate, a "disgraceful business" in the eyes of London society. But her mother had braved the gossip. And Mary admired her father for having changed his mind about marriage whilst always having eschewed it. A change of mind could be a powerful gesture; emotions had several heads and might turn and go the other way. So she, Mary Godwin, had been born in wedlock and her mother needn't feel ashamed. It mattered little however, for Fate was master in the end. Her mother had died just weeks after giving birth, and she, Mary Godwin, had lived, a motherless child with a distraught and inconsolable father. – And her mother had died so horribly! She closed her eyes and tried not to think. Her wonderful mother lay dead beneath the gravestone in St Pancras churchyard and her father had married Mary Jane.

It was the year 1814. There was a whole big world out there, people living their lives across land and sea, talking in different languages, yielding themselves up to whatever force might seize them. The elderly woman opposite leant towards her. 'Does your father expect you?' she asked. 'You are young to be travelling alone, and you have come such a long way.'

'My father?' said Mary, surprised. 'He knows I am arriving today. Do you know him?' She waited.

'We are acquainted,' the woman said softly. 'I have sometimes bought books from the shop. His own work is excellent.' Her husband nodded in agreement.

'Yes, he's a very good writer.' Mary said quietly, with pride. Her father and Mary Jane had opened a bookshop, sadly however, he seemed to be always in debt and often borrowed money from Shelley. As the eldest son of Timothy Shelley and the grandson of Sir Bysshe, Percy would inherit a fortune eventually and could easily obtain credit, which he regularly did while promising a high rate of interest. Shelley admired her father and even saw it as a privilege to help pay his debts. She gathered together her bags.

'Are you getting out?' asked the man.

'Very shortly,' said Mary. 'I have a trunk; the coachman will reach it down.' She rubbed her eyes. 'I am finally waking up. I've been dreaming. I always dream when I'm travelling.'

The man laughed loudly, then quoted something from The Tempest, *'"We are such stuff as dreams are made on, and our little life is rounded with a sleep"'*

Mary smiled and her mind fixed on Caliban, half beast half man, tormented by fate because he could not look like his fellow creatures, torment indeed to be ugly and different like that. And she thought again of her mother, in gratitude for the gift of life. Hyacinths, bluebells and buttercups would be out by her grave. She must go there soon. The flowers would quiver and the crows would make loud grating caws, but not a sound would she hear from her mother. The silence of the dead was merciless. Last time she'd talked with Shelley, they'd discussed Luigi Galvani, the Italian physician, who'd carried out experiments with electricity and discovered an electric charge could make a dead frog's leg try to leap as if the thing were a living creature. Might it not prove dead tissue could be brought back to life, Shelley had said excitedly, was it not a marvellous discovery? The 1751 Murder Act in England had given the provision that "for better preventing the horrid crime of murder" the bodies of executed murderers might now be used for experiments and scientists had turned from experimenting on animals to experimenting on human corpses. Shelley had talked of it intensely. People watching experiments had trembled; some had even fainted at the sight of jerking arms and legs.

Mary had read that the ancient Egyptians had experimented too, suffering shocks from electric fish, fish that could not be caught but might cure an illness if touched. Was it possible? Was matter in truth animated by natural causes? Was science after all the real creator, not God?

2

41 Skinner Street

Two eager figures waited in the doorway at Skinner Street as the coach driver stopped by the house. 'Home and dry!' he shouted getting out of his seat and lifting down Mary's trunk. She got out her purse and paid for the journey adding a little extra which her father had said she should do, always grateful to have her back safely in Somers Town. The man slipped the coins in his pocket then climbed back into his seat. 'Everything in order then, Miss?' he shouted. The horses stirred ready.

'I think so,' said Mary. She laughed excitedly, thrilled to be home.

'Good!' called the coachman, 'Job done!' and with a quick lash of his whip the horses were away.

Fanny stepped out of the doorway, also laughing, as Mary emerged from the dusk. 'It's been too long!' she said, suddenly woeful. 'Here, give me your hat and umbrella. Dear Mary, how good it is to see you!'

'Indeed,' said William Godwin, stretching out his arms. 'My pretty little Mary is home!' He looked her up and down, smiling. 'Though not so little nowadays eh, how you have grown.' He chuckled as they went inside. 'Mary Jane is in the bookshop and young William is with Claire upstairs. Come; let us go to my study.'

'It's wonderful to be back, Papa,' said Mary. 'We had a very good driver and made excellent progress.'

She glanced about and her father looked at her knowingly as she straightened her strawberry blonde hair. 'Only the cook and the maid today,' he said raising his eyebrows playfully. 'No Shelley. Charles is still in Vienna teaching. He sends us letters.' He frowned thoughtfully. 'Mary Jane fusses as usual. But the fellow must stand on his own two feet, never mind worrying his mother.'

Mary looked at him curiously. So Charles was a 'fellow' now, no longer a 'lad'. Time moved on quickly.

'Shelley came to see us yesterday,' Fanny said quietly. 'He's coming again next week.' She glanced at Mary and smiled.

'Ah,' said Mary. Her eyes widened with interest. 'Don't let me miss him, will you.'

'Oh, it isn't just to see me,' said Godwin. 'He'll talk to you all. And he'll want us to hear his poetry.'

Claire called from upstairs. – 'Mary, you're here! I've been teaching William French, he learns so fast. 'Il est très intelligent!'

Claire's spirits were high. Shelley had visited with Harriet, his wife, but they hadn't stayed long. Claire too was smitten. Normally Percy would talk with her father alone in the study, but it seemed they'd all had a chance to talk together in the kitchen. Shelley liked talking in the kitchen. He would fold his arms and sit down, spreading out his long legs, then deliver them his latest poetry and whatever gossip was on offer. But he wouldn't miss out on an audience with her father, who he saw as something of a Socrates, a Plato, a man with immense wisdom. Her father would call Shelley an inflated young scholar, only just into his twenties and with questionable habits of behaviour, conceding though that he certainly had a brilliant mind. He was difficult and argumentative however, and the University of Oxford had ousted him for publishing a pamphlet on atheism. Shelley had been a mischief maker and had often found himself in trouble. At Eton he'd shown a deep interest in science and liked to experiment. There was talk of him having had a kind of electric machine which he'd used to charge the handle of the door to his room, much to the amusement of his colleagues who must always be careful of potential electric shocks. And he was said to have blown up a tree on Eton's South Meadow with gunpowder. He'd lost friends rather than made them due to his pranks and people kept out of his way. But no-one could doubt his cleverness and he had done some excellent writing. He had written a novel called *Zastrozzi* in which his fearless atheistic views were made plain and some excellent pieces of prose and poetry as well. And he'd also published his notorious pamphlet, *The Necessity of Atheism*, which had meant he must stand before officials at his college and be made to depart, distressing his parents and causing them acute embarrassment.

Now there was a rift between Shelley and his father which widened by the year. Unbeknown to her family, Mary had read the pamphlet at the Baxter's and had marvelled at Shelley's bravery. But he was certainly in the bad books now with his father; what's more, he'd eloped with young Harriet Westbrook, the 16 year old friend of his sister, and more than that he'd made her pregnant. He seemed to be causing chaos everywhere he went, William Godwin had concluded. But he'd married Harriet, which was only right and proper, though he was such a restless spirit it was doubtful he'd abide by his vows. On hearing the story Fanny had felt sorry for Shelley and maintained he always looked sad, whilst Claire just said he was "beautiful, simply beautiful". Mary kept her own counsel, but she experienced a strange sort of suffering whenever he entered her thoughts, a sort of painful longing that wouldn't go away.

Claire was elated and vivacious as ever as they all found seats in the study. 'We are to eat roast lamb for dinner,' she said blithely. 'And roast potatoes too, just as you like them, Mary, charmant et croustillant!' She giggled like a child. 'Did you eat any more of that bubbly-jock you talked about in your letter? Mama didn't know what it was.' She had to do some research. 'It's a turkey cock isn't it? A big sort of chicken I think.' She broke into laughter. 'Mama says Shelley is a bubbly-jock himself, all that strutting he does and those noisy outbursts of poetry. He might well drop his wings and fan out his tail, oh, he is so dramatic!'

For a moment the room fell silent. It was evident Claire was entranced by Shelley; her face flushed as she rose and flipped the back of her dress, trying to imitate the fanning out of a tail.

'Did he bring any more poems?' Mary asked quietly.

'Poems?' Claire screwed up her eyes. 'I can't remember. He's a genius though, for sure. He knows it, of course. We are lucky to have a man of such rank come visiting.' She pressed her palm to her brow. 'Oh, that dreary shop, how I put up with it I do not know.'

'Why shouldn't he want to visit?' Fanny interjected, curious and cross. 'He is fond of Papa and reveres him. What's more, Shelley is an egalitarian. He strides the levels of society in ways the rest of us cannot. Our father for instance must conform to what is appropriate, even if he thinks otherwise. Not so Percy.' She braced herself and straightened her skirt.

Mary shrugged. 'I too am free spirited,' said Mary. 'But I hope I can live according to my parents' principles.' She glanced at her father. 'Shelley is no better than Papa. People ought to be equal.'

'Oh, that they were,' her father said, sighing. 'If only.'

Mary continued, talking ' . . . That includes men and women. Women must learn to be less dependent on their husbands. Mother emphasized that women should work towards becoming more rational, less emotional, more honest and genuine, not artful and coquettish like fish hooks out to catch a man.'

'A rich one, of course!' laughed Claire, brushing off Mary's words humorously. She would not have it that Mary's mother might be wiser than her own.

Godwin's eyes moved from Mary to Claire by turns. Mary took note. She knew her father's moods. He was sometimes unsure of himself, though men of distinction like Wordsworth and Coleridge admired him. He had come from a poor Norfolk family and must defer to the likes of Shelley, who'd been born into wealth and privilege. He must ask Percy for money, and Mary had seen the shame in his eyes and heard his murmured curses.

Fanny moved closer to Mary and whispered. 'Claire's behaviour with Shelley is ridiculous, she is much too forward. You should see it! Papa is often annoyed.'

'You can talk to Shelley next week,' said Godwin to Mary, watching them talking closely. 'Now please give your coat to the maid, my dear, and get her to empty your trunk.' He rang a bell and a young pleasant looking woman entered. She gave a brief curtsy.

The maid, who lived in the house, had been with Godwin for years. She brought them lots of gossip from round about town. The effect of Mary's presence had excited the whole household.

'My trunk is in the hall,' said Mary.

'I'll empty it Miss, right now,' replied the maid. And off she went quickly.

'Abigail is quite a dear,' said Fanny, smiling at Mary.

'Poof,' said Claire with a shrug. 'She lets the fires burn down so low they go out.'

'Fuel is expensive,' said Fanny. 'Abigail is prudent and efficient.'

'Abigail is trouble,' said Claire. 'She knows everyone's business in Somers Town.'

Godwin sat thoughtful as if contemplating the change in the family climate. Mary saw that her mother's portrait was still where it always was, hanging above the fireplace; an excellent picture and said to be a perfect image. A visitor had once remarked it was even better than a Gainsborough and that Opie was much more talented. A book lay open on the table; someone was reading *Candide*. A list of notes lay beside it. Other books lay on a low table by the fire; *Clarissa* by Samuel Richardson, *Camilla* by Fanny Burney and *Lyrical Ballads*. This was where Godwin wrote and indulged his intellectual life.

The maid soon returned and lit candles on the wall lights. An unearthly glow passed across her mother's face then flashed on the blue velvet curtains her stepmother had insisted on bringing from her previous home. They were thick and heavy and could block out the world, she'd said, in the blink of an eye. Mary thought it an odd thing to say, but Mary Jane said many strange things. Claire and Charles, her children, both had different fathers and she hadn't married either. Women gave birth and men sometimes disappeared, she said, as if denouncing them as worthless. Mary's father was raising children from several fathers. He was indeed a guardian angel.

She breathed in deeply and relaxed into her chair. She felt strangely renewed, as if she had a sort of Scottish self that hadn't been part of her before, the dark green verdure of the hills, the brown, the grey, the ferocious wind that battered the ships and the mountains, were all a part of her now, a part of her newfound strength. She gazed at her mother's portrait and felt as if they were at one outside of time.

'Ah, Mary!' Mary Jane cried, entering quickly, though without even glancing. She examined each of the wall lights. 'They have all been lit tonight, thank goodness for that. The girl would have us all go blind.'

'Candles are costly,' said Fanny. 'Papa has asked her to consider it.'

Mary Jane ignored her and spoke with an air of authority. 'Good afternoon, Mary. I've been very busy. I could have done with a little more help in the shop, but there we are, I am often overworked.' Claire took to looking through a book. 'Go and take care of William,' said her mother, sitting down. 'The boy must be supervised. You are not to leave him alone. ' Claire got up and sighed, then with a knowing smile flipped the back of her dress and went to the stairs. 'So what news do you bring us, Mary?' Mary Jane said loftily. 'I trust you enjoyed it in Scotland.' She turned to her and looked her up and down.

'Very much,' said Mary. Mary Jane raised her eyebrows in surprise. The knives were out, Mary could feel them in the air, her stepmother would prefer her complaining, but there was something magical about that gritty natural country, she loved its mountains and valleys and its wild fierce traditions. But not a hint of welcome did she get from Mary Jane. Mary Jane however was an excellent housekeeper and company for Mary's father and as promoter of the juvenile bookshop, the only female publisher of note in London. She might talk for days about a new translation she'd recently accomplished, inviting people to read it and say what they thought. That was all to the good. She was a clever woman and much admired for her abilities.

The maid came in with small beautifully cut sandwiches and tea. Mary Jane sighed. 'I am quite exhausted. I believe I carry the whole of this household on my shoulders.'

Mary and Fanny exchanged looks. The old family strains pulled on Mary's heartstrings. It was curious how her stepmother drained her energy. It did not happen to Fanny. But fanny wasn't their father's favourite. The swell of the family tide brought anger, spite and disagreements, Mary could feel them in her blood.

'How well your arm is healing,' said Fanny, pouring out tea.

Mary reached for her shawl and covered her shoulders. 'It does seem to improve somehow in Scotland. The air is fresher of course or perhaps it is the salt from the sea. Salt is healing, I think.'

'How could you possibly know,' Mary Jane said sourly.

'She can read,' Godwin interjected. 'And much can be learned from observation.' He took a drink from his tea.

'The Baxters have an excellent library,' said Mary. 'I thought myself lucky to use it.'

'Did you indeed,' Mary Jane snapped, looking down her long nose. 'We probably have more books than them, my dear. Claire and Charles are always reading. – Charles is teaching in Vienna, did you know?'

'I did,' said Mary. She glanced knowingly at Fanny. 'Papa told me earlier. Is he happy?'

Godwin nodded. 'Indeed he is. He is bright and alert, but there's something else . . .' He waved a finger. 'He is good at passing on knowledge, the most vital of skills in education. It's a sort of gift. However learned we are, passing on knowledge isn't easy. The receiver has to be ready and eager. Education is a two-way process or it is nothing. And the receiver must be rendered receptive.'

'That is the important part, Papa,' said Fanny. 'If the receiver is not receptive, it can often be a painful endeavour.'

'For both teacher and pupil,' Godwin said, nodding at Fanny.

'I am glad you are pleased with my son,' Mary Jane said to her husband, with an air of satisfaction. 'How much do you think he will earn?'

'Much more than we earn from the bookshop,' Godwin said, heaving his chest. For a moment or two they were silent. Godwin spoke again and looked directly at Mary. 'I'm afraid we are very much in debt.'

'Papa fancies Shelley will help us,' said Fanny, smiling awkwardly. 'You know how Shelley thinks the rich should always help the poor.'

'Ah yes,' said Godwin quietly. 'It is one of his mantras and a good one too.'

'I'm not so sure he is rich . . .' Mary Jane said sighing. 'His grandfather is for certain. As the 1st Baronet of Castle Goring, Sir Bysshe will have a fair bit of silver. Percy's father inherits the title when the old man dies, then he'll be Sir Timothy Shelley. A knight for nothing and the money starts rolling his way.' She shrugged irritably. 'It doesn't mean Percy will ever get to see a penny. The way he's behaved I should think his father will disown him. I heard they are barely speaking.'

'Well, I shouldn't worry about that, my dear,' said Godwin. 'Percy gets easy credit wherever he goes, which is more than I can say for myself. I'm sure he'll inherit, so I doubt he bothers too much.'

'I doubt he bothers at all,' said Fanny, sighing. 'He is quite careless with money. According to Harriet that is, she said so last time they came. He is far too generous apparently, but with money he doesn't yet have, that is the problem.' She glanced at her father. 'He brought us that expensive wine, remember. You haven't opened it Papa. Why don't you open it?'

'Oh dear, Fanny, I had better open it, hadn't I?' Godwin laughed.

'All I am saying,' Fanny protested, 'is that he lends freely and he spends freely too. He does not practise thrift. I think he would like you to open the wine, Papa.'

Drinking her tea, it was evident to Mary that Percy had enjoyed himself at Skinner Street. For a moment or two they were silent.

'I shall have to return to the shop,' Mary Jane sighed. 'I should not leave it unattended. There is an excellent market for stolen books, we must always be vigilant.' She rose and went to the door.

'You are quite a stalwart, my dear,' said her husband.

Mary Jane left and Godwin turned to Fanny. 'Dear girl, you are looking quite pale,' he said worriedly. 'You scarcely leave the house. Reading and drawing are excellent pastimes, but you need to take exercise too. Perhaps you should visit your aunts in Wales, what do you think?'

For a moment they were silent. Mary listened intently.

'Aunt Everina can be quite sour,' Fanny said awkwardly. 'I find her company unpleasant. She is rather difficult, you know, and I cannot talk with her about anything much at all. I haven't enjoyed my visits. However low I have felt, I return even lower. And they have little to say about you Papa that is good. I suspect they are none too fond of you.' She was thoughtful a moment. 'Aunt Eliza though refreshes my spirit. Yes, I am glad of Aunt Eliza. – But Papa, would you have me leave? You know I take care of you best.'

Godwin sighed. 'And you are unlikely to see Shelley if you go to see your aunts, are you?' He lifted an eyebrow and waited.

'"Shelley?"' she said, taken aback. 'Oh, Papa, I am scarcely noticed by Shelley. If we walk out it is to talk about Harriet mainly. I am a sort of confidante.'

'Ah,' said Godwin. 'I see. Well, you mustn't let him use you, my dear. Percy would have you take on his burdens in a flash. He does not face them as he should. He writes poetry about them instead. Excellent poetry, of course, but he avoids real issues.'

'Yet he helps us with ours,' Fanny said quietly.

'He does,' said Godwin, clasping his hands and frowning thoughtful. He smiled at Mary, and Mary smiled back contented.

3

Becoming A Woman

Returning to Skinner Street had been far less complicated than Mary had expected. She'd resumed her place in the household without ado. She read and sewed and occasionally assisted in the bookshop or helped take care of little William. But there were times she felt dejected; she didn't like living with Mary Jane and the skin on her arm reacted, reddening and inflaming.

Her mind teemed with questions. She adored Percy Shelley. But Percy was married with a child. Why did he treat his wife so badly, she wondered? Something bad must have happened, for surely he had loved her once. She had seen the pain in Harriet's eyes when he acted preoccupied and ignored her. Oh, that a husband should distance his wife like that. He appeared to have a strong disposition, but what of his true nature, what of his inner fears. She thought about herself and her own position in life. Now, at the age of sixteen, she had passed into womanhood. Men turned their heads on the street. To her father she was still his own pretty little Mary, and to her half sister Fanny she was a jewel. Their mother's celebrated book, had sold far and wide and she and Fanny both tried to live by its principles. Girls, Mary Wollstonecraft contended, wasted too much time and energy hoping for security through marriage and should realise their own potential. It was an undeniable truth with a long history of frustration and it pleased Mary that her father wouldn't attempt to match her with some older, though wealthy, bore. She knew only too well what her parents thought about marriage.

William Godwin's sentiments and those of her mother were clearly expressed in their work, but a few months into her mother's pregnancy, tired of the condemnation of English society they'd married to make Mary legitimate. Her father's reputation, along with her mother's had been very much damaged when he'd written and published her biography. Even her aunts, Eliza and Everina, had been shunned. On a chill grey winter's afternoon, at six years of age, Mary had seen the cold harsh truth of it all when people had crossed the road to avoid her illustrious father. In her mind she could feel his fingers tightening on her own as he'd quickened his pace, and she remembered his agonised face as he'd stared into the fire back home, Fanny's concerned eyes filled with adult understanding. And again Mary had suffered for having killed her mother simply by being born. Oh, how easily the pain gripped her. Fanny's birth had been easy. Well, at least there was comfort in that . . .

Mary braced herself and sighed. Was that why Fanny was always so poised and composed? She would look at Shelley and smile at him calmly, her dark hair twisted in a tidy knot about her head, her pale blue eyes always still and serene. She talked with him quietly and he spoke to her in deep soft tones. But they were not the tones of a lover, they were the tones of appreciation, the same appreciation as Fanny caused in their father. They were not the tones she wanted to hear herself. She went to find Fanny in the kitchen.

Fanny was getting the breakfast prepared with the maid. Shelley was expected that morning, she said, and his morning visits were early. 'I wonder if he'll eat with us,' she said as Mary came through. She cut into a crisp loaf of bread. 'Today he is coming on his own. We have good fresh eggs. We could boil him a couple. He likes boiled eggs.'

Mary felt anxious. 'I hope he will bring some poetry,' she said brightly, watching as Fanny sliced the bread, neatly, carefully, precisely. Her beautiful hands were always busy. Her head was bent in shadow, her lovely features were spoilt from the smallpox suffered in childhood, but her eyes shone with wonder. Especially today, for Shelley would soon be with them! He had taken on board their parents' philosophies on education, love, everything, and he believed in them utterly. And he thought himself a man of the moment, the urgent changing moment that was part of the future. Women, Mary Wollstonecraft had written, if lucky enough to have had any education at all, had received false teaching, acquired mainly from books written by men. It was wrong that women should learn from the thoughts of men her mother contended, and they should learn for their own benefit, not for the benefit of men, as Rousseau so offensively suggested. She thought of a passage she had learned by heart;

"*. . . the civilised women of this present century, with a few exceptions, are only anxious to inspire love, when they ought to cherish a nobler ambition, and by their abilities and virtues exact respect.*"

Women might be loved, even cherished, oh yes, like a pretty pet dog – but *respected*? Now that was different? Respect demanded a place in the bigger picture and knowledge of what it really meant. How could a man respect a woman who did not respect herself, and did not understand the important matters of the world?

She drew herself out of her thoughts and started at the sound of rapping on the door. Fanny went quickly down the hall. Percy's high pitched musical voice sounded out loud around the house. Mary listened and imagined. Most of her thoughts about Percy were imagined. She had imagined him a lot in Dundee, listening to the sea his arms about her like waves enveloping the shore. She recalled her father's words;

"*Without imagination, there can be no genuine ardour in any pursuit or for any acquisition, and without imagination, there can be no genuine morality, no profound feeling of other men's sorrow, no ardent and persevering anxiety for their interests.*"

Yes, she must think and imagine! For how could she not? She threw back her long flaxen hair as she heard him stride towards the kitchen. He had come to talk with her father. If he stayed the whole day, she might get to see him a while. He would talk with her father about freedom and the future and her father would include her. They would talk about governments and power. It was always wonderful to listen. Her father thought government a corrupting influence that prevented people from thinking and that better education and freedom of thought would create a better society. His hopes were high. He despised rule governed practises made solemn by law. And the words "private property" might send him into a fury. He and Shelley talked about such matters at length, and her father's letters to Dundee had often been filled with their ideas. Mind would prove stronger than matter, her father had asserted, mental perfectibility was indeed possible and would eventually become an intrinsic part of existence. She'd replied to her father's letters as best she could and had read the finest books in the Baxter's library. Her parents' thoughts and ideas translated to her soul. She was the daughter of Mary Wollstonecraft and William Godwin, but her own nature struggled as a seed must struggle to discover its own light, for she must be what her soul dictated, free from impulse and prejudice.

'Mary, dear Mary!' cried Shelley, looking her over with pleasure.

'Shelley!' she replied, feigning surprise. How well, he looked, how handsome.

'Well, it is Monday morning, and I am here with two lovely young women!' he laughed. 'I wonder what pleasures the rest of the week has in store!' He smiled at them both by turns.

'Have you had breakfast?' asked Fanny, taking his hat and cane.

'I have, my dear, I was up with the lark.' He threw out his arms and voiced some verse

> *"Hail to thee, blithe Spirit!*
> *Bird thou never wert,*
> *That from Heaven, or near it,*
> *Pourest thy full heart*
> *In profuse strains of unpremeditated art."*

'Something in formation?' Fanny enquired softly.

Shelley scratched his head. 'Yes, it came to me early this morning. What annoys me though is I keep on forgetting it. I do not know if it is finished or if it has only just started. That's what poems are like, they land and sometimes they melt.' He frowned. 'Yes, an intriguing business.'

'The thing is to catch them fast?' Mary offered quietly. 'Then sort of freeze them in your mind until you can examine them properly.'

'Is that so,' Shelley said pondering. 'You might be right. Catch them and freeze them, eh. But how is it done?'

Fanny led them to the parlour where a warm fire blazed in the grate. She placed a large pot of tea on the table and several boiled eggs in a blue china bowl by a plate of shining yellow butter.

'You were about to take breakfast?' he said, finding a seat.

'We were' said Fanny, 'but you are quite welcome to join us.'

'Yes, two breakfasts are better than one, are they not?' said Mary.

Shelley looked from Mary to Fanny, then back. 'Oh, indeed, two is always better than one.'

The maid came in with the bread Fanny sliced earlier. 'I can boil more eggs for Mr Shelley, if you wish,' she said, giving him a light curtsy. 'Or maybe he would like some mutton? Mr Godwin says it is good. He is in the bookshop with his wife and Miss Claire. They are busy.'

Shelley smiled at the company. He was tall and slender with a delicate charm. 'If these dear ladies do not mind,' he said, 'I shall simply sit by the fire and perhaps read a book while they eat. But thank you. In any case, I do not eat mutton. The poor beast was wandering the fields quite happily but months ago and then we decide eat it.' He gave a little shudder. 'The thought makes me nauseas. Most of our ills are caused by meat; we should all eat vegetables, not meat. I do believe that a meatless diet is best if we wish to stay healthy.'

Used to Shelley's impassioned speeches, the maid gave another light curtsy and left.

Mary and Fanny sat down by the table. Shelley was always an interesting and exciting experience. His words were uttered abruptly as if they were a sort of instruction. He was looking about, murmuring to himself and sighing.

It was a good sized parlour with two large bookcases. Shelley got up and went to take a look at the books. Taking one out, he sat down to read a chapter of *Waverly* then returned the book to the case. 'Very good!' he laughed. 'You are fortunate, that book is only just published, did you know? – Ah, I see you have finished your breakfast.' The maid came in and cleared the table. 'And so I have the pleasure of both a dark and light haired maiden. Scott would be delighted. He is constantly referring to dark and light haired maidens. He likes the contrast, I think. Would you not agree?' Shelley's eyes met Mary's then Fanny's. They both bent their heads.

'We do not know that the novel you have looked at is Scott's,' said Mary. 'It is published anonymously.'

'Indeed it is, but I think we know it is Scott's,' said Percy with a wink. 'I have a nose for that sort of thing. I can sniff out *The Lady of the Lake* in there as surely as I sniff out fire.'

'But The Lady of the Lake is a poem,' said Fanny, daring to challenge him.

'It makes no difference. I know things.' He straightened the ruffles on his shirt.

'You probably do,' smiled Mary. 'And Papa does too, he will know you are here and is bound to whisk you off to his study.'

Shelley leant forward towards her. Lowering his voice, he said, 'I *know* that you are lovelier than ever, my dear. Please believe me.'

Fanny rose slowly from her chair and went out quietly.

'So how is your wife?' asked Mary, looking at him straight. 'Is she well?'

'She is having another child.' Shelley frowned at the fire. 'She clings to me though. I do wish she wouldn't.' He ran his finger up and down the arm of the chair.

Mary looked surprised and frowned. 'But is it not yours, is she not your wife?'

For a moment they were silent.

'Of course,' said Shelley awkwardly. 'And babies come rather easily . . . It is a bit of a nuisance. Children tie you to the spot. To a given woman, that is.' He rubbed his face tiredly.

'But the child is yours,' she said, puzzled. She clasped her hands, watching him keenly.

Shelley furrowed his brow. 'Yes, I own it is mine. Harriet is loyal like that. Rather too much, actually. I would rather she weren't. People should be free to love whoever they want whenever they like. Do you not agree?' But he spoke his words to the ceiling.

'But she loves you. Do you not love her back?'

'Well, yes, in a way, but it isn't the same as . . .' He gave her a lingering look. 'It isn't the same as the way I might love *you.*'

She drew back quickly. 'Not so, sir,' she said with a deep intake of breath. She shook her head. 'That is impossible. You hardly know me.'

He leant further towards her. 'I know you well, dear Mary. I know you from letters and I know you from your father, from the things that are said in this house. I *know* and admire you.'

They both fell silent.

'You are no doubt aware of my thoughts about marriage,' he said, changing his position on the chair. He waited. 'There is something particularly wrong with it I think, this pairing up for the whole of one's life. What a terrible waste of love. What a pitiful waste of passion.'

Mary straightened and flushed. She could not deal with his boldness. 'I think I might rather love one man fittingly than lots of men superficially.'

He sat back in his chair and fixed his eyes on her firmly. '"Fittingly?" Do you mean *appropriately*, as in what is expected by society. That would be superficial to me. And in any case, Mary, need it be superficial if we love more than one person. I mean, cannot our love for a few be as worthy as our love for one?'

'You make it sound simple. I fear it is far more complex than that. My instincts would say so.'

'Are not animals creatures of instinct? Do they not work from a certain purity of intention? They do not marry or force themselves upon each other.'

'Not so. But some animals pair for life. And goodness knows how the males of the species can force themselves on the females. Human life is perplexing and profound. It bends and twists our nature, so that we often wander from the better paths we might follow and before we know it are lost.'

'And so we need rules?'

She nodded thoughtfully. 'Yes.'

'And we must bury ourselves in these rules – rules of law, rules of religion, rules of morality, rules made by others that vanquish our freedom and overpower us.'

He was breathing heavily, emotional and strange. She liked his attentiveness. It was as if she were all that mattered, all his feelings flowing just towards her. But just then, she heard her father's voice in the hall and the fast footsteps of Claire. She chilled and silenced. 'Father!' she said self consciously, her eyes widening. 'And Claire. – Good morning.'

Claire's eyes lit with pleasure. 'We have left Mama in the bookshop. It is not so busy at present.'

From outside there came the rhythmic sound of a coach passing the house. The life of Somers Town went on. Godwin took a seat and talked with Shelley about Napoleon Bonaparte. 'His day is over,' said Godwin.

'Oh yes,' said Shelley in his serious political voice. 'Who knows what will happen to him now.' He laughed. 'You might say Napoleon is now in the hands of the gods.'

Godwin laughed back.

'If ignorance of nature gave birth to gods, knowledge of nature is made for their destruction,' said Shelley nodding at the thought. 'I wrote about that in my pamphlet.'

Godwin put his hand on his breast. 'What matters is *feeling,* we must acknowledge the truth of our feelings.'

'There are feelings beyond this life, dear Godwin,' said Shelley with a sigh. 'They are bigger than us and belong elsewhere and they are capable of revelation if only we knew how it worked.'

'But are you not an atheist?' Godwin said frowning at the floor.

Shelley shook his head, looking confounded. 'It has nothing to do with gods. They are *my* feelings, mine. They belong to me and my soul.'

'So you do believe you have a soul?' Godwin raised his eyebrows waiting.

'I have a great deal of soul, my friend,' Shelley said haughtily.

'So where is it?' Godwin asked, sighing.

'Oh, everywhere.' Shelley cast out his arm. 'It exists in music far too splendid to hear, poetry beyond our understanding.'

'But what is the use of a soul that is remote from our being?' Godwin bit his lip, thoughtful.

Shelley screwed up his face as if struggling with a lingering thought.

'We need to talk further,' said Godwin, putting out his hand and directing Shelley to his study.

Claire slumped down in a chair looking glum and forgotten. The bright potency of Shelley was absorbed now by their father. But the spell that had fallen on Mary had lifted for now, and she was glad.

4

Heaven And Hell

The Godwin home was on the polygon, a triangular piece of land between the Pancras, Hampstead and Euston Roads in the parish of St Pancras. At the end of the 18th century due to a swelling community a fever for building homes had come to Somers Town. Houses went up fast amid fields and market gardens, and were still being built. Immigrants from France found solace there, bringing important skills, though paintings by Hogarth, a London painter and engraver, were notorious for showing the heaven and hell of life in England. Hogarth showed the lamentations of those who married merely for money and the sufferings of the poor who fell from grace through lack of it.

People on Skinner Street stood about gossiping on corners. Mary Godwin was home from Dundee, this time for good. And according to Abigail, the maid, William Godwin, the famous writer and bookseller, was lighter of step and easier of manner now his daughter was back in London. No-one could deny that Mary held a special place in his heart. He liked her at home for there was constantly something to curse and something to enjoy and the girl always heard him through. It was often a humorous business; other times grave, said Abigail, as she went about shopping for the family, for his daughter assiduously wrote things down and left her notes about the house. But bits of paper were easily lost, and Abigail became cross if blamed for the failings of others. Mary could be careless and often lost things, while Fanny was neat and orderly, or that is how

Abigail saw it. But she'd always liked Mary best, Mary, the one with the tumbling auburn hair and the soft hazel eyes that looked as if they were dreaming.

Mary Jane maintained that Abigail's tongue was too loose. Fanny said Abigail had no real purpose in life so fell to talking about others, which was only what maids did. She was seeing a youth from a nearby cottage, whose "purpose in life" was to dig the graves in the graveyard. He was often seen by the light of the moon after midnight with one or two others, Mary Jane said, and generally up to mischief. Mary Jane gossiped as much as the next, reasoned Fanny, and as others learned from her books Mary Jane learned from their talk.

It was early morning and Mary's thoughts were awhirl as she went about Somers Town with Fanny. The world was changing. People were always in a panic, there was a need for a little sobriety, said William Godwin to his family. But talk gathered like a storm, and people talked a lot about the French revolution. Men talked about war, and they waved their fists, incensed that their work was threatened by machinery. How could machines replace men? Mill owners even resorted to shooting at men who wrecked their machinery and some of the wreckers were hanged.

But who could dictate the music of time, soft or loud as it sounded. On a higher, more spiritual plane, Ludwig van Beethoven's 8th symphony had premiered in Vienna, a light piece of work, some said, with many accented notes thought to be musical jokes. Others called it a masterpiece amazed that a human being could create such heavenly sounds. And literature was very much alive. A novel named *Pride and Prejudice* had recently been published anonymously, a humorous tale about an English gentleman in Hertfordshire with his overbearing wife and five daughters and revealing hilarious truths about society.

Shelley was often at Skinner Street, most affable at meal times when he liked to sit beside Mary and talk. There was though a fair bit of rivalry for Mary's attention between Shelley and her father, who would cut into their conversations and frown if his daughter paid too much attention to the young aristocrat's opinions. But

Percy could be disgruntled if his ideas weren't taken seriously and Godwin complied in the main, for there was ever the thing about having borrowed money, and intending to borrow again he felt beholden. But it was always understood that Godwin was the master thinker and Percy the protégé. He would look at Godwin and breathe in deeply as if imbibing a patriarchal strength, for Timothy Shelley had lost all patience with his son and appeared to have cast him to the wind.

It was obvious now that 41 Skinner Street was of enormous interest to Shelley, who visited constantly in the main to court young Mary Godwin. Most days they walked to St Pancras churchyard to sit by her mother's grave with Abigail acting as chaperone, close behind, discreetly disappearing when they needed time on their own. More often than not everywhere was silent apart from a whispering breeze wandering the gravestones and the shrill cries of ravens. Percy would lead her through the rosebay willow herb, dazzling with fresh morning dew, the homes of snails cracking beneath their feet, cuckoo spittle staining her dress, and she would tell him how she'd learned to write as an infant by tracing the letters on her mother's gravestone where they sat to enjoy each other's company.

'She is beneath this stone,' Shelley murmured that morning. 'And we sit together above her.' He chanted some lines from *The Corsair,* Byron's recently published poem, fast becoming popular

> *"Remember me – Oh! pass not thou my grave*
> *Without one thought whose relics there recline:*
> *The only pang my bosom dare not brave,*
> *Must be to find forgetfulness in thine."*

'Ah, *The Corsair.* I read it in Scotland,' Mary said, catching her breath. 'You recite it beautifully.'

'The Baxters were quick to acquire it,' he said, looking surprised. 'I'm impressed.'

'Important works were there on the shelf in a trice,' she told him. 'They're a very literary family.' Her eyes were busy and shining. 'He writes of himself in that poem,' she said intently, 'the pirate anti-hero, fighting against humanity.' She laughed into the afternoon light.

Shelley gazed into space. 'You would think so wouldn't you, though from all I hear, I suspect he might like to keep himself out of his poems.'

For a couple of minutes they were silent, looking about at the forming afternoon shadows, then Shelley talked about his childhood in Sussex. 'Sussex is charming,' he sighed. 'I loved the village where I lived. That's where I learned how to fish and hunt. Father watched everything I did. He had such high hopes for me, you see. Damn it. I could never be the son he wanted.'

'And your mother?'

'Mother doesn't know who she is.' He sighed and met her gaze, his large eyes heavy with thought. 'She listens to Father. Always she listens to Father. Ah, let's not talk about Mama.'

'Why not?'

He shook his head. 'Best we talk about poetry.'

She stood slowly, then put out her arms, speaking dramatically into the still trees about them, reciting more from *The Corsair*, her voice echoing against the stone walls of the church

> '"*Such were the notes that from the Pirate's isle,*
> *Around the kindling watch-fire rang the while;*
> *Such were the sounds that thrill'd the rocks along,*
> *And unto ears as rugged seem'd a song!*
> *In scattered groups upon the golden sand,*
> *They game—carouse—converse—or whet the brand;*
> *Select the arms—to each his blade assign,*
> *And careless eye the blood that dims its shine . . .*"'

'Excellent,' he said, smiling, playfully. 'Very good indeed. You remember it well.' Sun swept the ground before them and lit up his face. He breathed in deeply. 'But I fear you admire him too much.' His voice was a little tremulous; there was anger in it and perhaps some fear.

'You are jealous?' she laughed, pleased and surprised, and again sat down beside him. Then her face grew serious. 'I do not wish to be stolen away, you know. You do understand?'

He smiled at the sky. 'Ah, you think I am a pirate.' He put his arm around her waist and drew her towards him. 'Well, perhaps I am. Do you know what – I shall tell Byron what you said. – Well, that's if I see him. He'll be pleased to know you read his poem, and I shall tell him how well you remember it. It's a long one my dear, though I will not examine you on it, I promise.' Mary had seen how he'd recognised the mould of her mind, the way she could memorise passages and quote them with feeling and vigour.

'Fear not,' she said softly. 'You are quite at liberty to ask me anything you like. *The Corsair* is new of course, and we talked about it a lot at the Baxter's. But I do have my own ideas about what he has is written, which is what Lord Byron hopes for I think.'

His eyes were curious. He gave her a long look and his arm tightened round her waist. 'So you think you know what Byron hopes for, do you? You are very courageous to imagine Lord Byron's hopes.' He sighed. 'But you are right; we cannot help but show ourselves in our work.'

She saw he was truly jealous.

Shelley continued. 'Byron's quite riotous, you know. But he isn't like me. Oh, he isn't as bad as I was! I felt repressed at Oxford, restrained like a sort of prisoner. But my good friend Hogg sustained me. He was a joy to have around. We nurtured new thoughts between us as if they were exotic plants. Hogg was utterly tireless in his desire for political reform. – You must meet him sometime. He would like you.'

'Does he write poetry?'

'No, not all, he is rather caught up with law. I was the poet.'

He spoke in earnest. Mary watched and listened. 'I haven't published very much,' he said, 'not yet.' He spoke of the way it was with his father and sisters. He did not speak of his mother. He was the eldest child of six and Mary wondered how it had been in his childhood, just as she wondered about her mother's childhood with her siblings. He talked on fast, seemingly lost, filled with all kinds of guilt too heavy for his mind to carry.

'No, Hogg doesn't write poems,' he continued. 'He's good with Greek though and as a matter of fact, he's a very good writer, though a little too taken with *me* I fear.' He brushed a hand down his sleeve and wafted some dust into the air. 'I fascinate him, you see.' He laughed quietly. 'He is rather interested in Harriet too. I believe he would like to be her lover. She has told me one or two things.'

Mary could hear the confusion in his voice. Did he want his wife to have a lover? 'I doubt Hogg's father was too happy about the pamphlet. – You wrote it together didn't you?'

'We did, and we are equally culpable, if that is the right word. We didn't see it like that though. We saw the work as enlightening. I suspect his parents can't stand me. And yes, I have been in trouble, I am often in trouble.' He was thoughtful for a moment. 'I once got a servant six months in prison for distributing and posting up papers, rather seditious stuff. What a lark. The verses were named *The Devil's Walk*.' He smiled at the thought. 'I was fired on once as well, though I do not know who was trying to kill me. I must have owed them some money.' His voice fell low. 'Oh Mary, I must always think for myself, not just believe what is fed to me. People have suffered for God, had their bodies ripped apart, fought wars, and yet this being stays remote. Unless we pray that is – ah, yes, we can always pray. And we hope that someone is listening. But why should we tire this being with prayers if he knows all things anyway and has us in mind? And if he is infinitely good, why should we fear him?' He rubbed his face hard. 'I have too many questions. Poetry, poetry is what matters. Through poems we can reach the truth; it is a sort of excavation. We mine our souls, which I believe are constantly changing.'

'Our souls are living entities,' she whispered. 'It is true; they change and grow as we do.'

He nodded slowly, frowning. 'So you see them as separate from us?'

'I'm not sure. I think so.'

Again they were silent.

'I dream of my mother,' she said softly. 'I see her coming towards me and I know what I want to ask her, but I wake. – Oh, how I hate it when the daylight takes her away!'

'The night abounds with such entities,' he said. His tone was nervous. 'I was full of fantasies as a child. I tried to sketch the demons that tormented me. The worst were horrific; I thought they might leap off the page. I spent a whole night once lying on a gravestone like this. I was hoping the wretched skeleton might rise from its slumber and I could ask it about the life hereafter. I'm intrigued by all that.' He laughed strangely, showing his perfect teeth. 'Life, death, it is all such a mystery. It is probably harder to enter life than it is to pass into death. It's amazing you know how fast we can die, just a couple of seconds with that guillotine.'

She could tell he needed to talk. It was one of the ways they were in tune with each other. He talked at speed and she listened. He liked to talk about his childhood and his schooling, the people he'd known. 'I hated Eton. Nobody liked me,' he said sorely. 'But the place was full of nonsense. I couldn't put up with all that business of older boys looking after young ones if they'd polish their shoes or something. But I did love chemistry; I thought it rather supernatural at first. Electricity excites me too, it sort of wakes up the psyche.' He laughed again. 'They called me "Mad Shelley", I might bite you see, or else stab you with a fork! – Oh, it's true, I have done it.' He turned to her. 'Oh, Mary, have you any idea how I love you!' He took her hands and kissed them over and over.

'But aren't you ashamed?' she asked, looking at him curiously.

'Of what?' he asked, frowning. 'We are here amongst the dead, two living creatures bursting with love, not a sound to be heard apart from the voices of ravens.'

'Ravens are ominous,' she whispered. She gazed at them as they flew about croaking.

Again they were silent.

'They are beautiful,' he said finally. 'Beautiful, shining and strong. – But tell me, my dear, what must I be ashamed of?'

'Your words,' she said quietly. 'You say that you love me . . . But what about Harriet, your wife?'

He folded his arms. His voice became hard and angry. 'How difficult it is to talk with you sometimes. We must follow the truth of our hearts, Mary. Harriet understands all that, we have often discussed it. Things are not good between us. Letting her sister live with us was a bad idea; it has brought us endless trouble. Harriet and I arc to separate soon.'

'But Percy, Harriet is pregnant with your child . . .' Her voice was unsteady. It hurt her to see the pain on his face, but she knew she must speak. His mind was open to love. But just how open was it?

'We *have* to be together,' he pleaded, gripping her hands. 'I have never before known such feelings, Mary. I never had feelings like this for Harriet. Before I knew it, we were married and I found myself bound like a prisoner.' He shivered slightly. 'Oh, I am always a prisoner! Just like Prometheus, that's me. But I achieved some excellent writing. *Queen Mab* is rather good, I think. Yes, it is quite an achievement. He recited some lines softly

> *From her celestial car*
> *The Fairy Queen descended,*
> *And thrice she waved her wand*
> *Circled with wreaths of amaranth;*
> *Her thin and misty form*
> *Moved with the moving air,*
> *And the clear silver tones,*
> *As thus she spoke, were such*
> *As are unheard by all but gifted ear.*

'Yes, wonderful,' she whispered. 'Is it inspired by Harriet?'

'No, no. Queen Mab is a fairy, originally invented by Shakespeare in Romeo and Juliet. The imagery is marvellous.' He put out his hand and splayed his fingers. 'The fairy's midwife is just the size of a finger. Imagine. She speaks of a Utopian society on earth, a perfect place where there are never any problems and everyone is happy. It could happen, you know, it really could.'

Mary shook her head. 'I doubt it Percy. Only in poetry. Is Harriet Queen Mab?'

He shook his head. 'I did not care for my life with Harriet at all. I was a hostage! I realised what had happened straight away. We rarely agreed on anything. She wouldn't even breast feed the baby.

She knew it was what I wanted, but I got nowhere trying to persuade her. Babies need their mother's milk; it's good for their health and their brains. But Harriet doesn't understand things.' He looked at her straight, his eyes bright with sincerity. 'I'm unburdening myself and I shouldn't. I'm sorry. I feel naked and weak with love, you see, just as it gives me strength, it weakens me. It's a sort of tragedy, the way that I love you, Mary.' He turned her towards him. 'And I know you love me in return. Tell me it's true.'

'This could destroy my father,' she whispered shakily. She felt angry with herself for even thinking of loving him. The natural, frank way he spoke to her now, compared to his exalted poetry confused her.

'You are a grown woman. Godwin has had his loves. It is your turn now.' He spoke firmly and precisely. 'Don't be afraid.'

She turned from him, silent.

'Your Father says life has changed you.'

'Does he?' she said indignantly. She and her father were normally loyal to each other. It was hard to imagine him talking to Shelley like that, but Shelley was seductive and persuasive. 'Rest assured, I am a child no longer.'

'No, you are not!' he laughed. 'You have burst from a chrysalis into something delightful and precious.' He pointed to some nearby nettles. 'There – look at that butterfly, what an extraordinary creature it is! It is a Small Tortoiseshell I think; there are a lot of them about. You often find their larva on nettles.'

'I keep my distance from nettles,' she stressed. 'They sting. And to tell the truth, I think moths are nicer than butterflies. They are dark and exciting.' She turned to him again.

He looked at her and narrowed his eyes. 'You like things dark and exciting, do you? You admire the ravens?'

His tone became gentle and soft, transcending everything about her. She drank it in.

'I don't like graves,' he continued. 'The thought of my bones down there in a box makes me shudder. I would rather be thrown into the flames, simply reduced to ashes. Ah yes, it would suit me much better.'

She looked down at the engraving on her mother's gravestone. Death was gloomy. It was terrible. And the way people died could be cruel.

'You are not too fond of Mary Jane,' he said suddenly, low and intensely, as if it were of great importance. It reminded her of her father when he was angry.

She frowned at his words and spoke quickly. 'My stepmother is good for Papa. Oh, she is glib and fussy and has no refined sensibilities. That much, I cannot bear. And she is jealous that Papa loves me. She wants him all for herself and Claire. How it annoys me when she stands about listening when we talk, and every new book in the shop goes to Claire before me.'

Shelley watched the butterfly closely. 'And what about Fanny? Your father loves Fanny, does he not?'

'Of course. Fanny has always been there for him. She is good. She is constantly concerned about the poor, always reading pamphlets about their sufferings. Since Napoleon was exiled on Elba there are so many aged and wounded soldiers on the streets of Somers Town. She worries about them and thinks she should solve the problems of the world. Poor Fanny. Papa loves her dearly. I remember when she was little, how he took her on his lap when Coleridge came to read his albatross poem. We were frightened of *The Ancient Mariner.* I clung to my father's arm and Fanny hid her face in his chest. 'I regularly looked for an albatross when I went to the sea in Scotland but I never saw any fly in.'

'I once killed a bird on purpose,' he said, frowning at the thought.

'But why?' She watched him pulling at pieces of grass by the grave. He tied them into knots and placed them neatly in a row on the gravestone.

His shoulders rose and fell. 'Oh, it was only a sparrow. A magpie had attacked it. I was there when it happened. Vicious it was. Magpies can be quite ferocious. They are always on the prowl.'

'And did it eat the sparrow?'

'Well no, it didn't get a chance. I shooed it away and stamped on the sparrow's head to make sure it was out of its misery.'

For a moment or two they were silent.

'And Claire?' he asked, waiting. 'How do you feel about Claire?'

She gazed at him, studying his smooth skin, his searching, intelligent eyes. She imagined his bare shoulders beneath his shirt, his chest . . . Ought a woman to have thoughts like that, she wondered, a woman of only sixteen. She breathed in deeply. It was getting quite dark.

He persisted. 'I don't think you like her either.'

'Whilst you?' she smiled looking up.

He scratched his chin. 'Claire? Yes, I like her. She has a certain kind of allure . . . But you, my dear, are *perfect*.'

'I was thinking about our *minds* . . .' she murmured.

'Of course you were,' he said smiling. 'I'm sure. 'But tell me, Mary, what must I feel ashamed of?'

She spoke in earnest, her hands locked tightly together. 'Your words to me. Such wonderful words, but what if Harriet were to hear them? What if she should *know*? What if the ravens should find her and tell her . . . as ravens do.'

Shelley looked at her warmly, meeting her gaze. 'Must duty come before love? All for the sake of a society that leads us astray. You love me too. I know it. And do not forget, my dear, you let me to kiss you yesterday, right here, long and deeply. I could have taken you then, it was dusk. – You wanted me to take you, didn't you?'

She did not speak.

He clapped his hands to his brow. 'Oh, I won't be Prometheus bound to a rock and have an eagle feed off my liver! I shall take my share of the fire! I will! I will! Ah, gods, gods, it is nonsense!'

'So would you be God yourself?' she asked quietly.

He answered with silence.

'You were expelled from Oxford because of the pamphlet,' she said awkwardly.

'Oh, don't go on about that, my dear,' he said, drawing her close. 'I have so many issues . . . I do wish I wasn't married. Oh, the church beats the drum for it loudly, but if married people stop loving each other, why should they stay together and . . .'

'Mother wasn't married to Imlay,' Mary interjected. 'Papa wrote her biography . . . And everyone knows what happened. There is an innocence about Papa and he never means harm, but he damaged mother's reputation. I doubt we will ever get over it. Fanny suffers most. She does not belong to Papa as I do. She feels she belongs to no-one.'

'But she belongs to *you?*'

'She does and I love her. But it isn't enough. Her father still lives, and yet he denies her existence.'

'Where is he?'

'Who knows? He is quite an expert at disappearing. He abandoned Fanny. But Papa has been her father in spirit. She loves him as I do.'

'And I have abandoned my father,' Shelley said abstractedly. 'He loved me once.'

'And no more?'

Shelley drew a breath and sat with his hands on his knees. 'No, it's a small child who remembers him now. I was born in the year of the Terror in France; I played on the floor with my toys and heard him arguing with guests who came to the house and my grandfather, a peer of the realm, he was strong in those days. They were such intense conversations, banging of fists on tables, all that. My father's eyes when he beheld me were soft and kind and I still remember his joy when he took me on his knee. He was part of everything I was. Sometimes it hurts to remember. I remember the lake where I took out my boat, and I saw how he watched me carefully. But I could not swim, ever. I was ashamed.' He placed his hands on his heart. 'There are things in here that long for fulfilment. But I am often weak and foolish.'

She smiled gently. 'I think you are brave, Percy. You are determined too and can cope with rejection for whatever you believe in. You manage your father well.' Her voice fell low. 'And I know you are able to love deeply and sincerely.'

'And you?' he asked softly.

She gave him a long look. 'I love like a red sunrise,' she told him smiling.

'I would never desert you,' he said. 'I shall speak to Harriet, she must know of our love.'

'"*Our love,*"' she murmured. 'Yes, it is true, it lives.' But she wasn't made whole by their love; it seemed to diminish her instead. But she needed his embrace and chilled at the thought of what life might be like without him. She would steal him from Harriet. She must!

5

A Summer Of Confusion

'But it's wrong,' said Fanny, talking with Mary in the parlour. 'He just can't do it. He ran away with Harriet, and now he wants to run away with you. I can't believe he is even threatening to kill himself if you won't comply!' She rose from her seat, flushed and bewildered. 'Oh Shelley, Shelley, what trouble you brings us!'

'Do you love him too?' Mary asked softly. She saw that Fanny had tears on her cheeks. There was a silence. She pressed on further. 'I believe you do,' she whispered. 'Even more than Claire does.'

'Not at all,' Fanny replied indignantly. 'How could you think it? And as for Claire, well it's all drama with Claire.'

'You are probably right, but with you it's different,' said Mary, watching as Fanny paced the floor. 'It's deep and serious, isn't it? Don't deny it. It doesn't matter, you see. It can't be helped, it happens and it can't be helped.' She breathed in deeply and turned away her face.

'If you leave this house and go off with him, who will console Papa?' Fanny said miserably. She placed her hand on her breast. 'Me, of course – *me*. Oh, Mary.' She sat down slowly. 'That's if anyone could. His beloved Mary, running off with a married man. – Oh, it would kill him. He would never forgive you. And I dare not imagine his anger . . . And Shelley threatening suicide again . . .' She shook her head troubled. 'He is always threatening suicide. Harriet told me.'

'He's talking nonsense,' Mary said sighing. 'I should never have told you.'

Again they were silent.

Mary spoke again. 'But what if he *did* because I said no?'

Fanny braced herself and sighed. 'He needs to grow up. He is twenty one years old and acts like a child.' She was trembling slightly. 'Yes, Mary, I care for him a lot, of course. We became quite close when he visited before . . . before you returned that is. He visited Papa on his own sometimes and we went out walking.'

Mary was thoughtful. Fanny gazed at the floor then lifted her head and smiled softly.

'Where did you go?' asked Mary. Had they been to the graveyard?

Again there was an awkward silence.

'No Mary, we didn't visit mother's grave. We walked in the fields. But when you came back, it was as if I had ceased to exist. I was suddenly sort of invisible.'

Mary sat listening while Fanny continued despondently. 'Well, it hurt me deeply. He ignored me. I am fully aware that I do not have your beauty. But I thought . . .'

'You thought what?' Mary interjected sharply, 'You thought you would have him for a lover? – No, you did not. Knowing he was married you would never have done such a thing. Not you, Fanny. That pantisocracy business he talks about, where everything is shared, even people, is farcical. People get jealous, people grow angry.' Her voice fell low. 'Percy is married to Harriet. You would always have it in mind.'

'Would I? You are quite sure of that, aren't you? I have to be good and leave all that is exciting to you. That is the truth of it, isn't it?'

'Fanny, don't say such things, it isn't like you.'

'You ask a lot of me, Mary, perhaps too much.'

Mary straightened. 'I do not possess your goodness, Fanny. Suicide is final and disturbing. I can't let Percy commit suicide.' Her voice fell low. 'And I know that he loves me.'

Fanny shook her head. 'I see from your eyes you are bound to do as he asks,' she said shakily.

Mary got up and walked across to the window. The tension in the room was almost palpable. She glanced at the door, fearing their father might enter. All was silent in the hall. Shelley had told her that the years of his marriage to Harriet had been tumultuous. She had accompanied him through England, Scotland, Wales and Ireland, all the while supporting his notions of how society should change, with both their families disapproving of their lifestyle and their impetuous way of living. They had argued intensely, and were constantly chased by creditors. Shelley would hide wherever he could, in a cupboard or even up a tree, he said. Sometimes men came with guns. He based his security for borrowing on the belief he would one day inherit and he always promised generous interest. His children would be taken care of through family money, he said, and rested assured at that, but his marriage to Harriet was over. Fanny's voice broke into her thoughts.

'He *will* do it,' she continued, pacing the floor. 'He will kill himself, I know it. He keeps a flask of laudanum in his pocket, it helps free his mind, he says, but he's often threatened to kill himself, he has a morbid attraction to death. And he gets so edgy when his father writes angry letters. Despite his beautiful poetry Percy's mind is chaotic. Father told me that one of his friends from Oxford said he had clothes strewn all about his room with pistols, papers, books and half eaten food. There were times he didn't eat all day. And he kept scientific equipment too, all kinds of things, vessels, microscopes and such, even a sort of electrical machine, though Papa can't think for the life of him what it was for.'

Mary felt disappointed seeing Fanny so troubled. She had hoped for her rational counsel. Fanny had obviously cared for Shelley immensely. And what about Claire, she would have to tell Claire. But come what may, she'd decided to elope with Shelley next morning and would tell him that very afternoon when they met in the graveyard. She knew in her heart that if he came with a carriage that minute she would climb inside it and he could take her wherever he wanted. She had encouraged him, undoubtedly, enjoying their walks along the paths at the graveyard, his deep moans of passion, even the way he spoke her name. And she had let him love her there on her mother's gravestone in the dusk and had welcomed his passion, his lips soft and urgent his warm hand on her thigh. She had not wanted to, indeed she hadn't intended it, but she had done it, there beneath the stars she had loved him. And each day she longed for his touch. She couldn't tell Fanny the truth, that she had made herself Shelley's own, and pretended it hadn't happened. It was far too bad to have happened. He wanted to take her to France, he said, and on to Switzerland after. He would leave Harriet and his child. He would leave them all. Yet still she loved him. He had written her a poem and she turned away from Fanny, speaking the words softly

> *"Upon my heart thy accents sweet*
> *Of peace and pity fell like dew!*
> *On flowers – half dead – thy lips did meet*
> *Mine tremblingly, thy dark eyes threw*
> *Their soft persuasion on my brain,*
> *Charming away its dream of pain."*

Was it not true that you should live with your heart's desire? she asked herself. She held tight to her feeling, it had to be right.

'You needn't say any more,' Fanny said quietly, sitting down. 'Your decision is obvious.'

'Oh, I beg you, Fanny, please keep it secret,' she pleaded, turning towards her.

Fanny raised her shoulders and dropped them with a sigh. 'I won't say a word. But you are going to hurt Papa. He enjoys Shelley's company and his adoration as well, but he loves you Mary.' She covered her face with her hands. 'A married man with a child and a pregnant wife – what can I say? Except that it's wrong.'

'But we love each other. What can be more *right* than that?'

'You are determined.'

'Yes,' said Mary miserably.

'I really don't know why you've told me,' sighed Fanny. 'But I'm glad you did. At least I can speak to Papa sensibly when he finds out. Oh, how life uses and abuses us!'

Claire came into the room. 'What's happened?' she asked, glancing about concerned. 'Is there some trouble? Tell me, I won't be left out!'

'Yes, there is trouble,' sighed Fanny. She rose from her chair and left the room.

'What is it?' asked Claire shakily. 'Is somebody ill?' She sat down slowly.

'No, not that,' Mary said quietly. Curious feelings went through her blood and made her feel dizzy. Already, she was being punished. She felt sick with the strain of the household. 'You must promise to keep it from your mother . . .' said Mary. She would have to disclose her plans to Claire or she was bound to badger her with questions.

'What do you mean? I am always discreet,' said Claire. 'I don't tell Mama everything. You know the way she takes on.' She moved in closer, her eyes wide and waiting.

Mary looked at her pensively. She had to tell her, it was a risk she must take. Shelley would come at first light tomorrow with a carriage; she had to be ready. They would leave for France straight away. As she delivered her story, she could see that Claire was jealous.

'Great weather for an elopement,' said Claire, peering out of the window. 'It's pouring with rain. I do hope it's dry in the morning.'

For a moment they were both thoughtful. Mary could sense Claire's annoyance. 'You mustn't blame yourself for loving him,' Claire said dramatically. 'Who wouldn't? And the fact that he says he will kill himself if you don't obey him is so romantic. But I doubt you needed much persuading. Why would you want to stay here, wandering that dreary shop with nothing but books for company?' She sighed and gazed at the ceiling. 'Oh, to be loved by Shelley!' For a few moments they were silent. Then she grasped Mary's hand. 'I want to come with you!' she exclaimed. 'Oh, Mary, please take me with you! I speak better French than you do, that would be useful, surely, and how wonderful to go to Switzerland, the land of my father!'

Mary recalled how her stepmother said Claire's father was Swiss, but the parentage of Mary Jane's children was shrouded in mystery. Shelley had said he'd been inspired by his reading and thought the continent a place of freedom and liberty, a perfect place for free love and intellectual growth. But to take Claire as well . . . the very thought was harrowing.

'I long to leave London,' pleaded Claire. 'And I'd love to get away from Mama for a while.' She frowned, petulant. 'She still treats me like a child.' Claire was almost sixteen; she had a shapely figure and long dark hair and believed she was very attractive. There were some who called her a beauty.

They both stared at the fire watching the flames. 'That would make it worse,' said Mary as Claire's words began to take hold. 'Your mother would despise me.'

'Have you told Fanny?' Claire asked anxiously.

Mary nodded. 'But she won't tell anyone else. She doesn't approve of it though, there are bound to be severe repercussions when Papa discovers what's happened.'

But Shelley doesn't love Harriet, everyone knows it,' said Claire emphatically. 'People need passion and feeling in their lives or their creative impulse dries up. Shelley has said so himself. He needs passion to write his poetry.'

'He has little self-restraint,' Mary said, suddenly thoughtful. 'But I have found that fault in myself.'

'You poor things!' cried Claire, her eyes filling with tears. 'What could be worse than having to deny your passion? It's just like holding back grief.' She leant towards Mary and kissed her lightly on the cheek. 'First light I shall be ready,' she whispered, 'first light. Now I must pack my things.' With that she hurried down the hall.

Mary sat thinking it over. What would Shelley say tomorrow if Claire climbed into the coach as well? They had very little money between them. They would have to rely on Shelley for everything. But perhaps he would be glad that Claire was so fluent in French. What a shock it would be for Mary Jane and her father to find they had left in the night. But Fanny would ease the pain. Fanny could always ease the pain.

6

Chase And Heartache

After dinner that evening, Mary sat reflecting in the parlour. She had eaten a meal with Claire and Fanny each of them knowing what would happen next morning, yet not one of them uttering a word. Mary Jane had been talking to Godwin about a cash register bought for the shop, it was imperative they had a new one, she said, for the drawer kept sticking in the other. She was rather pleased with the new one, she told him, it was made of good strong metal and a real pleasure to handle. Her husband had said the cash register would be very happy about that and they'd laughed in the way they sometimes did, which usually said things were looking up. And the books were selling quite well, she said, but they would still need to borrow from Shelley to help pay their debts.

Mary felt nervous, the secret had made her tense, and the fact that her father knew nothing about it upset her. She hadn't looked at him that evening for fear of meeting his eyes. But what must be, must be. She would have to be out at the crack of dawn with Claire and gone within minutes. She'd packed one or two clothes and in order to look their best they intended to wear their black silk dresses, fashioned in Spitalfields silk. The day would be wet and chilly, but their cloaks were heavy and warm.

Shelley knew nothing of the newfangled plan. It would be quite a surprise to find Claire had decided to join them. Mary Jane would be furious; she would call it disgraceful behaviour, say it was scandalous and wicked and probably rant and rave, but Fanny would calm things down.

Mary sat on her bed, waiting for the stroke of midnight from the Somers Town clock. As the thin chimes broke through the air, she reached for her cloak. They had to be silent as ghosts. She looked around her room. It seemed oddly unfamiliar and cold. And so she had crossed the Rubicon. Her soul had made a mighty leap. She might be ecstatic or she might be utterly miserable, but it was done, the agonising fight with her self was over, this would be her new life. She gathered together her things and put them in a bag, then blew out the candle and crept downstairs to the door.

It had rained heavily and she saw that the road they must travel was slightly submerged in water. She waited for a moment by the door then saw that Percy was beckoning. – But where was Claire? She didn't seem to be following. Perhaps she'd decided to stay with her mother after all. Percy took Mary's bags and helped her into the coach. Then they heard Claire's footsteps on the street. – 'Percy! Percy!' she cried, the shrill sound of her voice echoing down the silent pavements. 'I too, must escape!'

'Hush!' urged Mary. 'Not so loud. We have to be quiet.'

Percy looked confused. The sound of the wind and rain and the rattle of the horses' harnesses amplified the panic.

'I had no choice,' Mary said breathlessly. 'She forced me to bring her. I had no way of telling you.' She felt vexed and guilty. Shelley was known to be fickle. Would he change his mind?

'It doesn't matter,' he said, helping Claire with her bag. 'My dear Claire, you did right, we must always do as we wish. But the day will soon be upon us and all that goes with it, so get in the coach quickly.' He took Claire's arm and in no time at all she was sitting in the coach by Mary.

Mary shivered. How strangely unreal it all was. Claire settled down. Desperately tired, she leant against Mary's shoulder. The stillness of the morning and their whispering voices made the whole event seem dreamlike. Mary felt she was entering another world.

Shelley's world filled with excitement and daring, poetry and imagination, but could she manage its unruly terrain? When the moonlight fell on his face, his eyes showed a mind in turmoil. Time just now was of the essence, he said, they must get to Dover quickly. Mary saw that he kept on glancing back at the house, and she realised of a sudden, that not only did he revere her father he also feared him. 'Quick! – Quick!' he urged. 'We must fly!' His bags were slung on the floor of the coach, his trunk secured on the top. Harriet was probably fully aware of his intentions, thought Mary, he would have told her in cold blood. Mary imagined her pain, Harriet's fierce accusations, his child's cries and tears . . . But perhaps it hadn't been like that at all, perhaps it was all quite different, perhaps Harriet had wished him well and had accepted the new situation, the important new love he must have. It was also possible that she didn't have the least idea about anything, and he'd simply left the house like a thief in the night, stealing away her life and their son's security . . . But seated now in the shadowy coach with Claire and Percy, Mary had gone to her destiny.

All was far from well however at Skinner Street. Discovering her daughter and Mary had both left the house, Mary Jane concluded the only person who might possibly throw some light on the matter was Fanny. She marched through the house to find her.

Up, and helping the maid prepare breakfast, Fanny heard her stepmother's footsteps close and kept her head bent low. Then the door of the kitchen flew open. It was 6.30 a.m. The curtains were still undrawn and Fanny was brewing tea in her nightwear. She stirred the tea pot slowly, filled with pity for her father and a sense of loyalty to her sisters.

Then there came the tirade. Head tilted back and hands on hips, Mary Jane started. – 'They have left their beds and are nowhere in the house! Gone, it seems, even before the barrow boys had set out their wares. Where did they go? Tell me! This is all very sinister. Tell me right now what has happened. I can see from your face that you know!'

Fanny's features stayed still.

Mary Jane shook and trembled. 'Oh, come now girl, speak up! Or are you a rag doll? Mary and Claire have gone, now where did they go?'

For a moment or two the women stared at each other. The maid decided to sort out the kitchen drawer and rattled the cutlery. Fanny heard herself speak, but she didn't say what she intended. She spoke slowly and pointedly, 'Have you any idea how badly you treat me. I am older than the others, yet you . . .'

Mary Jane laughed scornfully. 'Oh, I have a very good idea what has happened, and you ought to have stopped it. They have both run away and heaven knows what will become of them.' She looked Fanny up and down and shrugged. 'Are you suggesting I treat you badly? You talk nonsense.' She waved away Fanny's words. 'But it isn't you I'm concerned about. My daughter has gone with that scheming sister of yours. Now where have they gone? – Oh, better she'd stayed in Scotland; she is wild as the heather!'

Mary Jane stared at the floor while Fanny brought out the teacups. 'This is all Shelley's doing,' she screeched. 'I can hardly believe that he's turned the head of my daughter; my girl is well bred and intelligent, she understands right from wrong, unlike our "pretty little Mary" who is empty headed.' She recovered herself on hearing her husband approaching, though she trembled with rage. 'Mary and Claire are not in the house,' she told him as he entered. 'I believe they have run away.'

'I heard the commotion from upstairs,' said Godwin coolly. 'Run away where, and why?' Then he looked at Fanny and frowned.

Fanny shook her head. 'I don't know a lot about it, except what I learned last night.'

Godwin stared at her curiously.

'So you *do* know something!' Mary Jane said, looking at her straight. 'Of course, you do. Now out with it.'

'Yes, I do,' Fanny faltered. 'I didn't think it right, and I said so . . .'

Godwin opened the curtains and stood looking out. 'Perhaps they have gone for a walk,' he said vaguely.

'What, so early? – No, no,' said his wife flatly. 'And their beds are cold as the grave. They've been gone for a while.'

Godwin stayed silent, still gazing outside. His eyes were fierce with anger. The way he'd rushed in though had made Fanny afraid. 'They are going to France with Shelley,' she said, pouring out tea. 'They left when the streets were still dark. I believe they hope to reach Switzerland.'

'"*Switzerland!*"' Mary Jane shrieked. 'Why are they going to Switzerland? – What did they tell you?'

'Nothing,' Fanny said quietly, concerned for her father.

The maid went out of the room.

Godwin turned and picked up his cup of tea. He took a drink then silently stared at the ceiling. Mary Jane continued her rant. 'They are two innocent girls who know nothing of the world!'

'Shelley!' said Godwin at length, white faced and furious. 'This is all Percy. He had better not let me catch him.'

Mary Jane drew herself up. 'Oh, I shall catch him!' she said. 'Just watch me. You will have to manage the bookshop and William. She looked from her husband to Fanny and back. I must get me a carriage to Dover straight away!'

'That could be difficult,' said Godwin. 'I shall need to get out of this nightshirt first.'

'You must get me a coach, *now!*' cried his wife. 'This minute. Osmond will be up. Send Abigail, and see he is properly paid.'

The maid stood gazing downwards meekly, her hands clasped before her. But she was in her day clothes, ready.

'To France and then to Switzerland eh,' growled Godwin, finding some money for the driver. His eyes narrowed with anger. 'How could he steal my daughter like that in the dead of night, and with such indecent intentions?' His voice trembled.

'And Claire as well,' Mary Jane groaned. 'My sweet innocent daughter. – Abigail, get me that carriage! I must dress and be off to Dover.'

'It's a long way to travel and the weather is bad.' Godwin said. 'But those girls must come back.' For a moment he stood at the window, looking on the dimly lit street, then turned. 'No doubt he threatened suicide again if they didn't go with him. Oh, the man has suicide fever! No-one can save him. He is lost. And my daughter will be lost too if she enters his madness.' He turned to his wife, determined. 'We'll go and fetch them together; that foolish young devil will have to be taught a lesson!'

'No,' said his wife. 'You stay here, you are far too irate. I can deal with this on my own.' She turned to Fanny who sat at the table thoughtful. 'Fetch me my warmest clothing Fanny, and I'll need you to manage the bookshop while I'm away.'

Godwin paced the floor in time with the ticking of the clock. 'I have finished with Mary for this,' he growled, as he heard the maid close the door. Very soon there came the sound of a carriage and Mary Jane threw on her cape and tied on her bonnet. Godwin stood in silent outrage as he watched his wife climb in.

The sound of the maid busy about the house was loud that morning as Fanny rested her head in her hands in the kitchen. The clock showed 7 a.m. Her father had gone to his study and Mary Jane was on the way to Dover.

The maid came through. 'I daresay Mrs Godwin will find them,' she said to Fanny reassuringly. 'What a to-do. She'll not have a scrap of patience with Mr Shelley.'

Fanny looked up. Abigail had learned a lot in the last few hours. 'I believe you are right,' she sighed. 'A to-do indeed Abigail, heaven knows what's going to happen.'

'Do I need to go out for groceries?' asked Abigail, wanting to get out of the house. The atmosphere was oppressive. Light spilled in through the windows, the day was upon them.

Fanny shook her head. 'We have provisions enough for now.' It was all too terrible to think of. She felt weak, empty and alone. She brewed more tea for her father and took it to his study, finding him sitting in his chair staring at space, his stare so sharp it could have cut poor Percy through. She tried to be strong in the disrupted and silent house. Feelings could destroy you, she told herself; she had learned that early, emotions had to be managed. She liked to seem calm and capable, but it seemed some fiend was inside her just now, some cruel spirit that Percy himself might have conjured. She felt she must guard her heart, protect herself somehow from a tragedy yet to happen. She hardened herself and went to fix her hair for the day.

'Well, at last I have found you!' Mary Jane gasped, finally alighting on the trio. They were seated together in an inn at Dover. They all three stared at her coolly, acting nonchalant.

'We are to cross the channel, Mama,' Claire said boldly, as Mary Jane joined them. 'Though the wind is too angry today, we are waiting for better weather. We shall probably sail tomorrow.'

Mary Jane laughed sarcastically. 'The wind is angry you say? Oh, never mind the wind, its anger is nothing compared to my husband's fury. And I am as livid as Lyssa!' Mary Jane's voice was loud amongst the company and made people look. She pointed at Shelley, who leant back leisurely in his seat and folded his arms. 'I forbade my husband to come, or he might have done you an injury, Mr Shelley. It's as well you didn't see his anger. – You think you've got what you want, do you? Well you're wrong.' She sat down heavily next to Claire. Shelley lifted his eyebrows as if in surprise, loyal to his arrogant self and Mary affected the same. Mary Jane continued with her warfare, shaking her finger and berating him. 'Oh my word, you scoundrel! How dare you steal away our girls?'

Claire spoke again, though calmer. 'Shelley did not procure me, Mama; I came of my own accord.'

'I'm sure you did,' her mother said sardonically. 'Do you think I'm a fool? I can understand Mary, she doesn't have a mother, but you my dear, why, the world has given you the best of its fruits. I thought you knew better.' She talked on breathless and tearful. 'This is very bad. But people aren't normally bad on their own, there has to be someone encouraging it, someone *inherently* flawed.'

Claire looked longingly at Shelley. Mary held on to his arm. 'We invited her to join us,' said Mary. 'We need to be free.'

'"*Free?*"' Mary Jane laughed. 'And what are you going to do? Where will you go? Oh, Claire, I really thought you were more intelligent than this. You were given a good education. You are well brought up. You can hold your own in any company. What will it profit you to run away with these fools?'

'I want to learn about the world Mama and become independent. I am too much . . .' her voice trailed off.

Mary Jane waited and pulled off her gloves.

'I am too much under your influence Mama,' said Claire, straightening. 'I am almost sixteen. Let me see the world, let me experience *life*.' Her voice trembled with feeling.

'What a good idea!' said Mary Jane. She smiled wryly. 'You will soon grow weary of that. Oh, the horrors you will discover in this thing called "life". Good heavens girl, you don't need to "experience" them, I can tell you all about them myself.' She laughed loudly, then turned her attention to Mary with a look of disgust. 'I can't begin to say how sorry I am that my daughter has been influenced by you. You cannot compare with Fanny, of course, who is loyal and kind.'

'You have treated Fanny very badly,' Mary said, quietly. 'You ignore her and speak to her roughly. What's more, you have grown quite fat.' Mary's temper was up and her cheeks were flushed with emotion. 'Don't you dare compare me with Fanny. You are not half good enough for that. And as for what you say about Claire's education, I too have a good education, an excellent education in fact. Much of it has been informal I know, but I am very well-read and . . .' She leant forward, facing her stepmother straight, 'I believe my father had intended to start the bookshop a while back, long before you put your nose in. – You made money enough from my children's story didn't you. It was very much liked.' Mary's eyes narrowed with rage as she spoke. 'Oh yes, a very clever book for a child of eleven, but you did not say so, did you. No, you wouldn't. I hate you.' She breathed in deeply. 'And you have tried to make Papa not love me. Don't look at me like that, it is true! You sent me to Scotland hoping he might forget me. But how wrong you were! Ha-ha. Papa will never forget me. I am his, much more than you are.'

Mary Jane replied in a whisper. 'Well, you see how she is Mr Shelley. Tantrums, tantrums.' She lowered her voice. 'Who knows what will become of you, Mary. You should try to control yourself, my dear.'

'I am not your dear,' snapped Mary. 'I never was. I am my father's dear, but not yours. He will always love me best.'

'Not after this, he won't. He will not love you at all after this. Oh no. You have made quite a blunder here.'

'And he won't love *me* either,' moaned Claire, wringing her hands. 'Not that he ever did. It has always been Mary.'

'And also . . .' Mary continued, shaking.

'Hush, hush, my darling,' said Shelley. He stretched out his legs and clasped his hands behind his head. 'Enough has been said I think.'

'Oh it hasn't,' Mary Jane insisted, standing. 'Wait until Claire gets home, their father will have lots to say then. – Mary, you must give up this nonsense right now and return to Skinner Street with me. I will hear no more.'

'Our minds are made up, Mama,' Claire said flatly.

The room was noisy with voices, but Mary Jane's voice was loudest. 'I say you come home, the two of you!' she shouted. 'And as for you, young man, I shall write to your father. You have left a pregnant wife and child.' She stood very straight looking at Shelley down her nose. 'I know your type. You are selfish and up to no good, writing your fancy poems without a care in the world for others. You will cause Mary to suffer I know, but never my Claire. You are trying to get your hands on her aren't you?' She looked at her daughter sadly. 'Please don't give yourself away to that good for nothing poet, my pet. You are sure to regret it.'

'You need not worry Mama,' said Claire. She smiled gently. 'You can depend on me to be sensible. And I must use my education for the world, must I not? You understand, surely. Or am I to stay in that bookshop for ever? – I am going to France, Mama. To France! And then to Switzerland. You told me my father lived in Switzerland.'

Mary Jane's face went pale with emotion. She frowned. 'Did I? Is that what I said?'

'The wind has dropped,' said Shelley peering outside.

'Oh, please don't take my daughter,' Mary Jane begged. She glanced about the room. It was busy with talk and laughter. 'I can find us accommodation. You might feel different tomorrow.'

'Well, I shall feel exactly the same,' said Claire with a look of resignation. 'This is my fate Mama.' She sighed loudly, as if her words brought great satisfaction.

Mary Jane turned again to Shelley. 'You are playing with fire,' she said bitterly, pressing her chin into her chest. 'And you are also ruining lives. I shall never forgive you for this. – What is to happen to your family, your child and the one that is yet to be born? Who will be there for your wife when she has to give birth?'

'She has family,' said Shelley dismissively. 'And as for Claire she'll be perfectly safe with me.' He smiled at her over the table and Claire smiled back.

7

Exploring

'I am free!' cried Claire as the trio ambled through France, her mother would have to think things through, she said, and realise her daughter wasn't her subject, she was a totally separate being. 'She thinks she's a queen!' said Claire walking along proudly, her hair pinned high on her head. 'Can you imagine Mama as a queen?' She laughed into the warm clear air. 'I doubt she'd be popular.'

'Well, the queen of France wasn't popular,' said Shelley. 'She went to the guillotine in a tumbrel. And after they'd sliced off her head, it was shown to the crowd, who cried, "Vive la République!"'

Claire shivered. 'I can't imagine Mama being guillotined; she would have found a way escape it.'

'Let's not talk about your mother,' said Mary, happy to have also escaped her. She wasn't interested in Mary Jane anymore, but she was still concerned about her father and wondered what he'd been told when her stepmother had returned to London.

They found good lodgings and resolved to see as much as they could of Paris, their world seemed suddenly bigger and more exciting, the scent of summer mingling with the smells of a country torn apart by war. The aftermath of the French revolution was evident wherever they went. Mary wrote in her journal

> *"The distress of the inhabitants, whose houses had been burned their cattle killed and all their wealth destroyed, has given a sting to my detestation of war …"*

Poor Paris with its broken windows and ruined monuments and general devastation brought the horror of the past close, though many of the people looked forward with hope. – "Paris est une ville merveilleuse! – Il n'y a nulle part comme Paris!" someone shouted, passing them by in a chaise. But a lot of French citizens still looked at English visitors with an air or suspicion; the revolution had changed their thinking. It had done away with the monarchy, the system of feudalism and the power of the Catholic Church, but the need for reforms lived on and revolutionary ideals were spreading fast through the world.

Mary thought a lot about her father, who she felt she had hurt and betrayed. Mary Jane had hated her at Dover, there were bound to be serious reprisals. She wondered if her father might disown them, or never let them back in the house . . . especially now she was pregnant. Oh, she was pregnant. How would she cope? What would it be like with a baby? She ought to have rejoiced, but she couldn't. She was far too young. There was a terrible sadness in her soul. Would Percy stay faithful? No he would not! He constantly looked at beautiful women when they passed and it made her afraid. Nothing bothered Claire; she was free as a bird. A natural antagonist, she did not suffer, for she did not love to excess and reserved her strength; she was as free spirited as Percy and the two of them talked without restraint in their Paris apartment. The relationship between the three of them was changing. Or perhaps it was becoming just what Percy intended. Breaking the news about her pregnancy to him, there'd been no delight in his eyes, only concern and disillusionment. She believed he still loved Harriet in his strange way of loving, but he could not manage the part of his life that contained her, and Mary knew it played on his mind. At the worst times when he grew wretched he went for the bottle of laudanum in his pocket and drank of it deeply, then he would turn to his writing. There was a great and powerful energy about him then. Mary wrote also, and when her candle threw shadows on the walls she would see the shapes of monsters looming about her, morbid silhouettes of her fears, then she would hear the agonizing creak of

Claire's bedroom door as he opened it and closed it behind him. In the early hours he would come to their bed, a bed often cold because she would not lie in it without him and sat in a chair throughout the night. Each day was a challenge. She had asked him straight if he loved her. "But of course," he had answered, looking at her curiously. "We shall experience what the world has to offer together. Dear Mary, we shall visit exciting places. There is more to life than London and Dundee, the world is a cornucopia of delights! – Mary, my darling, your heart throbs with passion. I know that Hogg would adore you, and I think you would return his feelings." "But I have no need of others …" she'd said, smarting with pain. "The right kind of love is what matters." "But love can never be wrong,'" he'd said, looking astonished. "There is only love. And love, and love. Let us live sweet Mary, let us live!"

Their stay in Paris was a flurry of writing and exploring. Percy and Claire often went off on their own making discoveries, Claire delivering a cascade of excited words after while Shelley scratched away with his pen. Shelley's vitality like Claire's was inexhaustible and he was up first light, eager and ready for the day. Sometimes her pregnancy made her nauseas and if they went out without her, she read or else wrote in her journal.

But it would not do. It wasn't what she'd envisaged. There was Harriet; there was Claire, and who else? She wondered how it was just now with Harriet and the child. Harriet's baby was due to arrive that autumn. How easily Shelley toyed with love, she thought, as if he were on a stage in his own theatre, love just a temporary pleasure, forgotten once the curtains drew closed. Try as she would, she could not share him with Claire. And she wondered if what she suffered had also been suffered by Harriet, and if Harriet too felt a dagger in her soul when she thought of her husband's betrayal. They could not speak of it for it irked him to think she might want him just for herself and he'd remind her then of their earlier talks about freedom.

But for all of that, she felt like a wife who would soon be a mother. But she wasn't a wife, Percy had a wife already. And she must now call upon Claire for assistance if she felt nauseous. She felt humiliated by it and helpless. She couldn't imagine her future. And she felt so treacherous too. She had betrayed her father; she had betrayed the cold white bones of her mother in the graveyard. But she couldn't turn back. Worst of all, she loved Shelley wholeheartedly and he had found his way to the centre of all she was. So much so that she had lost herself utterly. She must yield to his will, always yield. Ah love, sweet love! But she would not suffocate in it, and must always remember she was Mary Wollstonecraft's daughter, and remember her words.

'And so,' said Claire one morning, hand on hip like Mary Jane, and looking down on Mary as she lay on the chaise longue. 'You'll give birth to the child of a wonderful poet – what privilege? I do wish you looked more cheery.' She sat down heavily beside her. 'You always have the best of his love, you know. It is just the same with Papa. Mary, Mary, it is always Mary. Will anyone ever love *me*?'

Mary put out her hand and drew Claire close. 'Best not rely on Percy for love, his feelings are like the weather,' she murmured. 'He is spontaneous and devil may care. Who knows who he'll love tomorrow? He will always hurt us with love.' She gazed at the ceiling wistfully.

'He loves you most, I know,' Claire said with a hint of annoyance. 'But you don't see his brilliance like I do.'

'Perhaps he doesn't see mine,' Mary said quietly.

Claire laughed and stood up. 'Oh, Mary, please. You cannot compete with Shelley? He is a true genius. He has a marvellous imagination.'

Mary pondered. 'Yes,' she murmured. 'But what does it mean to be a "genius"? It would seem there are geniuses everywhere. – Byron is a genius; Coleridge and Wordsworth are geniuses, and others. Such men are said to be divinely inspired, but is it true?' She braced herself and sat up. 'I too have a great imagination,' she said flatly. But her pregnancy made her feel heavy and bloated, and when would she write her stories with the baby, if there was any genius in her it would never find its way into the world. For a moment or two she felt despondent. 'Shelley and I each have our own point of view,' she said sighing. 'Though a woman's point of view is all too often ignored.'

Claire looked at her and frowned. 'Shelley is very experienced and learned, whilst you, my dear have little of either.'

Mary looked at her straight. 'I believe I have wisdom,' she murmured. 'I have learned a lot from Papa, a man who Percy reveres.'

'But you were often in Scotland,' Claire said sighing. She rose and straightened her dress.

'He poured out his thoughts in letters,' Mary said earnestly. 'I am sure we know each other well.'

Claire shrugged. 'So you share Papa's ideas?' She gazed at Mary her eyes wide and curious. 'I didn't even know he wrote to you.'

'Of course. We wrote to each other often. But I do have ideas of my own. You see, Shelley and I see a need for social reform. People must think and change. There is too much pain and suffering in the world.' She thought of something she'd written that morning and said the word quietly

'I do know that for the sympathy of one living being, I would make peace with all. I have love in me the likes of which you can scarcely imagine and rage the likes of which you would not believe. If I cannot satisfy the one, I will indulge the other . . .'

'Is that how you feel?' asked Claire looking at her curiously and glancing across at the pages lying by Mary.

Mary gathered them up and went to put them in drawer. 'Those are the words of the wretched creature in my story.'

Claire sat rapt and attentive.

Mary looked her over slowly and continued. 'A man who has been delivered from the shackles of death and lives again amongst us, a creature that longs for love in a world that does not understand it.'

'A living demon?' Claire shivered.

Mary gave a loud sigh. 'Demons can come from the soul of things, straight from the living heart and soul of our fears.'

Claire looked perplexed and reached for her shawl. She sat on the edge of a chair.

'Dear Mary, why write a story that frightens you?' she said concernedly. 'Such writing would make me nervous.'

Mary smiled. 'I think I have something to say. Perhaps my story will help people see how it is.'

'How what is?' asked Claire frowning. 'You puzzle me Mary.' She gave an anxious little laugh. 'Oh come, let us join Shelley downstairs.'

Today they would leave and move on.

Leaving Paris, they hired a cart and a mule to help them on their way. But their finances were running low and Shelley was in need of a bank where he might negotiate credit. The most significant events had happened here in Paris – the storming of the Bastille prison in 1789, the execution of Louis XVI in 1715 and his Queen Marie Antoinette in 1793, the butchering of many citizens in the September massacres and the slaughter of thousands of others who had been pushed into the tumbrels and sent to the guillotine because they did not suit the revolution. No doubt the agonies of the terror still came to people in dreams, thought Mary, the sound of the tumbrels rattling through their city would echo in their minds for ever. They had barely been still and had seen the best and the worst: the Palace of Versailles, the Champs Elysées, The Tuileries Palace, a dismal place, where the king and queen had been as good as imprisoned after trying to escape the revolution. Wretched peasants peered at them from hovels while wealthy citizens passed them by in grandiose coaches. No matter that thousands of heads had been severed, inequality still held sway. Napoleon Bonaparte the powerful military commander who had taken power in France was exiled now on the island of Elba and it was rumoured he'd attempted suicide. But the dark days of revolution had gone and the people of France were determined their country would rise to power once again as in glorious days of old.

English travellers were still regarded suspiciously. It was evident that the black silk dresses worn by Claire and Mary would render them vulnerable, Shelley said cautiously, and they should keep themselves covered by their capes if they wanted to wear them, otherwise it would be best to wear something more plain. He was wincing and limping badly. He'd slipped off the cart and sprained his ankle badly, annoying the grouchy driver who claimed Englishmen were all *sans effet*.

Mary was searching through her bags on the floor of the cart, whispering. 'I can never replace those pieces,' she moaned.

He looked at her, and shook his head. 'What have you lost?' he asked tiredly.

'My box of writings,' she said, sighing. 'You shouldn't have rushed me.'

'I didn't,' he retorted. 'You are careless, my dear and you know it. It doesn't do to be careless; you should focus more carefully and not be so dreamy.'

She frowned defeated; she was forgetting things a lot lately. They were a good few miles out of Paris.

'All that writing,' said Percy, looking horrified. '– Your children's stories and the journal, have they all gone?'

She raised her shoulders and dropped them slowly.

Claire moved about uncomfortable, the cart was hard and the wheels were unstable. 'It's like sitting in one of those tumbrels,' she grumbled. She frowned at Percy as he tried to get down on his knees, looking for Mary's box, all the while wincing.

'You're not going to find it, it's in Paris,' Mary said flatly.

'Then we'll have to go back,' sighed Percy, struggling up. He rubbed his face and sighed. 'How could you lose your writings? Oh, Mary, it's a tragedy. Look, I must stop the driver this minute.'

'There isn't any point,' Mary said firmly. 'I asked the man at the desk if anyone had seen it and he told me the cleaners had cleared the room.'

'You mean they threw away your box?'

'I suspect that's what's happened,' she said feebly. 'Once you have given in the key they are free to do as they wish.'

'The cleaner wouldn't care a jot about your work,' Shelley said disgruntled.

Claire threw out her hands. 'Well Mary didn't care that much, did she,' she said, rolling her eyes at Shelley.

'What a nuisance. I must think more carefully,' Mary said, miserably. For a moment or two they were silent. 'Did you see it last night when you came in our room?' she asked Claire directly. 'It was there on the table by the bed . . .'

'*Me?*' said Claire, taken aback, astounded. 'Of course not. I didn't mean to disturb you, It was all that torrential rain and there was so much lightning. I'm terrified of lightning. That's why I got in your bed. You know how storms disturb me.'

Mary answered with silence. She hadn't been happy with Claire beside Percy in the night.

'Mon cher Percy, s'il te plaît, ne sois pas si malheureux,' said Claire, tilting her head on one side and looking at Percy sadly.

'Oh no, only I should be unhappy,' said Mary, 'not Percy.'

'Mary can write something else,' sighed Percy. 'The writings have gone and that's it. Let her alone for a while.'

Claire leant forward and touched Mary's hand. 'You will write better things,' she condescended.

Mary closed her eyes. 'If only I felt less tired.'

'It's a little too warm,' said Claire, glancing about, 'but at least it's not raining.'

Mary sat brooding.

'I shall always be here to support you,' Claire added brightly. 'I am strong as an ox. We are going to Switzerland! – Shall we be doing much walking?' she asked, turning to Percy.

'I'm afraid we must,' he said. 'That's if my ankle gets better. Damn thing. We can hire a chaise for some of the way, but we'll need good weather, it won't be an easy journey.' He gazed at his ankle worriedly. 'I think it's broken.'

'It looks quite swollen,' said Mary, 'and it's discoloured. 'But I doubt you've broken it Percy. – Where shall we stay?' She was annoyed that Claire had taken over.

'Oh, I know of some excellent inns,' he returned, more cheerfully. 'All will be well.'

He was rebelling furiously, thought Mary, against his father, determined to have his freedom.

'More to the point, how shall we pay?' asked Claire despondently. 'We left Paris without paying for our stay.' She smiled wryly. 'You've a nerve Percy, you really have a nerve.' She clapped as if to applaud him. 'You're a sot of highwayman aren't you?'

Percy sighed loudly. 'All is well. I can send them money later. Do not ask about my finances Claire. It is not your business.'

Claire frowned at the rebuke. 'Do you really think your father will leave you money after what you have done to Harriet?' She narrowed her eyes and folded her arms in a no nonsense gesture, irritated because Shelley sat with Mary while she sat opposite alone.

'I can always talk him round later,' Percy mumbled, stroking his injured ankle.

'"Later?"' Mary said curious.

'Once he gets used to my ways. It is taking him time to realise I am not like him. He obeys my grandfather's wishes, whilst I do not. I do as I want.'

'You are taking a lot of chances,' Claire said quietly.

'Life is all about taking chances, my dear,' he said flatly. 'Or what is it worth?'

Mary's heart pounded. What a pity she'd lost her box. And she wasn't ready for pregnancy yet, it made her feel full and clumsy, and it made her nauseas. She felt resentful that Claire was well and didn't get ill. She had summoned every fibre of her strength to avoid the pettiness of jealousy, but it had come to her now with the fullness of its hostility. She breathed in deeply and braced herself. She could do better, and she would.

Percy sat touching his ankle and wincing. ' . . . Oh yes, I am quite the rebel and my father knows it. I am an atheist and a cynic and I haven't a scrap of time for the aristocracy. Their wealth should go to the poor. I have always said it.'

'So how do people like you make money?' Claire said wryly. 'Will you start a business like Papa?'

'I can write and think,' Percy retorted brusquely, straightening and taking a breath. 'People like me shouldn't be made to earn money, we must write for the good of mankind.' He turned to Mary. 'Your father would say so, would he not? He also believes that people of wealth should support those who are gifted.'

Mary sighed. 'He does it's true. I doubt your father will support us now though, Percy.'

Shelley went on, intense and excited. 'My dear, I am Percy Bysshe Shelley. I see the world from quite a singular perspective. I am a . . .'

'You are a genius,' cried Claire, clapping her hands loudly. She laughed and leant forward, lowering her voice. 'We *know* you're a genius, Percy. Do give us some peace.'

'I have started two novels,' sighed Mary. 'I did not put them in the box, thank goodness. They are here in my bag, right by my feet.'

'Well, you'd better not lose them,' sniffed Claire.

'Am I to see them?' asked Percy, raising his eyebrows and smiling.

She shook her head. 'Not yet.' She knew the work wasn't ready. His own was quickly inspired and very soon polished. His gift was obvious, he could draw poetry from the ether, so much so that it came and went from him easy as the air he breathed.

'No, better not lose them,' said Claire petulantly. 'I don't know how you can write when you're always feeling sick.'

'I manage,' said Mary. She turned to Shelley. 'I saw you scribbling last night.'

He moved about uncomfortable. 'Oh yes, "scribbling" is the right word too. I was trying to write some poetry. I'm not sure there's any command in it though. Not yet.'

For a moment or two they were silent.

He turned to Mary and looked at her curiously. 'Your mother was in Paris for quite a considerable time? Fanny's father . . .'

'Indeed,' said Claire, straightening the folds of her dress. 'Another fellow who thinks he can leave his marriage at the drop of a hat.'

'He did not marry my mother,' Mary said quietly. 'It is known only too well.'

'I'm sorry,' said Claire. 'Not that it matters. It's a lot of fuss about nothing. Marriage is a miserable business.'

'Did your mother marry your father?' asked Mary, seeing that Claire was self-conscious.

'I haven't a clue. I have never asked her,' said Claire.

'I have brought my mother's works,' said Mary, bracing herself proudly. She touched the bag by her feet. 'I intend to read them while we're travelling.'

'You remember her books, but lose your own work,' Shelley said grimly. 'Not good, my dear, not good. Her travels tell of a brave adventurer, a sort of ancient voyager. Though she was searching for a ship, was she not, and its silver had been stolen by pirates. How we waste ourselves, you see.'

Mary felt uncomfortable on the hard seat of the cart. Claire was bold and it seemed cared nothing for anything. 'She did not find the ship with the silver sadly,' said Mary. 'I doubt Imlay thought she would. It was a bit of a fool's errand,'

'Are you saying your mother was a fool?' Percy lifted his eyebrows.

Mary shook her head. 'Only regarding Imlay,' she said quietly.

'I so want to see the Swiss mountains!' Claire said dreamily.

'. . . And you are writing about our tour,' said Shelley, still talking to Mary. 'I'm glad. You are a true searcher, a searcher of body and soul. Your inventiveness blooms with prodigious beauty, my dear.'

Mary warmed at his words, but he did not know the truth, her imagination was nothing like he thought. In fact it could be fearsome and ugly.

The driver moved on through the countryside, and they came to a mountain stream where Shelley said they should bathe. But Mary thought the driver watched too closely and the women declined. Claire complained there were too many buttons to undo on her dresses and too many petticoats to fuss with, and there was also the problem of their stays. They would wash at the next cottage, said Mary. The peasants were unkempt, but at least they would afford them some privacy for one or two coins.

Percy was soon naked, splashing himself with water and limping around in the stream, losing himself in the ecstasy of bathing his body.

He had long, beautiful limbs, thought Mary. He loved to have water on his limbs, but he also feared it. She remembered one of his poems

"My spirit like a charmed bark doth swim
Upon the liquid waves of thy sweet singing,
Far far away into the regions dim

Of rapture—as a boat, with swift sails winging
Its way adown some many-winding river,
Speeds through dark forests o'er the waters swinging . . .

Something frightened him in his soul, she thought, some dark spirit plagued him. Had he fallen in the water as a child and almost drowned? He did not speak of his childhood, but somehow he and his father fell short of what they'd wanted from each other and the matter was never resolved.

'I intend to be an actress,' Claire said languidly, as Percy got back into his clothes. 'I'm not sure how I shall do it, but I shall try my best to make contacts. I doubt I have very much talent for writing.'

Mary smiled at her. 'You write an excellent letter, Claire. I always enjoyed reading them in Dundee.'

'I'm glad,' said Claire. She reached for her bag beside her. 'I have brought Rousseau and Shakespeare to read in the evenings. I took them from the shop. Oh dear, Mama is bound to have noticed; she always keeps check on the stock. I expect she'll kick up a fuss.'

'I had thought to bring them myself,' Mary said blithely. 'But I saw they'd gone from the shelf. Now I know why. Will you return them?' She raised her eyebrows waiting.

'I'm not sure. I'd better not lose them though. Books like that are hard come by. I am rather more careful than you, I think. I value things more as well. I would never have lost that box.'

For several minutes they were thoughtful.

'Perhaps the proprietor thought it held jewellery and felt entitled,' laughed Claire.

'What about that then,' Shelley said smiling, his face red and shining from the vigour of his bathe. 'They thought it might contain treasure.' He laughed loudly, shaking water from his legs and drying his arms on his shirt, soaking the ruffles, the sound of his laughter ringing with Claire's in the air.

'And perhaps it did,' said Mary, handing him his stockings which he quickly pulled on his legs. She tried to remember what she'd written, the impassioned words from her dreams, the language of the sea in Dundee, the fanciful loves of beasts that rose from the waves and tried to mate with humans. But the writing had gone, just like her dreams. She had freed herself on the page and her heart had outrun the truth of her situation. She could not trust her lover; he had freed himself into life and she feared her future.

8

Paradise Grounded

'We are even poorer than these peasants,' Claire said dramatically as they walked through the French countryside. 'And we have nowhere to rest our heads.'

'Walk over there,' said Shelley, pointing to a smoother part of the path. 'And do help Mary with her things, I have all I can carry here.'

'The driver would have taken us further,' said Claire, 'That mule and cart certainly wasn't ideal, but look at us now, we are tired and you are still limping.'

'I have very little money,' Shelley snapped back. 'How many times must I tell you.'

They peered into cottages, looking for somewhere to stay. Hollow eyed rustics peered back suspiciously. 'How dirty they are,' Claire whispered. 'And they look so dumb and stupid. I wonder what they say to each other.'

'Wordsworth would have found poetry here,' said Percy. 'He'd find jewels in the minds of these rustics. I am not so inspired by this sort of life myself.'

'But you admire Wordsworth,' said Mary. 'You have often said so. He sees the beauty of the ordinary life where people may seem to have little, yet the important things like family and love are there in abundance.'

'Are they?' said Claire, in a tone of contempt. 'I'm not so sure. You can't do much without money.'

Shelley looked at Mary and smiled. 'Indeed my dear, you are right, and Wordsworth's poetry is often on my mind. But I do not enjoy, as you know, a lot of his inspirations, and I wonder if Coleridge does in general. For Coleridge the simple life is far too dull. Wordsworth's poetry is harmonious and beautiful indeed, but it does not have the flights of fancy that are found in the poetry of Coleridge. I like his flights of fancy.'

'I suspect Coleridge likes his laudanum too,' said Claire, looking at Shelley knowingly.

'Alas,' said Shelley. 'I do not feel the living body of rivers and mountains as Wordsworth does either or rely so much on metaphysical enchantments. Nature is both splendid and deathly to me.' He straightened. 'But I do feel social issues the same and need to address them if I can.' He fell to reciting a Wordsworth poem as they walked

> '"The world is too much with us; late and soon,
> Getting and spending, we lay waste our powers;—
> Little we see in Nature that is ours;
> We have given our hearts away, a sordid boon!
> This Sea that bares her bosom to the moon;
> The winds that will be howling at all hours,
> And are up-gathered now like sleeping flowers;
> For this, for everything, we are out of tune;
> It moves us not. Great God! I'd rather be
> A Pagan suckled in a creed outworn;
> So might I, standing on this pleasant lea,
> Have glimpses that would make me less forlorn;
> Have sight of Proteus rising from the sea;
> Or hear old Triton blow his wreathèd horn."'

Deep in thought they gazed about at the trees.

'Soon we shall be in Switzerland,' said Mary. 'We shall see the mountains. I'm sure you will feel their grandeur Percy in the way that Wordsworth does. You know that he has walked in the Alps.'

'Wordsworth is a strong fellow.' Percy gritted his teeth, still limping. For a minute or two they were silent.

'I am not poor,' he said, returning to Claire's earlier comments, and wincing at the pain in his ankle. 'I shall be rich eventually; however, people must sadly die before that.'

'"Eventually"', smiled Claire. She waved her finger. 'Voltaire argued money couldn't write poems, as if writing poems was better than having money. Fine words yes, but these peasants aren't interested in poems; they just want food for their families. They'll want silver Percy if they find us somewhere to sleep.' She sighed. 'I am tired and need to lie down.'

Claire talked on but Percy wasn't listening. Mary walked beside them, listening and looking. Claire was rarely silent and Percy's eyes looked troubled. He feared losing authority. Claire was too bold. She was also troublesome in an awkward and perverse sort of way, constantly putting them on edge with her dramatic outbursts. – They would be set upon by thieves, she and Mary would be stripped of their black silk dresses and would be forced to walk in their petticoats! The little money they had would be stolen and they would then have to beg. The sky was darkening and the sound of the wind in the trees threatened rain. Mary's eyes lingered on Percy. The thick bristle on his chin, combined with his brooding manner made him look fiendish. His mind was equal to anything, his imagination made him quite perfect, he might have been an angel or a devil, but in reality he was often confused and awkward. And nobody dared offend him for he might suddenly tremble and his eyes become mad with rage. They stopped for a moment and he leant against a tree. 'This ankle is purple as dusk, damn it!' he said, 'and twice the size it was this morning.'

'We have walked a long way,' said Mary sympathetically. She and Claire sat down on the grass. Shelley took out his laudanum and drank of it deeply.

'Mama says that will be the death of you,' said Claire. 'Don't you care?'

'What – about dying? Not at all. Death doesn't frighten me a bit. As a matter of fact it might be interesting.' He gazed at the sky and recited some lines of his poetry;

'O man! hold thee on in courage of soul
Through the stormy shades of thy wordly way,
And the billows of clouds that around thee roll
Shall sleep in the light of a wondrous day,
Where hell and heaven shall leave thee free
To the universe of destiny.'

Then he looked at the bottle in his fingers. 'I doubt it does me any harm,' he said, pressing the bottle on his cheek. 'It helps to speed up my thinking.'

'But your mind needs slowing,' said Mary. 'Not speeding.' She saw that his eyes had glazed over.

'If it happened though, if you died from drinking the laudanum, it would look like a kind of suicide,' said Claire. 'What must we do if you die?'

'Poor Claire,' he laughed. 'I am not about to commit suicide. Have no fear. Suicide has its place in life, of course. It is highly recommended sometimes.' The air felt suddenly cold. He picked up Mary's shawl which had fallen to the floor and handed it across. She wrapped it over her cape.

Mary was thoughtful. She hurt for Percy; he could not compete with Claire's directness. She had made him moody and perverse. The talk was inflammatory and she wanted to stop it, she gathered herself together and got up. Then the three of them carried on walking through the woodland gazing at the ground as they went. Mary recalled some words from another of his poems, *"There's not one atom of yon earth, but once was living man,"'* she whispered. '*Queen Mab*, of course. This woodland has made me think of it.' She looked around at the trees and smiled with pleasure.

'I haven't read it,' said Claire.

Mary told her how Queen Mab, queen of the fairies, helped sleepers give birth to their dreams. 'She comes from Romeo and Juliet, Percy has borrowed some ideas. I think it's exciting the way these magical characters are given such life through legend. Queen Mab delivers the desires of sleeping men and can be quite wanton.' She laughed quietly.

'So how is she wanton?' asked Claire, looking at Mary and Percy by turns.

'You must read it,' said Percy. 'I self published one or two copies and sent it about . . . I didn't look for a publisher, I didn't think I should, the poems wasn't really ready. I won't let it out there yet . . . I keep it in a file.' He turned to Mary. 'I had your father's theories in mind when I wrote it; I would like to see those societal changes he speaks of. I believe as he does himself, that many of society's evils can dissolve quite naturally in time through virtue and honesty.' He frowned. 'I need to get more experience to give that poem wings.'

He was talking quickly, his words disjointed. He drank more laudanum. Mary listened and watched him. Poetry was everything to him. More than her, more than his wife and child, more than his family, even more than his self, which he seemed to see as a kind of abstract entity, a sort of phantom that could live apart, changing and growing like something other. She asked herself if that was what happened to those who were truly captured by art, tortured souls lost in an abyss of pain where imperfection was never allowed. She leant towards him as they walked. 'You allowed me to read it,' she said, lowering her voice. 'Though it is dedicated to Harriet.' She wondered at his lack of sensitivity, the way he cut himself off yet burst through barriers of feeling in poetry so freely. He was out to discover the inner sanctuary of things, to have their veracity made clear, though his own true existence seemed vaporous.

'I have to think much harder,' he said. 'Napoleon's wars have changed a lot of my thinking. I do believe we can realise a perfect society in time.' He sighed hard. 'I suspect that poem might in some ways be seen as obscene. There would be someone on my trail for something or other. The government doesn't like poets. We tell the truth and we might say things they don't like.' He laughed at a sudden thought. 'My father hates me I think.'

For a moment or two they were silent.

'He probably suffers amongst his colleagues for the things you say in your writing,' said Mary looking at him straight.

'And the fact that you borrow lots of money hoping it will come to you later through him,' added Claire. 'It's a risky business, you know. You will be thrown into the debtor's prison one day.'

'Do you have any answers, dear Claire,' he smiled. 'How else do I provide for you and Mary? Do tell me? If you have answers please let me know, for answers are in short supply.' He laughed. 'My father serves the government in his work, you see, and I serve myself. I am a devoted enemy of religious, political, and domestic oppression and because of that he suffers.'

'But you caused him such bother with that pamphlet,' said Claire, in a tone of authority. 'It was foolish. They threw you out of Oxford for that.'

He frowned at her, annoyed. 'Universities are supposed to spread knowledge.'

'Of the right sort,' Claire said emphatically.

'It is good to disseminate ideas, and to challenge them too,' he said with certainty. 'There is no room for dogma in truth.'

For several minutes they walked in silence, gazing at the trees and cottages, searching for one that looked clean where they might stop and take rest.

'*Love*,' that is the thing,' Shelley said finally. 'To love as much as we can as long as we exist. I have often read of men who have laboured extensively, seeking their innermost selves by loving many women, and it's right. Love opens up the soul and in it are countless gems, some of which we see, others we do not. And some of them are ours. They know us, and we know them in return. There are wonderful words to be reached for, spiritual ideas and astonishing thoughts. We must find them!'

Mary thought of Harriet. How could he think high thoughts in poetry yet behave so badly in life? Was he wrong to have left her, or might it be right to leave love when it no longer lived. But she was still so young. Shelley was older; he had travelled and had loved before. She was building a new way of thinking piece by piece, she could almost feel it happening. Tears ran down her cheeks as she tried to balance her feelings. She lifted her head and stared at the woodland, everywhere was turning dark. She must not argue with Shelley, she told herself, for didn't he always know best.

She had broken her link with her father and now she belonged to Percy. But did she? Didn't she just *belong* to herself? What of the discerning woman she knew herself to be? She too had thoughts that needed voicing. A great sense of self surged in her daily, a pride equal to Shelley's, a pride inherited from her mother, and she vowed she would own it. She thought of the pain, of the laudanum, of her mother's attempted suicides. Then she tried instead to think of those beautiful times she'd shared with Shelley, their visits to the graveyard where they'd talked about wondrous things, and where they had first made love. All that, just now was silent in her mind and a lot of the time he neglected her. They each made their journal entries and continued to write. But what did she really know about this man she professed to love? 'He cannot . . .' she whispered. But the trees absorbed her words.

'Who cannot, what?' said Percy, turning to look at her. 'You are always whispering, my dear.' He drew her towards him. 'You remember such a lot of poetry. It's good to bring it to mind and quote it so readily.'

'I too can remember poetry,' Claire said loudly, folding her arms. 'I learned a great deal of Byron's *Corsair* on a quiet afternoon in the shop. I do love Byron's poetry.'

'I daresay you do,' said Shelley. 'That is apparent. He's a handsome beggar too, is Byron. Women fall at his feet. I suspect they will all have memorised that poem by heart!'

'I have heard of his beauty,' said Claire, passing her fingers through her hair. 'But no woman will ever have his love. I believe he is in love with his sister.'

'His *half* sister,' Shelley corrected. 'They only have the same mother.'

'Awkward though, falling for your sister,' Claire added thoughtfully. 'But I do believe he is a genius.'

They had come to a small village in the depth of the woodland.

'There are other kinds of geniuses,' said Mary, thinking of the genius of poets. 'What of the military genius of someone like Bonaparte, or the genius of Ludwig Van Beethoven, and then there are the artists and poets. Are there really that many geniuses?'

'There is room for them all, my dear,' said Shelley. 'Imaginations merge in amazing ways. Who knows what force ignites them, what essential spark makes art bolt forward into life! We poets are given possession of magic I think. We are blessed with incredible insights.' He breathed in deeply and swelled out his chest, then gazed at the darkening sky.

'So people like you and Byron are chosen by higher forces are you?' said Claire, half amused.

'I do believe we are,' he said grandly. 'As a matter of fact, Bryon, you know, had a very sad childhood. He lived above a Scottish perfumery a while. His father was rarely seen. Byron and his mother were destitute and lived in poverty. His father died in France. Suicide, I think. I doubt he ever saw his son. George Gordon Noel at ten years of age became sixth Baron Byron on the death of his great uncle. He went to Harrow and then to Cambridge University.'

'And he didn't write anything seditious,' said Claire. 'I suppose he had rather more sense.'

They walked on further.

'I heard the same at the Baxter's,' said Mary. 'Byron went to the Aberdeen Grammar school then he moved with his mother to Newstead Abbey, their ancestral home since the time of Henry the eighth. – But why are we talking about Byron?' She saw that Claire looked preoccupied.

Reaching the edge of the woodland a cottager standing in the doorway of his home summoned them over. 'Best come in 'ere!' he called. 'There's a mighty storm on its way!'

The rain fell fast and they all quickened their pace. The man's wife joined him at the door with three small children behind her. 'There's a good fire inside,' she said, 'an' I've a beef stew in the pot.'

Inside the cottage all was neat and clean. Mary and Claire took off their capes and bonnets. The husband took their bags and bade them sit down. 'Nous n'avons pas vu d'âme depuis des semaines,' said the woman. 'And now we are visited by ladies in black silk dresses!'

'We are from England,' said Claire, speaking French. 'Nous tournons.'

'And I am Percy Bysshe Shelley,' Shelley said bowing lightly. 'These women are my companions, Mary and Claire. Nous sommes très heureux de vous rencontrer! Travelling has been far from easy. As you see I have done myself an injury.' The woman looked down at his ankle and went for warm water to bathe it.

'You are kind,' said Shelley, as she laid soft cloths on the bruises.

'The swelling will be gone come morning' said the wife. 'Now you must wash and rest. – We need more wood for the fire!' she called to her husband. 'Go and find Horst!' She turned again to the company. 'Horst can chop wood as fast as a beaver! He is strong as a bear and has grown very big. They call him the giant of the forest. Some people fear him, though the man is gentle as a dove.'

The husband went out and returned within minutes then threw some logs on the fire. The children were playing with a kitten. The little black bundle hid then reappeared.

'Horst is obviously useful,' said Shelley as they all took a seat at the table. 'Perhaps he will come and speak with us? We need help to get down to the river, the pathway is steep.'

'Oh, he'll not row ye down the river,' the man said frowning. 'He doesn't like strangers. It's because of how they look at him, see. People call him a monster. There'll be somebody down by the waterside though who can help ye. Horst can help ye down the slope though.'

Mary's mind was busy. Poor Horst. Did he have a way to get back at his abusers, or did he just suffer. He was big enough to frighten them at least . . . '*Beware; for I am fearless, and therefore powerful,*' she murmured. 'Self-esteem is so important,' she said, but no-one was listening. She wondered how they'd survive for the rest of their journey. How would they pay the boatmen? Travelling by river however, cost less than other kinds of travel and they needed to return to London.

'We can't afford much,' said Claire, shrugging her shoulders. 'That's why we're going back to England.'

Percy sat at the table and tried to explain how he wasn't really poor but must wait to inherit from his father. 'We are short of money at present,' he said. 'But only for a while. Matters are rather complicated, you see, but they'll be very much clearer in time.' He bent his head, thoughtful. 'Life is rarely straightforward, eventually though I . . .'

'Always *"eventually"*,' sighed Claire.

'If I could only find a bank . . .' Percy continued.

'There's one on the way to the river,' said the woman. 'But now you must eat. We have more than enough to feed us.'

'I do not normally eat meat,' Shelley said awkwardly. 'But I intend to do so today for I am well near starving.'

'We can offer you beds for the night,' said the wife. 'The children can share.'

Mary saw it was a home of happy people acting of their own accord, living in a natural way. She fervently believed with her mother, that honesty and empathy, particularly as practised by women in a family would reform society and make people happy. Here, she could see it happening. After their meal, Mary checked that her pen and ink were safe along with her writing. She must make some notes that evening while the thoughts were fresh in her mind.

They all ate liberally of the stew, the children watching with wonder.

Shelley and Mary exchanged glances of relief.

And so they rested and replenished their strength in the perfectly kept little dwelling which was warm and busy. When the sunlight came in the morning, Claire and Mary awoke to the sound of the woman busy in the kitchen and the children laughing about the house while their father searched the hedges for eggs and the hens ran about clucking loudly with annoyance.

9

Back To London

The world in the meantime, continued to be wracked by politics, famines and war. Previously powerful kingdoms collapsed through invasions and internal turmoil, government systems once robust were destroyed within months, treaties were signed and new jurisdiction and controls changed the landscapes of life. Great Britain, with the defeat of France in North America and the conquest of many parts of India, was now an immense power and the ways of trade were rapidly undergoing change. And another revolution was beginning, an exciting flower of creativity had burst into being when the Scottish engineer and chemist James Watt, had altered and improved the steam engine, thereby providing for its abundant use in factories, mines and locomotives. And the world of literature was abuzz with the name of Lord George Byron, the beautiful aristocratic poet. His long poem *The Corsair* had sold 10,000 copies on the very day of publication, making him the most talked about poet in the land.

But the fugitive trio were filled with their own concerns, for there was Mary's pregnancy to consider, Claire's tendency to indulge in dramatic outbursts and Percy's urgent anxieties over the importance of social change, his love of justice, learning and freedom and his compelling need to write poetry. He had been to the bank the cottagers had referred to and had now secured a bagful of silver which he hoped would fulfil their needs until they reached London.

Mary took charge of their finances and was the cornerstone of Percy's existence, constantly insisting that his poetry came first over and above philosophy, politics or anything else that might distract him. Percy, she believed, had helped her live a freer existence and she felt she was growing in wisdom.

They had made good progress on their tour, noting in their shared journal what they had seen and done and keeping faith with their heartfelt ideologies whilst always affirming their dreams of a better society. Percy, convinced of his theories, included them in his poetry, and stayed within his dietary convictions. He would never take sugar in his tea, for it reminded him of slavery, he said, and most of the time he only ate fruit and nuts. Mary would ponder on it all, mainly humble with Percy, who she believed had immense talent and great knowledge. Should they argue, Claire would hold back for she could not rise to their talk, and if she divulged her own point of view, only to be found in error, she would not own to her words and claimed she'd felt tired. Percy would plead she should stay with her arguments and see them through to the end, and she tried constantly, but if she lost she would take the pins from her hair so that it fell in abundance down her shoulders and rendered him silent.

They had now reached Lake Lucerne and were in search of a worthy boatman who could take them down the water safely. That done, they went for provisions. The damp chilly air was uncomfortable and Claire complained about the mist, fretting the boat would get lost and they wouldn't know where they were. Percy stood gazing at the lake abstractedly. It was one of those detestable days when Mary knew he'd taken laudanum. He was nervous and edgy. 'The boatman says we must navigate a lot of sharp bends before we reach the Reuss,' he said anxiously. 'It concerns me. Boats have been known to turn over . . .'

'We need not rush,' said Mary. 'Why hurry? Nobody wants us in London and they do not expect us. Sit here and rest for a while until you feel better.' Mary knew that Percy would be nervous journeying on the great Lake Lucerne. She softened her voice. 'Once we are home you must learn how to swim, my love, I beg you.'

'The water intends to swallow me,' he whispered. 'I know it.' His voice broke as he spoke and he bent his head miserably. 'But we need to get back, a lot of things bother me . . . I asked Harriet to join us, you know. I did. I asked her in a letter. She preferred not to come. It's understandable, of course. She knows that I love you, and she couldn't have talked like we do. She has never seemed interested in poetry or philosophy and has little inclination to think of anything at all.'

Mary thought about Harriet. She too would give birth to a child by Percy very soon. Did he care? Did it matter?

'I am doomed, dear Mary, don't you see,' he continued. 'I have tried to tell you, time and again, but you never believe me . . . The water is fully aware of it though and waits.'

Mary was silent.

Claire stood thoughtful on the wet muddy path gazing at the towering mountains above them and the pine forests below. 'Did you not boat on the lake by your home in Sussex?' asked Mary.

'All the time,' Percy said readily. 'Often alone. I loved it. But the lake was always so still. I knew it was benign.'

She looked at him curiously. He spoke some verses from Coleridge's *Ancient Mariner*;

> *"And now there came both mist and snow,*
> *And it grew wondrous cold:*
> *And ice, mast-high, came floating by,*
> *As green as emerald.*
>
> *And through the drifts the snowy clifts*
> *Did send a dismal sheen:*
> *Nor shapes of men nor beasts we ken—*
> *The ice was all between.*
>
> *The ice was here, the ice was there,*
> *The ice was all around:*
> *It cracked and growled, and roared and howled,*
> *Like noises in a swound!*
>
> *At length did cross an Albatross ..."'*

She laughed. 'You really don't like that albatross do you? But Coleridge writes about the sea in that poem, this is a lake; it is not so wild and violent and the boatman is very experienced, do relax.'

He took out his handkerchief and drew it over his brow.

She hated his moods when he'd been taking laudanum. She felt lame when Percy was weak.

Claire came to join them. 'I heard you reciting,' she said, frowning at Percy. 'I hate that albatross too. There are all sorts of wicked forces in life, I often feel them, you know. Coleridge created a demon in that poem, for sure.' She glanced all around as they climbed in the boat. 'Albatrosses don't like poets.'

'Don't make Percy feel worse,' said Mary as they each parted with their bags. 'We've a long way to go. Nothing is out to get you, Percy. Enjoy the beautiful scenery and then we can write about it later.' Her words trailed off as she spoke. Perhaps it was true. Might Percy fall out of the boat? What if she couldn't save him? She imagined him struggling for his life, maybe finding the shore but then getting lost in the mountains, wandering like someone gone mad. She shook the image from her mind. Then she imagined a monster chasing him, a man larger than anyone she'd ever seen, a man like Horst the giant of the forest who lived in the village they'd left. She clung to Percy's arm as the boat moved on. A steep bank beside them led up to a high mountain where thin streaks of light like shining spears seared through the pine trees below. Apart from the sound of the water lapping on the side of the boat, the shore was almost silent. Percy was pale and shaking. She would have to find something to read to him until the effect of the laudanum wore off. They were to travel some 800 miles or so through many beautiful cantons, stopping at inns on the way. There would be much to enjoy.

The boat moved quickly as the full magnificence of the Alps came into view. The river flowed by castles high on the rocks, some of them ruined, crags and rich vegetation beside them. She imagined Wagner's Rhine maidens bathing on the rocks serenaded by lovely Oceanids. Here the Rhine grew busy and voices could be heard on the banks. Percy had fallen asleep, Mary had been reading from her mother's travels in Sweden, and Claire sat thoughtful. 'That ruined castle up there,' Mary asked the boatman, pointing. 'What is its name?' He screwed up his eyes to look, the ruins were too far away to identify their features precisely and a lot was hidden by pine trees.

'Ah,' he answered, taking a quick deep breath. 'That is castle Frankenstein. Un lieu de fantômes!' The boat strained with the current, the sun was low and deepening shadows made the castle remains look chilling. The boatman continued. 'A man called Johann Dippel was born there a long time ago, he worked as an alchemist and thought he had the power to make gold.' He laughed even louder and his voice echoed round the mountains. 'Oh, that he could! What friends he would have!' The boatman spoke with a regular boatman's knowledge and continued his tale. 'A very clever man. – Tu vois ce que je veux dire!' They say he made a special oil as well, the "elixir of life", he called it. Smooth it on your skin and you are immediately twenty years younger!' His voice fell to a whisper. 'Some say he carried out experiments on corpses from graves. It was rumoured he created a monster. Brought it to life, he did, with a bolt of lightning, but the thing ran away. It is said to be roaming the mountains.'

'"Brought it to life with lightning?"' said Percy, suddenly awake and sitting up. 'Yes, I do believe lightning has life giving forces yet to be discovered.'

Mary sat thoughtful, a light wind rocking the boat. She thought she heard a groan in the air, like the sound of a weary person lost in a kind of hell. Words went through her mind, painful agonised words – *"I, the miserable and the abandoned, am an abortion, to be spurned at, and kicked, and trampled on …"* The sky grew dark with menace and she gripped Percy's hand.

'Those ruins look eerie,' said Claire, looking up at the castle. 'You would probably be murdered in there and your body parts used for anatomy.'

Shelley smiled. 'I think you might be right, my dear. You would be cut to pieces in no time.'

Mary could feel the blood rising in her cheeks. The boat lurched on the waves and Percy grabbed the side, terrified.

'The water is rocky around here,' the boatman said calmly. 'But I have travelled this stretch many times. Have no fear, no-one will die.'

Once the journey was over and they had finally reached Gravesend, Mary's thoughts were all of her father at Skinner Street. Had he forgiven her, did he hate her, might he refuse to see her? Percy needed to seek out people he knew who might help him settle his debts. And Claire was lost in a world of her own fidgeting and moaning.

It was now September, a month Mary enjoyed, a time when she'd gone to gather blackberries with Fanny from the nearby woodland and they'd made preserves in the kitchen, a time when delicate primroses covered the base of the hedgerows and the market was brimming with apples. At last she was back in England! They hadn't been away very long but the clock had moved on. Once she was only a girl, she thought, as the three of them climbed in a coach, but now she was a woman and would very soon have a child. She hoped her father would understand and she knew how Claire feared her mother. To expect Mary Jane to forgive them though seemed futile. But hope they must.

The changing hues of the autumn leaves as the coach sped on made her wistful. How would her father greet her, what would she say to him now, so changed in such a short while? She felt like someone else, the girl who had left the Skinner Street household on that dull wet morning had gone. Sharp pangs of shame flooded her blood, making her tremble. No matter what Percy said, she felt she'd done wrong. What would happen to Harriet? What about his children? Claire sat silent clasping her hands, staring downwards as if in a trance, while Percy gazed out of the window. Mary took her journal from her bag. Perhaps it would interest her father? She had left her dear Papa, just as if she had vanished! All the time on their travels through France and Switzerland she had never forgotten him. He'd always been there in her thoughts, but would he believe her if she said so. She sighed as she turned the pages. What wonderful things they had seen and done. Percy's entries were beautiful . . .

'You are not to show it to your father,' he said, putting the flat of his hand on the journal on her lap. 'Seriously, my dear, I doubt he would wish to look at it anyway. I don't think he'll want to see *us*, never mind the journal.' He drew himself up and straightened his clothes. 'Heaven knows what we're to do. You and Claire will have to find lodgings separate from me. I can't be in reach of my creditors.'

'Or they'll take you to the debtor's prison,' Claire said shrugging. 'But at least you paid for the places we stayed coming back.'

'And now there is nothing left,' said Mary quietly.

'It's the debtor's prison for Percy,' sighed Claire.

'You are probably right,' he said haughtily. 'I could do some writing in there though couldn't I. And you dear Claire could be jailed for thieving from the bookshop if your mother proves difficult.'

'She only took a couple of books,' murmured Mary. 'And anyway they're being returned.'

Claire kept her head bowed low. 'Poor Percy, you always want freedom but you won't get it in prison,' she said quietly. 'I doubt you'd even get pen and paper in there. They wouldn't care a bit for your poems in prison. All you could do is despair.'

'My poetry is important,' sighed Shelley. He straightened. 'And do not speak so boldly. Remember, you are not my social equal!'

'Claire, do be silent,' said Mary. 'You are most unpleasant today. And we stayed at a good hotel last night. You've had plenty of sleep.'

'"Sleep?" Do you think I slept? For all you know, I might have been weeping all night.'

Percy shook his head with irritation. 'Mary was up at dawn, she knew there were things to get on with. No lying-in for Mary.'

'It was ever so dark last night, and I didn't even have any tapers,' moaned Claire. I undressed by the light of the moon.'

'Candle wax is costly,' said Shelley. 'The English can be very miserly.'

'Some of them,' said Claire with a shudder. 'Others are wasteful. But oh, it's so cold in England.'

Mary passed over her shawl.

'Mama is going to hate me,' whined Claire. 'We left so quickly.'

'Yes,' said Percy, scratching his head. 'We were indeed precipitous. But do grow up, my dear. You can't grow down, you know. At least I don't think so. If I remember, you were telling your Mama, that you felt you had reached an age when you knew what you wanted, now it seems you want her to hold your hand.' He frowned and looked downwards. 'I shall never bow and scrape to my father. I would kill myself first!'

'I believe you would,' said Claire. 'You always want to die. Perhaps you should have fallen from the boat after all, for you have many confrontations ahead of you. Dying might have been far preferable.' She looked him up and down. 'Your lovely silk waistcoat is creased and grubby and your trousers are crumpled.'

'Hush, Claire,' Mary said urgently. 'Percy's relationship with his father is something we can't understand, and we should not try. Percy has lived a different life from us. We must always consider it.'

'Well, he doesn't consider Harriet much does he,' sneered Claire, looking at him straight. 'Oh I do hope Mama will forgive me.'

'She certainly won't forgive *me*,' said Mary. 'And she'll have turned my father against me. Not Fanny. Fanny would never turn against me. She always understands.'

'There's a lot of bad stuff to deal with,' Shelley said, biting his lip.

'Oh, there is,' Claire said gravely, dabbing her eyes. 'It's all too terrible to think of.'

'There's been a lot of scurrilous talk,' he said narrowing his eyes. 'It's hard to believe that people are saying Godwin sold me his daughters. Hogg told me in a letter. Can you imagine?' He laughed. 'The things people invent. How much do you think you are worth?'

Mary felt angry. How could people speak of her like that, as if she belonged to her father and could actually be sold? 'That sort of talk could destroy Papa,' she said shakily. 'He has never got over the scandal of Mother's biography.' Hopelessness flooded her blood. Would her father keep them out of the house? What a horrible thought. Might he disown them? She shivered.

'No-one will speak to us ever again,' moaned Claire.

'I think that is probably true,' said Mary.

'So what will you do?' asked Percy, slumping back in his seat. 'Repair to the church perhaps, and ask forgiveness?'

'I don't know,' said Claire. She put her hands to her face. 'I could always sell flowers on the street for a while. – Well, a lot of girls do.'

'Mary sighed. 'Don't be ridiculous,' she whispered. 'Those flower girls are up at daybreak and must work like slaves for pennies.'

'Or I could find me a wealthy husband,' said Claire, her forehead tightening. 'An artist or a poet . . .'

'Poets are poor,' said Percy. 'You don't make money writing poetry. And in any case, why would you want to live in a cold dark house with servants, it's a dull old business.' He tied his cravat neatly and straightened. 'Find yourself a wealthy husband indeed. How absurd.'

'Byron made money with *The Corsair*,' said Claire.

'Oh Byron, Byron . . . He doesn't know if he's a poet or a politician.' He breathed in deeply then looked at her curiously, a vague smile on his lips. 'You fancy your chances with George don't you? I can tell. You'll be lucky. He has every woman in London falling at his feet.'

For a moment or two they were silent.

'Oh, what's going to happen?' Claire said fearfully as they closed on the Skinner Street premises.

'Let's wait and see,' said Percy. 'I doubt your father will come at me with a gun. He is far too dignified for that, and he's a reputation to think of.'

You never know,' said Claire. 'People act out of character under pressure.'

'Well, here we are,' said Percy, as the coach drew up by the door. 'Let me be first to speak.' He swelled out his chest and ran his fingers through his hair then made to get out.

Mary put her hand on his arm. 'No, Percy, I will go first,' she said firmly. 'It is I Papa will want to talk to. Though I doubt he will come to the door. He is likely to be working in his study.'

'It'll be Fanny,' said Claire. 'Or else Abigail. Mama rarely answers the door; she'll be back in the shop.'

'Abigail loves to gossip and has probably spotted us already,' said Mary, climbing out.

'That maid is so nosey, I'm surprised she gets anything done,' said Shelley, sighing and annoyed.

Mary loosened the strings on her bonnet, happy to be back in Skinner Street. She looked all around then rapped down the knocker three times. Soon they heard footsteps in the hall. Abigail opened the door, though she did not welcome them in.

Mary spoke first but her despairing tone betrayed her feelings. 'Claire and Mr Shelley are in the coach,' she said shakily. 'Can we come in?' It seemed wrong to her that the maid should be keeper of the door.

'I'll have to find out,' Abigail told her coolly. 'Oh, Miss Mary, you've been gone so long and you've caused such misery and commotion.'

Mary nodded. 'I can imagine,' she said softly. All was silent on the street as Abigail turned and left her. She returned quickly, alone.

So this is how it is, thought Mary, seeing the maid's expression as she came down the hall. Abigail shook her head. There would be no going inside. 'Will Fanny not speak to me?' Mary asked shakily, her eyes filling with tears. 'Not even Fanny?' Her heart beat hard till it hurt.

'I'm sorry,' said Abigail looking downwards. 'None of them want to see you Miss Mary.'

'You must tell them I'm pregnant,' Mary said, loudly. The sense of rejection was loathsome.

'Mr Godwin knows,' said Abigail. 'You told him in a letter and I heard him telling Mrs Godwin. I think you should go – quickly.' As she spoke, she glanced back down the hall. 'Go now, I beg you. Find lodgings and I'll bring you messages. – Dear Miss Mary, please go!'

Mary turned towards the coach and climbed back inside. 'We are banished,' she said shakily, though bitterness made her strong. Words screamed in her mind – "*I was benevolent and good; misery made me a fiend. Make me happy, and I shall again be virtuous . . .*'

10

New Plans

'Well done Wordsworth!' said Shelley. 'Excellent.' He folded Hogg's letter and laid it on the desk thoughtfully.

'Wordsworth?' said Mary, noting a tone of envy in Shelley's voice. 'What has he done?'

Shelley looked detached and uncomfortable. His pale cheeks flushed as he spoke. 'He's published a long poem, a sort of story apparently called *The Excursion*, and according to general opinion it's excellent. He works damned hard, does Wordsworth, always has something on the go.' They were in lodgings in Oxford Street living with Claire.

'So when can we read it?' Mary asked, handing him his hat.

'I'll try to get hold of it,' said Percy. He was about to go out and pulled on his coat. 'I ought to have published Queen Mab, you know . . .' He looked at her confused, frustrated by all his concerns.

'Mama will have Wordsworth's poem in the shop,' Claire boasted, coming from the kitchen. 'She likes to keep up. He's a great poet.'

'He is,' said Mary.

'It's mainly about nature and beauty,' said Shelley abstractedly. 'Pretty good stuff though.' He sighed and buttoned up his coat.

'Do I detect some jealousy?' Claire said wryly.

'I am by no means jealous of Wordsworth. He is indeed a wonderful poet. I have published some excellent work myself, as you know. And I intend to publish much more once I have sorted things out. Oh, that life would sort itself out! I am forever in a muddle.'

'You have only yourself to blame,' Claire said quietly.

He stood gazing at space. 'My dear Claire, I too can appreciate the natural world. It does not belong to Wordsworth alone. I too see its truth, its beauty, its cruelty . . . But my imagination is driven more by . . . well, by oppression and injustice, social issues and politics.'

'Politics are there in Wordsworth's work too,' said Mary. 'You can't get away from politics.' She spoke firmly, serious. She changed her position on the chaise longue and straightened the folds of her dress. 'You poets are very competitive. It is most unhealthy.'

'From all that I hear Byron isn't the least competitive,' said Claire.

'Byron, I believe, is often quite arrogant,' said Mary. 'I heard at the Baxter's that he boasts a lot about his swimming. He's an excellent swimmer.' She was in bad humour because of her father's hostility, and because Shelley was about to go out and leave her with Claire, intending to visit Harriet.

'Is he?' said Shelley with a laugh. 'Well, I suspect Wordsworth is an excellent swimmer too. I believe he was very athletic in his youth.' He smiled wryly. 'Bah. You are not to let anyone know I can't swim. I've told you before.' He spoke sharply and made Claire look up from her sewing. 'Did you ever meet Wordsworth?' he asked Mary.

'I think so when I was little, but I can't remember all the people who came to our house. Papa was extremely popular though, lots of people sought him out.' She looked downwards, suddenly worried. 'I could ask Papa, except I think he's disowned me.' She spoke shakily and looked away, thoughtful. 'I heard at the Baxter's that Wordsworth has one or two secrets . . . '

'Aye,' murmured Shelley. 'He doesn't deceive us though. There's a lot of fervour in his work, and he no doubt found passion in Paris.'

'Like when they were slicing off heads with the guillotine,' Claire said shuddering. 'The thought of those tumbrels makes me faint.'

'Oh dear,' said Mary, looking at Percy dismally. 'Let us not talk about slicing off heads. You say you are going to see Harriet and will be gone several days?'

'Yes,' said Percy, standing to attention like a soldier. 'I have a new born son.'

'And you rejoice, of course,' said Mary.

'Of course, just as I should.'

Mary was hurting, though she tried her best not to show it.

'I have to see Harriet about finances too,' said Percy, donning his hat. 'We've a lot to discuss.'

Mary sighed heavily. The joy on his face on hearing of the birth of his son confused her. 'That could be awkward,' she murmured, conscious of her father forever asking him for loans.

'It seems quite odd,' said Claire. 'I mean, it isn't as if you've shown much interest in Harriet, that is not until now when you are badly in need money, which Harriet gets from her father, of course. It's as well he's generous. Yours won't give you a penny.'

'You cannot know of the letters I have sent to Harriet,' sighed Percy. 'I even asked her to join us on our travels, as you know, but she declined my offer. What more could I do. My father is wrong to have stopped my allowance because we have parted. I parted from Harriet because I did not love her. He ought to understand, if he doesn't he needs to think harder. He has made life difficult for me now.'

'It's as well she declined your offer,' said Claire with a shrug. 'Less travels and more travails I would say. I doubt she'd have wanted to ride about in a tumbrel.'

'That's enough, Claire,' Mary said sharply. She turned to Percy. 'It's good that you visit her. You will want to see your son, it's natural, and your little daughter too.' A chill went through her as she spoke. The sad, sad, little children.

'Thank you, Mary, I'm glad you understand,' Shelley said flatly. He darted Claire a look of irritation, then turned again to Mary. 'I have arranged for Hogg, my friend from university, to come and stay with you a while. He is trying to publish a book and needs to be in London. I'm sure you will make him welcome.'

'You might have asked how we felt about that,' sighed Claire. 'Thomas Jefferson Hogg? – Isn't he the one who got you into trouble with the pamphlet?'

'We got each other into trouble,' laughed Percy. He turned to Mary. 'I thought it a good idea to let him stay here. There's the small empty room at the back. He only needs a desk and a bed. He says he'll pay the rent, so it'll save us some money.'

'But I don't know him,' Mary said quietly.

'Then you soon will,' Percy whispered, his breath close on her cheek. 'I am quite sure Hogg will adore you.'

'Whilst no-one will adore *me*,' Claire said moodily.

'Not at all dear Claire,' said Shelley. He went to her and lifted her hair with his hands, letting it fall slowly. 'This hair could captivate a king,' he murmured.

She shrugged. 'Kings are best steered clear of.'

Shelley laughed. 'You are right, kings don't get many compliments do they, and they are always in danger of someone trying to kill them.'

They were all three silent a moment.

Percy went on. 'But you will have to control your hysterics, dear Claire. They are enough to drive anyone mad. You must stop thinking that shadows are ghosts and that the bats flying by the window are trying to get you. Last night was horrendous, all that shrieking and writhing on the floor. I almost went for a doctor.' He turned then to Mary, 'My beloved. I cannot come here when I return. You know that my creditors are chasing me. We shall need some discretion as to where we meet up. I know of one or two coffee houses. I can send you messages.'

'Of course,' she replied. He kissed her goodbye and left.

A whole two weeks passed by, and Mary wished more than ever, that Claire had been embraced by her mother and taken back into the household, she was impulsive, difficult and loud. But Shelley liked to have her around. There was though a bond between the women. They both loved William Godwin and were concerned that he loved them back. Claire said Mary was good for Percy and Mary was in-clined to agree. But no-one was happy, and Mary was anxious, in her mind she could hear her stepmother berating her father and she could see his sunken expression, his misery because she'd betrayed him.

But just as she was captured by Shelley, her father was caught in a trap of financial despair. And Percy was very short of money himself. They could scarce get by and had little to eat, apart from the loaves and preserves Abigail stole from the pantry at Skinner Street. Abigail had been more than good. She didn't write much in the notes she pushed through the door, claiming her spelling was poor, but she did bake very good bread and scones and Mary and Claire were treated to her scones on Wednesdays. Bitter and painful to Mary, was the sight of her stepmother and Fanny walking together in the street and ignoring her, reminding her of how it had been when her mother's biography had been published and the whole family had been rejected. Fanny, she knew, would be in agony over what was happening. Her strange solitary ways could never be fathomed but there was often a sadness in her eyes that spoke of deep felt pain.

Mary looked at Claire, who that morning was repairing her stays and tying off the ends of her sewing. Claire wasn't at all romantic. She did not dream, and brought a harsh reality to Mary's existence that she could not find on her own. Mary believed Claire had often been intimate with Shelley, but it was unbelievable to her and she chose to cast it from her mind. To Claire it was of little consequence, she could take it or leave it. Mary gazed at her; there were tight lines around her mouth, determined and strong. She would never be bound like Prometheus was, she was the female Prometheus unbound and would screw the neck of the eagle so it might never spread its wings again. But she herself could never escape her chains.

They ate fresh bread and butter and good blue cheese from Skinner Street, discreetly looted by Abigail.

'I wonder if Mr Hogg would lend me some money,' said Claire, taking a bite of crisp, soft white bread. 'You know how Shelley says you have to take risks . . . well, you see, I have a plan.'

Mary met her eyes worriedly. Claire could be so impetuous.

'Do you mind if I don't tell you?' Claire was intense, her face strained with feeling, her large blue eyes excited.

'Well, I'm concerned. So long as it's sensible Claire. We are in plenty of trouble already.'

'No, it's all perfectly sensible. You needn't worry.'

'Poor Hogg,' said Mary. 'We are to pounce on him and ask him for money just as soon as he walks through the door.'

'I shall soon have money myself,' Claire said assertively. 'You see, I intend to marry Lord Byron.'

'What?' laughed Mary. 'Don't be absurd.' She sat pouring out tea. 'He is too much a man of the world to marry anyone. He has travelled to distant lands; through Greece and Turkey I believe. Who could count the children he might have sired? He is not to be trusted. He is always involved in some amorous liaison or other.' She lowered her voice to a whisper. 'And I have heard they aren't always with women.'

'He is a very colourful character,' Claire said abstractedly. 'I am drawn to him.'

'You don't even know him,' Mary said puckering her forehead. 'Don't be ridiculous, my dear.'

'I have talked with people, and heard things,' Claire said determined. 'Don't underestimate me, Mary. I shall get what I want. You'll see.'

'But how will you see him?'

'I shall seek him out. It shouldn't be too hard.'

Mary shook her head. 'His romantic adventure with Lady Caroline Lamb is talked about everywhere. But now he's engaged to Annabella Millbanke, the 11th Baroness Wentworth, soon to be Baroness Byron.' She tilted her head to one side and raised her eyebrows. 'Need I say more?'

'No, you need not. But none of that bothers me, you see . . .' She leant forward and laughed. 'I shall steal his heart.' She laughed very loud at the ceiling.

Mary smiled. 'That's if he has one to steal. But I should think he's lonely, having grown up without a father.'

Claire stared thoughtfully at space. 'It's strange, isn't it? Shelley has a father, but they're always at war, while Byron has no father at all. People are sometimes so foolish. I have no idea of my own father's identity, or if he is alive or dead. Mama doesn't speak of him. But I really don't give a hoot.'

'And I have betrayed mine,' Mary said quietly. She looked at Claire's comely figure and her long luxuriant hair. She was quite beautiful. Presently she added, 'Byron has a passion for politics. You must read them up if you wish to engage with him properly. He has a great social conscience and speaks in the House of Lords.'

'You need not advise me, Mary,' Claire said curtly. 'I shall speak in French and German too and impress him. I am quite fluent in both. And I am good at remembering poetry. I know a lot of *The Corsair . . .*'

Mary sat, pondering.

'Are you jealous?' asked Claire.

'Of what?'

'Of Percy going to see Harriet. – What if he stays and forgets you?'

'So be it,' Mary said softly. 'Percy will do as he wishes and Bryon will do the same.'

11

Thomas Jefferson Hogg

Thomas Jefferson Hogg was known to Godwin as 'a friend of Shelley's'. Born and bred in County Durham and a graduate from Oxford University, he often found his way to London where he enjoyed literary gatherings. He and Shelley had formed a friendship at Oxford and they'd collaborated on several projects, one of them being the notorious pamphlet which had resulted in getting them expelled. According to Shelley, Hogg had taken part excitedly in all his ventures and had shown a devilish willingness to behave mischievously.

And it seemed he liked Shelley's choice of women too. Mary had learned from the Baxter's that the wily scoundrel had set his heart on Harriet, though nothing had come of his advances. She suspected Shelley thought he'd want to do the same with her. It bothered her though that Shelley wanted to share her with his friend. He'd apparently shown jealousy over Hogg's romantic overtures to Harriet but now he showed only open encouragement when he talked of the prospect of herself and Hogg becoming lovers. The thought bothered her a lot. What was Percy doing right now she wondered, might he be making love with Harriet, might he . . . She cast the thoughts from her mind; the world of truth was cruel, but the world of imagination could be even worse. And Thomas Jefferson Hogg was living with them now in their lodgings. He had dropped right in like a hawk, his long limbs just about fitting in the narrow bed at the back. She was still suffering from the shock of

Shelley's departure and the need to befriend a complete stranger was difficult. This morning Claire had gone out. Having risen early she'd put on her finest clothes and gone off in a chaise without as much as a word about her errand. Mary though had a good idea what she was up to. She had made it plain she intended to seduce Lord Byron. Or at least she would give it a try, and she had probably gone to Newstead Abbey, where she hoped to find him at home. He would no doubt be alone, for his mother was deceased and gossip had it that he wasn't getting on with Annabella Millbanke. If luck was on her side, Claire would have him all to herself.

An unenviable task, thought Mary, wondering how Claire would find him in that great rambling abbey surrounded by so much parkland. Was he really that wealthy, or was it simply the grandeur of the abbey that gave the illusion of riches; the Baxter's had said it was in need of extensive repairs and he was desperately trying to sell it though they claimed he would never get anyone to buy such a gloomy old building, the hooting of owls from the parkland and the dark sad rooms with their stale damp air might have rendered the abbey a place of memories Byron didn't want to be part of. Aristocracy had its own headaches. As for Percy, she reflected, he liked to think he would one day inherit from his father, but hope of help just now was unlikely due to what he had done to Harriet. She shivered and rubbed her arms as the feeling came to her again, that awful sensation of guilt. Is this what she did, did she destroy people's lives – her mother's, Percy's, her father's . . . Why had he sent her to Scotland, was she really so hateful? But it wasn't possible to be perfect, she reasoned, human beings were parts of other people and sometimes the parts didn't fit, they might become monsters despised by the people they loved. Had Byron become a monster like that? Was Shelley a monster beneath his beautiful exterior? How did Byron live? Many of the nobles living in their great houses had been exposed as virtual beggars all told. And what if Percy didn't inherit at all like her stepmother so often implied, what would he do, how was he to live? Would he land in the debtor's prison? Never! Never! It could not happen!

She set out her writing materials and turned the pages of her novel. She was inspired to work today. But the story was in bits and pieces. Nothing fitted together as she wanted, just like her hopes and ideals. The parts of her story had seriously separate entities, yet they disturbed her with their togetherness, their words, ideas and sentences. Did not that on its own qualify for good writing, for it came from the very same soul? She sighed. Not today. She tidied up the pages and returned them to her file. Hogg was making an appearance.

Percy had been coming and going. He had taken lodgings elsewhere and was stealthily avoiding his creditors. His letter said he wasn't far away, but she was lonely.

Hogg came towards her and smiled. It hadn't taken long for Claire to let down her hair and empty their lodger's purse, Mary reflected. Alone, in his little room, at the back, he had possibly wondered how she'd done it. Hogg was susceptible to pretty young women, Shelley had said, and Claire was pretty and alluring. It was curious to Mary to have this man, who was almost a stranger, going about their lodgings without wearing his cravat and with his sleeves rolled up to the elbow, though he paid their rent and brought food. Shelley had said he hoped she'd find Hogg attractive. She'd been hurt and amazed. Hogg was kind and pleasant and often made her laugh, but she would never make love with anyone other than Percy and was embarrassed by the way Hogg's eyes followed her about. But she liked his kindness and was softened by his generosity. He probably had a generous spirit too, she decided. And she needed that generous spirit just now, for the lodgings were bare and cold until Hogg lit the fire and they both sat reading. Her pregnancy, she thought, was a good enough excuse to keep her distance. She did not want to upset him or have him report bad feelings to Percy, but she would not, could not, sleep with him. Free love to her was betrayal and nothing would ever change her mind.

12

Newstead Abbey

Nottingham's Newstead Abbey, built in the 12th century, had once been an Augustinian priory; its meandering paths and landscaped gardens, roaming deer, waterfalls and lakes were a joy to behold. In the reign of Henry VIII, the Pope was head of the Christian Church and the Roman Catholic faith dictated that marriage was for life, but Henry wanted to marry his beloved Anne Boleyn and argued his marriage was against God's will because his wife, Catherine, had been married to his late brother, but the Pope refused him a divorce. In consequence Henry sold the monasteries, priories, convents and friaries in England, Wales and Ireland, and in a fit of anger created the Church of England. In 1816, Newstead Abbey was the home of the 6th Baron Byron, more commonly known as Lord Byron, poet, peer and politician, and something of a philanderer as well.

But the Abbey was 'home' in name only to Byron who would rather have been without it, for trying to manage his financial concerns was a constant frustration.

Lord George Byron wasn't well and often shouted out in the night during his dreams. It was a very disturbing predicament, Frederick Llewellyn the gardener said to his wife, Gertrude. – 'I ask you, my dear, the ghost of his mother wandering the rooms; he swears he sees her at night time!' Gertrude Llewellyn expected the obese old woman to appear of a sudden in their midst and was often turning to look. The abbey held so many mysteries.

That grey November afternoon, Claire made a lonely figure standing by the gates. She glanced about nervously as the carriage departed; a hollow echoing sound of wheels on the stony highway. She settled her single bag at her feet to reflect. She'd arrived at the abbey, and now what next? She took deep breaths. She'd followed her plan precisely but the overwhelming inertia at the sight of her destination fixed her to the spot. The chaise had gone and apart from the sound of a few birds singing in the high trees about her, everywhere was silent. What was she doing? It was sheer stupidity to think she could seduce Lord Byron, she who hadn't a penny to her name other than what she'd begged from Hogg, and living in lodgings with Mary Wollstonecraft Godwin and Percy Bysshe Shelley? She felt strangely remote amidst so many naked trees and cold still stones.

Lord Byron was no fool; he was bound to perceive her intention. She straightened and rehearsed her role. She was strong with a splendid figure, and her hair might captivate a king according to Shelley, let alone a baron – though a baron reportedly impoverished. But she did not believe it for a minute, as her eyes sped over the magnificent grounds, beautiful, even in November. What would those splendid grounds be like in summer, she wondered, when the trees were in blossom and everything returned to life? She picked up her bag and made her way down the path. Then came a voice from behind her. 'I do beg your pardon, ma'am, but does his lordship expect ye?'

'What?' she said, turning. 'No, I am not expected,' she said, bending her head, embarrassed. 'You are a gardener, I take it.' He leant heavily on his spade at the edge of a lawn.

'A gardener? Well, I suppose I am. It'll do for now anyway. Why are ye here?' He was frowning, curious.

She breathed in deeply the dank November air. 'I am Claire Clairmont, a friend of a friend of Lord Byron's.'

'Ah,' he laughed. 'His lordship has lots of friends of friends.'

'That friend is a poet he admires,' said Claire, bracing herself while still looking ahead. 'A man named Percy Bysshe Shelley.'

'A poet you say? Ah, I'm none too fond of poets. Far too fanciful, they are, an' they're allus gettin' depressed. His lordship's a poet but writin' poems makes him moody. He's been havin' it bad of late.'

She was glad to find he was talkative; talkative people were useful and he wanted to talk about Byron.

'I am the *only* gardener,' he continued, casting his eyes over the estate. 'These grounds run wild. His lordship is lucky to have me.'

'And does his lordship pay good wages?'

'He pays as it suits. But I've been tendin' these grounds for years, like my father afore me. My wife takes care o' the kitchen and we allus have a lot in the cupboard.'

The cold was penetrating her coat. She shivered. 'And what is Lord Byron like?' she asked, daringly.

He gave her a long look. 'Now that's a difficult question. He's not like anyone else, for certain.' He laughed at the sky.

He was a man in his mid thirties, she thought, healthy and strong. The wide path she stood on ran from the gates to the doors of the abbey. She saw he was burying bulbs. They looked like little pyramids of onions, and she recalled that onions were known as *cepa* in Latin and linked with the ancient Greek word *kapia*; the fibrous delicate roots were already reaching out and had long awaited the earth. Byron would like it if she talked about Greece, she thought, to all accounts he was fascinated by all things Greek.

'Them's daffodils and crocuses for spring,' he said, seeing her looking. 'I plant 'em where the light can easily find 'em. M'lady liked 'em round the lawns, but she's passed on now. There's only his lordship and his wife.'

She started and glanced at the abbey. '"His wife" – is he married?'

'Only just recent. But I doubt he'll be married long. Her ladyship is always disappearin'. She's been gone a good two weeks; his lordship is difficult to live with.'

'Please don't tell me anymore,' Claire said shakily. She'd rather discover Byron's foibles for herself.

'The daffodils keep on returning,' Frederick Llewellyn said abstractedly. '– Did you say you were called Clairmont?'

She nodded. 'Daffodils,' Claire murmured warmly. She liked daffodils. She looked down the long path, her mind racing. She hardly believed for a minute she could steal Lord Byron from Annabelle; after all, she herself was only a shop-girl from London and had nothing to offer. Perhaps she should just turn back? But she straightened and braced herself instead. She knew she had a good figure, and according to Shelley, had hair that could captivate a king. Take courage, she told herself. *Take courage*!

'Well now,' the gardener said, looking her up and down. 'You ask what he's like . . . Well, he thinks he's spawned from the devil. He were born with a deformed foot, ye see, and his mother had mocked him for it.' Frederick Llewellyn shook his head sadly. 'She were a bit overweight poor woman, anyhow he mocked her back. Now she comes to haunt him at night time an' it's made him half mad. He's like a dark phantom, wanderin' the grounds in his nightwear.'

'Goodness,' gasped Claire. She looked away, smiling. 'He had better not wander through the gates.'

'Aye, right enough ma'am. You're a wise woman.' For a minute or two he looked at her. 'So what am I to do wi' ye then?'

She peered ahead at the abbey. 'Is there a butler or anything?'

'No butler. Not today. Brenton's in London trying to sort out some problems for his lordship. But he's leavin' us soon. Nobody works for his lordship long. He forgets to pay ye. He employs folks if he's 'avin a party, but not now in November. Everywhere's silent just now. An' to think o' those empty rooms wi' nobody in 'em but ghosts, while there's folks as are sleepin' in hedgerows along wit' hedgehogs and snakes.'

The abbey loomed large ahead. She had taken off her bonnet and was removing pins from her hair; it fell heavy down her shoulders.

The gardener frowned. 'You've a walk to find him, even once you're inside. An' he's probably writin' some poem or other. Ye might catch the maid though, she's my wife. She gets in provisions and helps keep his lordship's apartments clean and tidy. There's a cook as well, but my wife does a lot o' the cooking. They both let me in on the gossip.'

'"Gossip?"' The gardener left his spade in the ground and they walked together up the long tree lined approach. The tall stone building looked dark and ominous before them. A little bewildered she cast her eyes across the windows. They were dark and dusty and there was something gloomy and menacing about the old grey stone, as if it were made from at least a thousand gravestones. They had walked a good way, the gardener carrying her bag. What had been only a dream was now a reality. She was here and soon she would approach Lord Byron. Her thoughts moved fast. She'd decided to talk about her stepfather's books, good enough books for anyone interested in politics. They had made him famous and talking about them would make her sound clever; she had learned some passages by heart. 'So what do you think of Lady Byron?' she asked.

'Oh, her ladyship comes and goes. She might as well pluck the petals off a daisy for one day she loves him and the next she doesn't. Or that's what I learn from Gertrude, my wife. His lordship would rather visit her house than 'ave her come 'ere. He's embarrassed about the state o' things at the abbey. There's mould on a lot o' the walls and the stones are loose in places. A couple of windows blew in earlier this month, a wicked east wind it was. His lordship's been to one or two auctions lately tryin' to sell it, but nobody's interested.'

'Quite a problem,' she sighed, wondering if Byron would live there forever in the cold and lonely abbey.

Someone called out from the entrance. – 'Frederick Llewellyn! I saw you from my study. Who do you bring to the abbey?' Byron beamed with pleasure.

Claire drew back. The gardener leant towards her. 'He allus calls me by my first and second names, though I don't know why. We'd best make haste.' He quickened his pace. Claire followed.

Reaching the doors, she saw that Bryon looked unkempt, his dark curled hair was matted on his forehead and long down the back of his neck, and his silk waistcoat was stained. But the indubitable beauty she'd heard of was there, the dark penetrating eyes, the full sensual mouth and the proud superior countenance. As he walked towards them, she saw that he limped slightly.

'It is a lady from London your lordship,' said the gardener. He stopped for a moment and directed Claire on her way, then he bowed and returned down the path.

'Lord Byron – it is good to meet you,' said Claire, making a slight curtsy. 'I am Claire Clairmont, stepdaughter of William Godwin. I have come to see you.'

'Ah, the stepdaughter,' he smiled, narrowing his eyes as he looked at her. 'How good of you to come. I enjoyed your letters.' He murmured from one of his poems

> *"She walks in beauty, like the night*
> *Of cloudless climes and starry skies;*
> *And all that's best of dark and bright*
> *Meet in her aspect and her eyes;*
> *Thus mellowed to that tender light*
> *Which heaven to gaudy day denies."'*

Claire met his gaze, her cheeks were hot and flushed. 'A wonderful poem, Lord Byron. I would have joined you in it had it not been written for a woman. I would though like to join you in reciting *The Corsair* sometime.'

'You can recite *The Corsair*?' he gasped. He spoke with admiration as they went through the entrance of the abbey.

She nodded. 'Je peux certainement.'

'Je suis charmé,' Byron replied dramatically. 'It is a very long poem, Miss Clairmont. It is hard to believe you can recite it.'

'Au contraire,' Claire said blithely. 'I recite it well.'

He cast out his arm and directed her. 'Come to my study. November is a cruel month.' The cold white sun fell suddenly on her hair through the window.

'I would like your hair for my pillow,' he murmured, 'along with dewy red roses.'

'You could gladly sleep on my hair Lord Byron . . .' she said softly. She placed her hand on her breast. 'You might even sleep on my heart, if you could promise to treat it kindly.'

His eyes widened and he gave her a long look. 'You would let me sleep on your heart, Miss Clairmont, so quickly? Why, the hand of the clock has scarcely moved five minutes.' He laughed loudly, his voice echoing on the high grey walls as they went.

She checked herself; she was going too fast, excited by her success.

They went up a narrow stone stairway. He was slow, helping her on, carrying her bag all the way. 'This bag is rather heavy; it seems you intend to stay.' He smiled wryly. 'It is the way with a lot of women. Once a man becomes famous they want him. Not when he is poor and unknown.'

'Are you poor?' she asked, glancing at him sideways.

'I'm not sure.' He frowned at the stairs. 'It seems my poetry is popular. I need to speak with my publisher.' They walked on higher up the stairs. 'Just look at the steps on this stairway,' he said. 'I often wonder who walked here. They are worn by the feet of so many persons – maybe even a king.' He fell to thinking on his words. 'I would like to be in love,' he said softly, in a tone of sincerity.

'And you are not?' She was taken aback by his candour. She wondered about his relationship with Annabella.

He put his hand to his chest and sighed. 'Lady Byron has left me.'

She talked on quickly, saying she was seventeen years old and had an older brother abroad who she did not see, but she said it strangely, blankly, as if she talked to herself. He was lost in a world of his own, and she did not feel he was listening. He was taking her up to his rooms, so he obviously liked her. She was thrilled by his look, his black heavy brows and lashes, the dark indifferent stare in his eyes.

'I want to know all about you,' he said as they entered his study. It was a warm room and the fire burned brightly. There was a plate of sweet meats and a large bowl of fruit on a table. He bade her eat as she wished.

She took off her coat and picked some grapes from the fruit bowl. 'This is luxury to me,' she laughed. 'Mary and I are living with Percy Bysshe Shelley in lodgings, as I said in my letter. Mary will have his baby come spring. We have very little money and eat when we can. The maid from Skinner Street brings food. It is just as if we are prisoners. Percy is all but a vagabond, constantly avoiding his creditors and also his dishonour, of course. He is not yet divorced and is visiting his wife this very week. She has just had a second child, a boy, and the baby is his.'

For a moment or two they were silent. Byron nodded slowly.

Claire carried on. 'There isn't a lot to say about me. Mama lives with Godwin and that dreadful portrait still hangs on the wall. Perhaps you have seen it.'

He smiled but made no comment.

'And so . . .' she continued pursing her lips. 'I am living with Shelley and Mary and Papa has disowned me because I went off with them. He has disowned Mary also. We are banished.' She laughed at the dark window. It was getting quite late. 'He doesn't always live according to his writings, you see.'

'Ah yes, his famous writings. Shelley must know them backwards. He is a big follower of Godwin. I am cautious myself. Life is rarely as it seems. It tricks us. Or it does if we don't watch out. Ideas are one thing, truth is another.' For a moment or two they were silent. 'And so you are living with Shelley,' he murmured. 'And are you under his spell?'

'What do you mean?'

'Shelley's spell, of course. He works magic. You must be under his spell.' He bit his lip thoughtfully and narrowed his eyes.

'I am a long way away from him just now,' she sighed. 'I own he is attractive, even beautiful according to Papa, but he isn't for me. And in any case, he belongs to Mary.'

Byron laughed and poked his fire. 'He wastes no time our Percy. I would have thought he belonged to Harriet not Mary, if he wishes to belong to anyone.'

'Possibly,' sighed Claire. 'That remains to be seen. He was going to see Harriet when I left. I expect he is with her now. Thomas Jefferson Hogg is with Mary at our lodgings. You will no doubt know him.'

'Thomas Jefferson Hogg alone with Mary? Well, well, well!' He laughed. 'There is a lot going on in London it seems.' His features twisted into mockery, for there was nothing he did not know about the ways of London. 'I am lonely here, as you see,' he said quietly. 'I hope you will stay for a while.'

She felt a quiver of excitement as she answered. 'Of course. I have wanted to talk with you a while. Things are quite sad in London.'

He rang his bell and a woman came running.

'Gertrude – do light a fire in the guest room for Miss Claire. And ensure that the linen on the bed is fresh.'

The woman gave a brief curtsy and left.

Claire sat down by the fire and warmed her hands. 'So many books . . .' she said.

'Too many,' he grimaced, glancing at his book shelves. 'And I must read them too, that is the problem. When is there time? I have a library also. You must see it. Books, reading, writing, that is my life, a dismal business indeed.' His eyes passed over her and he smiled. 'But you have made this day very pleasant, Miss Clairmont. And thank you.' He shrugged and straightened his waistcoat. His face stayed serious, as if harbouring a long lived pain.

'You have blessings, Lord Byron,' said Claire, nodding at him slowly. 'Your mother would be proud of your work.'

'I am more than my work,' he said quietly. 'That is the trouble; sons must always succeed, whilst daughters can do as they wish.'

'It is not so,' she murmured. 'You must read Mary Wollstonecraft's Vindication.'

'Ah, that, yes. He sighed. 'We are so governed by books. Read this, read that, think this, think the other.' His voice fell low. 'Well, I shall always think thoughts that others would never dream of.' He laughed quietly. 'Wollstonecraft didn't like men very much did she. She would surely hate me for I am not deemed fit to walk the earth according to some. Ah yes, she had a very bad time with that Imlay fellow, didn't she. He left her high and dry, and I believe he is still on the run. Sad thing for his daughter. Fanny, I think she was called. I would never leave a child of mine like that; I suspect the girl felt abandoned.'

'I suspect she did, though Papa takes care of her now. He is good and takes care of us all,' Claire looked away sighing. 'But Mary and I have disgraced him. Fine thanks for his kindness and protection.' For a moment they were silent and thoughtful. 'I believe you are connected with Drury Lane Theatre,' she said, her eyes lighting up. 'You have influence there.'

He gave her a knowing look. 'Do I? Well yes, I suppose so. Why do you ask?' He smiled wryly.

She straightened. 'I would like to be an actress,' she said flatly. She threw back her hair. It glistened in the light of the fire, then she took on a theatrical pose and lowered her eyelids. 'I am quite dramatic,' she laughed. 'Mary thinks I could do it. Though she is not too fond of actresses, considering Fanny's father took off with one in the end.'

For a moment or two there was silence.

'Shall we run away?' she asked softly, leaning towards him, 'and leave everyone wondering where we are? That's what Shelley did with Mary.'

He raised his eyebrows and smiled. 'Cela pourrait être intéressant Mademoiselle Clairemont.'

They laughed quietly together and talked for a while, then he rang again for the maid.

'Go along with my maid,' he said as she entered. 'See Miss Clairmont across the landing will you and up the thin stairway. It is rather steep – oh, and don't forget her bag.' Byron pointed to Claire's bag on the floor.

Claire followed the maid. 'Do you wash clothes for his lordship?' asked Claire, because Byron looked shabby.

'I do at the moment, the laundry maid left us,' Gertrude Llewellyn said flatly.

'I see,' said Claire, striding the stairway behind her.

'Will you empty your bag yourself?' asked the woman.

'Of course,' said Claire.

'I must first get fresh linen for your bed and see there's a decent fire. After that I will leave you until I am called by his lordship to bring him his dinner. He eats in his study. Will you join him?'

'Yes,' said Claire, 'if I may.' But she did not think she would be using the bed, however fragrant its linen.

13

The Reality Of Existence

Thomas Jefferson Hogg was now ensconced in the trio's lodgings and had quite settled in. Shelley was often away and Claire might go off for days on her own, returning quiet and withdrawn. Shelley said she went to see Byron, but Claire told them nothing. Her manner had changed fundamentally. They knew she'd been going to the abbey but she was guarded. It was no doubt a sad tale to tell, thought Mary, for she didn't think Byron would ever love her as she wanted, and there was always the fear of Lady Byron returning. Claire, it seemed, was bound emotionally to Byron now for he had taken her vital energies and she wandered their lodgings like a wraith, a shadow of her former self. Mary could tell that her half-sister was in love. There was a certain passion in her movements, she held things differently, she touched things differently, she was different.

Mary had been preparing the layette for her baby that day and had been busy through most of Christmas; Abigail brought her baby clothes she'd made with Fanny, and Hogg gave her money and would occasionally take her to the shops to buy whatever she needed. The gossips, she decided, would probably say Hogg was the father of her child, for Shelley was rarely in evidence. She had come to enjoy Hogg's visits, his conversation and laughter, but she did not sleep with him as Shelley would have wanted. It wasn't convenient, she said, she was pregnant and needed to rest. She had good solid excuses, but she never had any intentions of sleeping with Hogg for she did not love him. Shelley was free to come and go as he wished but he could not force her to do what she shrank away from. A lot of the time she didn't know where Shelley had gone. He might be with Harriet, other times he might be with Claire, but he rarely came back to the lodgings. He came to borrow money from Hogg and would glance about the rooms saying how cramped they were and that they'd have to find somewhere bigger. But where would they go? It was January and bitterly cold.

The room was silent that morning. She longed for Shelley, and wondered sometimes if he might be deliberately avoiding her because she would not sleep with his friend. She liked Hogg a lot and enjoyed his company, but whenever he touched her she recoiled. In truth she felt Shelley had abandoned her and she feared what had happened to Harriet might now happen to her. Was it the way of men? Was it what happened when a man no longer desired you? She felt dazed with the weight of it all. Shelley was hard to understand, he had rigid values that held with the force of his feelings, yet she felt he was lacking in virtue. She recalled a conversation she'd heard him having with Hogg.

"You hate the landed aristocracy, dear Shelley," Hogg had laughed, "Yet are you not one of them yourself, and you continue to enjoy its privileges. – Ah, but you do, you do." And he had neared on Shelley shaking a finger at him closely. Shelley had been indignant, but he knew how Hogg liked an argument. It was often the way with lawyers and he'd replied calmly. "I enjoy very few privileges Hogg as you know. My father has stopped my allowance and I have very little to live on, which is why I am always needing help. Why must you make me feel worse? I loathe the way the poor are exploited and I might receive nothing at all from my father if he turns nasty. That's how it is. I think I try to be fair. Forced labour has built the aristocracy, as well you know, and very much supported it, too. The way the rich look down on the poor is despicable – have we learned nothing from France?" Hogg had continued tiredly. "We who have all the answers should practice what we preach," "And I do," Shelley had retorted. "You injure my pride with your words!" And he'd narrowed his eyes angrily. – "And you no doubt still blame *me* for what happened to poor Margaret. The woman was insane, yet you would still have us write that poem." "Oh, the poem, yes . . .' Hogg had tipped back on his chair, staring up at the ceiling. "Heaven help us, Shelley, she had attempted to stab King George! She said he'd usurped the throne and that she herself should be queen! I should think there were one or two others who felt like that. Thank God the king took pity." "Love made her mad" "There were problems with her lover . . . " Shelley had murmured. "If you remember, he . . ."

Always problems with lovers, thought Mary. Life was all bits of truth and lies and could never be the Utopia Shelley longed for. At least not seamlessly, life was constantly straining, mourning for the loss of something precious, its separate souls trying to find their way. She had seen it, she had heard it, she had felt it.

Just now the room was silent. She shuddered with cold and put more logs on the fire then she brought her writings to the table. She gazed all about her. Today the walls seemed closer to her than before, as if they were moving in. She felt bound by her pregnancy, somehow confined where she sat. But her best escape was writing. She dipped her pen in the ink and wrote on quickly, *"When falsehood can look so like the truth, who can assure themselves of certain happiness?"* Now where did that come from, she wondered, where did it fit? In her hearts of hearts she knew life fitted together somehow, all its pains and sorrows a complete united whole. But how? This was most obvious when she wrote. She could deliver the fullness of truth on the page and create a whole from the parts. Or that's what she hoped for. But truth metamorphosed and soon became lies, for people must be saved from themselves, human beings could be cruel and thoughtless and history could never be trusted. She wrote on quickly, recounting her continental travels with Claire and Shelley . . . though other thoughts moved in . . .

"Sometimes my pulse beat so quickly and hardly that I felt the palpi-tation of every artery; at others I nearly sank to the ground through languor and extreme weakness. Mingled with this horror I felt, the bitterness of disappointment; dreams that had been my food and pleasant rest for so long a space were now become a hell to me; and the change was so rapid, the overthrow so complete!"

Who was feeling such terror, she wondered. A story pounded in her blood. She straightened and blinked, trying to clear her mind, then settled again to her work. She must write about their travels on the continent, the things they'd experienced and learned. But Burg Frankenstein rose in her mind, the old broken castle on the rock . . . She braced herself, she would not dwell on it, she had promised Shelley she'd make progress with their journal. She bent her head and went through the pages, looking for Shelley's entries, oh, such beautiful writing, no struggle, no pain, just beautiful splendid words. And yet his life was filled with confusion, it was as if he were somehow waiting, hoping for a better life to find him.

Nowadays she went alone to her mother's grave, trembling with pride over the baby growing within her, wishing her mother were there to share her happiness. She would sit by herself in the deep dark quiet of the graveyard, on the cold hard stone of her mother's gravestone. It healed her feelings of hurt. She had given Percy her love and he'd abused it, he had wanted her to sleep with his friend. Free love was the mischief of dark bored angels, she thought, for it taunted and mocked with its power. Sometimes Percy looked at her curiously as if she were someone else, and perhaps she was. He had fallen in love with Mary Wollstonecraft Godwin, a pure, auburn haired girl, who had returned from the hills of Scotland bringing him romance and excitement, a girl in a Scottish tartan and she had set his heart on fire. Then everything had moved quickly and she had gone along with it all.

14

New Ways Of Thinking

Mary was alone with her secret. The loss of blood overwhelmed her. And she felt a terrifying deadness within her for the child wouldn't quicken! – 'Out damned spot! Out I say!' she shouted, tears on her cheeks as she burned the cloths she had used to wipe blood from her thighs. 'I shall be punished like Lady MacBeth!' The blood signified her guilt – what she had done to her father, what she had done to Harriet, what she had done to herself. And now he had this formidable pain in the very pit of her being. She slumped in a chair, *'What's done cannot be undone,'* she whispered; Shakespeare was indeed discerning.

Pregnancy was new to her and strange. She felt like a sort of curiosity. Claire's spirit was free whilst her own was captured. She'd imagined freedom and wanted it dearly, freedom from her father's vigilance and her stepmother's jealous control, freedom from expectations . . . but she felt no freedom now. She had rarely fallen sick, but now each day she felt weak and anxious. Would the child die in her body even before she gave birth? She had heard it could happen. She braced herself and tried to think rationally. Was it not common to have a show of blood near the end of a pregnancy? But she wasn't near the end. Perhaps her baby would be early? She felt frantic and there was no-one to share her fears. Abigail came and went quickly and in a clandestine fashion, but Mary couldn't send her troubles back to Skinner Street, alarming Fanny. She thought about telling Shelley, but having to meet him briefly in Coffee

Houses and taverns jarred on her nerves and there had never been the right moment. Shouldering her fears alone was a burden, especially now when the afternoon light was fading; and she hated gliding through the gloomy streets to see him in the evening or early morning. He was young and feral, fired by passion and poetry, a pale and beautiful aristocratic poet who constantly raged about injustice, but her soul shrank from his easy infidelities.

She drank some water and tried to steady her nerves. Hogg was to visit her tomorrow, it would cheer her; he was always good-humoured and caring. Looking in the mirror that morning she'd noticed her features held a look of resignation, a fallen defeated expression. Oh, where was the young Mary Godwin, the fierce pride she had known when Percy had fallen in love with her? She breathed in deeply and straightened. No-one would know how it was, she told herself firmly and she would strive to find herself again. She would not let herself go. There were times when she hated Claire, Claire who could take the stairs as fast as a hare, Claire who was bold and free. She had gone to stay at Newstead with Byron, she said, but would return at the weekend. Was it the truth, was she really at Newstead, or might she be with Shelley instead? Mary sat wringing her hands. The outside world could be savage and she lived a lot in her mind, finding solace in memories, the sounds of the wind and sea in Dundee, laughter at the Baxter's parties. She needed the wisdom of her parents and went to reach down her father's book from the shelf, he had great wisdom and a mighty heart which she felt she had shattered. Did Shelley have such a heart? She turned the pages and murmured some favourite lines

"The method is, for a thoughtless and romantic youth of each sex, to come together, to see each other, for a few times, and under circumstances full of delusion, and then to vow to eternal attachment. What is the consequence of this? In almost every instance they find themselves deceived. They are reduced to make the best of an irretrievable mistake. They are led to conceive it is their wisest policy, to shut their eyes upon realities, happy, if, by any perversion of intellect, they can persuade themselves that they were right in their first crude opinion of

each other. Friendship, if by friendship we understand that affection for an individual which is measured singly by what we know of his worth, is one of the most exquisite gratifications, perhaps one of the most improving exercises, of a rational mind. Friendship therefore may be expected to come in aid of the sexual intercourse, to refine its grossness, and increase its delight. What opinion ought we to form respecting infidelity to this attachment? Certainly no ties ought to be imposed upon either party, preventing them from quitting the attachment, whenever their judgement directs them to quit it. With respect to such infidelities as are compatible with an intention to adhere to it, the point of principal importance is a determination to have recourse to no species of disguise. In ordinary cases, and where the periods of absence are of no long duration, it would seem that any inconstancy would reflect some portion of discredit on the person that practised it. It would argue that the person's propensities were not under that kind of subordination which virtue and self-government appear to prescribe. But inconstancy like any other temporary dereliction would not be found incompatible with a character of uncommon excellence. What, at present, renders it, in many instances, peculiarly loathsome is its being practised in a clandestine manner. It leads to a train of falsehood and a concerted hypocrisy, than which there is scarcely anything that more eminently depraves and degrades the human mind ..."

Ah, her dear father! The room grew dim as she carried on reading until it was time to light candles and prepare for the night.

Next morning just after seven, Hogg came knocking and she went to the door to greet him. He took off his hat and placed his cane in the corner, then went to warm his hands by the fire, it was bitterly cold.

'For a moment or two they were silent. 'Am I dead?' she whispered. 'I feel as if I am dead.'

He stared at her perplexed. 'My dear, of course not. How ridiculous. What are you thinking?' He looked at her concerned. 'You need more company. You shouldn't be alone, like this.' He glanced across at the table. 'I see you've been writing?'

'Yes. I mustn't stop writing.' She talked on tiredly, as if in a dream.

'Have you been unwell?' he asked worriedly. He leant towards her. 'You are pale, my dear, and alone.' He glanced again at her work on the table. 'It's true what you say and you must keep the writing flowing, let the words leave your mind. They are safer on the page I think. What tortures live in our minds.'

She nodded slowly, searching his eyes for news. Had he seen Shelley that week, was he with Harriet? Had he seen Byron – had he in fact, seen Claire? She felt cut off from the world, cut off from the life about her, even the life within her that seemed to be bleeding away. But Hogg's look offered no answers.

'He's in lodgings just out of London,' Hogg said finally. He sat in a chair, hunched in his frockcoat, the laughter she knew so well was absent. 'You might be glad of it, dear Mary, he isn't in the best of moods and I see you're exhausted. He is never in the same place long.'

'I'm a little tired, it is true,' she said quietly. 'And I would very much like to see him. He left me food and drink last time he came, but it's almost gone.' She spoke wistfully. 'And the fire goes out all the time. I must ration the logs.'

He stared about abstractedly, then nodded at his bag on the floor. I brought some food.' He stood and clapped his hands. 'And I propose to brew us some tea!'

'Do tell him to come to me soon,' she called fearfully as Hogg went into the kitchen. 'You will remember, won't you?'

Hogg called back to her laughing. 'Oh, Mary, he doesn't need telling. He speaks of you constantly, and I am sent by the speed of light!' He returned with the tea, his manner was earnest and eager. 'And Claire is with Byron, of course. You know about that.'

Mary felt relieved and sighed. 'I doubt he'll endure her hysterics,' she said, smiling as he poured out the tea.

He hadn't seen Shelley for a while, he said. Last time he'd seen him on the street in London by himself, walking so fast he'd had to chase him. He frowned. 'Byron married Miss Milbanke for money, oh, no mistake about it. He's in very deep trouble financially, and he can't sell the abbey. A man can't make a living out of poetry. He has made his name with *The Corsair*, but I heard he doesn't take money for his poetry, though I do not believe it. They're an arrogant lot these poets.'

He spoke in a dull low tone that surprised her. 'You don't like him?' she said.

'I haven't really considered it,' he said shrugging. He wiped his hands on his handkerchief. The talk had made him emotional. He took off his frockcoat and loosened his cravat. 'We must try to lighten our spirits, Mary. Do drink your tea.'

Mary smiled, though the atmosphere had changed. On his visits she'd rejected his advances, but she doubted he'd accepted her excuses. And they weren't really true. Had she been well and not pregnant she would still have refused him.

He drew a breath and spoke again. 'I do not see why women fall in love with Shelley so easily, you know. But they do, all the time, I have seen it. Harriet is lovely, and you, my dear, are adorable. He has both of you tethered to the spot, whilst I . . .'

'I would never be tethered,' Mary said quickly. Though it was right, she did feel tethered both to Percy and to her pregnancy.

He laughed quietly. 'But you *are*, my dear. As regards my own affections . . . well, you know about them. My work, as a lawyer, however, sends me away far and wide. We men must work one way or another.' He raised a finger in the air and made a sign like a finger going round a clock. 'Time, time, we are always so short of time.' He clapped his hands. 'But I am far too practical anyway to constantly have my head in the clouds in the way of poets! – Oh Byron and Shelley, how they swagger – and more than that, the way it influences women astounds me. Those poems are just like spells.' He laughed loud at the ceiling.

She liked his laughter and smiled at his words. But he was obviously jealous and annoyed. She knew he had fallen for Harriet, and that she too had rejected him. 'An important part of a woman's life is spent having children,' Mary said softly. 'It takes its toll on the body if it does not kill them. And children are tiring. Having children though is a vital part of a woman's existence, is it not?' She waited for his answer. His eyes agreed, and fell on her swollen body. She looked downwards and smiled. 'I wonder what it is like in the water with no way out. However do they survive coming from the womb into air. It is quite a journey?' A cold chill ran through her as she thought of the blood she kept losing. Was her baby trying to escape? Some babies were early; others were late, some even died. Her nerves were very unsteady.

Hogg frowned at her curiously. 'They don't exactly "think" in the womb though do they,' he said abstractedly. 'Well, not as we know. I mean these babies just keep growing according to some magical instruction. It's quite remarkable.' He was thoughtful a moment. 'Once they are born it is all quite different, however. Life can take you by the throat after that and destroy you.'

'How long are you here for?' she asked.

'I'll stay till tomorrow if you like.' He looked at her and smiled. 'But I doubt you will like me any better if I stayed for a year.'

'I couldn't possibly like you any better Hogg,' she said, trying to laugh. 'But you see how I am. And I have yet to think longer on Percy's ideas about relationships.' She looked at him straight. 'Tell me the truth – is he with Claire? – You say she's with Byron, but I know that Shelley has her heart, I see it in all she does.' She shivered as she spoke.

'And you have mine,' he said, hopefully, dropping his voice.

She asked him again.

'I don't know everything, Mary. I'm sorry. I know that Shelley will be here very shortly. He said so.'

'That's good. And you?'

'I told him I would visit you.' He gave her a long look.

She met his gaze and her eyes searched his own.

'What is it?' he asked. He leant forward.

They were silent a moment. She felt much older than her years, her hair was shining and beautiful but her features were drawn. 'I feel a little weak,' she said. 'Abigail brings me food and messages sometimes, but I don't leave the lodgings very much.'

'I brought fresh bread and butter and some apples and cheese from the market. I've put them in the kitchen.'

His air of benevolence and concern made her feel safe. They drank the tea and sat quietly a while. Then he rose from his chair thoughtfully. 'I need to wash my face; the London air is filthy.'

She watched him walk to the bedroom where there was a bowl and a jug of water. She heard him splashing his hands in the water. He had gone from her now, only to the bedroom, but it bothered her. 'Don't be long,' she called apprehensively, afraid of the bleeding.

'Is there something you ought to tell me?' he said, returning. He leant on the back of her chair. 'Whatever it is, do let me help you Mary.'

She smiled and rested her head on his arm. 'I am quite all right,' she whispered. She could not tell him the fears she had about her baby, nor could she disclose her sometimes horrifying dreams. But he made her food and talked to her, then read to her from her favourite books in his soft melodious voice. She enjoyed how he moved about the lodgings, much slower than Shelley, as if she might stop him and talk about her concerns. Shelley's mood was intense and his voice high pitched. But it was only Shelley she longed for.

Next day she felt better, her eyes shone and she'd eaten well. And more than that, she hadn't bled.

'Now then, Mary, might I be a little daring?' Hogg asked early that morning.

They were sitting on the chaise longue. Mary gathered her shawl further round her shoulders. Hogg's voice softened. 'My treasure, might I hold you, only for a minute? It would mean so much to me. Please let me hold you.' He smiled and recited her some Shakespeare

> *'"Come what sorrow can,*
> *It cannot countervail the exchange of joy,*
> *That one short minute gives me in her sight."'*

Then he placed his arm around her shoulder and moved in closer. But there came a rapping on the door. He rose and went across, opening it on a very distressed young woman. 'Who are you?' he asked frowning at her curious. The girl peered around the door.

'It's Abigail,' said Mary, coming to join him. 'She is the maid from Skinner Street.' She invited the girl inside, looking at her perplexed.

Abigail stood in her cloak, the hood half covering her face. 'I am not their maid any more,' she wept. 'Mrs Godwin dismissed me, for I ought never to have brought that food. She says I have stolen from the kitchen.'

'And have you?' said Hogg, astonished.

'I brought food for Miss Godwin,' she sobbed. 'She's been starvin'. An' her with child an' all. That poet never feeds her. I brought some raisons for him as well. He only eats nuts and raisins.'

'Hmm, that's true,' Hogg said quietly, swelling his chest. 'The man eats like a bird. – Do calm yourself, my dear; I'm sure we can help. You say she has dismissed you?'

The girl stood nodding, dabbing her eyes with a hanky. 'They sent me away.'

Mary listened and wondered. Had Abigail lost her work all because of bringing them food? It hardly seemed possible. Matters were worse than ever. 'Come and sit down,' she said. 'You are as fine a maid as anyone could hope for, Abigail. I'm sorry.'

'Miss Fanny wasn't in an' I couldn't come 'ere without tellin' 'er.'

'Had she gone to shop?' Mary asked curiously.

Abigail looked at her worriedly. 'No, not that. – Am I to tell ye Miss?'

'But, of course. Why do you hesitate?' She moved in closer.

'Mr Shelley came to see her, an' she was cryin'. She had to go out with him to talk because if Mr Godwin should see him I think he might do somethin' silly, he hates him ye see.'

Hogg frowned and drew back. 'You are probably right,' he murmured. 'Shelley makes people do very silly things indeed. People have shot at him before.'

'But did she come back? Mary asked anxiously.

'She did, but she went to her room. I don't know what happened after that, Miss, because Mrs Godwin dismissed me and told me I should never return.'

'"Never?"' said Hogg, clapping his hand on his forehead.

'Never. She said she couldn't stand thieves. But I didn't take a lot, just so as she wouldn't notice. But she watched me close and caught me.'

'Oh my days, people like her would notice a thing like that,' said Hogg, pacing the room irritably. 'Every morsel, I should think. It isn't much fun being poor.'

'My father isn't poor,' said Mary a little annoyed. 'He is going through difficult times. Tell me, Abigail. Have you any idea where Shelley went after. Did Fanny not tell you?'

'No Miss, I didn't talk to her. Mrs Godwin just told me to go. No questions, nothing.'

'Do you think she knew you were stealing the food for us?'

For a moment there was silence.

'I think so, Miss. I think she knew all the time.'

Mary shook her head. A sudden shame came over her. And an anger too, that she'd been so diminished in the eyes of her father's maid. How long would they live in lodgings like beggars without even enough to pay the rent? And why had Percy gone to see Fanny? That was very odd indeed. She took Abigail's cloak and put it in the kitchen. When she returned the girl has stopped crying and Hogg stood beside her, smiling.

'You're a very thoughtful girl, my dear,' said Hogg. 'And Mrs Godwin threw you out, did she? Well, forget her. I'm sure you are an excellent maid.'

'She didn't throw me out sir, not exactly,' said Abigail shakily. 'But when she was having her tirade, she frightened me ye see an' said I should leave as soon as possible and never come back. So I thought, well, I'll go right now, you silly old witch!' She stopped and took a breath. 'But how can I ever get work if she says I'm a thief? And I don't have a man anymore. He's gone to another city and isn't coming back.'

'Oh dear, Abigail, your world is turning upside down,' said Mary.

'But Mr Godwin said the world just goes round, Miss,' said Abigail.

'Indeed it does,' smiled Mary.

'As a matter of fact,' said Hogg thoughtfully. 'I know of someone who is very much in need of a maid like you.'

'An' I can cook as well,' said Abigail quickly, looking more cheerful.

'But Hogg, you are leaving shortly?' said Mary. 'You have hired a coach.'

'Indeed I have,' said Hogg. 'And the coach will be empty but for me. Now if Abigail would like to keep me company I shall feel much better.' He turned to her. 'Do you need to collect your things from the house? I shall find you an excellent home.'

'I don't have much, sir, and I hope I've seen the back of that house.'

'I can't say I'm surprised,' sighed Mary.

'Well, never mind,' said Hogg. 'The lady I am thinking of is lonely and lives by herself. She is very comfortably off and will buy you nice things to wear. I'm sure you could be of considerable help to her, Abigail. Yes, she'd be delighted to have you.' Hogg looked through the window. The streets were still busy. But his coach wasn't due for another half hour. Abigail sat by the fire, her features bright with life. She would leave with Hogg that day. Mary would wait for Shelley.

15

More Complexities

It was a cold January morning as Mary waited for Shelley in the lodgings. He had promised to come that day. She stood gazing through the window on the silent, winter's day. Against the white sky not a bird could be seen, the trees on the fields looked tired and grey and several had fallen in recent high winds against abandoned shovels and tools left by the builders. It seemed as if the whole of London were longing for spring.

No-one had been to enquire about Abigail, who had now gone off with Jefferson Hogg in a coach. And Claire had been absent for weeks, even through Christmas, which Shelley and Mary had shared alone. She was probably with Byron, Mary decided. She would hardly have returned to Skinner Street. But what was happening with Fanny? Was Fanny with Shelley right now? Percy was full of surprises. But Mary would soon give birth; surely he wouldn't neglect her so close to her confinement. But he'd neglected Harriet, who'd been placed in the same position, so why not her. He'd deserted his pregnant wife and child. He might do anything.

The world felt dark about her and she hated the night time alone. She felt lost. Percy's love was like the sunshine, marvellous when he was with her, but cold as a shadow when he wasn't. The long agony of waiting to see him was wearing her out.

She comforted herself. She hadn't lost any more blood and felt quite well. At night time the baby fluttered, only a flutter, but a true flutter of life. The delirium of thinking it was dead had gone, her baby was alive and moving. The sun came in through the window and lit up her face, then she heard the longed for footsteps on the stairs. She stayed where she was as he entered, shocked by his shabby attire. And he looked so wretched. 'My love, you are back,' she whispered.

He pulled her towards him. 'I have been gone too long, dear Mary, you have forgotten me. I have almost forgotten myself.' He pushed the hair from her face and kissed her. 'But I've been trying to borrow money – oh, from everyone, everywhere, at ridiculous rates of interest as well. People are good to me though. It's as well I have a charming manner!'

But she could hear the torment in his voice.

'Oh, Mary, Mary let us lie down.' He took her hand and led her to the bedroom where he pressed his lips to her cheek. 'My love, how I need you,' he murmured. 'You always do what is right. Oh, my precious, I love you so much.'

'I feared you had gone for good,' she faltered, tears in her throat.

'Indeed,' he said, sighing. 'There have been times when I've needed to pinch myself just to prove I exist.'

'Me too,' she said. relieved he was back. 'I have felt quite dead without you.'

He kissed her throat and opened the top of her dress.

'Percy,' she whispered. 'I must tell you . . .'

He waited.

She sat up slowly. 'I'm concerned.'

He waited, suddenly frowning. He hadn't yet taken off his frockcoat and unbuttoned it slowly. 'What is it?' he asked, shakily.

'I've been losing blood . . . Not too much, but enough to cause me to worry.' She was trembling slightly as she spoke. 'No-one was here. I thought it might never stop.'

'But it did?' he inquired urgently.

She nodded.

They sat together on the edge of the bed. 'I saw Hogg. He didn't tell me.'

'He didn't know,' she murmured. 'Why would I tell him?' She would never have revealed such intimate details to Hogg.

'So, how are you now?' he asked, stroking her hair. 'Have you seen a doctor?' He looked at her concernedly.

'No. Apart from losing blood for a while, I am well. Anyway, it's stopped. I believe I am strong.'

For a minute or two they were silent. Again he kissed and caressed her. 'My dear, I'm so glad. I must manage things better.'

'Abigail came . . .' she said presently.

'I know,' he said, sighing. 'Ridiculous business.'

'You heard?

'Yes.'

Mary waited. 'She left with Hogg.'

'I know that, too.'

'So where are they now? she asked, curious.

'I cannot say, for I know not a thing about that. He took her somewhere or other. To get her a post I believe, as a maid or a cook or something. I did not see her.'

'And so she has gone from our lives?' Mary said softly.

'So it would seem.'

Again there was silence.

'She told me . . .' Mary said quietly. 'She told me that . . .'

He turned to her, waiting. She did not want to hurt him or damage their love, but speak she must. 'She told me you'd gone to see Fanny.' She heard him breathe in deeply. 'I was surprised . . .'

'She told you that did she?' He stared at her, worried. 'She told you when she came here?'

'Of course.'

'And what else?'

'She said you'd gone out into Somers Town with her . . .'

Again they were silent. He straightened the cuffs of his frockcoat.

Mary continued. 'And that Fanny had been crying?' The words came anxiously. 'Why was she crying?' The coldness in her tone made her distant. But his acceptance of all she said brought him closer, his beautiful eyes filled with sadness and pain. 'Tell me, my love,' she urged. She fell into talking quickly. 'Why did you go to see her? – Were you trying to make her go away with you, in the way you left Harriet for me? – Did she say no, because of me. – She would, you see. Is that why she cried, because she didn't want to hurt me?'

'No, no,' he said quietly. 'You have it all wrong. I *did* go to see her . . .' He wiped the tears from her cheeks with his fingers. 'Of course I did.' He bent his head and sighed. 'You see – oh it seems like a long time ago, before we two fell in love. But I thought I loved her, you see. She was quite splendid then, but little by little Mrs Godwin wore her down, until she was almost a shadow, something ate her away, and now she is quiet as a mouse and has somehow forgotten who she is.' He clasped his hands tightly, the knuckles shining and white. 'I went to see her – I suppose it was a sort of goodbye.'

'Do you still care for her?' Mary whispered, tracing the lines of his strong heavy brows with her finger.

'Well, of course. But it isn't the same. And I told her.'

The same as what?'

'The same as with us.' He turned to her. 'Please believe me, Mary. Nothing is the same as us.'

'Is that *really* how you feel?' she badgered, still afraid.

'Yes, oh yes.'

'And where is Claire?'

He shook his head. 'With Byron I think at the abbey. Or that was the last I heard.' He gave her a boyish smile. 'You worry too much.' Again, he kissed her. 'We are lovers, you and I. – We are lovers.'

She turned from him quickly. 'Which is probably what you said to Harriet? I trust she knows everything now. You have told her I am due to have your child.'

He covered his face with his hands. 'Mary, I went to see my son. Harriet is well and the baby is thriving. I needed to see my son.'

'Did you stay?' She shrank from her words. But she felt her fears were the cause of her having bled. She had to voice them, but she trembled.

'For a while, of course. I had to. I wanted to see my children. I needed to hold the baby. He's a fine looking boy. – Oh, for pity's sake Mary, need you spear me with all these words?' His tone was mean and cruel. He talked on quickly. 'We must go to another part of London.' He rubbed his face wearily. 'A good way from here. I must find us a bigger place to live . . . Claire might come back, you see. We will need to find room for her with us.' He sighed again and drew himself up. 'She will never get Byron to love her. She is quite deceived.'

16

Awakenings

And exactly as Shelley had expected, Claire arrived back next day, though there was little room to indulge the flood of her talk. She constantly delivered her hopes, her fears and her terrors in a torrent of words. Byron was a pretty bad lot.

Shelley opened a book, while Mary and Claire talked on, their voices almost a whisper. – 'Oh, Mary,' said Claire. 'Please don't look at me like that; it's no use saying bad things. Haven't you done worse yourself, you will soon have Percy's child and he is married. You are quite good-humoured and kind so long as others applaud you. You hate being criticised, but you're hardly perfect, are you?'

Mary glanced at Percy, at the other end of the room, seated at the table writing, his back towards them. They talked together in whispers. It was late afternoon.

'Well, you know too well how powerless we are against love,' Claire said flatly. 'And Byron is extremely fickle.'

Mary grew indignant. She didn't like to be criticised, that much was true, for she constantly criticised herself. Claire was saying she had nowhere to live. 'I should forget about Byron,' said Mary, having listened for a full ten minutes. 'You are wasting your time. I suspect you are only one of many.'

'But I can't forget him,' whined Claire. 'I want to be with him. And you're wrong; he cares for me more than you think.'

'Did you try to return to Skinner Street?' dared Mary.

Claire flushed frustrated. 'I thought about that, and one day I sort of half got there, but I don't want the bother. Mama's face haunted my mind.'

'Do you know about Abigail?'

Claire shook her head and waited.

'She went with Hogg to live somewhere else,' said Mary. 'She'd argued with Mary Jane, about bringing us things to eat. I felt so sad at first, but Hogg made it all work out.' Mary told her the story while Claire looked on curious. She didn't know if Abigail had informed Mary Jane she was pregnant with Shelley's baby, and Fanny would never betray her, it was enough to be living with a married man, she said, let alone become pregnant by him.

Claire shrugged. 'So you think Byron doesn't want me.' She threw out her arms. The tone in her voice was desperate. 'I tried so hard to make him want me, but I think you are right.'

'Claire, Claire,' Mary said, impatiently. 'How can you throw yourself like that? Where is your pride?' They talked in hushed voices. Shelley still bent to his work.

'But I am pretty, Mary, you have said so yourself. I thought I could win him.'

'You have no money,' Mary said flatly. 'Byron wants money. Annabella Milbanke has money in abundance, that's why he married her.' For a moment they were silent.

'I might go away . . .' Claire murmured.

'Where to?' Mary looked at her curiously. 'You really mustn't trail after Byron.'

Claire dried her eyes with her handkerchief.

'I'm afraid I shall have to go out,' Shelley said suddenly, rising from his chair. 'I have business matters to attend to.'

Mary straightened, and a rush of fear went through her. He had only just returned. 'But where are you going?' she asked shakily. 'It is almost night time.' She pressed her hands on her stomach and felt the baby stirring. Did he think of it, ever?

'I don't know yet. I must find us some bigger lodgings.'

'How long do you intend to be gone?' Mary asked, standing to face him.

'Two days,' he said, biting his lip. 'I need two days.' He threw on his frockcoat and donned his hat determinedly then grabbed some clothes from the bedroom and flung hem in a bag. 'My dear Mary, do you not see how I am! Let me assure you, I am no more happy with this awful situation than you are. I am doing my best.'

For a moment or two they were silent. Shelley held Mary and kissed her. He glanced at Claire, then went out.

Claire was wrestling with rage. It seemed she hated them all just now, her mother, her stepfather, Mary, Shelley, Bryon, everyone. 'Nobody loves me,' she whispered.

'Life is often intolerable,' Mary said softly. 'The soul enjoys serenity only in passing, but it returns to a state of agitation all too quickly. That is what I believe.'

They took to their reading. The street through the window was noiseless. They sat silent, abstracted. But the two of them knew there was no going back from the place they had now arrived at.

Mary was restless; she could feel the bulk of the baby urgent and strong. The pain she'd felt when the blood had trickled from her body had returned, and was becoming gradually worse Then she felt a quick flood of water wetting her gown. 'It's happening!' she moaned, 'the child is coming and Percy has left us! – Claire, bring me some towels.'

'But it isn't due?' Claire said fearfully.

'It will come as it wants,' cried Mary. Slowly, she stood. 'Help me get to my bed. – Come Claire, please!' She put out her hand and Claire took hold of it nervously.

'I am not fitted for this,' Claire said pitifully. 'Oh Mary, your dress is soaking.'

'The waters have broken,' moaned Mary. 'The labour is taking over. She lifted the dress above her head, all the time wincing with pain. 'I shall need a midwife!'

Claire gasped frantically. 'But where can I find one?'

'You can bring the doctor,' said Mary. 'You know where he lives.'

'Yes, I have been with Mama. I know where to find him. Oh, I wish Mama could be with us!'

Having removed her dress, Mary lay in her petticoat, panting.

'We must do things ourselves,' she said, calm as she could. 'The doctor will come to help us. – Now go for him Claire, make haste!'

Claire ran out and fled down the stairs.

Ten minutes later she burst back into the room with the Somers Town doctor, a small serious looking fellow with quick intelligent eyes who assessed the situation quickly.

'My baby is almost here,' cried Mary. 'I feel it. But the child is early. Oh do let it live!'

'Rest assured,' the doctor said firmly. 'I shall do my best.' He swiftly removed his coat and hat, then requested Claire bring hot water and towels. She immediately did his bidding and followed his every instruction. The daylight was fading fast and dusk crept into the room. Claire lit candles as the doctor went about his work.

Time passed by intensely, until the cry of a child broke through the candlelit room. 'You have a beautiful daughter,' said the doctor.

Claire wrapped the tiny baby girl in a clean white sheet, Mary smiling and happy. It was a very small baby, thought Mary, like something out of a fairy tale, a Queen Mab baby perhaps, but it was quite perfect and well.

'You must put her straight to your breast,' the doctor said gently. 'She will grow. A mother should always breast feed her new born child.' He smiled as if hoping for agreement.

'Her father is of the same belief,' Mary said softly, overwhelmed. Saying the words "her father" to the doctor felt strange. She stared at her little creation.

The doctor washed his hands and put away his things. 'I take it Mr Shelley is away?'

'Not for long,' murmured Mary. 'A couple of days, no more.'

'She is not as strong as I would like,' the doctor said sighing. The baby was struggling to suckle. 'But if she feeds, then all will be well.'

'We have no money to pay you,' Claire faltered, looking downwards. 'At least not yet. . . . If you could . . .'

The doctor waved away her worry, they could pay him when matters were more sorted out, he said. 'I'll slip a bill through the door. You know where I am if you need me.'

It was 8 o'clock in the evening. Mary felt relieved. She now had a baby daughter, Percy Bysshe Shelley's daughter. But the speed with which life changed track amazed and confused her. The child's eyes were closed, so she could not see their colour or get a glimpse of any emotion. She ran her fingers through the soft auburn hair, the colour of her own, and cradled her baby tenderly. Percy had another daughter!

Claire was back and forth to the fire, burning the bloodstained cloths from the birthing and steeping Mary's dress in water.

'It went so easily,' Claire said, sighing with relief. 'Nothing like what I'd imagined.'

But still the child wouldn't feed.

17

A New Direction

The very air felt tight with tension that day as Mary bathed the face of her baby and Claire stood ironing its linen. The sound of the iron, crunching on the coals of the fire as Claire took it back and forth, and Mary's occasional sighs were the only sounds in the room. The baby was quiet. She couldn't have had much energy, said Claire, for she only fed spasmodically. Mary was constantly at her cot ensuring she was warm and comfortable; Now and again gasps of desperate breath came from her tiny lips. Mary determined not to worry, though the baby had not the least eagerness to live.

Shelley had been gone four days. During this time, Mary had been up and out of bed, while Claire went shopping, covering her head with her shawl and hoping she wasn't recognised. She feared colliding with her mother and didn't know what she would say if she did; they were so estranged. Mary and Claire talked at length about Byron.

'I should respect him more if he accepted his responsibilities,' Mary asserted. 'Whether or not she is with him, he is married to Annabella Milbanke now and has certain obligations.'

'I doubt they will ever be together' Claire replied boldly. 'From all I hear, they're not suited.'

Mary lowered her voice, for what she had to say might be hurtful. "I believe Annabella is pregnant," she said quietly, 'I heard it from Hogg.'

Claire started at that, and Mary looked the other way, immediately aware of her mistake. It wasn't common knowledge that Byron's wife was expecting. And as for Byron accepting responsibilities, it was hardly likely. Byron was much like Shelley, what mattered most was poetry, first and last.

Late afternoon, Shelley returned to the lodgings.

'He is going to have such a surprise,' said Mary, hearing his footsteps on the stairs. Her heart thumped hard with excitement as he opened the door and came in. Claire put aside her book and went to her room. The candles were lit, the baby asleep in her cot, and Mary felt excited, though the need to be up in the night trying to feed her had been exhausting. She felt stronger today however, as he entered and oddly on a par with Harriet now, for she too had a child by Shelley and believed he loved her best.

The fire crackled in the silence. She leant back in her chair and waited, the child in the cot beside her. 'My love!' he cried, bursting in. 'The baby has come already!' He laughed with joy and went to look in the cot.

'It's a girl,' she whispered. 'She's lovely.'

'Indeed, she is,' he gasped. 'But my darling, I wasn't with you!' He looked her up and down. 'You are well, I take it?'

Mary nodded slowly, taking him in, each look, each gesture. 'I'm as well as can be,' she laughed. 'She wasted no time in arriving. Claire was here to assist me. She went for the doctor. I was lucky, it was all so easy.'

'I'm glad Claire could be with you,' he murmured.

'I thought we might call her Clara,' Mary said, eager to see his reaction. The name was quite like "Claire".

He touched the baby's fingers. '"Clara", yes Clara. Why, she's delightful. And look at her tiny hands; they're the hands of a cherub! And her face is so small and pretty. I had better not lift her yet, she seems so fragile.' He stood for a moment looking downwards then fell into a chair. 'My dear, I am useless.'

Mary thought he looked unwell. He did not know where he belonged; he was always hurrying, writing frantically, talking at speed and thinking too fast. That or else he was silent, staring at space. He could not relax. 'You have not kissed me,' she said softly.

'See, what I mean,' he said sighing. 'I do not kiss my dearest love. I forget.' He was earnest. 'And you *are* my dearest. You know it, do you not? Please tell me you know it.' He reached for her quickly. His kiss was long and tender.

'Where have you been?' she asked, anxious to know what he'd done in the last four days. He took off his frockcoat and flung his hat on the table.

'Everywhere,' he said, frowning and rubbing his brow. 'To hell I think. – But as you see, I broke free. I am no bound Prometheus.'

'Have you been to see Harriet?' she asked. Her new child made her daring.

'No,' he said, flatly. 'I didn't even call on her. I've been to see one or two people in London; I'm desperately in need of money, my dear, as you know. I am quite sick to death of myself. Oh Mary, I feel I have diced with death for I was almost knifed for my purse.' He laughed at the thought. 'Not that there is anything in it.'

'And did these friends oblige?' she asked guardedly. Though she knew he'd have bargained, he would have got what he wanted in the end, he usually did.

'Well, someone did.'

Her eyes widened curiously. 'And who was that?'

'Do you really want to know?' He looked away as he spoke. 'I'll tell you if I must.' They were silent a moment. He went on. 'I was staying at somebody's house and a letter came delivered by hand. It was sent by Harriet. She knew where I was. She sent me some money. Wasn't that good of her? A fair bit, too. She got it from her father, he is always obliging, but he wouldn't have known it was for me.' He breathed in deeply then gave her a brief look of shame. 'She knows our situation. Harriet is a dear when it comes to it, you know. But she remembered I'd asked her to join us. I never pushed her out. And she's given me a new baby son.' He shook his head then moaned woefully. 'What a mess it all is. But I love you, Mary, I really do.' He straightened and attempted a smile.

'Yes,' murmured Mary. 'It's a mess. But it was good of her to send you that money.' Mary felt jealous. Her own father borrowed, Harriet's father gave. 'But she doesn't really know you, does she.

Not in the way that I do. She stays where she's comfortable and doesn't believe in your ideas . . . or so it would seem.'

He looked at her straight. 'No, she doesn't. She isn't like you, my dear. Oh, I realise that.' He went to the kitchen, returning with a glass of water. Forever restless, he drank it at once. He looked thin, she thought, and ashen. She knew he'd been taking laudanum. 'Sit down,' she said, 'and rest. We shall have to stay here a while longer, just until the baby is stronger. I must teach her how to feed from my breast. She is not too good at it, you see.'

'Oh we can't stay here,' he said, looking alarmed. He shook his head. 'I've found us another place much bigger and better. Hogg helped me find it. He's also paid the first month's rent.'

She looked at him steadily, waiting. There was always the sense of a life in suspension as if the real life waited to be lived.

'And you do not care for him?' Shelley asked, frowning.

'Is that what he said?'

'He told me he felt he could not hope for your love.'

She smiled. 'Did it please you to hear him say that?'

He came to her and knelt beside her, then rested his head on her lap. 'Oh, my dear sweet Mary, I could scarcely bear the thought of you making love with Hogg. You have been with child, so I was safe. But now . . . is it possible you might think again about loving him? Do I need fear it?' He looked at her, holding her gaze.

She did not like the look in his eyes. If only he knew the truth, she thought, that she did not agree with his thoughts about sexual relationships. When ideas were young they could easily fragment, she thought, and Shelley's ideas throbbed with youthful passion but might easily collapse in an instant. She had listened to him ardently so many times, his politics, his anger, and his love, his eyes shining and his voice filled with intensity. A sound came from one of the bedrooms.

'It's Claire,' said Mary. 'She is with us. It has all gone wrong with Byron.' There was a moment's silence, then Mary continued. 'She supported me during the birth. She is kind. Perhaps Harriet and Claire are kinder than me.' She frowned then smiled awkwardly.

He kissed her forehead and wound his fingers through her hair. 'She will have to come with us. I rather expected she might.'

'Yes,' Mary said quietly. 'When must we go?'

'Tomorrow,' Shelley said decisively, standing up straight and frowning with thought. 'We have no choice. If we don't take the rooms tomorrow we will lose them. We can walk there, it isn't so far. I won't pay another penny for these lodgings; they are far too damp and cramped.'

Mary gazed at the cot. 'But the baby is so new and tiny and the streets are icy. I could hardly see through the window this morning.'

'Do you have a decent blanket?' asked Shelley; his tone was hard and urgent.

Mary closed her eyes. How she wanted to sleep. 'I have something,' she said.

Claire came to join them from the bedroom. 'We are leaving tomorrow,' said Mary. 'Can you help me gather our things? I shall have to feed Clara and see she is well wrapped up.'

Claire looked at her perplexed. Mary looked back in earnest. 'I shall need you more than ever,' she said. 'I fear for my poor little daughter.'

'And the paths are slippery,' said Shelley, peering through the window. 'They are thick with ice. We must be careful. Yes Claire, you will have to help us.'

Mary glanced at Shelley who turned and stared at the fire. It seemed Claire was indispensible.

18

Life And Loss

'This ice is hellish!' Shelley exclaimed. He was carrying the child in his arms, Mary and Claire treading carefully beside him. It was early morning. – 'Claire, can you take her?' he asked, passing her the child. 'I feel quite ill and am none too steady on my feet, and Mary is recovering from childbirth.' He was irritable and tense because they had left in a hurry. To reach their new abode would take about half of an hour, he'd said, but that was in decent weather, not now when it was cold and the pavements were frozen over. Mary saw that Shelley was pale and gasping. He needed a holiday she thought in a warm sunny climate, but how could they ever afford it? Again Hogg came to mind. They went slowly, Mary glancing all the time at Claire who was nervous with the child.

There was a curious silence on the streets. Everyone was inside. They made their way cautiously, passing the doors and windows, hoping not to be seen. Mary was glad that their things had been delivered earlier.

'This blanket is far too thin,' said Claire. She held the child closer. 'Babies can't take the cold like us; their bodies don't know what to do. I have often heard Mama say so. We ought to have stayed where we were.'

'Impossible,' Shelley said sharply. 'Now Claire, pay attention. Hold the child tightly. Not much further.'

Mary stayed silent. She knew Claire was capable and efficient. But Shelley was struggling and kept stopping to catch his breath.

They were paying too heavily for their freedom she thought, and living from hand to mouth, with little thought for the future, and there was more winter to follow.

'I'm done for,' moaned Shelley. He blamed the ice for being slippery and his body for making him sick.

'You must rest,' said Mary. 'You eat so little, my love, it's hardly surprising you're ill.'

'There is something going on inside me,' he said hoarsely, pointing to his chest. 'Some terrible germ has got me.' He walked with bent shoulders, shaking slightly and feverish.

'You need sunshine and something decent to eat,' said Mary.

He put his hand in his pocket and drew out his laudanum. 'It helps,' he said, seeing her look.

'Laudanum is bad for you,' warned Mary as he leant on a wall and took a drink.

'Who says so?' he retorted brusquely. He looked at her knowingly. 'We are free, Mary, free to do as we wish! And freedom is good.'

'I'm not so sure,' murmured Mary.

The landlady met them at the door. It was starting to rain.

Next day, as if by magic, the ice had disappeared and the rooftops shone with sunlight. Claire went out to get nuts and raisins for Shelley. But she was ill at ease and unhappy, constantly telling Mary she felt sure that Byron would love her in time for she was far more interesting than Annabella Milbanke who was dull and plain and didn't have beautiful hair. It had become a constant refrain. But she plodded about the lodgings washing and ironing, doing whatever she could, though constantly saying life was unfair and how horrible it was to be poor.

Shelley's health was worse than ever and he ate very little. Mary had decided they must force him to take some broth. He did so quietly and mechanically, pulling at pieces of bread, though loath to swallow anything at all for he said his chest hurt badly. Mary fed Clara from her breast. But the child fretted and the sucking grew weaker. Time passed by, day, then night, then day, then night, but there was little life to be had in the tiny infant. They read and talked and attempted to write, but a sense of doom lingered about them and they knew the baby would not live.

'You are overjoyed by your son,' Mary said to Shelley begrudgingly. 'You say he is healthy and robust. Not so my Clara, however.' There were tears on her cheeks. 'I am sure Harriet must miss you.' She spoke resentfully, tired and dispirited. But she was sorry for having said it and felt sick with contrition. She knew he feared for the baby. Added to that, he was in no fit state for arguing. Both her lover and her child were sick, her life was collapsing around her.

Shelley lifted his face from his writing. 'I know how you feel about Clara and as her father I share your suffering. He rested his head in his hands and moaned.

'I do not feel any life in her,' Mary said shakily. 'She is almost weightless in my arms.'

For a moment or two they were silent. She returned the child to her cot. Claire had gone out and they were on their own by the fire. 'And your own father, Percy, do you actually *know* him?' she asked. Her voice was hesitant as if releasing long guarded words. 'I mean, do you *really* know him, other than that he is your father? He is father to several children. And yet . . .'

'Mary, I know my father's history. You cannot tell me anything about my family. It's quite a big one actually.' He leant back in his chair and looked at her curiously. 'I know my father well. And you know that we do not get on. Much is expected of me, of course, for I am the eldest.' He braced himself. He always straightened when he spoke of his father, and she noted the struggle in his eyes.

'I heard from Hogg how much he had tried to guide you,' Mary continued.

'Did you indeed. The truth is my father despises me. He has no idea what's in here.' He put his fingers to his head. 'My mind is like a tempest to Father.'

'Hogg has told me a lot.'

'Hogg talks too freely.' He frowned, his face flushed from the fire, his eyes glazed from loss of sleep. 'Though he is more in the way of trying to find things out. He is clever with that.'

'But do you respect your father, Percy, in the way that I respect Papa, for all his recent anger I still respect him.'

Percy replied with silence. Mary continued.

'It interests me, you see. I would like to do what is right by our child . . .' She frowned at the fire and sighed loudly. Percy's opinions were so important; she had put herself at his mercy, almost as if she served him. He sat before her, his waistcoat slung on the chair, his white throat bare. He seemed to need her. But did he? Did Percy need anyone at all?

'I do wish you wouldn't speak with Hogg about my family,' he sighed. 'You don't know the details, and neither does he.'

'But that's what I wanted. I *wanted* the details, you see. I thought he might know things.'

He looked at her keenly. 'And did he?'

'Yes, Hogg knows a lot.' She thought for a moment, Hogg could be quite formidable.

'You do believe in me, Mary, don't you? he said anxious, and a little afraid. 'You have often said so.' He held her gaze, waiting.

She was slow to reply. 'There are things I don't understand . . .'

'And you won't, because I don't understand them myself,' he frowned, suddenly annoyed. 'Harriet loves me, yet she knows that I love you, the most important thing in the world is denied her. *My heart*. It is yours Mary, always.' He rose from the chair and paced the floor. 'Can you not see how that hurts her?'

'Please sit down,' she told him. 'You are very intense when you pace.'

He ignored her request. 'I must find my strength, it has left me and I have much to do. I could land in the debtor's prison. Mary, I could land in prison! Do you not realise!'

She spoke quickly. 'I believe you told Hogg you were happy to share your 'common treasure. – I thought it offensive. You were meaning me, of course.' Her skin tightened as she spoke. 'Hogg is as generous with talk as he is with money sometimes.'

'I must speak with him about that,' Shelley stopped in his tracks, his hands clasped behind his back. He frowned and peered through the window. 'I know he is taken with you, Mary. He likes my women.'

For a moment or two they were silent.

'Alright then, my dear,' he said presently, slumping down in a chair. 'You are right, you are our common treasure. Indeed you are! But you know it of course?'

She worked her fingers together by way of comfort.

Shelley's features tightened. 'Do not goad me, Mary. Have you nothing better to do?'

She changed her position in the chair. 'I have plenty to do with the baby. And as a matter of fact I am reading Ovid.'

'Are you? Well done, I hope he will teach you some sense.'

'I have plenty of sense, too,' she said quietly. 'Rather too much of it, probably.'

Again they were silent.

'And I'm also reading Wordsworth,' she added more cheerfully.

'Ah, Wordsworth, yes. His very bones are carved from rock. Cumbria is an ancient land. There is something ancient about Wordsworth. I am told he sleeps on the hills in summer. "Ars goin owwer yonder fer a kip."' He laughed quietly. 'He is very good friends with farmers you know and vagrants. He listens to their songs and they inspire him.'

'He is an excellent poet.'

'He certainly is. And so am I, half a chance. It takes time and energy to bring forth the genie, my dear.'

'Wordsworth and you interpret the world differently,' she added thoughtfully.

He looked away abstracted. 'Yes, the way we poets interpret the life around us is strangely subjective. Wordsworth though, has always been interested in politics, like me, of course, and Byron. But poetry ought to transcend all that. It should reach for something profound, something that is all embracing.'

'Something metaphysical?' She lowered her voice. 'Wordsworth does that splendidly.'

'Yes,' he murmured. 'Poets search for meaning. If I write a poem I like to think it can be *felt*. You might offer some words about its meaning, but the feeling is a different phenomenon. If I asked you how you *felt* about it. Would you be able to tell me?'

She smiled, thoughtful. There was always the battle with words and ideas, the constant searching for truth. 'Might it not be wrong to know more than our lives can allow?' She spoke pensively. 'Perhaps there are things we shouldn't know. Matters beyond us, a ground we should never walk on. – Oh, Adam and Eve and the apple, the story resounds in my mind.' She loved to sit with him like this, exchanging ideas.

He stared at space for a moment then suddenly cried, '*Depart not – lest the grave should be, like life and fear, a dark reality*' – The dreamless sleep, that's what I need. Sleep is no escape if we are captured by nightmares.'

'And are you?' She waited.

'Not so much me, but I do believe you are, my dear. You often call out in your sleep.'

'Yet you never ask about my dreams?'

'I never know if I should. Dreams like yours are best forgotten.'

Mary pulled on a shawl. She hated the cold winter weather which seemed to suck the life out of everything about it. Its silence spoke the words of death. How she longed for the spring. 'Wordsworth is at one with the natural world. It has no desires or greed,' she said flatly. Shelley's thoughts about Wordsworth's poetry were always complex.

He smiled wryly. 'Oh, it has greed alright. If you see how ivy takes over the woods you are well aware of nature's greed. There is always a line of dominance in life. It leads to injustice and unfairness. We writers and poets should try to speak the truth for humanity.'

She looked at him perplexed. 'An impossible task.'

'Much would seem impossible, he replied, lowering his voice to a murmur. 'Poetry seeks to find truth within the savage wilderness of life.'

For the next half hour they sat reading. There was a wind on the street, rattling the window. He stood and went to inspect it. It was the wood, he said, the window was in need of repair, it did not close as it should. He took his handkerchief from his pocket and folded it, then fixed it into place, stopping the noise. 'I wonder what's happening out there,' he murmured. 'It would be good to know what your father is up to. Perhaps he has heard about the baby from Hogg. He won't be too happy about that.'

'It doesn't matter. I am happier than ever when I have you close beside me.'

'But you're unhappy today, my dear,' he said turning to her. His voice was full of gentleness; he knew her every mood.

'Perhaps a little,' she faltered, trying to hide the feelings showing in her face. 'There are always struggles and problems. Who can possibly avoid them? But you find things out through unhappiness,' she said.

'Finding things out is tiring when you don't discover anything worthwhile,' he said, shrugging. 'Hogg is good at all that. Not me. I watch and observe, but only discover poetry, not the nature of demons as Hogg does.'

'But you find out everything important,' she smiled. 'You, Shelley, have found out wonderful things and put them into your poetry.'

'I have, you are right,' he said relaxing. 'But I rebel against ideas about gods and such; not a single thing do I discover that makes me think different. And science – now where is love if everything is maths and molecules? Where is passion and longing?' For a moment or two he was thoughtful. 'Some say the science of electricity will deliver us the answers, and perhaps it will. It is one of my theories. But a theory is far from a truth. Perhaps life could be created with a lightning bolt – pure energy transmitted from lightning to a corpse. Just imagine.'

'But what of the soul?' She spoke abstractedly.

'Souls, ah yes . . . Strange things, souls. Take courage, I say. Think and think some more.'

'Tell me, my love, do you know why you write your poetry?'

For a moment or two they were thoughtful.

'I'm not sure why I write my poems, I have never considered it.'

She watched him carefully, it was a moment of profound revelation and she saw how he struggled.

He continued slowly. 'They grow from somewhere inside me and need to be born, like flowers, children or anything else that is born and unable to help it. Poetry is a part of what I am. And it helps me understand things.'

'Most people don't care to understand things much; they are far too busy surviving,' she said tiredly. 'Only the rich have time for thought and reflection.' She drew a breath and looked at him curiously. 'Do you think the poor get depressed?' She spoke abstractedly. 'I mean, the way they have nothing to hope for.'

'If they have love from their families, then that is worth a lot . . .' murmured Shelley. 'Wordsworth writes poetry for the poor. But a lot of what he says is all embracing, and so he is loved.' He clapped his hands and smiled. 'Well, I think we've thought it all through!'

'I doubt it,' she smiled. 'Problems might be solved temporarily, but history says they keep on returning and people are vessels for that. – I talked about Swedenborg once with some people in a coach returning from Dundee.'

'And?' He looked at her with interest.

She was thoughtful. 'According to Swedenborg, when we remember things we didn't actually experience it isn't our memory at all, it's the memory of a spirit within us, someone might return after hundreds of years and inhabit the body of another.' She chilled at the thought. 'Swedenborg thought angels got depressed like we do. They cease to love God and get depressed.'

He smiled wryly and shook his head. 'Pah! Depressed angels! Fallen angels! Perhaps they are poor. I mean, really, Mary, what do these angels do when they don't fly about?'

'Love and wisdom like the sun is forever trying to reach us,' Mary said, hopefully.

'And some travellers on the coach from Dundee told you this?'

She smiled. 'Not all of it. But they got me thinking and reading.'

'And they laughed when they said it, did they?' he smiled.

For a minute or two they were thoughtful.

'I do believe there is a link between moral and physical health though,' he said. 'An animal diet can lead to all manner of depravities. I would rather eat fruit and nuts. He pulled out a tattered piece of paper from his frock coat pocket and recited some poetry;

'A Sensitive Plant in a garden grew,
And the young winds fed it with silver dew,
And it opened its fan-like leaves to the light.
And closed them beneath the kisses of Night.

And the Spring arose on the garden fair,
Like the Spirit of Love felt everywhere;
And each flower and herb on Earth's dark breast
Rose from the dreams of its wintry rest.

But none ever trembled and panted with bliss
In the garden, the field, or the wilderness,
Like a doe in the noontide with love's sweet want,
As the companionless Sensitive Plant.'

He smiled and returned it. 'It isn't ready. It needs sorting out. I think I might work on it this evening.'

'It's beautiful,' she said. But the pain she felt over her father's rejection still hurt her. 'My father's love has turned sour,' she murmured.

'Your father will never forgive us, Mary. Now forget it, or you know how I'll be.'

Mary sat silent. She felt her father had forgotten her since she'd left him. It was as if she had left him for Shelley.

'It's 2 pm, said Shelley. 'I wonder why Claire isn't back. She said she'd be home by noon. Perhaps she has gone to see her mother.'

Mary shook her head. 'I doubt it.' They both sat tense by the fire. Mary sighed loudly. 'I'm trying hard to be rational,' she said, lifting her shoulders and dropping them slowly. 'It's what my mother would have wanted. Best be rational and not be ruled by emotion.'

Shelley gazed at the ceiling. 'In terms of morality, trying to be rational suggests that we humans are wicked and depend on rationality to save us.'

'Well yes. If men were more rational perhaps there would be far less war,' she said flatly. 'People would love each other better; families would get on with each other.'

She got up and went to the cot. For a few moments there was silence, a terrible formidable silence that sounded out loud, as if it might continue for ever. Mary gave a cry of agony, like an animal caught in a trap, and Shelley ran to her quickly, dreading the alarm in her voice. They looked together in horror at their now lifeless baby.

'She is dead,' wept Mary, fearing to touch her. 'I knew it would happen. But minutes ago she was with us and now she has gone. I am punished, Percy. And oh, how cruelly!' She slipped to the floor and sobbed.

He looked at his dead baby daughter and lifted her slowly from the cot. She was cold and still. 'We missed it,' he whispered. 'I think she convulsed. Such a lonely, silent little death.' He stroked the soft pink cheek still flushed from the baby's struggle.

'I knew she would leave us today,' said Mary. 'A mother always knows. I have felt it coming.'

Shelley looked at the child, bewildered and afraid. 'She must be wrapped and buried,' he said. 'Oh, my love ... I must find an undertaker quickly.'

Mary rose slowly then held the child to her breast. A great rush of failure flooded her. 'Oh, that we could bring back the dead,' she moaned. All life about her seemed suddenly remote just then. She too felt dead. Shelley placed his arm around her shoulder, and she wept heavily, the dead baby between them, warmed by their living blood.

19

Deep-Rooted Changes

There was a strained atmosphere in Godwin's bookshop of late. People from Somers Town were indulging in scandalous gossip, whispering behind the bookshelves. Today Mary Jane had needed to get up close to hear what a group of women were saying in a corner. She fell to tidying up the shelves. She knew that Mary had given birth to a baby daughter that month, her pregnancy had been common knowledge in Somers Town, but had the child actually died? She felt deeply sad about that. The memory of how the girls had fled still chilled her. She wished no harm to Mary, in fact she only wished her well, but both Mary and Claire, her very own daughter, had brought shame on their parents and a great deal of heartache. Now it seemed something terrible had happened. Mary's baby was dead. Mary Jane felt shaky as she thought of it. Her husband was despised by a lot of the Somers Town community, for Godwin, they said, desperate for money, had sold two of his daughters to the false-hearted faithless poet Percy Bysshe Shelley. Was it not right and proper, they said, that their mother, Mary Jane Godwin, should find them and bring them back home. Those women should be taught some morals! Mary Jane had tried to be polite in the shop, though a lot of asides made her angry, and she supposed she'd behaved with dignity, and she had certainly done her best, for she'd tried to intervene at first, though without success. Stories came right, left and centre in bits and pieces and people assembled them as they would, often arriving at monstrous conclusions nothing like truth. But what could she do? She and her husband had exhausted all words and emotions. And Fanny didn't say a word, going about in silence, carrying on her work, or she might disappear into Somers Town bending her head, her cape drawn close about her. She did not talk to the locals. In fact, she didn't talk to anyone. But Mary Jane knew that Fanny's feelings were deep, for sometimes on passing her door she had heard her weeping. *Her as well*, she had thought, for Percy Bysshe Shelley had stolen the hearts of all three girls at once, but as luck would have it, Fanny had been left behind. And good for her, Mary Jane thought, she is better off without him; the man was nothing but a cad! She wondered if Fanny knew about Mary's baby. William would no doubt find out in the way men did. And in any case, they had their own young son to take care of let alone the shop. She would have to get on.

Shelley's creditors chased him wherever they went, but Mary too felt pursued. She felt as if she were watched when she left the lodgings. There were days she lay on the chaise longue staring at the fire, unable to read or think. Her baby daughter was dead and she could not bear it. She felt ill and knew she looked weary. Also her hair lacked lustre and wouldn't stay in place however she tried to dress it. But the summer would return its shine she thought, and she tried not to dwell on her pains.

She had written to Hogg about Clara, telling him she got not a bit of support from Shelley who seemed to have gone into a panic, walking about in circles. "Please come to see me Hogg," she'd pleaded, stressing how important his calmness was and how much she needed him. They were now in the month of March, but spring was slow and Shelley had said the cold weather had delayed it. He'd remarked that even flowers hated cold, not a bird, not a flower could be seen. But she'd seen a little blue butterfly that morning, she'd said, trying to find somewhere to land. It was more like a moth, but were moths ever bright blue? She had never seen one like it before and wondered if it might be the spirit of her baby living again as something else. And she contented herself that her baby could fly and be happy in its new existence, quite a nonsensical thought, but it made her feel better. In her journal she wrote of a haunting dream she'd had recently

"Dream that my little baby came to life again—that it had only been cold & that we rubbed it before the fire & it lived. Awoke and found no baby. I think about the little thing all day."

She pulled herself together, Hogg would understand and sympathise, please let him come to her soon.

When he finally arrived she delivered him all her concerns in a rush, and in his thoughtful and kind way he heard her out. Shelley and Claire had gone walking. 'They often go out without me,' she fretted. 'I can't bear it when the lodgings are silent and they have taken their coats without telling me where they have gone. Hogg, shall I go mad?' She had no-one to confide in, she said, and often thought she might go mad. She felt wretched and worthless. Hogg was gentle and considerate, but deep down she felt angry with Shelley. She described to Hogg an unpleasant scene from yesterday.

"So you want to be rid of me, do you!" Claire had exclaimed dramatically, when Mary had suggested she should look for alterna- tive lodgings. "Not at all", Percy had interjected sympathetically. "Mary is talking nonsense. And in any case you are very helpful, my dear. I can't imagine why she speaks so bitterly." Mary had argued she felt better and didn't need Claire's assistance and that Claire should be more independent. But neither Claire nor Shelley would have it and Mary had felt defeated. Her relationship with Percy was languishing and she was weary of Claire, her laughter was always too loud and her words must always be heard.

Sitting with Hogg on the chaise longue that evening she smiled and reached for his hand. He moved in closer towards her, his eyes heavy with desire. His fingers were thick and strong, not long and elegant like those of the man she loved. She tensed as she felt him slip his arm about her waist. Would she have him take her to bed, could she let him make love to her in the way that Shelley wanted? She had left herself now; her soul had fled and she trembled slightly at the thought of her future. But what was happening, really? Did Percy love her like he said, did Claire really love Percy, and did she love him in return, did Hogg in truth love Percy too which was why he wanted to sleep with her, and why Percy promoted the idea? Questions, questions! Free love was achingly complicated. And if she did not choose to accept it, what then? She drew away from him quickly.

'Well Mary, I think I should go,' said Hogg, slowly making to rise. 'I have matters to attend to in the city. But I trust our talk has been useful. Write to me soon and I'll come if you need me.'

Mary sat quiet and troubled. She watched him walk across the room, heard him open the door and go down the stairs. Again she was alone.

Later that week with Shelley in their lodgings she became decisive. Claire was lying in with a headache. It was early morning and they had just finished breakfast. 'Claire has to go,' she said firmly. Percy sat writing at the table.

'What?' he said turning. He put down his pen and faced her.

'Claire must move out. You know how I feel. We can't live all three of us together. It's too complicated Percy, and what's more it's making me ill.'

He frowned and rested his hands on his knees. 'Mary, oh Mary,' he sighed. 'It's been a terrible time for you, I know, indeed for us both. And Claire has understood. You have to admit she has made herself enormously useful.'

'It does me harm to have her live with us,' Mary said flatly. 'Surely you see it.' She would not state the obvious, that Shelley's relationship with her stepsister had become too close. 'And I do not wish to take Hogg for a lover,' she added firmly.

For several moments they were silent. 'Claire must leave,' she continued fixedly. – 'That is unless you simply cannot bear to lose her.' She smiled wryly as she said it, annoyed at the conversation.

He looked at her straight.

She met his eyes miserably. She felt such a piteous creature sitting there complaining, but she knew it had to be done, and she was growing contemptuous of him now. 'She will break us apart. It's best if she goes,' she insisted.

'I can't discuss it just now,' he said, frowning. 'I'll talk with you later.' His manner was cold and detached. He turned again to his work and wrote on quickly.

'I always come last,' she pleaded, speaking into his back. 'But Percy, I matter too. We scarcely speak to each other.' He turned to her again. She put out the flat of her hand. 'Oh do not stop your work just for *me.*'

'Try to be kinder, my dear,' he said softly. 'Claire suffers too; she has problems of her own. Think about what you are saying.'

'Well, I'm glad she confides in you,' Mary said sardonically. 'For it seems I cannot.'

He sat for a moment biting his lip and frowning.

'So you want her to stay.' Mary said, shrinking away. 'You like her around. You enjoy her company. It is better than mine, is it? Claire and I are two very different women. She is lively and amusing while I am more earnest and thoughtful, but . . .'

He shook his head slowly. 'Mary, Mary, you know how I love you. Your mind excites me, while Claire's lightness of spirit gives me respite.'

Mary flushed with indignation. 'Oh, how I would love such lightness of spirit, but I am stern and steady and can be no other.'

Percy rubbed his face with his hands. 'Oh, this is so tiresome. And don't raise your voice. What if she hears and comes out? I wouldn't want to unsettle her.'

'Oh, we mustn't unsettle Claire, Mary doesn't matter. I can't tell you how you hurt me, Percy – your easy talk about your son with Harriet, the hours you spend away when I have no idea where you are. If it wasn't for Hogg . . .'

'"Hogg?"' he interjected quickly. 'But you have made it plain that you do not care for him. He told me.'

'I cannot sleep with him, and that is the end of it.' She stood and paced the floor. Unable to collect herself she talked in quick sharp whispers. 'Claire goes off to see Byron at Newstead. I wonder what she tells him. She is often indiscrete.'

'Is she? What will she tell him that matters?'

'Everything. She will tell him about Papa and the way things are. My father likes things private. Nothing is private with Claire.'

155

'Your mother's biography wasn't private,' he sighed. He narrowed his eyes and waited.

'I know,' said Mary. She straightened. 'He knew he'd done wrong with that and he suffered. You see, revelations can cause such suffering.'

Percy sat gazing at space.

For a moment or two they were thoughtful.

She saw he wasn't wearing a cravat, his neck was bare and he looked unusually unkempt. He was suffering from the loss of the baby and he feared the debtor's prison more than ever.

'Byron would have bored her, he'd be talking about liberating Greece from the Ottoman rule and the struggle for Italian nationalism,' Percy said grandly. 'He won't want to hear about Skinner Street.'

Mary continued. 'Annabella Milbanke is a very clever woman. He wouldn't want to be challenged by a woman like her now, would he?'

Shelley tipped back on his chair. 'She has money, my dear.' He smiled at the ceiling. 'And the man needs money. Oh he likes to pretend he is some sort of demon. It's that twisted foot. He rather makes too much of it I think.'

Mary threw back her head and stared at him boldly. 'I am told he's in love with Lady Caroline Lamb. Well, there you are, Hogg told me that. Though I fear the woman is crazy.'

'In love with Caroline Lamb? I don't think so.' He shook his head. 'Perhaps he sports with her a bit, that's all. But a man might love a number of women at once.'

'That is quite plain,' said Mary. 'And it isn't the least bit wrong, is it?'

Again they were silent.

Mary continued quietly. 'He damages his body with laudanum too, like you do.'

'Well, he's writing some excellent stuff,' Percy said dismissively. '*Childe Harold* is selling very well. But I believe he gets quite irate about things and shouts in the House of Lords, especially about the Elgin marbles . . .' He shook his head at the thought and put away his writing, sighing. 'It's not so much he's impassioned by old marble sculptures, but more what's happened to Athens.' He fell to quoting a passage from Byron's poem

> *"Dull is the eye that will not weep to see*
> *Thy walls defaced, thy mouldering shrines removed*
> *By British hands, which it had best behoved*
> *To guard those relics ne'er to be restored.*
> *Curst be the hour when from their isle they roved,*
> *And once again thy hapless bosom gored,*
> *And snatch'd thy shrinking gods to northern climes abhorred!"'*

'Good,' she said. 'All good. But I believe the Earl of Elgin had permission to bring those sculptures to England. I heard it at one of Father's dinners.'

Shelley shrugged his shoulders. 'No proof has been found to that effect. Hogg will know though, I'm sure.' He clapped his palms on the table. 'Very well then, my love, I'll see if I can find some lodgings for Claire in Pimlico; anything to make you happy.' With that he reached for his coat and hat and went out.

As Claire went off to live in Pimlico, Hogg came to stay. And again, Percy disappeared, to look for a house, he said, possibly in Windsor. He was a lot better off now, Sir Bysshe Shelley, First Baronet of Castle Goring, had died at the age of 83, leaving Percy an excellent annual income of £1,000. Now he could relieve himself of many of his debts, and an allowance had been made to Harriet too which eased his concerns a great deal. But until he inherited from his father, he said, he would still be in need. Poet, philosopher, genius as he was, Mary found that like her father, managing money wasn't one of Percy's talents. But she believed in his poetry wholeheartedly. He would write great poetry for the world and she would always be there to assist him.

Several days passed by then Shelley returned to the lodgings, talking excitedly of houses he'd liked and wanted her to see. But none of them took her fancy and they spent the summer happily alone in their lodgings enjoying one another's company. And again she became pregnant. It thrilled her to know that the river of life still rushed in her, yet an odd and terrifying sense of sterility held her. Words from the bible came to her with warning

> *"When the woman saw that the tree was good for food, and that it was a delight to the eyes, and that the tree was desirable to make one wise, she took from its fruit and ate; and she gave also to her husband with her, and he ate."*

Each day she brooded about the history she and Shelley were making, for whatever they did was discussed by the people in Somers Town and would always reach her father's ears. Percy was often late back, acting detached and indifferent, and she believed he went to see Claire in Pimlico. Did he take her with him to the city? Did people see them? One afternoon when Hogg came to visit he talked about matters far removed from their concerns. He too was seeking escape and wanted to talk about the fields near Somers Town speaking with a strange gravity about moles that were "churning up the earth". 'It's all very odd,' he said frowning. 'They don't usually surface when it's cold, but the ground has been soaked. Those fellows building the houses are really weary of the moles . . . I used to think moles were blind, you know, but they're not, they sort of see through their skin. – But how can we know if a mole can or can't see, those creatures can't tell us? I need evidence!' He laughed loudly, sort of hysterically.

'Of course,' said Mary. 'Evidence is the thing, dear Hogg. So often we work from our feelings which can often be badly informed.' She went along with his talk, for it made it easier not to have personal contact. Today he looked older and seemed to be walking more heavily. He had put on a little weight during the winter. He was talking about moles, about agriculture and food, how certain cities fared better with their produce than England. He told her about a volcanic eruption that was causing a lot of pollution. – 'The East Indies, that's where it happened, the dust travels everywhere.

No wonder I'm constantly coughing.' The harvests in Europe would be bad, he asserted, there'd been so much rain and cold. He looked at books in the lodgings then turned to her. And she saw from his eyes he still wanted her, but she could not respond. When it was time to leave she leant to him and kissed his cheek and his eyes searched her own. He was very much alone like she was. But she knew she could not give him what he needed. He left silent as a shadow, slow, heavy and resigned.

20

Claire And Lord Byron

New Year delivered Mary a son called William, named after William Godwin her acclaimed father. A doctor had been in attendance and the child had entered the world without the least ado, a source of immense relief and joy to Mary who always had in mind the terrible plight of her mother who had died from a cruel parturition. But the sun had rarely been in evidence that month and the sound of heavy footsteps crunching through the icy streets constantly reached her ears through the thin glass window of their lodgings bringing back painful memories. It was a dark and soulless day, a bleak and wintry welcome for baby William, and she wondered where she and Percy would live, for Shelley was eager to find new accommodation. And Claire would have to come with them, for Shelley claimed she was needed more than ever. Mary had reluctantly agreed. But she was filled with fear and doubt. But the die was cast, baby William was healthy and strong, a little sweetheart from the first, thought Mary, but thoughts of dead baby Clara still preyed on her mind. She shuddered with cold and put more logs on the fire. The dead were so long gone . . .

Over in Nottingham, the wind moaned through the trees of Newstead Abbey as Claire climbed out of the coach. She was a frequent visitor to the abbey now and had decided it was quite an achievement to have Byron accept her so openly into his home. And also into his bed. And this was her secret. He was separated now from Lady Byron and Claire had been taking her laughter and gaiety to the dreary old abbey for a month. Frederick Llewellyn, the gardener, had said his lordship had gone to a great deal of trouble to try to revitalize the place, but he feared it would never be sold. Times had changed and he could never keep up with repairs. Also, what was the man to do there other than give parties he did not enjoy for people he did not like? His lordship didn't like parties nor did he dance, but it didn't take money or space to sit and write poetry, and apart from giving the occasional address to the House of Lords, most of the time he wrote poems.

There was little help to be had at the abbey, Llewellyn told Claire, but his lordship was glad of her company, he'd been unhappy with Lady Byron coming and going – talk about rows – why, they even disturbed the pigeons in the highest windows of the abbey! And she'd packed her things and returned to live with her parents. Frederick's wife cooked and kept his lordship's living quarters neat and tidy, and they had both remained loyal servants, even helping him organise a break in Switzerland, which was soon to happen. The poor man needed a change, said Llewellyn, and not before time.

Frederick moved fast up the stairway, he was a strong and able bodied man, but he cursed and swore like a trooper. But none of that bothered Byron; he was as easy going as a snail. His lordship thought himself a miserable sinner, however, said Frederick, a product of evil. But the Llewellyn's were used to his ways and took him as he came, for George Gordon Byron was a fellow of many parts. Frederick's wife helped out with his lordship's nightmares too, for Byron thought the abbey was haunted, and visitors often confirmed it. Even his beloved pet dog, Boatswain, who had died of rabies in 1808, and was buried in the grounds, was sometimes heard howling from its grave. Oh yes, it was true, Frederick Llewellyn had experienced that disturbing phenomenon far too often for comfort. And he knew by heart his lordship's poetic mumblings about the 'the hall of his fathers,' even reciting the words himself as he went with Claire up the stairs

"Thro' thy battlements, Newstead, the hollow winds whistle: Thou, the hall of my fathers, art gone to decay."

But such was the way of old castles and abbeys said Frederick. Reading about old buildings was one of his hobbies. The old abbey, he said, had never been an abbey at all. It had first been an Augustian priory, founded by King Henry II in the twelfth century, a penance for the murder of the Archbishop Thomas Becket who'd been murdered in Canterbury cathedral. According to the king, the church was subject to the law of the land, but according to Becket, the Church was higher than him and the king had made angry protestations in front of his knights. Misunderstanding what the king had actually been saying, and thinking he wanted rid, four of them had galloped at speed to the cathedral and murdered Becket at the alter. The king had called it an appalling mistake. Llewellyn shook his head while delivering the story to Claire. It was wrong to kill an archbishop, there was bound to be retribution! As time passed by the abbey had been left to George Gordon, a ten year old boy, who then became the 6th Baron Byron. In time George Byron grew tall and handsome and was constantly pursued by women. Claire heard a hint of warning in Frederick's tone, as if she were just one of many and ought to take care. But nothing daunted Claire Clairmont and she'd determined to have this peer of the real for her lover. She had though found herself pregnant.

Much of the ice had melted and the streets were clear and dry as Claire took a carriage to Somers Town and called on Mary and Percy. There was such a lot to report. The fact of her pregnancy had made her feel proud for she too was now adored by a poet, and a famous poet at that. She explained with breathless pleasure that Annabella had gone for good and that she, herself, would probably be the next Lady Byron. She laughed triumphantly and went to look at the baby in its cot. 'I too shall soon have a child,' she said triumphantly, 'and what a noble child it will be. – Lord Byron loves me!' She sat down and straightened her skirts, in a noble, superior fahion. 'You might think it most unlikely, Mary, but we've declared our feelings for each other. I told you I would win him, and I did.'

'Dear sister, take care,' smiled Mary. 'You will never win a man like Byron. He will always be off to the bed of some other woman, or even the bed of a man, he is quite liberal in his tastes. And according to Annabella his sexual inclinations are gross.' She bent her head and frowned. 'But you will have to ask Hogg about that.' Mary lifted the baby out of his cot. 'So there he is,' she said fondly, cradling the new baby boy, 'my precious gift to the world. He is quite perfect.'

Claire looked on. 'How can you speak about Byron like that, when you don't even know him? You know how Hogg likes to shock. Byron might well be my husband soon. I shall endeavour to correct his faults when I . . .'

Mary laughed. 'Annabella was of the same opinion, until she became disgusted. But opinions are of little use. I do not like what I hear of the man, though I own he is a great poet and perhaps my judgements are unfair for I only know what I hear. Shelley however is eager to befriend him. It is natural of course that poets of such stature would want to talk to each other.'

'Well,' said Claire, stroking the baby's forehead with a long elegant finger. 'If you think I can't help him, you must think me of little worth.'

Mary answered with silence and returned the child to his cot.

Claire shrugged and went on. 'Our Shelley isn't that wonderful, you know. All the time I have been with Byron, I suspect you thought I was with Shelley. – Oh, I know you did! You thought Percy was with me, didn't you. Well, he wasn't, you see. Byron has been reading his poetry to me, and has even let me be critical. He values my opinion.'

'You have criticised Byron's poetry in his presence?' Mary said aghast.

Claire straightened. 'Of course. He is happy to receive my advice.'

'You have given Byron advice on poetry?' Mary shook her head astonished.

'Oh Mary, do stop it. I am quite learned, you know. I think you forget.' Her tone turned angry. 'You don't know what is in my head, do you, you have no idea. You might be surprised. Byron and I have talked at length about Shakespeare. You know how well I remember passages of poetry. He was most impressed.' Claire wound herself down from her high pitched tone and spoke more slowly, faltering slightly. 'Byron will be wealthy once he has sold the abbey. Or that is what he thinks.' She frowned. 'It is something of a problem however.' She looked downwards, thoughtful. 'What is to become of the place if he cannot sell it?' She spoke anxiously and frowned. 'And Annabella is pregnant too. Oh dear. But his life with her is over. They will soon be divorced.'

Mary saw that Claire was serious. She wished she could support her hopes, but from what she'd heard of Byron she did not feel he could ever make a woman happy, or indeed be sincere in his affections. And he didn't seem the least romantic. 'I wonder if Byron has ever known joy?' she said thoughtfully. 'I mean *real* joy like we see with Percy. He seems so morose.'

'Everyone feels joy sometimes, 'said Claire, though a little irritably. 'The joy of a beautiful day, the joy of being loved, the joy of the sublime . . . He must have felt joy when he published *The Corsair.*'

'Do you think Annabella loved him?' Mary said keenly. 'Or was it just his poetry?'

'I think she loved him very much. But their temperaments weren't suited. He did not like her conversation, he said. He thought her extremely dull.'

'Is that what he told you?'

'Of course, why should I invent it? Oh, Mary, you never trust me.'

For a moment or two they were silent.

'He was loved by his mother, surely,' said Claire, sighing. 'Though he doesn't like to talk about his childhood. – He was certainly loved by his dog.'

Mary smiled. 'And it seems he adores his sister, though rather wantonly I'm told. I can't believe much good can come from that.' Mary raised her shoulders and sighed.

'I'm not going to think about it anyway,' said Claire, her eyes hard with decision. 'I doubt there is any truth in it at any rate. People hanker after scandal.'

Mary looked at her quizzically. Claire was always so certain, so eager, so naive. She was bound to get hurt.

'I believe in free love, I definitely do,' Claire said loud and firmly. 'I will not stop him loving others if that is his wish. And I shall do the same . . .'

Mary looked at her straight. 'Without caring how others might suffer?'

Claire threw out her hands. 'Do *you* care how Harriet suffers? No, you do not. How you deceive yourself sometimes.'

'I do not know the full story of that. Percy has been badly treated. Harriet too has lovers. Or so I am told by Hogg.'

'I do not believe it, Hogg wanted Harriet for himself. Percy has said so. Hogg should be writing, writing about imaginary people instead of making up stories about people he knows. That would be far less dangerous. He does not work from a lawyer's mind at all. – Where is Percy today?'

Claire was standing in the middle of the room. She looked odd and unfamiliar now. 'He has gone to stay with a friend in the city,' said Mary. 'He is trying to sort out his finances and find us some-where to live. He hates it here. Matters have slightly improved since his grandfather's death.'

'He has almost gone mad. He needs to get away.' Claire pressed her palms together and closed her eyes as if praying. 'How wonderful it was when we wandered on the continent!' She sighed. 'Oh, Mary, do you recall how Percy loved it when we wandered?' Then she threw out her arms and twirled around the floor like a girl.

'I remember he damaged his ankle and did a great deal of moan-ing and groaning,' said Mary, wondering at Claire's enchantment.

Claire sat down and continued. 'Well, Byron has left for Geneva now. He will live in a villa by the lake and what's more, I am going to join him. He wants to see you and Percy too. Might Percy rent a villa nearby then we could all be together a while – what do you think? Oh, Mary that would be wonderful!'

The thought made Mary less tense. The lodgings were so oppressive. How she needed an adventure. 'Has Byron gone alone?' she asked, wondering who he might be taking with him. It was all so sudden, but Percy liked sudden happenings.

'Not entirely. Two servants from Newstead have accompanied

him, a man called Frederick Llewellyn who works as a sort of butler and his wife Gertrude who looks after Lord Byron's rooms. He has also taken his personal physician, a Doctor Polidori. Byron believes the devil is out to get him and he likes to have Doctor Polidori close by.' She sighed and laid her palm on her forehead. 'What an imagination! His nightmares are quite disturbing, even more frightening than mine. He shrieks so loudly you would think he'd awaken the ghosts! Polidori helps comfort him. I believe Polidori is something of a writer too and is intent on writing a novel. – Oh, Mary, do come and join us!'

Mary decided the idea was irresistible and she knew Shelley would agree. It was hard to know what sort of society Byron liked to move in though. He didn't stay away from the abbey for long and was something of a clandestine figure.

'It's just an idea,' Claire said hesitantly, looking at the child in the cot. 'It might be too much with the baby ... As Percy and see what he says.' She went towards the door. 'I must visit the landlady in Pimlico. I owe her some rent. How good it is to actually pay up. And Percy has sent money for the doctor who delivered baby William.' Her eyes shone with excitement. 'Oh, I hope we can take that holiday together Mary. The better weather will be good for us.' She glanced about the lodgings. 'Is there anything I can do for you, my dear?' She went to look at the child. 'He doesn't look much like Percy, does he?' She frowned thoughtful. 'Perhaps he is going to be a Godwin. Poor thing.'

Mary narrowed her eyes with annoyance. Claire's manner had become condescending. It was almost as if at the least opportunity she would catapult her back to Skinner Street. She braced herself, she did not want to turn into a creature of habit, consigned to domestic routines and forgetting to lift her pen. She did not want to lose her own distinctness, that special quality she had which she knew had made Percy love her. Her breasts were heavy with milk and she must feed her baby, that done, she would settle to write!

Part Two

21

Villa Diodati

Having thought about it and talked about it, argued about it and finally come to a decision, the trio were at last in Geneva, Shelley and Byron in lively debate with each other in the grounds of Villa Diodati, the mansion Byron had rented for his holiday on the shores of Lake Geneva. They were sitting together on a bench, the fresh air drifting about them and the gentle splashing of water on the embankment in accord with their sense of serenity. They might walk by the lake that evening, said Byron, weather permitting, the mountains at night time were inspiring, and the still dark water lit by moonlight was capable of rich enchantments. He murmured some verse

> "'. . . That iron is a cankering thing,
> For in these limbs its teeth remain,
> With marks that will not wear away,
> Till I have done with this new day,
> Which now is painful to these eyes,
> Which have not seen the sun so rise
> For years— I cannot count them o'er,
> I lost their long and heavy score
> When my last brother droop'd and died,
> And I lay living by his side.'"

'Something you're writing?' Shelley asked, listening curiously.

Byron leant to him and whispered. 'I get these moods, you see, where I feel as if I am somewhere else, apart from my body . . .'

169

'But where?'

'That's it. I don't know. But I would like to find out.'

'It's as if you are dreaming, you mean?'

'Something like that.'

'It happens to me when I've taken laudanum,' Shelley said thinking on the words and looking a little disturbed. 'But it's good to neither die nor sleep but to sort of drift away for a while . . . Yes, I do rather like it.'

Byron nodded and smiled. 'The mind has great magnitude, countless seas and shores, many many lands yet to be discovered – thoughts, feelings, memories . . . Sometimes I'm afraid to pursue them. I fear the deepest caverns.'

'Poets can be very peculiar,' Shelley said, taking a deep breath and changing his position on the bench. 'We do as we feel don't we, and that's the end of it.' He batted away a flying insect that had come too close.

'Or the beginning,' Byron said dubiously. 'We shouldn't try to understand it, just belong to it as water belongs to the sea.'

'Indeed,' murmured Shelley. 'It would be good to belong to something. I mean really belong.'

Shelley had rented a villa nearby with Mary and Claire. They had come to Switzerland to spend time with Byron and better acquaint themselves with the now celebrated poet who had become Claire's lover. The women were in Byron's villa, the baby needed attention and Claire, now pregnant, was resting.

Claire was pleased with herself. She had engineered the holiday perfectly and all was going extraordinarily well, but word travelled fast and intruders came close, creeping up by the mansion and daring to look through the windows after dark, hoping to catch a glimpse of "the mad, bad and dangerous to know" Lord Byron from England with his friends.

It was a chilly damp day, but surrounded by trees and mountains the beautiful frontage of the villa was a perfect place for the coming together of two quite singular minds. The weather had brought nothing but rain and more rain, but a brief spell of sunshine had enabled them to sit outside. Byron had grown serious over breakfast;

as if he there were something important he needed to say. "It isn't that simple," he'd muttered, "In fact it is rather difficult." "What is?" Shelley had asked him. But he'd declined any further confidence. "I'm in a bit of a predicament," Byron said at last as the women left the table. "And so am I," said Shelley. Then Byron changed the subject and Frederick Llewellyn brought them another pot of tea. Mary had said it was probably about the abbey and that he wasn't able to sell it and didn't know what to do. But they'd continued to talk about politics. They were two very different men and each wrote singular poetry.

'We are sharing the sky with the Alps,' said Byron, casting his arm about the landscape with a look of wonder. Shelley listened in silence. 'Magnificent things mountains,' Byron continued. 'How wonderful to walk them.' He shook his head. 'I must always consider my devil's hoof however. Accursed thing.' He laughed and put out his leg.

Shelley looked surprised. Byron's aristocratic bearing would suggest he was far too proud to be bothered by a limp. 'It's hardly noticeable, you know,' he told him flatly. 'And you walked quite far the other day.'

'Some days are worse than others,' said Byron, suppressing a wince. 'Too much damp about today, it's damned painful I can tell you. I am by no means crippled however.'

There was an awkward silence.

'Wordsworth is a very strong fellow,' said Shelley abstractedly. 'So much walking. I marvel at his energy.'

'Quite so,' said Byron. He clapped his hands and disturbed some swans on the lake. 'Those creatures dance for you,' he laughed. 'It's quite extraordinary; if you're lucky you might see a ballet.'

'They're beautiful birds,' Shelley said admiringly. He murmured some lines from a poem

> *'My soul is an enchanted boat,*
> *Which, like a sleeping swan, doth float*
> *Upon the silver waves of thy sweet singing;*
> *And thine doth like an angel sit*
> *Beside a helm conducting it,*
> *Whilst all the winds with melody are ringing . . .'*

'You and I have much to offer each other my friend!' said Byron. I have been thinking about it a lot, the idea, you know, that some human beings are destined to produce music or art, or something else that is important to the world. People like us fight against becoming automatons. I will often do exactly the opposite to what is expected; just to prove that I serve myself and not some force that compels me.'

'Oh, I know exactly what you mean,' said Shelley, folding his arms for certainty. He frowned seriously. 'The predominant feeling in my heart just now is fear. That's very odd, don't you think. I don't even know what I fear, I just fear.'

'Life itself perhaps?' offered Byron.

Shelley looked out into the distance. 'Water is very powerful,' he pondered. 'How many sailors has the sea swallowed up? The sea is a sort of monster.'

Byron's face was brilliant with sunlight, but storm clouds were threatening. Mary had told Shelley that he and Byron were like brothers, knowing one another's thoughts. She had said it with assurance in front of them, and they had both agreed. Shelley saw that Byron was scribbling something down in his notepad. 'What are you writing?' he asked.

'It's the third canto *Childe Harold*,' Byron said in a whisper. 'I'm inspired by your presence.'

Shelley smiled. 'Oh, we'll be good for each other, I'm sure.'

There was silence as they pondered the mountains, the water, and simply being together. Polidori was inside with the women, writing madly in his usual intense way, determined to write something of value. Frederick Llewellyn came out with a bottle of wine and glasses then departed quickly. Byron poured drinks. 'Mrs Llewellyn works wonders in the kitchen,' he said. 'She has been my cook several years.' He touched his stomach. 'Her food is bad for the physique, however.' For a moment or two they were silent. 'Do you fear the water?' he asked Shelley.

Shelley replied with a sigh.

'It's just a perception,' said Byron. 'One or two things you have said would suggest it.'

'You are right,' said Shelley reluctantly. 'This lake is enormous. I enjoyed boating in Sussex, but here there is so much water it bothers me. And death has come close of late.' He screwed up his face awkwardly, showing his beautiful teeth, then bent his head, embarrassed. 'I was never able to swim, however I tried. If I had the least belief in reincarnation then I know I wasn't a fish!'

'What a pity,' said Byron, with genuine concern. 'Swimming is wonderful. Perhaps I should teach you. We must take a boat ride together. There are some great sights around here. – Or we could visit some interesting places on horseback. I am told you like riding?'

'I am less afraid of horses than water,' Shelley said frowning at the thought. 'Water has its own ambitions; it would swallow us back into its depths half a chance, I'm certain.'

'You are probably right,' said Byron with a sudden quick frown. 'It does not frighten me though, for I swim very well. Yes, dear Shelley, I might have been a fish.' He laughed. 'That or a bull. A really bad tempered creature, like a bull would suit me, for I do find one or two people irksome. How good it would be to gore them!' He poured more wine and they drank. 'This wine is some of the best I've tasted,' he said. 'And I like my wine.' His strong, muscular arms were bare to the elbow, though the afternoon air was breezy. He did not bother about the weather too much, he said, and was neither too hot nor too cold.

'Human beings have a difficult existence I think,' Shelley continued. 'If truth be told, I'd rather be a bird – how wonderful to just spread your wings and fly away!'

'And where would you fly?'

'I really don't know. Do you think birds have a plan? I mean when they take off, do they know where they're going?'

'A lot of them disappear in winter.' Byron said thoughtfully. 'Strange.'

'Perhaps they just disappear, no more than that. Maybe our lives are an illusion. Something conjured by our minds.'

'But we have family,' Shelley said, frowning. 'They know us. Are they an illusion too?'

'I dare not think of my ancestry,' Byron whispered.

Shelley looked at him curiously. 'Why not?'

Byron's voice fell low. 'It enters my dreams. The tales of how my family inherited the abbey fill me with horror. But my dreams are never far away from my daytime activities. I sort of exist in two worlds, or perhaps I am somewhere in between, in a place I am not aware of . . . Perhaps I am dead and don't know it.'

Shelley gazed at him thoughtful. 'An intriguing idea,' he said, frowning at the clouds gathering deep purple above them. 'I wonder what it's like being dead. There is a great distinction between the living creature and the dead however. There is something about life that keeps us wondering about it. My poor dear Mary would have little Clara return from the grave if she could. She still hears her crying in the night. The dead constantly haunt us.'

'Indeed they do,' sighed Byron. 'I am even haunted by the barking of my dog back in the grounds of the abbey. We buried him there, but at times he barks us into waking.' He pointed at the sky. 'A storm is brewing. Soon there'll be a flash of lightning. – Now, where does it come from I wonder? Might it be the source of life, a lightning flash to bring insentient things into being? Ah, this stuff prevents me from sleeping.'

'Galvani's work has offered us valuable insights as to the ways electricity might be used to give life to the dead,' said Shelley. 'Science, of course, wonderful science.'

'Or magic,' Byron jested. 'How we fear the supernatural.'

Byron drew himself up stiffly then nodded at the villa. 'I have an interesting book in there, *Phantasmagoria*, a collection of supernatural tales, horrific stuff, but great for a dreary evening.'

Shelley listened with interest. Byron went on. 'Damn it, my man, it's June and look at the weather. But at least the air is warm; the dampness was bad in Aberdeen where I spent my childhood. But the climate kept me from exploring my demonic nature. For I do have one, you know. Oh I do, I do. Cruelty and spite have nurtured it. I hated the way I was bullied as a child.' He braced himself. 'Now that I'm famous, it's different. People are afraid of me now. They think I'm rich, you see. I despise hypocrisy.'

Shelley looked at him straight. 'I know how you've fought for the right to say what you believe in, whether it is love or politics, you will say what you think, and for that I admire you. You have done much travelling, a source of inspiration I should think.'

Byron touched Shelley's hand. 'You are a good companion,' he said quietly. 'We can speak from our hearts to each other. That is how it should be. You will stay my friend, I hope.' Then his features loosened and he laughed, looking towards the mountains. 'How I wish I could dance. If I could dance, we might have a party. I presume you dance, a fine fellow like you is bound to have rhythm in his limbs?'

'I can if I wish, but I am not too fond of prancing around. Mary is an excellent dancer however, but I doubt she will dance this holiday.'

The lake glistened like ice and the air seemed chill with portent. The night would come and then the day would be over. 'The day is darkening,' Byron murmured. 'Ah, night terrors pursue me.' Sometimes, he felt like a lame horse that could go no further, he said, and the pain in his foot felt worse when he was anxious. Then he would stumble towards sanity hoping it would meet him halfway, for he was never quite sane, he said. 'I have done much wrong,' he faltered. 'I know it.'

Shelley sat listening in silence. How often Mary said the same. His throat tightened with feeling. Byron lost himself so quickly, as if he were drifting away, desperate for something to cling to. 'Relax, my friend,' he said. 'You are a great poet. The horrors of life belong to evil itself.'

'Indeed,' sighed Byron. He breathed in deeply. 'Perhaps later we might imagine some horror tales ourselves. I like a good ghost; we have quite a few at the abbey. Let us think up some phantasmagorias – skeletons, demons, all that.' And he gave the strange low laugh Shelley was coming to know, as if there were untold secrets in the depths in his soul.

They sat in silence for some minutes. 'I believe Claire is pregnant with your child,' Shelley said presently. He looked at Byron keenly. 'You acknowledge it?'

Byron moved about uncomfortable. 'I'm afraid I must. She suddenly arrived at the abbey, just like one of the ghosts. She was there before I knew what was happening, just like an apparition. I was feeling distraught. What is a man to do when a woman offers herself like that?'

Shelley gazed at him with interest. Byron poured more wine. 'She was in my bed within seconds. I behaved rather badly I'm afraid.'

Shelley rubbed his face with his hands. The blood had drained from his features. He hoped Byron would keep his distance from Mary; the man was a magnet to women and Mary throbbed with passion. Her outer life was calm and serene, though her inner life was quite tumultuous. Claire was very different. Byron had spoken already about her hysterics, seeing them as mere dramas that were best ignored. Perhaps he knew best.

Byron continued. 'I do not love her however, and I have told Augusta, my sister, in a letter,' He looked downwards pondering. 'I have always shared my feelings with Augusta.' Again he gave a low troubled laugh. 'They called our father "Mad Jack Byron". It does not bother Augusta, but she knows I fear going mad. I might, you see, they say these things are inherited. Lady Caroline Lamb tells everyone I'm mad. Though I think she is mad herself. She will chase me into my grave.' He waved a finger in the air. 'I was weary sick of Caro.'

Shelley stared at him absorbed. 'Are you in love with your sister?'

For a moment or two they were silent.

'Some have said so,' Shelley added quietly. 'That is why I ask.'

Byron shrugged, then quoted some lines from his poetry

> '. . . *Thy soft heart refused to discover*
> *The faults which so many could find.*'

'She is a half-sister actually,' he added uneasily. 'But yes it is true, I love her dearly. She is married, of course with children, but I have always adored her.'

Shelley met Byron's gaze. 'Just to go against the grain?'

Byron smiled wryly. 'Well, there it is. I am very bad indeed and so is Augusta.'

'Are you lovers?' Shelley kept his eyes on Byron, waiting for his answer. Shelley was always direct.

Byron frowned and looked away. 'Do not talk about Augusta like this, for I will not answer,' he said, a sharp tone in his voice. Then again he stared at the sky.

'I do not wish to aggravate you, Byron,' Shelley said standing and straightening. 'I am only trying to learn about you, that is all.'

'I am a bundle of ideas struggling for survival whilst strangling each other to death – half revealed images I can't quite grasp, voices from strangers who I think belong to my mind. No more than that.'

'Perhaps we can find ourselves through dreams?' Shelley offered. He fell to reciting

> *"We rest. – A dream has power to poison sleep;*
> *We rise. – One wandering thought pollutes the day;*
> *We feel, conceive or reason, laugh or weep;*
> *Embrace fond woe, or cast our cares away:*
> *It is the same! For, be it joy or sorrow,*
> *The path of its departure still is free:*
> *Man's yesterday may ne'er be like his morrow;*
> *Nought may endure but Mutability."*

Byron gave him a long and serious look. 'From your poem, *Alastor*?'

'Yes, Mary enjoys it. It pleases me to know she likes my poems. She looks to me for a lead. But I don't want to lead her astray. I think I might be an incubus, sometimes, like the one on the belly of Fuseli's wife in *The Nightmare*. Now there's a horror if you want one!'

'You talk very well with Mary,' Byron's tone was thoughtful and detached. 'I have heard you. I have never had a woman to talk with like that.'

'But you talk with your sister?'

'But not like that. You are lucky,' said Byron, enviously.

'I am,' said Shelley. 'It is normal to enjoy reading and writing with Mary. We were reading from Milton's Paradise Lost last night.' He quoted some favourite lines;

"Did I request thee, Maker, from my clay
To mould me man? Did I solicit thee
From darkness to promote me?"

'Ah yes, haunting words. But what do you believe yourself?'

Shelley folded his arms and looked into the water. He spoke quietly. 'I am trying to find out. Mary is trying to find out. We are all trying to find out. For you see, it seems we must believe in something, even if that is nothing.'

Byron laughed. 'Yes, I like that idea very much.'

Shelley continued. 'We were talking about Galvani too and the idea of bringing back the dead with a flash of lightning.'

'Does Mary believe it possible?'

'I think she does. But there are dangers . . .'

'What dangers do you envisage?' Byron lifted his face, frowning curiously.

Shelley was becoming restless. 'Too many to talk about now but perhaps we can discuss them later.'

'And what of an after life?' Byron asked abstractedly, making to rise.

Shelley stood silent and thoughtful. 'Who knows?' he said finally. 'What if it's just an endless frustration like this? Who would want it? What if it is nothing at all? What must it be like to experience nothing, to become like a stone.'

They might have talked some more, but it had started to rain.

22

The Genesis Of Frankenstein's Monster

Over the next few days it was warm and dry. Sunshine coming through the clouds in bursts of glorious light encouraged Byron and Shelley to take boat rides together on the lake, while Mary and Claire set to planning events for their holiday. Baby William would soon be weaned but at present it was only Mary's milk that nourished him, and she must constantly attend to his needs. But between her duties she read and got on with her writing. The business of taking care of her child though was uppermost in her mind, grief for her dead baby never left her and she was only mending slowly. Shelley could set himself apart and never had the look of failure in his eyes that she saw in the eyes of Byron. Some days it seemed there was a deadness in Byron as if much of his life had been stolen leaving him bewildered, his real life that was, for he was ever a man of the mind, wandering the villa murmuring, standing outside and gazing at the heavens as if some ministering angel might deliver him from a terrible fate.

It was chilly that morning when he walked into the parlour and pulled up a chair to join her by the fire. The baby was sleeping, Claire was reading in the bedroom, Polidori was hidden away writing and Shelley had gone out walking.

'Are you cold?' Byron asked Mary, lifting her shawl from the chaise longue and placing around her shoulders. 'This room has scarcely warmed up. I shall have to ask Frederick Llewellyn to put more logs on the fire.'

'I've been reading another story,' she said, setting aside her book.

'You are reading Phantasmagoria. Better to read it in the evening I think.' He laughed his low strange laugh.

'Shelley lit the fire,' she said cheerfully. 'He isn't too good at lighting fires. The night was so stormy, neither of us slept. We came into the parlour and decided to write instead.'

'There's an art to lighting fires,' Byron said thoughtfully. 'Frederick Llewellyn makes very good fires.' He stared at the withering flames. 'I can't seem to do it myself. Making a fire needs careful thought and patience. I always want the heat straight away. A weak flame is depressing, don't you agree.' He turned his attention to her book. 'The stories we read last night have whetted your appetite.'

She smiled. 'Those tales are harrowing. But I like supernatural stories. I had an interesting conversation once with an elderly couple in the coach returning from Scotland. We talked about Emanuel Swedenborg. He believed higher knowledge came to us from angels.' She gazed at Byron curiously, interested to know what he thought.

'Swedenborg, ah yes. He was lucky enough to take spiritual journeys with angels. I am not permitted access to angels myself. They avoid me.'

'He thought angels led us to advanced ways of thinking,' she said, waiting.

'Otherwise, our thoughts are inferior?'

'Inferior to what?' she said lifting her eyebrows.

'To the thoughts of angels.'

'But how do we know what their thoughts are, or even if angels exist?'

He narrowed his eyes and nodded. 'Well, there you are. Higher thoughts, lower thoughts, what do they actually mean in the end. *"Out out brief candle"*. You liked the ghost stories though?' He flicked through the pages quickly, and smiled wryly as he spoke. 'These stories go deep, they explore our innermost fears.' His shoulders rose and fell as he spoke. There was a touch of annoyance in his tone.

She pulled her shawl closer about her shoulders. 'The stories last night were exciting. Claire couldn't sleep. She was screaming.' She smiled as she spoke, though Claire's antics were tiresome and often woke the child.

Byron nodded. 'It is something she does. She enjoys frightening herself; she has a passion for terror. There are a lot of people like that.'

'Last night you suggested we should each attempt a frightening story.'

'Indeed I did. And Polidori was up first light, he has been busy with his pen ever since. I saw him earlier, he is writing a tale about a vampire. I promise you'll enjoy it.' His eyes were dark and assured. 'I know Polidori's mind. He has a vivid imagination.'

'Yes,' she said quietly. 'I think there is something exciting about Polidori.'

'Do you, that's good. He would like to think so. He is a creature of the night.' Byron leant forward and gave her a serious look. He was intense.

She drew further away. 'And you say he is writing about a vampire, a being that sucks the vital essence from the living? Who would believe it possible?'

He stretched his arms above his head and yawned. 'You might well if you were me. Something sucks my blood from my body each night. I feel its loss profoundly.' He frowned. 'What is it grows so strong from my weakness I wonder?'

They were silent and thoughtful a moment.

'And you, dear Mary, were also writing at daybreak.' He nodded towards her papers on the floor beside her. 'Your story?'

She quickly gathered up her jottings and laid them on her lap. Her story was taking shape. She had remembered the glittering leaves in the sun when returning down the Rhine River, how her eyes had wandered to the ruined castle on the mountain, and she heard again in her mind the loud voice of the boatman. – "That is Burg Frankenstein. Un lieu de fantômes!" – Her protagonist would be Victor Frankenstein, a scientist, who believed the force of electricity could return dead flesh to life; this was Victor's mission. But no-one could play at being God and Frankenstein would suffer and his dreadful creation also, for once the creature had received the life giving force and lived, there would have to be a reckoning.

She would show how society laid waste the best of what human beings might be, how cruelty itself created monsters. Her eyes passed over some words on a page of her story

"I saw—with shut eyes, but acute mental vision—I saw the pale student of unhallowed arts kneeling beside the thing he had put together. I saw the hideous phantasm of a man stretched out, and then, on the working of some powerful engine, show signs of life and stir with an uneasy, half-vital motion. Frightful must it be, for supremely frightful would be the effect of any human endeavour to mock the stupendous mechanism of the Creator of the world."

Her heart beat heavily for the agony of the monster and the suffering of the man who'd created him. But she could not stop what her pen must deliver. There was something important to be said and she would carry her tale right through to the end. 'I began it last night,' she said, holding her papers close. 'Just after midnight.'

He frowned curious. 'How well Phantasmagoria and the wicked weather have rewarded us!'

'It came from a bad dream.'

'And you won't let me look?' said Byron crossly. 'See how you hide those papers.'

'But you'll want to know more,' she said smiling and determined.

'Oh, I will. You are a fascinating woman, Mary.'

They sat in silence for a moment. She knew she had made a connection with Byron. She was real for him in a way Claire wasn't. She could fetch the dreams from her mind and build them into stories. She could use her entire imagination. It pleased her to see he understood, and she did not fear his power, for she felt she was equal in strength. He leant back in his chair and grew silent with thought.

'Tell me about this dream,' he said at last.

'It was a nightmare. I have had such dreams before, but never so intense.'

'And did you tell Shelley?'

'Of course. I always tell Percy everything. Well, mostly. He knows what I'm writing, and he will see how my story develops.' She straightened, serious. 'But the story is mine, not his. And let me tell you, I can explore the darkest depths of thought as vigorously as any man, and what I have to say might surprise you.' She straightened, holding his gaze. Just then the mountains, the lake, even the bright morning sunlight that crept through the room, was hers. Byron sat silent in shadow.

Next day brought a dull morning. The skies were grey and again it was cold. But Frederick Llewellyn had built a good fire in the parlour and it blazed on heartily. Mary looked out of the window at the muddy paths by the villa, the little pools of water that ran about busily. There was scarcely a dry place left. Claire complained that her skirts were filthy, everything smelt musty and her pregnancy made her feel sick. Did Byron ever enquire about her welfare, she asked? Claire replied that he did not. And he would not sleep with her either and she felt he had a sort of pleasure in rejecting her. It was all about Augusta, she said. No woman on earth could ever compete with Augusta.

'Do let it go,' Mary said quietly. 'You will find a way through. Do not lose your dignity, it is what he expects.'

'But am I not pregnant with his child?'

There was no sound in the room, apart from the crackling fire and the two women talking. Suddenly Claire started crying. 'It's easy for you,' she said. 'It's obvious Percy adores you. I am not loved in the least.'

Mary sat down. 'Oh, you do go on, my dear,' she said softly. 'You have nothing to gain from making a fool of yourself. It isn't good to let loose your emotions so freely, others will exploit them.'

Claire looked up quickly. 'You think I am making a fool of myself by caring?'

'Yes. You have to be sturdier. A lot of the time circumstances form our characters I think. We have choices, but circumstances limit them. You are in danger of becoming a child again Claire. You are a grown woman, soon to be a mother. You mustn't let life shape you into someone you fear. We are easily made into monsters.'

'Please don't tell me I'm a monster,' Claire moaned wearily. 'You make me sound vile.'

'I'm sorry,' Mary murmured. 'I'm a little extreme sometimes. I didn't mean to hurt.'

'I see you've started your story,' said Claire, drying her eyes on her handkerchief. She glanced at Mary's papers on the table. 'What is it about?'

Mary sighed. 'It's about the dead,' she murmured. 'And the great gift of life. We are wont to abuse it, you see. We destroy each other and ourselves in the cruellest of ways.'

'Oh the ghost story,' Claire said frowning. 'I'd forgotten about that, I haven't even started.' She spoke brusquely, trying to regain her strength. 'Can I see what you've written?'

Mary laughed lightly. 'Not yet. I don't feel it's ready.'

'What, not even a bit?'

Mary shook her head.

'Byron will find it,' said Claire. 'I saw him reading Percy's writings yesterday. And without permission too.'

Just then Shelley's quick footsteps could be heard coming down the path.

'You are back!' Mary cried happily, as he strode into the room towards them. Byron was still in bed. He took off his coat and hat and fell into a chair.

'I was asking Mary about her story,' said Claire. 'She won't let me see it.'

'Won't you?' said Shelley frowning. 'Why not?'

'Stories, poems, lose strength once we discuss them,' Mary said quickly. 'Byron asked to see it too, but I wouldn't comply. I must know what it's about properly myself before I divulge its secrets.'

'I know what it's about already,' said Shelley, folding his arms. 'You told me, remember . . .' And he quoted a passage

'"Many times I considered Satan as the fitter emblem of my condition; for often, like him, when I viewed the bliss of my protectors, the bitter gall of envy rose within me."'

'How mean of you, Percy,' said Mary, glancing at Claire. 'Do I have nothing of my own? You must not speak my lines. They're not ready I tell you.'

But Claire ever vigilant was eager. '"Protectors?" What do you mean, and why do you speak of Satan?' She spoke shakily, rubbing her arms, chilled.

Shelley's eyes rested on Mary and Claire by turns. Then he glanced at them both and laughed. And Mary wished she had kept the story to herself from the first, she perceived she had now thrown Claire and Shelley together in a pattern that had become familiar. How easily he fell into her stepsister's moods; she entertained him, flattered him and made him feel lighter of heart. She rose from her chair then took her papers to the bedroom. For all her love, all her will, Shelley would never be her own.

Percy followed her quickly. But anger glowed in her eyes. 'You shouldn't do it,' she murmured.

'I know, I know,' he said, kissing her cheek. 'My dear, I've upset you.'

'No more than usual,' she said sighing. The mother in her came to her aid and she pulled away from his hold. She had been a mother twice. And she thought at times she must also be a mother to Percy and Claire, for they could fall so quickly into the easy springtime of life. Times like that she felt alone and remembered the death of baby Clara, and she was glad of Byron's company for he was always aware of the burden of his foot which reminded him that life could be cruel. When they were alone, Byron might talk to her softly and tell her his mysteries, quickly becoming silent should anyone come near. How awful to have had to limp as a child when other boys were strong and able, and how lonely he was with such a cold uncaring mother, for it seemed she had never understood him and had even felt ashamed. The horror of his childhood never left him. George Byron was often unhappy, he did not know his father and his foot had been a curse. But it wasn't his fault, any more than it was Horst's to be called the giant of the forest and to be shunned so wickedly, such rejection could cripple the soul. She went to lift her child from his cot.

'He'll feel better if I hold him,' she told Shelley as he followed her across and she gathered the little body into her arms. For several minutes she sang to the baby softly.

Claire wandered in to join them. 'Byron is at last out of bed. But he will not dress. He will wear his dressing gown all day if we don't leave the villa. Mama would never allow it.'

'But Mama isn't here,' said Shelley triumphantly.

'He looks so manly unshaven,' Claire said smiling. 'I have always liked him better unshaven. He says he's been writing.'

Shelley looked at her curiously.

'Oh, I don't know what. Some poem or other I expect.' She glanced through the window. 'His peacock is roaming in the rain. Do peacocks catch cold? And that monkey in his room makes such peculiar noises. Why must he have these animals? They are such a bother.'

Shelley lay back on the bed and clasped his hands behind his head. 'He does what he wants, it's his way. Fredrick Llewellyn looks after the animals; Byron just plays around with them. Poor Frederick!' He laughed. 'He tells me that monkey is Byron's familiar.'

'Ah, a supernatural entity that assists him with magic!' said Claire in a screechy unearthly voice. 'I wouldn't be at all surprised.'

'You never know,' said Shelley. 'Take care. That peacock out there is a lovely woman in disguise. One who will seduce him. He began to quote some lines from Alastor, his recently published poem

> *'His strong heart sunk and sickened with excess*
> *Of love. He reared his shuddering limbs and quelled*
> *His gasping breath, and spread his arms to meet*
> *Her panting bosom: ...she drew back a while,*
> *Then, yielding to the irresistible joy,*
> *With frantic gesture and short breathless cry*
> *Folded his frame in her dissolving arms.'*

'Peacocks and poems are both prey to vanity!' said Claire, shrugging. She was filled with bitterness. Did she matter to anyone at all? She knew that her mother loved her, but did anyone else? She considered she was always helpful one way and another and insisted that whatever faults she had, she was good and caring at heart and put herself last. In a couple of weeks they'd go home. What then? She would be bigger with her pregnancy and people were bound to notice. She was filled with a burning fear. She couldn't go back to Somers Town where everyone gossiped and her mother might learn she was with child. Where could she go? Fanny's letters suggested she too was unhappy. She hated her life in London, for it was hardly a life at all. Mary Jane had said it was time she tried to find work. Teaching was talked about, but Fanny had cringed at the thought. Sometimes Fanny's writing was difficult to read, for her words were so small, pushed in as they were at the bottom of Godwin's letters to save on paper. Godwin's letters were usually unpleasant too, he was still furious with Percy. Fanny understood all that and always tried her best to smooth things over, saying that her father didn't always consider how he said things and only meant well. 'Fanny imagines us having an idyllic existence,' she said with a shudder. 'If only she saw this rain. I try not to grumble when I write to her, or to admit I am sometimes bored. But my nerves are terrible.' She paced the room, her hands pressed against her stomach, her features tight and strained. Her face looked thinner and she did not eat as she ought.

'We shall have to return to England soon,' said Mary. Claire sat biting her nails. Shelley had closed his eyes and fallen asleep.

23

Bath

'You'll be staying over there by the abbey,' said Shelley, pointing from the window of the coach. 'I cannot be with you, you do understand?' It was dusk. The city of Bath was darkening; but contrary to London, it was a quiet place at night time and they were glad of the silent streets. The journey from Geneva had been long and tiring.

'It's all so upsetting,' said Claire. She spoke rapidly, making quick little gestures with her hands, something she did when nervous. 'Mary must hide away too, all because of me. – It is all too horrible to contemplate.' She pulled on the strings of her bonnet. 'Oh, this wretched bonnet, it has shrunk in the rain! I shall choke – I shall die!'

'I'll buy you another as soon as I can get to London,' said Shelley, reaching down the bags then helping them out of the coach.

The baby lay silent. Mary wrapped him more firmly in his warm woollen blanket as they stood together by the lodgings. 'Wilmouse has been so good; he scarcely makes a sound. My lovely child gets dearer and sweeter every day.'

'What a silly name for a baby,' Claire said irritably. But for the odd incurious looker-on, the street was still. 'Why not call him William?'

'So who will you see in London?' Mary asked leaning to Percy.

'I'm not sure yet,' he answered frowning. He knocked on the door of the lodgings. 'I'm hoping one or two people will help me out. The money's run out, and of course I must keep my head down. There has no doubt been a great deal of talk about what we've been up to in Geneva. And a lot of invention too.'

It was evident that Shelley didn't know where to go next. 'We can't concern ourselves with that,' Mary said softly. 'But don't be away too long, will you.'

Shelley stood thoughtful a moment. 'Claire's pregnancy must remain hidden,' he said firmly. 'Not a word.'

Claire looked at him moodily. 'Oh, I know what you think. You think I'm not good enough for Byron, don't you. Well, I'm every bit as worthy as Annabella Milbanke. It's just not fair that people have money and others are poor.' She shrugged. 'To love freely whoever you like as it suits is excellent for men, but it is not so good for women!'

'Do calm down,' Mary said tiredly. 'You are better off without him anyway. You'll have quite a few problems ahead though; trouble follows Byron like a plague of locusts. We were spied on a lot in Geneva. Every time we went out women were pointing fingers.' She looked at Percy seeing his preoccupied expression.

'I will send you books and money,' he said. 'The landlady here expects us, the rooms will be ready. Why isn't she answering the door?'

'And what about Wilmouse?' Mary asked quietly. 'What does she say about the baby?'

'She isn't averse to babies. But she thinks we are married, so leave it at that. This is good old England, my dear, bear it in mind.' He sighed. 'She hasn't asked about Claire but now that she's starting to show we had best lie low.'

'Oh, just talk on. I'm invisible,' Claire said sighing.

Shelley glanced about. 'Listen. I don't want people to bother you, but I have many things to attend to.' Mary nodded, Claire gave another deep sigh.

'Must we stay inside?' asked Mary. 'Wilmouse will need fresh air.'

'Oh, you can't become prisoners,' Shelley said frowning. 'We must think of the child's wellbeing.' He stamped about on the pavement, looking tense.

'But we brought all this on ourselves,' moaned Claire. She looked at Percy with narrowed eyes as if nursing a secret hatred.

Percy ignored her. 'Make sure you cover your heads if you leave the lodgings,' he said. 'You won't be here very long. Hogg might visit. He has the address and will no doubt pass it to Fanny.' He looked at Mary concernedly. 'You *will* want to hear from Fanny won't you, my dear? The woman is so alone and she takes the brunt of all the irritation in that household.'

'I wonder sometimes what you say to Papa in your letters – and Fanny too,' Claire added heatedly. 'It would help if you could speak the truth, Percy.'

'What on earth do you mean?' Shelley straightened his cravat. 'Are you calling me a liar? Dear Claire, you know better than that.'

The landlady was taking her time.

Claire spoke again. 'From what I have heard your letters are full of half truths about Harriet and such. Mama has no time for you, especially since you stole me away.'

Shelley shook his head incredulous. 'Stole you away, did I? You almost broke a leg to catch that coach. But you'll think what you like.' He was getting annoyed, looking at the upstairs windows of the lodgings. He knocked again.

Mary knew that what Claire had said was a familiar accusation, but Shelley cared nothing for his faults, he saw them as part of his creative spirit and she rescued the truth from his fables as best she could. 'So will you go to see Fanny?' she asked, holding the baby tightly.

Shelley composed himself and took on the air of his class. 'I do not know. I dare not call at the bookshop, of course. Your father's hostility is severe. But he ought to remember I have saved him from the debtor's prison. Yes, I must somehow remind him of that. But the way things are going we might be in there together.'

Mary gazed about abstractedly. 'And Harriet? Will you see Harriet?'

'Mary, I have children with Harriet. Do not torment me. I shall do what has to be done. And you must do the same. Take care of yourself and Wilmouse. And see that Claire doesn't scream or run about in the night. We don't want the landlady panting upstairs with a candle.'

190

The landlady opened the door and they all went inside. Seeing the child, she clapped her hands with pleasure, saying how lovely the child was and hoping all was in order. Mary saw that Percy was examining the lodgings with his eyes. She stood very close, it was harder than ever to be separated from him now and she was still dazed from the journey. For several minutes, the landlady talked aside with Shelley and Mary saw that all was well.

'We have only just arrived and you're going,' moaned Claire. 'We shall see you again, I hope. Or will you just leave us for good? I wouldn't be surprised.'

'I wish you didn't have to go,' said Mary as they followed the woman upstairs.

'But I must,' he said shakily. He kissed her and held her close. 'Goodbye, my dear,' he said to Claire, smiling briefly. He glanced once more at Mary then fled down the stairs.

It was autumn. A soft orange light lit the glittering honey coloured limestone of the city where people stood talking in the streets of Bath and the leaves on the trees were a brilliant array of colours. It had been an interesting summer filled with a great many feelings and activities, and some very special writing for Mary. Her novel lived in her daily, constantly demanding her pen. Whenever she could she sank into its urgent embrace, for it truly was just like a lover and she abandoned herself to her tale body and soul.

Just now the city was peaceful. But some 200 miles away in Ely and Littleport, the rising cost of grain and high unemployment had caused protests and riots that May. Property had been ruined and men maddened by drink and anger had started to rampage and fight. Hearing the city dwellers talk, Mary had been reminded of her mother and the French revolution. Could it ever happen in England, she wondered anxiously, it was certainly possible. The poor might tolerate their lot if their families didn't go hungry, but if that were to change, what then? Might they rise up in fury just as they had done in France? And so they should, Shelley and Byron had declared firmly, people should fight for their rights! Poor relief had been organised to try to appease them and a minimum wage had been ordered, rioters were tried and sentenced and five had even been hanged. People trembled at the thought of the French revolution and their souls were fearful. The revolution had been bloody and vicious. But weren't the French more easily roused to passion in ways that couldn't happen in England? It helped to think so.

Mary and Claire went walking with the baby in the nearby countryside. October's birthstones were tourmaline and opal and its birth flower was the calendula, an herbaceous plant from the daisy family, commonly known as a marigold. They had gathered them in bunches from the fields. The blisters on Mary's arm that year had been nasty and the landlady had shown them a way to make oil from the flowers that would lessen the pain. There was much to be said for the smooth sweet smelling oil, thought Mary, and she had certainly found it beneficial. They had walked round the Royal crescent, 500 feet of splendid terraced houses in glistening Bath stone, delightful to see. The crystal masonry lent a glow of peace to the beautiful surroundings. In Bath she thought of her mother who had lived there a while and she wondered if they trod the very same ground. Mary was waiting constantly for Shelley to return, but when he did it was only briefly. He was all too soon back to London. Claire would settle to read, but she too was waiting, waiting for impossible things, like Byron walking through the door and declaring his love.

The lodgings were quiet and the baby was always good. Mary and Claire filled their time reading and writing. Mary felt pleased. Her novel was flowing superbly and she thrilled at her own invention. Victor Frankenstein, her scientist, a brilliant young man, was courageous and fiery on the page, a man full of ideas and her pen worked swiftly. *Frankenstein* told how Victor created a living human being from parts of dead men and brought it to life with the magical power of electricity. It was a daring, provocative idea and she'd thought about it a lot, imagining the chaos that might ensue when man interfered with creation. There was a lot of talk and excitement about electricity, how it might be a life giving force if it were possible to harness its potential. She had read with Shelley about the work of Luigi Galvani, the Italian physician and physicist, who'd discovered animal electricity and had stunned his students by causing the leg of a frog to jerk as if by a kind of wizardry. But her story would show how creating such a being could prove to be a hideous mistake and ultimately catastrophic. She would show the awe that ensued as the creature pulsed and lived. Oh how its being would hurt, how lost it would be, how lonely and afraid! And how terrified Victor would be by what he'd created.

Writing her lines had sometimes caused her to shudder and she'd needed to put down her pen and take deep breaths. Victor would be repulsed by his creature, and his creation in turn would be hurt and dismayed, destined to wander lost in body and soul, even becoming vengeful. Did it not happen to mankind, she concluded. Men sought supremacy and in the event caused terror and destruction. Was it not a fact that only the true transcendent being understood the heart of his creatures and would man not violate some sacred law by trying to commandeer that potency? Her creature had feelings and thoughts, and through them must somehow live, but his mind was clouded with suffering . . . Her monster feared its existence! What must this man of cold deceased parts do with himself if he could not be loved and cherished and have others to hope for his happiness? He was a monster, and he was ugly. But could he not be good and noble? Yes, yes, he could! At first, that was, until life itself corrupted him. She would show how it happened . . . Victor might make such a being, but he did not bargain for the creature's free will, its emotions, thoughts and needs! There was a heavy price for such conceit. She wrote on rapidly for an hour, until the sound of the landlady's footsteps on the stairs alerted her.

'A woman came to see you,' she said breathlessly as Mary opened the door. 'You were out. I didn't know where you were . . .' She handed Mary a letter.

'Who was she?' Mary asked urgently, thinking it might have been Harriet.

'She left no name. She was wearing a cape. Her face was hidden by her hood. She kept her head down. A wraithlike creature she was. She seemed unhappy.'

'How long was she here?' Mary asked, reading the letter quickly, and discovering it had come from Fanny.

'Only a couple of minutes. I said you were out and she brought it out of her pocket.'

Mary looked at Claire who stood by. 'It's a letter from Fanny. But it isn't like her to just come and go like that. I wonder what's happened.' The landlady looked at them in silence a moment, then turned and left.

Mary and Claire sat down passing the letter between them, then stared about abstractedly. What did it mean? What were Fanny's intentions? In it she claimed she was not loved, that she could not live with Mary Jane and was simply a burden to them all. Claire and Mary wondered at her words. Fanny wasn't someone who indulged in self pity, but that's what it seemed like now. Why was she so defeated? She had thought to live with her aunts in Ireland, she said, and work as a teacher, but her aunts were cold and reserved and she feared being lonely. She constantly lamented that Mary and Claire had left her and gone with Shelley, now she must cope with her father's distress on her own, for he was almost bankrupt and constantly in despair, there had been many arguments at the shop and endless turmoil. One way and another, her stepmother had tried to raise money, trusting Percy might help them but he had not. She wailed on the page that she couldn't help feeling responsible for everyone's misfortune, and having had a visit from one of her aunt's friends, who had related such endearing tales about her mother, she had felt even worse –

"I have determined never to live to be a disgrace to such a mother . . ."

'What a disaster!' sighed Mary. 'I am cross with the landlady, she ought to have kept her here until we returned. How could she just let her go, she must have seen how she was.' The two of them were white with worry. They both felt guilty about Fanny. The letter was a plea for love, which they had not given. They had selfishly gone their own way and forgotten her.

Shelley returned next day. He had scarcely sat down, before Mary thrust the letter before him. He played about with the paper, his fingers tracing the words, his eyes narrow with thought. 'What have we done?' he murmured. For several moments they were silent. 'I had no idea . . .' He looked from Mary to Claire and back. They both bent their heads. Shelley continued his voice humble and low. 'Your father had requested money, but this time I could not help. I'm sorry.' He looked at Mary and bit his lip anxiously. 'I do my best . . . I intended to . . .'

'Mary Jane has had a hand in this,' Mary insisted. 'She is always finding fault with Fanny. My dear half sister can never do anything right.'

Claire nodded. 'It's true.' She looked at Shelley with both a hopeful and guilty expression. 'Perhaps Fanny should come to live with us. I know how Mama can bite.'

'No, no,' Percy said flatly. He leant to the fire, stirring the logs into flame. 'It would not suit her. And in any case your father needs her.'

'But she can't be his slave,' Mary said annoyed. 'She is a free human being.' She threw back her head proudly. 'A woman has so few choices. My mother always said so.'

Shelley rose decisively. 'There's an address at the top of this letter.' He held it out for them to see. 'She's in Bristol. She intends to take an early morning coach.' He screwed up his eyes, thoughtful. 'I must find out where she is going. We have neglected her! Do you not see what we've done – she, who asks for so little, has been neglected! I must leave straight away!'

Mary spoke again. 'It has pleased Papa to keep her at the shop to deal with unpleasant matters and help with the business, but he too has failed her. Everyone has failed her.'

'Not yet,' said Shelley, donning his hat. 'I shall find her and all will be well.' He waved the letter in the air. 'There is something sinister in this!' He turned from them swiftly and left.

'Poor Fanny,' said Mary as Shelley dashed down the stairs. 'She cannot protect herself at all. She bends to the will of others so easily, and hasn't the least cunning . . .'

'Like us . . .' said Claire, dabbing her eyes with her handkerchief.

Mary sighed and sat down. Everything seemed suddenly different. How had it happened? Claire continued to grumble about how it had been at the shop, how she'd been glad to get away, and how it was a wonder she hadn't been driven insane.

For a moment or two they were silent. Everything was so obscure; anything could happen now. 'We have lived very different lives,' said Mary, thinking of her time in Scotland while Fanny had been in Somers Town with her father and his new family. For it *was* a new family. She felt she had never really known them, not even Claire properly, who constantly surprised her. She'd been taken aback to find she'd gone to see Byron at Newstead Abbey and had boldly seduced him. She had brought him to heel with her power. But her audacity had been her downfall. The anger she suffered now and her pregnancy with all it entailed was far too heavy a price to pay for fleeting sexual pleasure.

Claire went off to her room, and Mary went back to her writing. Her monster's life was as nothing if he could not love and be loved . . . Someone must pay! She wrote on quickly

> *"I was like a wild beast that had broken the toils, destroying the objects that obstructed me and ranging through the wood with a stag-like swiftness. Oh! What a miserable night I passed! The cold stars shone in mockery, and the bare trees waved their branches above me; now and then the sweet voice of a bird burst forth amidst the universal stillness. All, save I, were at rest or in enjoyment; I, like the arch-fiend, bore a hell within me, and finding myself unsympathized with, wished to tear up the trees, spread havoc and destruction around me, and then to have sat down and enjoyed the ruin."*

Presently, she lifted her eyes and stared at the cold white ceiling. Fanny had turned so quiet of late, so strange. She seemed to have lived through the three of them, Shelley, herself and Claire, through their letters, their dreams, even their thoughts of the future. Everything except their blood. She had followed them in her mind, down into the darkness of her soul, and they'd all been unaware.

Now, it seemed, she had nothing left to hope for. They had made her as good as invisible. Mary put down her pen and rested her head in her hands. Where was Fanny intending to go from Bristol and what would Shelley discover?

24

The Terrible Truth

The chemist stared curiously at the anxious young man standing and talking at speed before him. – 'I do believe she was here,' the chemist said nervously. 'I sold her a bottle of laudanum. – What? Oh, no sir, no, I never ask questions. I advised her as to how she might use it, nothing more.' He bent his head and frowned. 'I was though, rather concerned, she didn't look well.'

'Didn't she,' said Shelley shakily. 'I see.' He fixed his eyes on the chemist who stood looking thoughtful at his counter. 'Did she give her name?'

The chemist shook his head. 'And I did not ask for it either. I have to say, she was in no fit state for questions. She intended to catch the early morning coach to Swansea and purchased a ticket from my assistant over there. I keep them for the coach, it is often quite full.' He frowned concerned. 'It's a long and unpleasant journey but the sad little creature was determined. She said she would stay at The Mackworth Arms . . .' He reached in his drawer. 'Now, I wrote the address down somewhere . . .' He drew out a small piece of paper. 'There – do take it. I am sure you will help her.' He gave a sigh of relief. 'I am glad you have come to find her.'

The look on the chemist's face made Shelley ashamed. He bent his head pondering.

The assistant came forward. 'Yes sir, I sold her the ticket,' she said, worriedly. 'But the coach left yesterday morning. You'll not catch up with her now, and you must take the ferry on that journey as well.' She shivered. 'Oh, the weather has turned so cold.'

Shelley was soon on his way, oddly aware that there was something nasty ahead, something he would have to fight. He knew too well that Fanny loved him. Would he argue with her, hold her in his arms, tell her how wonderful she was, but try to explain that he could not love her in the way he loved Mary and that she could not fit in with his life. Fanny understood herself well, but she walked alone. He could never have influenced her in the way he had influenced the others. She was though good and kind, all her experience had been in the service of others right from the start, but what had happened to her now? Where had she gone and why?

Now he was close! He breathed a sigh of relief as the coachman dropped him at The Mackworth Arms, the Coaching Inn on the main Swansea road where Fanny intended to stay. For a minute or two he stood silent, looking about. The inn was close to the exchange for fish and vegetables and the street was busy with traders. The stench from rotting vegetables and decaying fish made him gag for a moment and he leant for some seconds against a wall. Finally he turned to the Inn, braced himself and went in.

He would try to atone for his wrongs, he thought, he would beg her forgiveness for having used her for counsel, for warmth and indeed rationality, for she was always straight and honest, but he could not love her in the way she needed to be loved. Fanny, dear Fanny, who never caused any distress and had always been there for others, was now in danger. She had borne so long the misery of life in the gloom and it seemed the shadows had absorbed her. But *Laudanum?* A cold shiver ran through him when he thought of what she might do. She hated laudanum, and had constantly chastised him for keeping it in his pocket. He could feel the hardness of the bottle against his hip as walked towards the man at the desk. Laudanum could kill if taken in large amounts. Fanny's mother, Mary Wollstonecraft, had tried to kill herself with it, that was well known. Oh, the pain of it hurt him to the quick! He tried to compose himself.

'Is she . . . Is she here?' he faltered. 'I mean the woman . . . a young woman, a slight young woman, rather shy? She is quite upset, you see. None of us meant it. It just sort of happened, the way things do.' He gazed about the foyer. Apart from himself and the proprietor, the place was empty. 'Oh, do please tell me where she is! I really must see her.' He could hear his voice shaking.

'Of whom do you speak?' asked the man, looking Shelley up and down. A maid came to join them.

'A woman in her early twenties . . .' said Shelley. He indicated Fanny's height with his hand.

'I take it you are a relative – or a friend?'

Shelley spoke haltingly. 'Yes, yes, I am a friend. We know each other well.'

Hesitant at first, the inn keeper passed across the details as Shelley bent forward his shoulders hunched his eyes glassy from tiredness. He took off his hat and held it in his hand, his cravat hung untied. 'Thank you, my man,' he said, tapping the inn keeper's arm. 'Thank you, so much.'

'She hasn't been out,' said the inn keeper as they went to the stairs. 'In fact, we haven't seen her at all. And I don't know how long she is staying. She was a finely dressed woman and I presumed she would pay when she left.' He nodded towards the parlour. 'She sat in the parlour a while and drank tea. She didn't want anything to eat. After that she went to her room. I think she was tired. She said she would put out her candle herself and we weren't to disturb her. I am though, concerned. She does not answer her door and must surely be hungry.'

They arrived at the door of the room. The man knocked twice, but no answer. He placed his key in the lock and allowed Shelley inside. That done, he returned downstairs.

Closing the door behind him Shelley slowly stepped forward . . . He gasped and dropped to his knees. It was all too late . . .

Un-cried tears sped through his blood as he returned to Bath in a coach. He was trembling hard. What he'd discovered was all too dreadful to think of. And what must he say to Mary? Fanny, poor

Fanny. Had the fact that he carried laudanum and had often threatened to use it, encouraged her? But it was very easily acquired and in common usage; they even gave it to babies to help them sleep. It was only dangerous if used to excess . . . Ah, used to excess!

Arriving at the lodgings, his body felt heavy as he made his way up the stairs. He stood for a moment by the door, trying to steady his nerves. Not a sound could he hear, not even the cry of the baby. Finally he went inside and found Mary alone by the fire, Claire had gone out with the child and Mary had stayed behind awaiting his return. The afternoon sun fell on her hair from the window. Oh, Mary, his own true love! His own splendid Mary! How he needed her now! 'I'm so sorry,' he stammered, falling into a chair. 'So very, very sorry . . . And all because we didn't understand her. Or worse than that, didn't care.' He rested his head in his hands.

Mary put aside her book. 'What's happened?' she whispered. 'Percy, please tell me.' She touched his hand and waited.

'Something too awful to speak of,' he said quietly. He clasped her hand and pressed it to his lips. For a moment or two they were silent. 'Fanny is *dead*,' he murmured. 'I found her in a room at an inn. There was any empty bottle of laudanum beside her . . .'

Mary gasped in horror. 'Oh, Fanny!'

'But your mother was saved,' Shelley said straightening, immediately knowing her thoughts. 'Imlay saved her, whilst I was too late!'

'He saved my mother, but he could not save his daughter,' Mary added weeping. 'He never cared about Fanny.'

Shelley lifted his head and looked at her strangely. 'There was a letter . . .'

She searched his face, waiting. 'A suicide letter?' A great dread was upon her.

He nodded.

'Fanny had much of our mother in her soul,' she whispered, ' . . . that intelligence, that deep sensitivity and that debilitating sense of defeat that comes over us sometimes, Fanny had it all. And how awful that she never felt loved? – I always loved her, and I thought Papa did too. But did he really? Who did she have to talk to, to share ideas with and help shape her mind?'

'She ought to have been with us,' said Shelley, his face white with grief. 'She said in her letter that the best she could do was to die, she believed she was a burden to us all.'

Mary dried her tears on her handkerchief. 'Have you got the letter?' she asked.

He shook his head slowly. 'No, I left it where it was. It seemed the right thing to do.'

'She was well and truly abandoned,' Mary murmured.

He leant towards her and reached for her hands. 'Mary, I could do no other. What was I to do? – Oh, death is so cold and miserable, why would anyone want it?' He held her hands tightly. 'We shall have to tell Claire.'

They were silent for several moments, staring into space.

'She'll be back very shortly,' Mary said finally. – 'And there's Papa. Percy, you must send him a letter, or else go to see him at Skinner Street. You will have to. – My love, do take your coat off.' The room was warm from the fire. 'And you must eat, you are tired and shaking.'

'I'm not hungry,' he said raising his shoulders and dropping them slowly. 'How can I eat after this?'

They heard Claire's footsteps on the stairs as she returned with the baby. 'And I must feed Wilmouse,' said Mary, as Claire came in through the door. Mary took the child in her arms. 'I'll feed him in the bedroom,' she said, looking at Claire miserably. 'Percy has terrible news.'

Claire looked back at her frightened then took off her cloak. 'What is it?' she faltered, sitting down slowly.

'Percy will tell you,' said Mary. There was noise outside on the street. Children were laughing and talking as they passed. The last of the afternoon sun came in through the window, then the room fell into shadow as Percy delivered her the news.

Claire grew big with her pregnancy. It disturbed her a lot that Byron might possibly ignore the birth of their child at New Year. She secretly hoped he'd come running, for surely it would appeal to the softer part of his nature, she said. Mary marvelled at her step sister's continued naivety. But it was one of her endearing qualities. Shelley had written to Skinner Street, and had delivered the news about Fanny achingly on paper to Godwin. Godwin had said he had known how Fanny had felt, and had also had a suicide letter. Much of the tragedy was due to her disposition, claimed Godwin, and the nature of her personality. But Mary knew that neither Percy nor her father would own to their respective faults, for there were too many disputes between them. There was though now the problem of how Fanny should be buried. And everything would have to be secret. It would be scandalous if her suicide came to be known. Her death was reported in the paper though no name had been revealed; it had been torn off her suicide note. Fanny had simply been recorded as just "Found dead."

To Mary it was all unreal. Shelley said nothing, but there were nights when he wept loudly. That evening, she laid the baby in his cot then read once more the letter she'd received from her father

"Do nothing to destroy the obscurity she so much desired, that now rests upon the event. It was, as I said, her last wish . . . Think what is the situation of my wife & myself, now deprived of all our children but the youngest [William]; & do not expose us to those idle questions, which to a mind in anguish is one of the severest trials.

We are at this moment in doubt whether during the first shock we shall not say she is gone to Ireland to her aunts, a thing that had been in contemplation . . . What I have most of all in horror is the public papers; & I thank you for your caution as it might act on this."

Shelley had made his choice and Fanny's body had never been claimed. She had been buried in a pauper's grave.

25

The Death Of Harriet Shelley

Harriet Shelley had been heavily pregnant. But who was the father of her child? It might have been the man who called himself her husband, the landlady at Harriet's lodgings said to the curious housemaid, for that man had often called in. Though she did have other callers too. A plumber named William Alder had helped move her out of her parents' home in September. That was something of a puzzle, the landlady said – had her family forced her to leave because she was pregnant, or had she gone of her own accord? 'Harriet Smith', as she called herself, had been doing a lot of crying, but she'd had plenty of money to get by with and had seemed quite healthy. She was obviously weary of mind however, the landlady said sympathetically, and spent much of her time in bed. She'd called herself 'Mrs Smith', but a lot of people knew exactly who she was and that her husband lived with two single sisters, one who had borne him a son and the other one pregnant to boot. Percy Shelley was talked about a lot. Those aristocratic types did just what they wanted without the least thought for tomorrow. Whatever had been in that poor woman's mind the day she went missing was a mystery, the landlady said. All she could say for certain was that on a bleak November day, Mrs Harriet Smith had simply disappeared, leaving all her belongings.

A body had been found in the Serpentine River in early December, reported as that of 'a respectable female', wearing a valuable ring, thereby suggesting it hadn't been robbery or murder, but some terrible mystery instead. The unfortunate woman had been 'far advanced in pregnancy', and the body had been floating for weeks. The confused and despondent plumber, William Alder, had been called to identify the corpse, and Shelley was informed in due course. Harriet had left a suicide note, though it didn't make for easy reading since the writing was mostly illegible.

"When you read this letr. I shall be no more an inhabitant of this miserable world. do not regret the loss of one who could never be anything but a source of vexation & misery to you all belonging to me . . . My dear Bysshe . . . if you had never left me I might have lived but as it is, I freely forgive you & may you enjoy that happiness which you have deprived me of . . . so shall my spirit find rest & forgiveness. God bless you all is the last prayer of the unfortunate Harriet S—"

Fingers were pointing fast again at Percy Bysshe Shelley. Where had he been when his poor sad wife had needed him, for Harriet was still his wife, was she not? And surely that was important – and what about his motherless children. Harriet's death was recorded the same as Fanny's, the woman was simply, 'Found dead', and her name was 'Harriet Smith.'

Shelley felt wretched. Two deaths from suicide and both the women had loved him. He went into a fierce panic, telling stories wherever he went. Harriet had ensnared him, he said, and she'd thought she had him for life, but he'd sprung right out of her grasp! Shelley liked to think she'd been driven from her parents' home because of her headstrong nature, and as for himself, he constantly maintained he'd been nothing but upright and honourable regarding Harriet.

'It isn't your fault,' Mary insisted one morning. The effect of the suicides had started to show in his eyes, which now expressed a strained look of anguish. They walked down a lonely path in the still December woodland. Nature today was peaceful and calm, just stillness, silence and peace. 'You must only listen to what you believe in your heart,' she told him. 'You have done no wrong, and if people decide to kill themselves, is it not their own choice?'

He gazed at the clear blue sky. 'I am quite awhirl with it all.'

'I shall always support you,' she persisted. 'No-one will vilify your name in my hearing.'

'And does Claire feel the same?' he asked miserably.

'We haven't discussed it, but I know she is loyal. I doubt she'll be thinking about the deaths. She is quite obsessed with Byron and will soon give birth to his child. New year, new life! The way life starts is magical. I look forward to seeing the baby.'

'I shouldn't think Bryon does,' murmured Shelley, he was breathing hard between his words. His chest was hurting, he said. Mary said he was far too liberal with the laudanum. It made him sleepy and unbalanced.

'As regards Harriet's ruin, I know who is being blamed,' she said, sighing. 'It is bound to be *me*. No girl with the least bit of decency would have hurt her like that.' Her voice faltered. 'Even my father has disowned me.' He put his arm around her waist and drew her towards him. She looked at him and smiled, then laid her head on his shoulder as they walked. She had given herself to Shelley, both mind and body. Come what may, she was his.

With Harriet gone, the way was clear for Shelley and Mary to marry, Godwin told his wife in the shop. 'We can now be rid of the shame. I hope she realises she could now clear things up.'

Mary Jane shrugged her shoulders. 'If she is so inclined.'

Godwin went on. 'Mary has let me down very seriously, I know. Who would have thought it?'

'I would have thought it,' said Mary Jane plaintively. 'And we'll never stop the wagging tongues. They were busy enough before, now they caw like a thousand crows at twilight.'

'So my name is stained with blood?' Godwin whispered dramatically, throwing out his hands. He looked at her straight. He was always a fighter, he told her, there were few who would take him on – just let them try.

'C'est tragique,' she murmured.

He pressed her hand gently and frowned. They were silent a moment. 'How can it be, I ask myself, that Shelley can work such sorcery on women so easily. For one way and another that is just what he's done.'

Mary Jane's eyes were glassy from loss of sleep. She had hardly recovered from Fanny's suicide, and now there was this. 'I always thought Harriet a fine young woman, you know. Neither she nor Fanny said much about how they were feeling.' She rubbed her eyes and blinked. 'But look where it gets you – dead, nothing but dead. And when you are dead you are done for.'

'*For ever?*' Godwin murmured. He gazed about abstractedly then talked about his second novel *St Leon*, the tale of Count Reginald de St Leon, a young French aristocrat, who'd lost his fortune in a life of debauchery. The guilt of what he'd done had haunted his whole existence. A stranger had given him the secret of the elixir of life and the way to multiply gold. What better gifts could a young man wish for? But Godwin had shown how none of it had served St Leon in the least and how life was fraught with complexities. In order to gain goodwill from others, St Leon was forced to lie; for people frowned curious – how had he acquired such wealth, where had it come from, what was his past? And the man didn't age? He was watched and monitored, even brutally punished and in time became lonely and depressed.

'It's a very good book,' Mary Jane said. 'But that poor fellow could never succeed whichever way he turned.' She shook her head and sighed. 'Money is very important. But you were right to show how an excess of wealth can bring misery. The French know all about that.'

'And if life is too easy we waste our time and resources,' Godwin added sagaciously.

'There is no elixir,' Mary Jane concluded, sticking her chin in her chest. 'Try as you will you cannot create one, even in a story.'

Deaths, calumny and broken hearts had caused Shelley to reap the whirlwind. But he followed his own best interests as usual, which at present meant marrying Mary. It served him best with Godwin and it served him best with his father, for it would seem to be sensible if he hoped to have custody of the children he had fathered with Harriet. – And Mary was pregnant again. Shelley's radical beliefs, encouraged by Godwin's *Political Justice*, had resulted in him being estranged from the whole of his family. Mary Jane claimed he was quite at sea with his avant-garde ideas and had caused considerable heartache, and probably worse. He had though helped them financially, believing in her husband's brilliance and for that she was grateful.

But the poor in England had a rankling poison in their blood, poverty and starvation loomed everywhere. Children were starving and work was in short supply. There had been serious public disorder at the end of 1816 and in the last few years of his reign George III had been unwell and could not rule his country. People whispered he was mad. The end of the Napoleonic wars had led to a fall in the economy, mass unemployment and hunger, and the popular radical speaker Henry Hunt had been brought to address a gathering at Spa Fields in Islington. The rioters had hoped to take the Tower of London and also the Bank of England then petition prince regent George Augustus Frederick for electoral reform. They were dead set on justice and their bitterest energies were harnessed. Guns were stolen and troops appeared at the Royal Exchange. Then came the gunfire. – "English poverty, French poverty, the rich get richer and the poor get poorer!" the rioters had shouted. "It is now time to get even!" But guards had refused to surrender the Tower and the crowd had finally dispersed. Matters moved fast after that, new Acts were brought into being, circulars were sent around the people with the message that anyone who printed seditious material would be severely taken to task. Horrors of the French revolution were never far removed from the thoughts of the English government. The people listened and watched, ready for anything.

On January 12th 1817, Claire Clairmont had given birth to a baby daughter in Bath. She delighted in her child and was intent on seeing Byron, who must realise his responsibilities! That evening she talked with Mary in their lodgings, Shelley had gone to see friends in London and little William lay sleeping in his cot. 'What is to happen,' Claire said wistfully, cradling her tiny infant, 'now I am mother to this child? Byron is living in Venice and I am left here with our baby.'

Mary was writing at the table. She put down her pen and lifted her eyes from her novel – just a few more paragraphs and she'd done. She turned slowly, relieved to have come to the end of its twists and turns, she had worked her emotions so rigorously! Her monster had shown enormous fits of anger, suffering and despair, and great feats of love and compassion. He lived inside her now and demanded her energy. She braced herself. Claire looked sad and afraid. 'Well, I hope he sees sense,' sighed Mary. 'Little Alba will need her father. I believe like the Faustian noble, Manfred, in the play he is writing, Byron is searching for peace with his past; perhaps he can find it in Venice.' She returned to herself gradually and put away her pen. She'd been writing a lot that day. She stared for a moment at Claire and the child, then away into space. 'A supernatural play like *Manfred* is bound to do well in these times,' she said abstractedly, it sounds exciting. 'I should think it will be most profitable. It offers vicarious speculation and fear. You must frighten people, you see. That's what they like. Frighten them and force them to think.'

Claire winced. She had a pain in her groin, the labour hadn't been easy but she'd managed without too much suffering and her breast milk was flowing well. 'I suspect Shelley is still reading *Don Quixote,'* she said, stroking the baby's cheek. 'As regards Harriet and Fanny, he won't spend long depressing himself about the deaths of women who have loved him. He'll have forgotten them both already.'

For a moment or two there was silence.

'Do you really think Fanny loved him?' Mary said frowning. They hadn't talked about Shelley like that before. Fanny and Shelley together didn't make sense. And Fanny had never said much about Shelley especially. Her love though would never have been returned. Perhaps she had tried to find out and couldn't take the truth. To discover the truth, the real truth of how it was, might have been far too painful.

'Of course, she did,' Claire said quietly. 'I always knew she loved him.'

'But she never said so,' Mary said, deep in thought. She rose and walked about the room.

Claire gazed down at her child. 'Your father is tormented,' she whispered. 'He tries to talk to spirits in his writing.'

Mary watched her in silence.

'Manfred was ravaged with guilt over matters torturing his mind,' said Claire, smiling wryly. 'He was trying to summon up spirits to help him forget.'

Mary could hear a touch of triumph in her tone. It was quite a victory to give birth to Byron's baby, a lot of women would be jealous, particularly Anabella Milbanke, who also had a daughter by Byron but had left him and taken the child. 'I wonder if the babies look alike.' Mary said curiously. 'Perhaps they resemble each other.'

'They probably do,' Claire said quietly, gazing at the child's perfect features, the beautiful rosebud mouth and the high intelligent forehead. 'But it's doubtful Alba will ever see Augusta Ada. Annabella has gone and will never return to the abbey.'

'Percy said Byron has a buyer,' said Mary, recalling a recent conversation. 'He'll be glad to be rid of it.'

'Not to mention the ghosts,' said Claire with a shudder.

Mary looked at her and smiled, recalling what Claire had told her about hauntings at Newstead. 'Yes, he'll be very happy in Venice, I'm sure,' she concluded, though a little facetiously.

For a moment or two they were silent. 'I really must see him,' Claire said miserably. 'Surely he will love little Alba?'

Mary shook her head. 'Who can know the mind of a man like Byron, but how good it would be for him to see her. We must speak to Percy. Perhaps we could live in Italy a while. Percy needs a change of environment. I'll see what he says.'

'Could we?' Claire said hopefully, bracing herself quickly. 'Oh, could we, Mary? That would be wonderful. I long to see George.' Her spirits cheered as she thought of it. 'I feel I belong to him now.' She gazed at the child fondly. 'We need to be together as a family.'

Mary braced herself; it was "George" now, was it. She had never before heard Claire refer to Byron as 'George'. She smiled. The lodgings were silent and lonely. Fears came up in her again. Would Claire live in Venice with Byron? It seemed unlikely. What if Percy never returned and just disappeared? She looked through the window at the gathering dusk; he still wasn't back. His London friends would delay him, enjoying his company. Perhaps he'd be back tomorrow.

26

Venice

Hoping to publish Manfred that spring Byron was busy with his writing. Apart from his animals, his manservant Frederick Llewellyn and his wife Gertrude, plus a few hired servants he lived by himself in the grand Venetian palazzo. He liked to have his animals about him for they afforded him a kind of peace, he said, and helped him escape from the world. Half a dozen peacocks roamed about outside, while two mastifs lounged at his feet and three monkeys climbed about the furniture, two red Burmese cats sprawled lazily on his bed and a falcon perched on the head post. He'd been making good use of his time writing, riding and swimming and felt sharply alive, proud of his strong body and always determined to never let his twisted foot get in the way of his life. He sent and received letters from England about literature and politics and looked forward to seeing Shelley sooner or later. From time to time he sighed with relief that he had now sold Newstead Abbey with its miserable associations. Friends from abroad had been visiting, bringing him news, enjoying his generous hospitality, gasping at the sight of young Italian women meandering through the palazzo half naked and animals wandering his rooms.

Frederick Llewellyn's wife told everyone she knew that the mother of his lordship's new daughter had called her Alba but his lordship preferred her called 'Allegra', which meant cheerful and brisk and was related to the Italian word allegro. That was how she would be known when she arrived in Venice, and she would very soon be with them.

Frederick's wife kept her head held high and was all glowing and approving when she spoke about Byron's new daughter for she knew how much his lordship hated being criticised, and he was certainly criticised for the way he behaved with women. He had treated Lady Byron shamefully, and now she had left him and taken his daughter with her. But now he had another, and they hoped he might behave a little better. Judging however, from the number of women who came and went from the palazzo, it was doubtful his lordship would change, said Gertrude Llewellyn, who knew him only too well.

He was though in better spirits since moving to Venice. That day in the kitchen with her husband, Gertrude commented she hadn't seen his lordship so relaxed in a good few years. She didn't like seeing him unhappy. He'd had a hard time with his mother at the abbey, but she and the abbey had gone, and Gertrude had seen a certain freedom in his manner. When the time was right, someone would bring his new little daughter to see him – she would not come with her mother, he couldn't bear the mother, he'd told her, and the Llewellyns remembered how she'd literally thrown herself at his lordship, and her a daughter of William Godwin as well, the famous writer in London. 'She seduced him,' Gertrude Llewellyn trilled to her husband as women came and went from his rooms.

'Aye, but seducing his lordship wouldn't have been much of a problem,' said Frederick said smiling knowingly. 'There were plenty as did it before her and plenty have done it since.' Frederick laughed as he plucked the feathers off a hen he'd sacrificed that morning. His lordship wasn't too keen on meat in general, but he did like a nice slice of chicken. Frederick pulled at the feathers and they flew about the air.

His wife looked at him irritably. 'You know I can't chase them,' she said, gathering as many as she could from the floor. 'Feathers have a life of their own.'

Her husband braced himself and nodded. 'You asked me to pluck the feathers from the hen and that's what I'm doing. We can sort the mess out later.'

'And did you remove the innards?' she asked stretching her neck to look. 'You sometimes forget, and you know I can't bear to touch them.'

'They're over there in the bucket.' He pointed. 'Keep them away from the monkeys though. Those monkeys eat anything going. I caught one of them gorging a lizard yesterday on the steps.'

For a moment or two they were thoughtful. 'I was thinking,' said Gertrude. 'All his lordship's problems grow from the very same root.' She leant towards her husband and whispered, *'He has a passion for his sister.'*

'Well, it's hardly news, but you keep your nose out of that,' said Frederick, giving her a look of disapproval. 'There isn't a scrap of proof to be had anywhere. It's a sort of sport to tell lies about his lordship, and you know it. He put his hand on her arm. 'I've warned you before. Now do be careful what you say, my dear. – And watch those monkeys.'

The year 1817 passed quickly, spring soon became summer, and in no time at all it was winter. Then it seemed everything had changed. Harriet and Fanny were dead; Shelley was married to Mary who had given birth to a daughter named Clara that autumn, while William was now "a mischievous young rogue", according to his grandfather Godwin. Now Mary was married to Shelley, she found it easier to visit the shop on Skinner Street, though eyes looked the other way if Claire and her tiny daughter came too, for who was the little girl's father? People raised their eyebrows and smiled at each other. They whispered and invented stories. Claire withdrew from the gossip and Mary grew haughty. But life continued amidst the voices and footsteps, for there was always some matter to attend to. And Mary recalled wistfully, how it had been with her father in the past. It seemed like a long time ago when he'd written those beautiful words on his travels

> *"Tell Mary, I will not give her away, & she shall be nobody's little girl, but Papa's: papa is gone away, but papa will soon come back again, & look out at the coach-window, & see the Polygon across two fields, from the trunks of the trees at Camden Town. Will Mary and Fanny come and meet me?"*

He'd been warm and loving those days compared to how he was now. A cold and resolute expression had taken the place of his smiles. Shelley sent letters to Venice giving Byron news of his daughter; she was a good little creature and healthy, their lodgings were depressing, he said, and they were planning to see him very soon; Mary was eager for Italy. Shelley wrote of his hopes for a better existence in that lovely accommodating country; the climate would be better for his chest, he said, it was often so damp in England. As far as England was concerned, he couldn't recommend it as a good place to live just now, and Byron had been right to get away.

Thoughts of Italy made Mary feel more at ease, and she indulged herself with the satisfying thought that *Frankenstein* was finally published! But the book had been published anonymously, which always led to frustration and bother in Mary Jane's shop with people constantly enquiring as to who was the author. The gossips speculated wildly but Mary Jane's tack was to shake her head and look baffled. The book had been rejected at first but had finally found a home with Lackington, a small, undistinguished House who had liked it. It would make them a fortune in time, Godwin had said assuredly. Lackington, Hughes, Harding, Mavor, & Jones of Finsbury Square, was owned by a self-made man who focused on selling books to all classes of society. An apprentice shoemaker and a man with vision, he had gone to London in 1773 in the hope of making his fortune and had started selling books as Lackington & Co. the very next year. He now had a good sized store in the mall on the corner of Finsbury Square which he'd named "The Temple of the Muses", designed, Godwin would laugh, by the very same man who had designed Newgate Prison. All three volumes of his daughter's book however had sold far less than she'd hoped for and that was a bit of bad luck. 'Timing!' Godwin had said, shaking a determined finger. 'Timing is vital. They will publish it again later on.'

But Mary felt resentful. She very much admired her husband's work, and was even flattered at first when people suggested the astonishing tale had been written by Percy Bysshe Shelley. But she wondered if she would ever feel the pride of having been the author of *Frankenstein*. The book was hers not Percy's! The gossips talked without restraint, making faces and despising much of what she'd written. – "What gruesome ideas! What a hideous story! How could anyone imagine it?" they said. It was little wonder Shelley's family had disowned him, why, the fellow was quite depraved, and to think what he did with those girls, not to mention his first wife's suicide, a very strange business indeed.

There was a great deal of talk about Percy Bysshe Shelley and if people hadn't heard of him before they certainly heard of him now. But Mary's emotions ran riot and it was hard to quell her annoyance when people made spiteful remarks about *Frankenstein*. And they criticised Percy viciously. But she didn't want to distress him, and kept her thoughts to herself, for he was constantly chased by creditors and terrified of the debtor's prison. Worse than that, he was sick at heart for the court had decided he was no fit father to have custody of his children by Harriet. Mary bent her head as she went about the streets, annoyed at how life had turned out. She'd be glad to depart for Italy as soon as they could.

'Harriet's family is at the back of this custody thing,' Shelley said to Mary one morning.

'Oh, custody, custody, I'm annoyed too,' said Claire, lifting her head from her sewing. 'Byron wants custody of Alba. But he won't get his way, not ever!' Claire was determined, and she was proud. She loved being a mother, and it gave her immense joy to take care of her baby.

Mary knew Claire would never do just as the lofty lord Byron commanded. But Byron had power and now that he'd sold the abbey he could safeguard the child fittingly and see she had a good education. Claire had nothing to offer but love. Would Byron love Alba as he should, asked Claire, if she must live with her father?

Neither Mary nor Shelley answered. They were both thoughtful.

'I can change his mind if I see him,' Claire said intently. 'I know it. We can raise Alba together.'

There was a great deal of fault to be found with Byron, thought Mary, he had a bad reputation and Claire's life had been shamed. He was also said to be "dangerous". But Claire was a problem for all of them now. Mary Jane's attitude had changed; Claire must suffer the consequences of her own mistakes her mother had declared firmly, she could not bring them to her. Mary too, hoped Claire would find strengths of her own, for she followed behind her so closely she might have been a shadow. 'Raise her together?' Mary said looking at her sadly. 'I wish it were true, but I fear you would be bad for each other. Byron can be quite demonic, and you, my dear, are inclined to be too dramatic.'

'We can't help the way we are,' Claire said moodily.

For a moment or two they were silent.

'Perhaps he thinks he can redeem himself in Venice,' Claire said sighing. She turned to Percy who had bent again to his book.

He closed the book with a clap then stood. 'Living in Italy will be good for us. – We shall go to Milan, then after that I shall go to Venice and Alba can see her father. – Claire, Claire, please don't be difficult. Do stop frowning. Byron wants to see his daughter, and so he shall. Is it not fair he sees her? But he will not keep her.' He threw out his hands and gazed at the ceiling. – 'Italy, oh Italy, what life, what colour, what warmth! I hate the smoke of the cities in England and the noise.' He shuddered and continued. 'And the chilling fogs and rains that conspire to kill us. Bah! I shall be glad to leave them behind for I am well near dead.'

So Shelley's party left for Italy. Much of the anguish they'd suffered lifted as they left the shores of England behind them, though each felt a sense of failure. But they held to the belief that life would be better in a gentler warmer climate and with the prospect of starting afresh. Following the defeat of Napoleon in 1815, Italy now had heavy border controls and scrutinized the details of any foreign travellers, but Percy's eloquence, and the sight of the little children silent in the arms of the women helped persuade officials to be kind.

The first place they stopped at was Turin, then on to Milan where they hoped Byron might join them. But Shelley thought it most unlikely, Byron was established firmly in Venice now, railing against English traditions and proprieties. He was very well known and much admired for his poetry and intellect, but condemned for what people called his "abject debauchery". They claimed he was as unconstrained as the sea, which Byron said would always embrace him if all else failed. His daughter would live with him, he said, but only with him, for Claire, he maintained, would corrupt her. His sister? – Of course, he adored Augusta, but what if he did, he could not help it, he would ride on the crest of the highest wave, no less. Augusta was an important part of his life and he hoped she would meet Allegra.

Claire had tried hard to build a bond between herself and Byron, and she believed he loved her, which was only a fiction to Mary, but Claire would hear nothing but her own counsel of hope. And she went about in the same daze of love she'd experienced on her first day at Newstead. But Mary maintained she was reaching out for an echo, an echo that was fast fading. All she had been for Byron was a source of amusement. Alba had been a mistake and as regards her battle for the child, she had well and truly lost. It was a horrible cruel truth which Claire refused to accept. But in the end she had had no option and despite her countless protestations and tears, was forced to admit Byron didn't want her. But at least he wanted his daughter. The decision she must make felt brutal, and she knew she must make it alone.

> "I send you my child because I love her too well to keep her," she wrote finally, as she prepared for Alba's departure. "With you who are powerful and noble and the admiration of the world she will be happy, but I am a miserable and neglected dependent."

'This isn't how it should be,' she moaned to Mary. 'But the nurse is good and can be trusted. She promises me news.'

'I so feel for you,' said Mary, tying on the child's small bonnet. She glanced at Claire guiltily. It seemed wrong to let Alba go living with strangers. But what could be done? It was the best course of action all told. 'I love this child as if she were my own,' she murmured. 'She'll be well taken care of, I'm sure. It's the best you can do for her now,' she said, as the child gazed at her trustingly. 'When she is older she'll thank you.' She had other thoughts too, but she kept them back just then. She felt a terrible sensation of pity for Claire. Who did Byron think he was that he could treat her so badly? It was rank, of course, he was a lord, and he was also a man.

'But I can't even visit,' Claire whimpered. 'She's only just walking and must live with those peculiar Llewellyns. And what about all those animals? Allsorts of animals live with him. She doesn't fear cats and dogs, but I'm not so sure about monkeys and the rest.' Claire rubbed her arms and sighed. 'And dogs can be vicious if they're hungry.'

'I doubt he will leave them hungry,' Mary said, thoughtfully. She was tired and her spirits were shattered. The children were still so young and demanding, two year old William, Clara, almost a year, and Alba just fourteen months, were all very much loved. To lose Alba would hurt them deeply. 'A good education will help her,' said Mary abstractedly. 'She won't be dragged down by her father's contemptible lifestyle either. She will grow to be sensible and good. Alba is a precious little creature. Who knows, perhaps she can save him.'

'Perhaps,' Claire said quietly. 'Having a child makes us brave,' she added straightening. 'I am brave enough now to give her up. – I *am* being brave, am I not? Oh, Mary, tell me I'm brave. For when is bravery weakness and when is weakness bravery?'

'We do what we do,' said Mary. 'Some women are simply plucked from the tree as if they were ripe red apples and devoured by life in an instant. Beauty can be deathly. My mother thought a lot about that. Oh, how we women hope. It is one thing to have ideals, but they cannot always be realised.' She sighed despondently. 'Life can make it impossible. Civilisation itself holds us in bondage.'

Whatever shortcomings Alba's father might have, with the patter of tiny feet and the clicking of the nursemaid's shoes, Alba left Milan for Venice.

And just as Mrs Llewellyn had predicted, as time passed by his lordship increasingly enjoyed his little daughter and was always on his best behaviour. He was, said Gertrude, attempting to right his wrongs. He played with the child and made her laugh; he even brought a tortoise out of its bed, a sleepy fellow which the child found enthralling as it leisurely moved about the floor its legs sprawled awkwardly outwards. And she would reach for his lordship's embrace and did not hesitate to quickly cross the floor and tug at his breeches for attention.

But experience told Mrs Llewellyn that this ideal relationship could not last; his lordship would want his time to himself again soon, and it seemed he wished for Allegra to live with Richard Belgrave Hoppner, the consul, and his wife, who also resided in Venice and with whom Byron had become friends.

As month followed month, the little girl's confidence grew; she would open drawers and take things away, careless of her nurse's reproaches. Sometimes she hid his lordship's pens, and the monkeys were blamed till the pens were recovered. The child needed lots of managing. And it was always hard to chastise her, for her large brown eyes looked sorrowful as a puppy's and his lordship could only clasp her to his chest and kiss her. It was the triumph of heartfelt feeling over intelligence, Frederick Llewellyn said, a great triumph indeed. But he knew that deep in his heart Lord Byron was very disturbed. His nightmares grew worse and he constantly shouted his political concerns over dinner while banging his fist on the table. There was so much unresolved violence in the world, he said, so much war and death. Frederick said Byron's mind was crammed with poetry and it interfered with his thinking. One day when he'd gone out with the child, Frederick chanced to glance at a poem on his desk. 'He has brought out his *Darkness* poem,' he whispered to Gertrude. 'The one he likes to chant.'

'Well, he doesn't let darkness go away,' said Gertrude, sighing and leaning in to look

> "*I had a dream, which was not all a dream.*
> *The bright sun was extinguish'd, and the stars*
> *Did wander darkling in the eternal space,*
> *Rayless, and pathless, and the icy earth*
> *Swung blind and blackening in the moonless air;*

Morn came and went—and came, and brought no day,
And men forgot their passions in the dread
Of this their desolation; and all hearts
Were chill'd into a selfish prayer for light:
And they did live by watchfires—and the thrones,
The palaces of crowned kings—the huts,
The habitations of all things which dwell,
Were burnt for beacons; cities were consum'd,
And men were gather'd round their blazing homes
To look once more into each other's face;
Happy were those who dwelt within the eye
Of the volcanos, and their mountain-torch:
A fearful hope was all the world contain'd;
Forests were set on fire—but hour by hour
They fell and faded—and the crackling trunks
Extinguish'd with a crash—and all was black ..."

'No wonder the man has nightmares,' said Frederick, scratching his head. 'He fills his mind with misery.'

'That or else women,' said Gertrude.

Frederick looked his wife over; she was a pretty woman. Rather too old for his lordship's fancy, thank goodness.

'You wanted me to wash your shirt,' said Gertrude, frowning at the stains down the front. 'It's soiled from seeing to the animals. Now take it off and go and get another.'

'And he's translating two of St Paul's epistles into English,' Frederick went on, undoing his buttons. 'He might learn a thing or two from them.'

'I didn't think he was religious,' she said, helping him pull off his shirt.

'No, you wouldn't. I think he's a bit confused about religion.' Frederick wriggled his arms from the sleeves and continued. 'He holds with that Calvinist thing, him being raised in Scotland and all. We are all sinners, you see, whatever we try to do we were born sinners. Even little Allegra is a sinner. But his lordship champions liberty, liberty in works and deeds. And that is all to the good.'

'I can't say I'm religious myself,' Gertrude said staring at the floor a little worriedly. 'I suppose it makes me frightened of dying, but if God lets all sorts of terrible things happen to innocent people, how can he love them. And isn't he in league with the devil if he does nothing to stop them?'

Frederick laughed. 'His lordship thinks he is one of the devil's own. You should hear him talk. But it's all poetry. He likes to shock people. Him and Mr Shelley have a lot in common I think.'

Frederick sat down by the table, bare-chested. Nothing seemed to matter in Italy; he would never have exposed himself as boldly as that at Newstead. 'He thinks a lot about war though,' he continued. 'And he often gets angry when he's drinking. Then he starts talkin' about countries where people get abused by their rulers and can't break away. He wants to liberate them, see.' Frederick threw up his arms and raised his eyes to the ceiling. 'Freedom! Freedom! Freedom!'

'Oh, stop it,' cried Gertrude. 'I know how you always hear him out, sometimes till daybreak too. But best not get carried away.'

'I listen and learn. He likes me to learn.' Frederick nodded his head for certainty. 'I am quite an educated man, you know. And I can write a proper letter.'

'You must try to look smart tomorrow,' she told him dismissively. 'Mr Shelley is coming. They're staying somewhere nearby. He wants to take Allegra to live with her mother a while. It won't be for long. His lordship watches like a hawk. He'll not be coming with Miss Claire.'

Frederick Llewellyn frowned. 'Oh no, that's forbidden.'

'But what shall I prepare for his dinner?' said Gertrude thoughtfully. 'He doesn't eat meat.'

'Give him a good cheese salad. The Italians make marvellous cheeses. There are several kinds in the larder.'

'And we must keep the monkeys shut away,' she warned. 'He might not be happy to have them leaping about on the table.'

Frederick remarked that Italy wasn't just famous for cheese; it was also famous for its music and arts, which Mr Shelley would most certainly indulge in. Venice throbbed with passion and was recognised as a city where love might be enjoyed to the full, a perfect place for their concupiscent lord to live. The Venetians were quick of mind and dressed and ate as they pleased without any concern for formalities. No man carried a weapon; women walked about without servants, even officials walked the streets without attendants. Its inhabitants were intent on pleasure. There were also good bookshops and coffee houses where people could talk about important events. And Italy embraced great painters and great musicians. People went to concerts, the theatre and the opera; Venetians loved singing, even in the streets. His lordship thrived in his new environment the Llewellyns told each other happily, and the Venetians liked having him, love him or hate him they relished the gossip he gave rise to. He was a wild creature, a man who couldn't be trusted when it came to women, half demon half man, women should keep a guard on themselves if Byron was in the vicinity for his dark eyes had you captured in seconds and you were lost.

27

The Communion Of Poets

Shelley climbed from the gondola and crossed the path to the palazzo. So much thinking on the journey had given him something of a headache, but he was eager to exchange ideas with the now illustrious Byron. Byron's residence was four large buildings linked together, originally built for the wealthy Mocenigo family, some of them Doges of Venice between 1413 and 1763. Byron lived on the right-hand side of the central palazzo where the day brought the best of the sunshine. He suddenly emerged with his dogs.

'Shelley!' he cried, clapping his hands with pleasure. 'You kept your promise; I see you have come by yourself. It might have been difficult otherwise.'

Shelley bowed briefly then stretched out his hand. 'All is as planned, dear Byron. We are grateful Claire is to have some time with Allegra. Even a couple of weeks will make her happy, she misses the child dearly.'

'I'm sure,' Byron said quietly, watching the water before them.

'I hope she will come without fuss,' said Shelley. 'She is fond of her mother; of course, Claire is rather disturbed though at the arrangement.'

Byron answered with silence.

Shelley continued. 'Mary will travel to Este with the children in the next few days to the place where you've arranged for her to stay and I shall take Alba to Claire who is waiting to see her. Alba – or as you prefer, Allegra, is an uncommon little creature, is she not?'

'Ah yes, and the child likes being with me, so don't keep her long.' Byron spoke in a firm and resolute tone. 'She rather likes Venice too; there are lots of festivals here. She enjoys a festival.'

'Of course,' said Shelley, looking at Byron curiously and startled by his obvious emotion.

'Your look suggests you are surprised,' laughed Byron. 'I do have a heart, you know. I have another daughter somewhere, but Annabella doesn't let me see her. She thinks I am bad, you see. Well, perhaps I am a little bit. But I would like to see my daughter . . . You do understand, don't you?'

'Oh certainly,' said Shelley. He was suffering the absence of two of his children with Harriet and feared they were lost to him forever. His letters were unanswered and they probably thought he was dead.

Shelley glanced about the splendid sparkling palazzo. The great mastiffs at each side of Byron were silent as mice. 'So, you are very happy in Venice?' he said.

'Ah yes, this magical city rises out of the water!' said Byron, casting out his arm. 'I adore this place. The women are glorious, everything here is wonderful. The silence of the canals is bewitching and the simple lapping sound of the passing gondolas is very relaxing.' He recited a verse of his poetry

> *"I stood in Venice, on the Bridge of Sighs,*
> *A palace and a prison on each hand:*
> *I saw from out the wave her structures rise*
> *As from the stroke of the enchanter's wand:*
> *A thousand years their cloudy wings expand*
> *Around me, and a dying Glory smiles*
> *O'er the far times, when many a subject land*
> *Looked to the wingéd Lion's marble piles,*
> *Where Venice sate in state, throned on her hundred isles!"*

'My dear Shelley, you too have fled from England, and who could blame you.'

'I have fled from the weather,' Shelley said straightening. 'And other things too I have no desire to speak of.'

'So how is Mary? Is she thriving?'

'She is strong, but the children are very hard work, my baby daughter cries constantly. My precious Mary does her best, but little Clara sweats heavily in the night and she will not feed as she should. My other two children in England have been robbed from me.' He breathed in deeply as if defeated.

'"Robbed?"'

'Absolutely, they won't let me have them, ever. I am not a fit father, you see. In the eyes of the world I have done it all wrong.'

'Likewise,' said Byron quietly. 'But poetry consoles us, does it not. I believe you are busy with *Prometheus Unbound* ?' Shelley nodded in answer. Byron continued. 'I am lost in the cantos myself. I was stuck with a part of the verse this morning, but now it flows freely, thankfully. I have suffered such terrible insomnia.' They walked through the spacious building, drenched in sunlight and shadows. 'I am in very bad spirits if the words get stuck in my mind and will not come to the page.'

'Indeed,' said Shelley. 'And moving from one state to another bothers me. Poetry puts me in a sort of trance which is hard to get out of, which I must if there is pressing business. The state of dream and the state of reality are quite separate with me. Mary suffers the same.'

'*Frankenstein* has now been published!' said Byron, raising his voice with pleasure. 'I know the story, of course, but it would be good to hold the book in my hands.'

'I'm afraid it has sold rather badly,' Shelley said sadly. 'Godwin thinks they will print it again later.'

'Yes, you said in your letter.' Byron looked at him concerned. 'Lackington didn't get it right. He isn't an experienced publisher. But at least he was wise enough to know he had something special. Yes, a second publication is the thing.'

'And because it's anonymous everyone thinks it's mine. Quite a conundrum. Mary gets furious sometimes.'

'And will you reveal the author?'

Shelley looked downwards and frowned. 'Next time perhaps. I'll talk with Mary about it.'

Byron helped himself to cherries from a bowl on a ledge and offered the bowl to Shelley who took a handful.

Frederick Llewellyn met them in the hall and bowed lightly. 'Mr Shelley, can I get you a drink?' he asked him.

'You certainly can,' said Shelley. 'Good man.' He looked sideways at the monkeys dashing about the hall, strong, muscular and disturbing. 'Do they go wherever they like?' he asked Byron.

'Well, yes,' laughed Byron, watching them bounding about. 'I can't say I notice them much, but I like them around.'

Byron was slightly shorter than Shelley and heavier. His busy brown eyes looked ahead as if at his thoughts. His dark thick hair fell softly curled about his ears. His body was taut and strong, quite opposite to Shelley's, whose build was elegant and lithe. Shelley had the advantage in height though he lacked a certain power in his frame and bent his shoulders when he walked, he was almost ghostlike and his pale questioning eyes searched everything around him as he went.

'Yes,' said Shelley, bracing himself. 'Claire is keen to see Allegra, but it's right that the child lives with you. You can give her what Claire cannot.' He lowered his voice and spoke abstractedly. 'Claire is in need of financial support . . .'

'And does Mary keep well?' Byron said, ignoring his comment.

'She is a little tired and is always busy with the children, yet she still finds time for writing. And she reads constantly. She has read *The Corsair* on our journey, and other works of yours she enjoys.'

'Are you jealous?' He glanced at Shelley who gazed about abstractedly.

'What? Oh no, not at all, she likes the works of other writers too. She has recently read Scott's *Rob Roy* and speaks of it with admiration. She's annoyed however he thinks *Frankenstein* was written by me, but he gave it a good review. She is grateful for that.'

'*Frankenstein* is an excellent novel,' Byron said quietly, as if to himself. 'Though I can see why some would think it yours.'

Shelley looked at him straight. 'How so?'

'Well, the story exhibits a pronounced atheism doesn't it. Let us be honest, my friend. It challenges the idea that man is created by

God, and rather suggests science is the answer to why we are here. You do realise that readers will pounce on that.'

'I know,' said Shelley. He sighed, thoughtful. 'But let them.'

'Indeed,' added Byron, shaking a finger at the air. 'Very courageous, but dangerous too. It's as well the book is anonymous. You have a reputation for atheism my friend, and having whisked Mary and Claire down into the bowels of iniquity you have lost the custody of your children with Harriet.' His shrugged and sighed. 'Awful business this custody thing. Ah, fathers, fathers, yours, mine, let us not talk about fathers.'

'I wrote the preface,' Shelley said quietly. 'Only the preface.'

For a moment or two they were thoughtful._'Scott knows nothing of Mary's brilliance,' said Byron, drawing a deep breath. 'I know of it myself, of course.'

'Do you?' Shelley looked at Byron sideways, surveying him up and down.

'I think so,' Byron murmured. He smiled at Shelley and nodded for certainty. 'Mary is a prize.'

'She is,' said Shelley as they walked along the marble floors, the echoes of their footsteps sounding out as they went. 'And she is happy. Or so it would seem. She writes letters to friends and to Skinner Street, though I do not see them.'

'How long will you stay in Italy?' Byron looked at him and lifted his dark eyebrows. 'Do you intend to settle?'

'I am not too good at settling.'

Byron shook his head. 'You might settle here though, you will never get bored in Italy. There is riding to be had, concerts to attend and the theatre. There is much laughter in Italy, oh yes, much pleasure, much life.'

'I have to say, my breath comes easier here,' said Shelley, biting his lip thoughtfully. 'It is a most agreeable climate and the people are easy. You must understand though how difficult it was for Claire to part with Allegra. I have to tell you. But I know that you love her, the child shines in your eyes. I shall console dear Claire. I intend to take her to parts of this country she is eager to see, such as Rome, Florence and Naples. Their beauty might help distract her.'

They went up a flight of stairs. 'Beautiful, yes. But there is much poverty in those places,' said Byron. 'It is shocking to see. Prisoners are made to clean up the streets and take care of the landscape. They are worn to shadows.'

Shelley replied with silence, thinking on Byron's words.

Byron turned to him. 'They are chained,' he gasped. 'Don't you see? – They are chained like slaves! They must work constantly and are forced to provide sexual favours. They have no freedom at all. Be ready to witness the sheer sadness of their souls. Ah, it appals me!'

For a moment or two they were silent.

'I have much to explore and not enough time to do it,' Shelley said plainly, rubbing his face tiredly. 'We must find the truth of what we must do with our existence. It has to be somewhere.' He looked at Byron quickly. 'Do you not agree?'

Byron looked downwards. 'I don't know,' he said, murmured. 'We must constantly search. Sometimes poetry offers truths that prose cannot reach, prose is so often self serving.'

'And poetry too is self serving, is it not?' Shelley watched him and waited.

'*True* poetry is true; it is inspired,' said Byron sagaciously.

'You are right,' said Shelley. 'Oh yes. I do believe poetry is an instrument for good.'

'Whatever good is,' Byron murmured.

They went through room after room, Shelley asking questions about the ornaments on dressers, strange looking objects Byron liked to collect. It was an eclectic mixture, suited to his eclectic mind with a sort of classic harmony that created a mysterious magic. Byron talked as he picked things up and examined them, for each had its own story.

'I can't be long,' Shelley said, disturbing the ease of their discourse. 'Mary gets worried.'

'She fears you will leave her?' Byron laughed quietly. 'You have left a wife before, and could do it again.'

'I do as I like,' he retorted. 'I shall never leave Mary. – I suspect she thinks you will do me no good,' he said half serious.

Byron sighed. 'I could do you a lot of bad if I wanted. Or such is the opinion of Venice, me being spawned by the devil.' He laughed loudly.

'As regards Allegra,' Shelley said, softening his voice. 'Claire will be thrilled to see her.'

'Well, just for a while.' Byron said cautiously.

'She is her mother,' said Shelley, frowning at the marble floor. 'It hurts not to see her child. She must know she is safe and well. I promise you she will only stay with us briefly, and then I shall return her here.' They stopped by a small table with a chair at each side; a window looked out on the water and distant mountains. Frederick Llewellyn brought drinks then left.

'And how do I know you won't *steal* her?' Bryon fixed his eyes on Shelley. 'I mean keep her and never bring her back. I am not a conventional father, I know, but am I not free to let my child live as she wishes. She plays with the animals; she wanders the palazzo at will.'

'And what if she falls in the water?'

'She knows to keep away from the water. The child takes well to instruction, her nurse and the servants watch her.'

Shelley looked surprised and dismayed. 'She is only an infant . . .' His brow tightened with tension.

'*You* fear the water my friend, because you have never mastered it,' Byron continued. 'It will challenge you for that. But you should not fear it. We are created in the waters of the womb. My daughter swims wonderfully well.' For a moment or two he sat brooding.

Shelley could see from his manner and the nervousness in his fingers that Allegra's spirit was strong in his life and belonged to the palazzo. 'I shall return her myself,' he said quietly.

'Why do you look about so nervously?' Byron asked curiously. 'You are safe from the English here.'

'I am never safe from myself,' murmured Shelley.

Byron took a drink from his wine, his dark eyes gazing at space. 'Thank you for taking care of my daughter,' he said. 'She was happy with you, I can tell. You have bought her beautiful clothes and fed her. I am grateful for that.'

'A mere trifle,' sighed Shelley. 'I am sure she loves Venice just as you do.'

'I do indeed,' said Byron, straightening. Frederick Llewellyn brought cheese and salads and laid them before them. 'I do not care for the autumn mist at night time though, it gathers up from the water like the very breath of hell, and the dark streets echo with the voices of ghosts, melancholy voices, like the sounds of abandoned love . . . Oh, I hate it then. There is much lost love in Venice. That or else anger.'

Shelley drew a breath. 'This place is built on water,' he said curiously.

'Yes, it is quite lonely at night time when the moonlight falls on the water.' Byron frowned. 'Newstead was lonely, you know. Ghosts like to wander in loneliness. You do wonder why.' He looked at Shelley and met his gaze. 'Remember how Mary has her monster want a female companion.' He laughed quietly at the thought. 'Even a monster needs company. A good woman is worth a lot. You have one in Mary.'

'Yes, I do,' murmured Shelley. He saw that Byron's spirits could change quickly; he was one minute serious, next he was laughing.

Byron went on. 'The mind is a great cavern; many of its corridors are dark and unknown, even to us.'

Shelley looked away, thoughtful. 'Yes, we don't really know who we are, do we. Perhaps we can only know ourselves when we're dead.'

'"*Dead?*"' laughed Byron. 'I suspect there is nothing after death. Perhaps some essence of us wanders like a sound receding, nothing more.'

'A ghost?'

'Perhaps . . . I am haunted by ghosts, though they are probably born from my own preoccupations.'

Shelley fell to reciting

> '"*Our life is twofold: Sleep hath its own world,*
> *A boundary between the things misnamed*
> *Death and existence: Sleep hath its own world,*
> *And a wide realm of wild reality,*
> *And dreams in their development have breath,*
> *And tears, and tortures, and the touch of Joy . . .*"'

'*The Dream*,' laughed Byron. I wrote it at Villa Diodati on that wonderful evening. Storms can create magic!' He nodded slowly with approval. 'You recite it well. Though it is far, far longer than that. – Do you remember it all?' He turned to Shelley and looked at him with questioning eyes.

'I probably do,' said Shelley. 'I like that poem.'

They started to eat. Byron requested more wine and Frederick Llewellyn complied. They drank freely. 'Italian wine is excellent,' said Byron, smiling. 'It is easy to over indulge.'

'Tell me, Byron. Do you believe there are forces that punish us for having done wrong?' Shelley spoke anxiously; it was something he'd thought about a lot. He emptied his glass and Byron poured him another.

Byron looked at him curiously. 'They are certainly with us in dreams,' he said quietly. 'I am quite familiar with that. But why are you acting fearful? Fear has been with you since the minute you arrived. What is it?'

Shelley straightened and took a breath. 'Is it so obvious?' Byron watched him, waiting. Shelley continued. 'It's a woman . . . It's all very odd . . .'

Byron narrowed his eyes. '*A woman?*' he whispered. 'Does she live here in Italy? What is her name?'

Shelley drew himself up and breathed in deeply. 'I have no idea . . . But she comes to me. I know she is there, she is behind me, and when I turn to look she is there in the shadows. But she disappears within seconds.'

'A stranger?'

Shelley ate a forkful of food. 'I don't know . . . It's a mystery.'

'Do you think she knows you?' Byron looked at Shelley worriedly.

'I doubt it – unless she has followed me from England.' He put his hands to his face. 'You know how women fall in love with us poets . . .'

'Is she young?' asked Byron. He leant back in his chair and gazed at Shelley curiously.

Shelley screwed up his eyes as if he were thinking deeply. 'Yes,

I can tell she is young, and she isn't alone. She carries a baby, you see, a very small baby in a blanket . . .'

'A newborn?' Byron frowned and pursed his lips.

Shelley looked uneasy and nodded.

'Oh, oh,' laughed Byron. 'Take care. There are many deserted women in Italy and they are often carrying babies.' His voice fell to a whisper. 'She probably thinks you are a wealthy gentleman from England who will banish all her concerns and adopt her baby. Will you talk to this woman if you see her?'

'No . . .' Shelley moved about uneasily. He lingered over his answer. 'You see, I don't think she's really there.'

They both looked at space for some minutes, silent and brooding.

'You mean she's an apparition?'

'Not quite. But I might have dreamt her.'

'Ah, that,' murmured Byron. 'Dreams, imagination; how these states torment us.' For a while they sat quietly eating.

Byron scribbled down some notes. Shelley stared ahead. 'Perhaps I have taken too much laudanum,' he said, admonishing himself, 'for I have needed it a lot lately with Claire constantly weeping and Mary trying to comfort her.' He felt a chill against his neck and sensed someone near! Oh yes, she was near . . .

Later that day as they both relaxed by the fire, Frederick Llewellyn hurried to Byron with a letter. Byron cast his eyes over it quickly then put it in his frockcoat pocket. 'Damn them!' he whispered angrily. 'I sincerely hoped it would not happen! How ingenious they are, these people! I didn't even get to say goodbye.'

'What is it?' asked Shelley.

Byron rose from his chair.

'So they took her early this morning?' Byron said to Frederick Llewellyn, who stood by waiting.

'Yes, my lord, at daybreak.' Frederick spoke with a slight tremor in his voice. 'The maid has gone with her, my lord. But it is only what you expected. Did you not say the nursemaid was far too young – that she could not manage the child? – Did you not say it was good that the consul should take her, that the Hoppners would be good for her to live with? I believe it was what you wanted. You have often said so to the Hoppners. I thought . . .'

'I know, I know!' snapped Bryon. 'That's what I said some weeks ago, but matters have changed. – Let me think.'

Frederick stood nervous and emotional. He spoke again, quietly. 'You were sleeping M'lord. I did not want to disturb you.'

Bryon ran his hands through his hair, his skin tightening with anger. He stood quickly. 'Hush. Frederick Llewellyn! Bah! My child has been stolen away!' He turned to Shelley and flung out his arms. 'So you cannot have her at all, my friend, not even briefly. – "*My fate cries out, and makes each petty artery in this body as hardy as the Nemean lion's nerve.*"' He paced in a trance of confusion, cursing the consul and cursing Frederick Llewellyn.

Shelley sat quietly listening, looking bewildered. So Allegra had gone. Claire had been defeated. He must return to the women without delay.

Back at the villa, Baby Clara was sick. Her lips had whitened and despite the raging heat she trembled as if with cold. Late in the night Mary had been roused from her sleep by strange little cries, distant sounds, which only a mother might hear and she had gone to the cot quickly. Fearing a convulsion, she had taken the child in her arms and attempted to soothe her. She'd been packing to travel to Este with Claire and the children, where they intended to stay in one of Byron's villas until Shelley brought them Allegra. Though her heart was heavy, for the journey would be long and hot and she feared for the baby's health.

Claire was up too, sitting about in her dressing gown holding a candle. She had scarcely slept for fretting. 'I do hope he doesn't let me down,' she whispered. 'I have to see my daughter. I doubt her father gives a single thought to my suffering.'

'Let's not talk about it now,' said Mary. 'Everything is worse at night time. We must sleep; we've a long way to travel tomorrow.'

Both Mary and Claire felt tired setting out with the children. The heat and loss of sleep made them listless and the baby would neither eat nor drink on the meandering and tiresome journey.

Arriving at last in Este, they found their way to the villa and rested. But the baby scarcely drew a breath. Sitting quiet and obedient, Wilmouse watched over her constantly, a pensive look in his young innocent eyes. Mary's faith in herself as a mother was diminishing rapidly. She was struggling like never before. Must she fail her child yet again! Claire sat lonely by the window.

The villa at Este might have been a welcoming place, filled with light and beauty and an air so sweet Claire insisted she could taste it, but the women were both preoccupied. Time passed on, Mary nursed her baby and attempted to feed her, but it seemed the child existed elsewhere in a place between life and death. Claire looked lost and Mary felt fearful. How she needed Shelley! She could not, dare not, lose another daughter! There were moments when the child stopped breathing and Mary patted her cheeks to try to awaken some colour in her features. But her eyes closed all too often and for far too long. She wondered if they should try to find a doctor, though she wasn't familiar with the small Venetian town and they hadn't yet spoken to the locals. Wilmouse clung to her knees. 'Your little sister is ill,' she told him shakily.

'She is very cold. What are you going to do, Mama?' asked the boy.

Mary shook her head and sighed.

'Will she die?' Wilmouse asked, in a strangely adult voice. 'Babies often do.'

'Not always,' she said, bracing herself and stroking his soft brown hair. '*You* didn't die, my treasure.' He too looked to the door for his father. 'We shouldn't have come,' Mary, said sharply to Claire. 'You forced me.'

'But she wasn't so bad before,' Claire protested, tearfully. 'Oh, Mary, what are we to do?' She found herself a chair by Mary and clutched at her stomach. 'I have to say I am not too well myself. I think I am about to be sick. Shall I end my days in Este?'

Mary ignored her and held her child even closer. She didn't dare look at her baby's face, afraid of what she might see. Every nerve in her body tightened with terror. A bird sang by the window, a beautiful, beautiful song; there had been no birdsong on the death of baby Clara, only cold grey skies, silence and ice. Here in Venice with unbearable heat it was all quite opposite. But death was death wherever it occurred; that long eternal silence was inconceivable. 'Please let my baby live, please let her live,' she prayed as the baby lay still in her arms. What a blind fool I have been, she thought. Wiser to have kept with her own counsel, a better counsel than Shelley's! Then came four little gasps. Mary knew them too well. 'No, please no!' she murmured. 'She dare not die!'

'I wonder if anything dreadful has happened to Shelley?' said Claire. 'What if he's fallen in the water and couldn't reach the shore?'

There was a silence.

'Byron doesn't have the least fear of water,' Claire continued.

'And neither does Clara,' Mary said quietly, tears streaming down her face. 'She has gone beyond fearing anything.'

The villa was silent when Percy strode through the hall. Numb with despair, the women were silent as he entered.

'Where is Allegra,' Claire asked, seeing him alone.

Shelley fell into a chair and shook his head dejectedly. 'She is in the care of the consul. – I'm sorry. – There has been an arrangement. – They arrived at dawn and took her away.'

Claire stared at him confounded, while Mary looked downwards her hands clasped tightly in her lap.

Shelley continued. 'Byron wasn't too pleased – and neither was I.' He threw out his hands. 'There is no way of getting her back.'

'Oh there is, there is!' cried Claire. 'You ought to have gone for her before! Where have they taken her?'

Shelley looked at her horrified. 'I am not to blame for this. I have done what I could . . .'

'He never wanted me to have her,' moaned Claire. 'It is all Byron's doing!'

'No,' Shelley said softly. 'I do believe there might have been one or two other things happening. Those Llewellyn's, you know, perhaps they are not too happy with Byron's ways.'

'Do you think they might have encouraged the consul to steal her?'

'Well,' Shelley said sternly. 'I cannot bear Mrs Llewellyn myself; she is a gossip of the worst order. But the Hoppners appear to say more than is sensible to others it seems. Stories abound.'

'But the Llewellyns are loyal to Byron. They worked for his mother before him, and I think they are fond of him,' Claire argued. 'They will want the best for Allegra.'

'But perhaps they think he doesn't look after her properly,' Shelley said straightening. 'He allows her to roam by the water . . .' He shuddered slightly. 'I thought it a very bad idea when he said she had total freedom and could roam as she liked. He ought to consider accidents.'

'Such as?' Claire said nervously, fixing her eyes on him straight.

'Such as *drowning*. Is it not right that parents should be responsible?'

'I believe it is,' Mary said quietly. 'But we fail.' She spoke in broken sentences. 'You see, we fail so miserably. We try to do what is right, but it . . .' She put her hands to her face. 'All of us fail.'

Claire rose from her chair and left them.

'Poor woman,' said Shelley, as she closed the door to her room. 'The consul will . . .'

'I don't want to hear about the consul,' Mary said, tears in her throat. 'It is done. Allegra will be happy with those people I'm sure . . .'

'I've been gone too long, my love,' he said, taking her hand. 'I have failed indeed. I am so sorry . . .'

She shook her head sadly and met his eyes. 'We have far worse things to consider,' she said shakily, struggling for words.

He glanced towards Claire's bedroom. 'She weeps so loudly,' he said. 'You are both weeping.'

'We have much to weep about,' Mary said sympathetically. 'But at least Claire's child is alive.'

'Shelley sank to his knees by her side. 'Mary – where is Wilmouse? – Where is the baby?' His eyes moved fast to the cot in the corner.

'Wilmouse is sleeping,' she said. 'Do take your coat off. You are tired from your journey.'

He unbuttoned his frockcoat slowly and stood very still before her. 'And Clara?'

'It is a wicked spirit pursues us, my love. See for yourself,' she sobbed. She pointed to the cot.

'It cannot be,' he whispered.

She followed him slowly. 'The doctor will call on us soon,' she wept. 'I have tried to be strong.'

He stroked the smooth white brow. The tiny body was inanimate now and cold. He trembled, gazing at the child. 'Another dead child,' he wept. 'How can we bear it?'

'Candles, Percy,' she whispered. 'Let us light candles.'

28

Guilt

Baby Clara was buried on a beach in Lido, a small sandy island between the Venice Lagoon and the Adriatic Sea. For several weeks Mary and Shelley turned their backs on the world, for they felt it had lashed them bloodily. Now they were dizzy with pain. No headstone solemnised their baby daughter's passing and only the sound of the sea offered condolences.

Trying to recover in Este, Mary kept Wilmouse close, evermore fearful of the unseen forces that might try to snatch him away, for how she believed in them now! Must she suffer for Harriet's suicide for ever? She had stolen Percy from his wife and children that much was true, and she felt accursed, like the monster in her story. Guilt rang out in her blood like an army of stinging scorpions! Her arm erupted into fierce weeping blisters like never before, whispers came on the breeze, horrible, taunting and mocking and she feared the lurking energies that sought to wreak vengeance upon her. She thought of a passage in her novel where Victor is chased by his monster after promising him a female companion

" . . . I trembled, and my heart failed within me; when on looking up, I saw, by the light of the moon, the daemon at the casement. A ghastly grin wrinkled his lips as he gazed on me, where I sat fulfilling the task which he had allotted to me. Yes, he had followed me in my travels, he had loitered in forests, hid himself in caves, or taken refuge in wide and desert heaths, and he now came to mark my progress, and claim the fulfilment of my promise ..."

Ah, evil deeds had needs of their own and demanded payment when a pact was made with their master. She screwed up her eyes and looked through the window, seeing the distant mountains, bold, proud and indifferent. The mountains seemed like military strongholds guarding the sky, restraining some evil potential. She shivered, suddenly chilled, she ought to have been more insistent, she told herself and refused to take Clara across Italy in such blistering heat, she had known what could happen and had gone against her better judgement! Yes, she must learn from experience! She said little about her torment; for she could not find a language to speak of her suffering. She had written to her father trying to explain her feelings but reading his reply that morning had given nothing in the way comfort

> " . . . *it is only persons of a very ordinary sort, and of pusillanimous disposition, that sink long under a calamity of this nature . . . We seldom indulge long in depression and mourning, except when we think secretly that there is something very refined in it, and that it does us honour.*"

Wrong! Wrong! Her father was wrong, for grieve she must until her mind had exhausted its pain.

Autumn was passing fast. She sustained herself with her son and her hopes for the future, yet a light that had glowed in her had dimmed and she had lost her vision of happiness. It was Shelley's fault, it was all Shelley! But no, she too was to blame for her lack of will, for surely she should make her own decisions? Was it not her mother's mantra? She had trusted that day followed night and night followed day that calm followed the storm, she had trusted that all would be well. But no, it was not. And now she must pay! – They must all pay!

She began to think about Claire. Her desire to see Allegra was relentless, more so since the loss of Clara. She *must* see her daughter she said, if only for a brief few days, and insisted Shelley go find her and bring her to Este as promised. They would keep Allegra for a fortnight then return her safely to the consul. She pleaded it had to be done. They were all drifting away from each other now, lost in their own concerns. In their sadness they went about silent. Where could their sufferings go?

Wilmouse had cried endlessly, bewildered and hurt by the awful mystery of death. Shelley reached for the laudanum again and again, and went about in a dream. After some difficult letters and stumbling negotiations, he succeeded in bringing Allegra for a brief two weeks in Este. New found friends brought her gifts which she laughed and danced for. And she played with Wilmouse happily, who at three years old was now in his first pair of breeches and delighted to have her company. Claire took the child out walking and they visited ancient buildings which had once been significant in Este in medieval times. She pointed to major monuments and famous works of art, desperately hoping the two year old child might chance to marvel at their beauty and learn in some small way. But she marvelled only at the movements of her own body and her freshly awakening life, preferring to dance and listen to the echoes of her voice in the old buildings.

It was now the end of October and most vegetation in Italy was tired and dying. But the child delighted in the bloom of her own existence, running about, talking nonsense to statues, her small fists clenched with excitement whilst following Claire's instructions – "This way! – Now that!" The little girl was quite perfect and had intelligence well beyond her years, said Claire. So much of Byron was in her; at the core of her little soul she was all Byron and would accomplish wonderful things.

It was only a brief stay, but she ate well, slept well and laughed without care, and she cried when she had to say goodbye, holding Claire's hand as if she might never let it go. After the tears she went with Shelley quickly and disappeared in the autumn sunlight.

As October bowed out Byron wrote thanking Shelley for the safe return of his daughter to the Hoppners and also offering condolences over Clara's death, adding however how foolish it had been to have travelled so long with a baby in sweltering heat, words that left Mary even more gloomy and troubled.

'I'm glad she is safe and sound,' Frederick Llewellyn said to Bryon bringing him breakfast one morning. 'The days are shortening and winter will soon be upon us.' His wife had missed the little girl, he said. 'She liked to do up her hair. – I hope the child will be happy with the Hoppners.' Frederick Llewellyn frowned as he said it.

'My daughter has very good hair,' said Byron, passing his hands through his own thick dark locks. Yes, she was indeed a Byron. 'And quite right, we shall lose a lot of the daylight soon.' He narrowed his eyes thoughtfully. 'The darkness is sometimes depressing and reading by candlelight can often be difficult.'

Frederick moved from foot to foot uncomfortable. 'I do not like dark nights in Venice, your lordship,' he said, lowering his voice. I do not like them at all. The moonlight seems to laugh on the surface of the water.'

'Does it?' said Byron, raising his eyebrows curiously. 'Well now. It has plenty to laugh about of course.'

Llewellyn continued. 'My wife won't go out. The quiet footpaths are spooky.' Frederick shrugged. 'Mrs Llewellyn gets nervous, you see.'

'And you?'

Frederick Llewellyn shook his head. 'I like feeling scared. I usually read a good spooky book in winter, but the wife isn't keen. She never liked Newstead at night time. Too many ghosts at Newstead.'

'You will have to read *Frankenstein*,' said Byron with a laugh. 'It is a very spooky tale indeed, and written by Mrs Shelley. I remember when she first thought it up. It was a cold stormy night in Geneva, perfect for a tale of horror. Oh yes, it is certainly a tale of horror.' He leant back in his chair and folded his arms, remembering the night when the story of Frankenstein had first begun to take shape. 'If you are looking to read something scary, then there you have it. I am hoping for one or two copies from England shortly. You can borrow one once they arrive.'

'I should be most grateful your lordship,' said Frederick, deeply intrigued. He was putting out leaves for the monkeys which they snatched up quickly then sped up the stairs.

Byron's voice came low. His heavy brows drew together quickly. 'Oh, that book will set you on edge Frederick Llewellyn I promise you. The very idea of making a man from bits and pieces of corpses is chilling, then to have him spring into life with a spark of electricity right before your eyes, well . . .' He breathed in deeply and straightened. 'You can't get more frightening than that.'

'"Electricity?"' gasped Frederick, his eyes opening very wide. 'Electricity is magic. I know of a tree that was struck by lightning and split into two. Oh, a terrible sight it was. It fell to the ground in flames just like an evil omen.' Frederick pursed his lips at the thought.

'Interesting,' Byron murmured. 'And did you witness this phenomenon?'

'I did your lordship; it happened in the woods where I lived. I was only a boy at the time.'

Byron found a piece of paper, then forgetting his breakfast took up his pen and scribbled some words in silence. Then he lifted his head. Frederick Llewellyn still stood before him. 'So it would seem electricity gives life and takes it away . . .' Byron murmured abstractedly.

'If electricity can ever give life to the dead, that is,' murmured Llewellyn. 'I have to say I am doubtful . . . '

The monkeys leapt about Byron's table, enlivened by the urgent conversation. Byron shrugged his shoulders; *Frankenstein* was indeed a fascinating novel. 'That story is like no other,' he whispered. 'I wonder what happens after death. Might we return to life, or is everything over?'

'I hope the Hoppners take care of her,' said Frederick quietly.

'Allegra? – Oh yes, they'll take care of her.' For a moment or two they were silent

'They are not like us though,' Byron said thoughtfully. 'I mean easy of manner and letting her play as she likes.'

'No,' Frederick said, frowning. 'I have to say though, the child is very adventurous and it is . . .'

'I know,' said Byron, pouring himself more wine and sighing. 'But captivity could make her ill. They really must allow her to play. The mind is in charge of the body I think, unhappiness is a sure murderer and I want the child to be free. But enough now Llewellyn,' he said, waving him away. Then he leant back in his chair and for a while sat thoughtful.

It was a still and pleasant evening when Shelley returned to Este. Claire had gone to her room to rest, and Mary sat quietly with Wilmouse. The room was busy with shadows. 'Did everything go as it should?' she asked him anxiously. Shelley gazed down at the boy asleep by her feet. 'He didn't want me to move him,' she said. 'I tried to take him to bed but he cried. He can't understand that Clara is dead.'

'I don't suppose he can,' Shelley said quietly, taking off his things and sitting down. 'Neither can we.' For a moment or two they were silent. Shelley continued. 'Yes, all went according to plan.' His eyes rested on their son. 'You are right to let him lie near.'

Mary thought Shelley looked pale and even frailer than before. But his face held its usual timeless air of immortality, his skin shining and smooth as if he were carved from marble. His eyes though were glassy with a far away look she feared. Death beat relentlessly on the doors of his soul, she could almost hear it. 'Everything is slipping away,' she whispered.

'Do not be defeated, my love,' he said tiredly. 'We have both suffered.' He reached for her hand and kissed it, then glanced towards Claire's bedroom. 'Has Claire gone to bed?'

Mary nodded. For a moment or two they were absorbed in their own thoughts. 'I am afraid for Wilmouse,' she murmured. 'He would not eat today and is far too silent. Always I fear for his life. It is natural, of course. I have lost two children.'

'We should leave,' Shelley said sighing. 'Este is bad for us. We need to go somewhere different.'

'But is that wise?' said Mary, with a questioning look. 'The weather is cooler now, but we . . .'

They both felt helpless and haunted.

'I cannot cope very well just now,' Mary said quietly, rubbing her face with her hands. 'My mind is a mess. You are right; we must leave, but when? And what can we do about Claire, she is so unhappy.'

'She has much less to be depressed about than you, my dear,' he said, drawing her close. 'She does not have your strength, dear Mary. Her feelings always command her; but I have promised to take her to Naples and Rome. A change would energise us all.'

Mary drew a breath and straightened. They all felt lonely. Their lives just now were a mockery of what they had hoped for, and the awful misery in Shelley's eyes was hard to bear. He was often preoccupied as if he had a secret existence, another life he led without her knowledge, a sad one filled with despondency, the creative part of his soul, she decided where his mind grew mystified and baffled and he must bring his thoughts to poetry to relieve his passion. There were days he seemed absent, seized by something other. They were close and intimate and yet they were also separate, she did not absolutely know him. Together they guarded Wilmouse closely and were both anxious for his welfare, and it was she who Shelley turned to when voicing his most serious concerns. Though she saw through their glances there were parts of him Claire knew better. She shuddered inwardly at that, and didn't dare think of the feelings the two of them might share. But she loved him more than Claire did, of that she was certain. Claire loved Byron and wanted him, but he did not love her back.

The journey to Rome was tedious and they all felt weak. Mary feared madness lay in wait for her should she succumb to the worst of her fears, it was important to try to keep sane. She held her son tightly; her heart burning with dread, for vengeance knew no boundaries and might make its way across continents.

It was late November when they finally arrived in Rome, and they were met with miserable weather. Most of the way, Wilmouse had been silent and only Mary's rhymes and songs had kept him from sleeping. Shelley was ill and complained he felt nauseas, but he'd managed to find them a decent hotel where they rested and renewed their strength. Mary's nerves were raw and many painful thoughts plagued her – Shelley's whispers to Claire, the glances she didn't understand, baby Clara's untimely death, but mostly her son's silence. It was not like him to be silent! What had happened to his essence, his vital curiosity? Her body felt clumsy in its sadness as if it were separate from her being, but suffering had to be endured, she decided, and everyone's pain was different; no-one could truly share it.

There was an excellent view of the city from their rooms and that morning Shelley sat looking out of the window. There was a lot of activity outside. Excavations were taking place though it was raining, and the ground was unsafe in places, they would have to take care walking out. And just as Byron had said, men were working like slaves, and it surprised him to see that indeed they were chained together. Rome was a shambles just now. Much of the city's Imperial past was still majestic and beautiful whilst other parts were broken and abandoned, cattle grazed in the grounds of ancient monuments while women gossiped in the rain beneath their umbrellas.

'The workmen look filthy,' said Shelley, grimacing with dismay. 'And they're exhausted. Will we never get away from bondage?'

Mary smiled at his words. 'We are in bondage to fate,' she whispered. Some days she felt hidden inside herself like a hunted animal, it was a strange and disturbing sensation. But she was thankful they'd made it safely to Rome and that her son still breathed as before. The sense of impending doom however would not leave her, and Claire's constant hysterics set her on edge.

The rain drew to a halt and their thoughts turned to walking as sunshine burst through the window. 'Why not enjoy the sights,' cried Shelley clapping his hands. He turned to Mary. 'What do you say, my dear?'

Mary sat on the chaise longue with the boy. The sun had reached her and glowed on her hair. 'I should like it myself – very much,' she said hopefully. She turned to the child who sat playing with a toy. 'What do you say, Wilmouse? How do you feel?'

'I am well, Mama!' he cried, sitting up straight.

'Excellent!' said Shelley. 'And so you are, my boy. You are as well as can be.'

Suddenly the child was bold and strong and Mary looked on with wonder as he ran straight to the door and tried to pull it open.

As they went about the city the old stone walls echoed with the sound of their footsteps and voices. From time to time, the boy grew weak and reached for his father's arms.

'But why did we come?' Claire said irritably, walking heavily beside them. 'You knew he wasn't well.'

'I thought the fresh air would be good for him,' Mary said meekly. They were now returning to the villa. Shelley carried the boy on his shoulders a while. 'He'll soon feel better,' said Mary.

'I do Mama, I feel better already!' he cried, always concerned for his mother. And he asked his father about the broken statues all about them. The truth seemed absurd but Shelley's simple stories satisfied his questioning mind. But Mary's faith in herself and Percy was shattered. Just like the broken statues she felt she was being dismantled, broken into bits and pieces. She didn't dare think of the future and wanted to obliterate the past. But what of the present, who was she and how should she live? She couldn't continue to live as she did just now with Claire and Percy; something must change.

29

Towards Naples

And again the boy fell ill. 'Mama, why must I always be sick?' he asked anxiously. His eyes were shot with blood and he was pale and frightened.

'I should never have taken you walking,' she said, and a flood of desperate feelings came to her. 'Today you must stay in bed.' She was weak with weariness. And the guilt rose up in her again that she had taken him out after rain. Was it not damp? Was the damp not dangerous?

His father paced about the floor, frowning. Shelley was in a quandary. He could not write; he could do nothing. Mary pointed to the window. 'Percy, will you open it a little and let us smell some of the morning.'

Shelley did as requested then sat down. 'Do go out,' said Mary seeing him frustrated. 'Have you not promised Claire, she would see as much of Rome as was possible in the time we are here, you saw so little the other day. Wilmouse will soon recover.' But her voice was low and distressed.

'I cannot leave you,' said Shelley despondently. 'We have suffered the loss of two of our children; I cannot indulge myself like that.' He threw out his arms dejectedly, tired with despair. He could not think and he missed his baby daughter. He even missed the noise of her crying, he said, though it had often stopped him from working. 'The empty cot reminds,' he said woefully. He reached for the little silk dress resting on the chaise longue and held it close to his chest.

'She had such a pretty face,' he whispered. 'Her hair was beginning to grow; I loved the colour, it was very like yours . . .'

Mary replied with silence. Tears came into her eyes. Along with her concern for Wilmouse, she could not cope with Shelley's emotional needs which weighed heavy along with her own. And he was reaching for his bottle of laudanum far too often.

Claire sat huddled in a chair biting her knuckles and making strange little sounds like the sounds of a wounded animal, whispering of ways she might procure Allegra from the Hoppners, some of them silly and dangerous. Mary warned her that the Hoppners were powerful people and she might land in serious trouble if she tried to steal Allegra in the night. But Mary knew it was just another drama and that the Hoppners home would be guarded. Percy sat staring at space. Both Percy and Claire were elsewhere in their minds and Mary was forced to take charge as ever. Her son's health was unpredictable, he was full of energy one minute, next he wanted to sleep. They had been in Rome four days and might have spent their time more productively had the boy been in better health; today he had a headache and complained of pains in his stomach. Again, she addressed her husband. ' . . . And besides, my love, you will surely benefit from the exercise,' Mary continued. She looked at Claire for support. 'Please persuade him, my dear.'

Claire spoke slowly, as if from the depths of her thoughts. 'I don't think I should. Someone might come with a message.'

'What sort of message?' asked Shelley, giving her a curious look.

'A message about Allegra,' she said irritably. 'I need to know things.'

'But *I* shall be here,' said Mary. She glanced outside. The sun streamed in through the window. 'What good will it do if we all stay indoors being miserable.'

'The weather is excellent just now,' said Shelley bracing himself. He went to his son and placed his hand on his forehead. 'You are hot,' he frowned. 'But Mama is right, for are we to stand about all day like this? Will it not make you feel worse?'

'It will, Papa,' the boy said weakly. 'I am sad when I can't get better and it stops you enjoying the sunshine.'

'You'll be better very soon,' smiled his father. 'It is normally the way. You set us a heavy task, my boy with your health. Why, you are in and out of it fast as a shadow. Claire and I will return to you with much fresher faces.'

Claire looked thoughtful. 'But Mary, what will you do while we've gone?' She gazed at her sympathetically.

'I shall write,' Mary said firmly. She wanted to write in her journal.

Claire looked at her concerned but reached for her cape and bonnet. 'We'll do as you say, you are always so wise, my dear. – Percy, come, we must obey.'

Shelley nodded and donned his frock coat and hat. 'Let us explore then Claire, for we shall soon be away to Naples!'

'I wonder if the artist will be painting again by the water,' said Claire, as they went to the door. 'He captures the mood of the city so well.'

'He certainly does,' said Shelley, relieved to be putting on his coat. 'It is very clever work. If the picture is finished, would you like me to buy it?'

Claire shook her head. 'No, no, not at all. I'd like to do some painting myself though sometime. I was good at it once. Mama threw away my easel.' She glanced at Mary resentfully. 'It was her new life, you see, she wanted me to help in the shop. Mama is good at living; I am not so good at it myself.' She stared downwards looking sad.

'We must cross the Pontine Marshes tomorrow,' Mary said quietly. 'They call them "malaria marshes".' She chilled at the thought and frowned. 'There is something quite sinister about them.'

'What?' said Claire, abstractedly.

'"The malaria marshes",' Mary repeated. 'We must cross them tomorrow. They are very much feared.'

'How horrible,' said Claire wincing. 'And what else do you have in mind for us Percy. I think of myself as a very brave woman, but really – marshes and malaria?'

'Don't be afraid,' said Percy, straightening. 'All will be well. Our driver tells me he has been through those marshes many times. And I can always assist him if necessary.'

Claire smiled wryly at Mary. 'Does Percy mean he will help the driver haul us out of the marsh if the carriage gets stuck? I rather doubt he has the strength.' Mary knew Claire had a grievance against Shelley; there was something she wanted that he could not give. Mary thought it might be love. She could scarcely bear it when Claire stomped about the house, thumping down into chairs and sulking over things he'd said. She had lost her pride by throwing herself at Byron, now she was difficult and weak.

But they would have to make their way through the marshes and Mary felt concerned. The area had turned into swampland because water from the mountains couldn't find anywhere to go. The territory was forest in the main and dark muddy pools, few people lived there. But she'd heard there were ways of getting through for experienced drivers and Percy had troubled to find one. She felt suddenly cold. If only she didn't worry so much, she thought crossly. She was always imagining something terrible would happen. Claire didn't worry for long. She would moan or have a fit of hysterics but then she would be back laughing and entertaining Shelley. Mary pitied her in a way; her manner was often childish, though she wondered if Shelley liked the contrast between her and Claire, her own serious nature might otherwise overwhelm him, he enjoyed Claire's flamboyance and flirtatious behaviour and she doubted she could ever have captivated Byron as Claire had, however briefly.

As she thought about it all, seeing them both go off, she wondered if Claire's kind of love might be a better love than her own. Her own could be dark and inflexible. Her stepmother had said she was stubborn but she believed she was single-minded and reliable. She was Mary Wollstonecraft's daughter and understood her mother's nature from her writings. There were times however when Claire had made her feel inadequate; she recalled her laughing freely with Byron at the Villa Diodati while acting out Frankenstein's monster, though at the same time insisting Mary was a wonderful writer. Yes, there was always that, Claire praised her work and did not begrudge her the admiration that came from Shelley. She recalled the night when *Frankenstein* had seeded in her mind, and she thought of Doctor Polidori, a very attractive man, a man she might have taken as a lover had the holiday lasted longer . . . Love was an exciting phenomenon; it had its own being and went entirely its own way.

It was another day and a half before Wilmouse showed signs of improvement. That morning he was bright and alert, trying to button on his boots and saying he felt much better. They were all delighted with his progress. He was a good and fascinating child. His health though was still unstable and between his bouts of walking and highly strung behaviour he fell on the floor and slept. They went with the way of his moods, for there was much to do as they set about packing for Naples. He ate and slept very well, but Mary was always conscious of the easy way he fell ill, and she must watch him carefully, feel the heat of his brow and listen to his shallow breathing in fear of it suddenly ceasing, but he constantly fought to restore his more potent spirits. Setting out for Naples, he plied his father with questions.

'Where are we going Papa?' he asked as the coach rattled on.

'To Naples!' Shelley said jubilantly. 'You will like it. Napoli è meraviglioso! It is a very old place. What's more the tomatoes are splendid. I know how you like tomatoes.'

'And I hear the wine is excellent,' added Claire.

Looking out of the window, Shelley shook his head and frowned. 'Ruins, ruins, so many ruins? There is something wrong with people radically. They always want to destroy things.'

'But why?' asked the boy, his eyes dark and serious.

'A very important question . . .' sighed Shelley. 'I only wish I knew. People have wars, you see. There are greedy kings and queens who want everything for themselves.'

'People like breaking things too,' said Claire. 'They build things and then they break them.'

'How strange,' the boy said frowning.

Shelley gave a loud sigh. 'You might wonder about it forever.' He changed the subject and pointed to the mountains. 'They say there are goddesses up there, living at the tops of those peaks. I am told they make healing potions.'

'Perhaps they could make me better?' the boy said hopefully.

'I can't say I know where they are,' sighed Shelley, 'or I'd take you. They belong to stories, dear Wilmouse, not life as we live it.'

'And is there a difference?' asked the child. He gazed at his father and waited.

'I'm not sure . . .' said Shelley. 'Maybe not.'

For several minutes they were silent. The boy, still thoughtful, turned to his mother and leant against her arm. Mary smiled and passed her fingers through his hair. 'He questions everything,' she said. 'It is the way of intelligent children.'

'And we shouldn't tell them lies,' Claire said frowning. 'It's wrong to fill their minds with falsehoods.'

'Life is full of fabrications,' Mary said, straightening. 'He enjoys his papa's stories.'

'Not half as much as his father does,' Claire said crossly.

The boy slept against her arm, and Mary thought about Naples, its beauty, its sufferings, its history. She reached for the guide book beside her and read through some of the pages.

. . . By the end of the 17th century, Naples had had some 300,000 inhabitants and was home to all kinds of artists, philosophers and writers. There had been a brief revolution in 1647 and a subsequent Neapolitan Republic but it hadn't lasted long, the old Spanish rule was very quickly re-established. Half of the people however had died just a few years later from an outbreak of bubonic plague. People still spoke of it in fear. It was a part of their past they did not want to forget. The elderly in particular talked of ancestors who'd died from the curse, for the plague had caused terrible misery and some believed it wandered their bloodline. But the whole of Europe had been plagued yet further by the French revolution, and in 1799 the French army had subjugated Naples and formed a republic. But the old order came back into being just as soon as Napoleon was defeated. After Napoleon's departure, Italy had been left quite dazed, but the people had found new energy and the Italian soul had reasserted itself triumphantly. They made new laws;

people talked about culture with passion, about artists and musicians, greatness, talent, would be recognised and applauded. Italy would reach for the stars! The Italian soul was resourceful.

Mary peered out at the sky, that great expanse of universe she didn't understand, and she tightened her arm around her son. He was shaking slightly and they were yet to cross the marshes . . . She braced herself and took deep breaths, she could not weaken. She was a wife and mother. She had to be strong. As she looked at the sleeping boy a great flood of anguish went through her and tears fell down her face. Percy's way of life had consequences. But he didn't seem to think about that. Sometimes he sat for hours labouring over his verse and probing the depths of his mind for beauty, passion and liberty which he believed he could find through the power of imagination. Perhaps it was possible, but there was a great deal he gambled on too.

They crossed the Pontine Marshes, the driver commanding his horses through the frayed edges of the road, the marshland snatching at the wheels of the coach which clattered defiantly onwards over mud and stones, passing soldiers on foot and on horseback and the odd savage looking wanderer. After a while on a smooth stretch of road they stopped and got out to take the air. The child slept on in the coach. Seated on a dry patch of grass Mary found her journal and scribbled down some notes.

> *"Cross the Pomptine Marshes. . . . There are no houses or villages to be seen in the whole extent if you except 3 miserable post houses – the people you meet have all a savage appearance – they appear to gain their livelihood by sporting or robbing when they dare – We meet many solders as patroles both on foot & on horseback."*

It was a good fifteen minutes before they got back in the carriage. Further on the road, they stopped at the Riviera di Chiaia, a beautiful esplanade on the coast of the Gulf of Naples, a place with a bay and marvellous views of the mountains. The air was clear and sweet and it pleased Mary to breathe it, knowing her son breathed it too. How he needed good air, neither too hot nor too cold, extremes were bad in all things.

Everywhere was golden and splendid, the light so bright, Mary thought the mountains might be heaven. Shelley found them lodgings where they ate and rested, and in the evening they sat and talked. The child was well, Claire was in better spirits and Mary had resolved to put her best foot forward. The night fell softly about them and they escaped a while from their concerns, telling each other stories and singing to the child. 'Sono molto felice!' Shelley cried out to the darkness. 'Sono molto felice!

Next day was a day for exploring. The avenue where they lived curved round to a causeway which led to the Castel dell'ovo, a famous historical site. It had taken its name from a story about Virgil, the poet, who had once placed a magic egg in the bedrock of the castle hoping it would bring him good luck. Mary smiled hearing Percy's rendition of the tale, the child walking beside him. 'Oh,' she murmured suddenly, turning and catching her breath. 'Here, in Naples! I can't believe it . . .'

'What?' he asked frowning. 'Is something the matter?'

She leant towards him. 'I think we are being followed,' she whispered. Glancing behind she saw the shape of a woman, carrying a baby.

"Followed"?' he said, suddenly nervous. They both turned slowly, someone was definitely there but they could not see beyond the blurry haze of sunshine.

'I think a woman is trailing us,' she whispered.

The boy ran ahead to join Claire.

'Surely, you are wrong,' he said tensely.

'She is following us, I know it,' Mary said flatly.

'No, no, you are mistaken, my dear,' he said; walking on calmly. 'It is merely a trick of sunlight.'

Mary put her hand on his arm. 'She knows I have seen her.'

He was annoyed and curious. 'Oh, Mary, why would somebody follow us?'

'I don't know. She is carrying a baby . . . I have seen her before. I have thought to speak with her, but she turns and is gone within minutes. – She has followed us from Este.'

'"From Este?"' he said, panic rising in his voice. 'But why?' He turned again and screwed up his eyes to look through the sunlight.

'Do you think I've invented her?' Mary said curtly.

'Not at all, it's just that it's odd.' He smiled awkwardly.

For a moment or two they walked on thoughtful.

'She's had plenty of time to approach us if she wants to make contact,' Percy said dismissively.

'She was carrying the baby before.'

He gazed at the floor as they walked.

'Is there something she wants to tell you?' Mary asked firmly.

He gasped astonished. 'I rather doubt it is me she is after, I have no idea who she is.' He pulled off his hat and wiped his brow with his handkerchief. Then he glanced at Mary annoyed. 'You saw her before and never said?'

'I'm surprised you haven't seen her yourself,' Mary said calmly. 'I think you should talk to her.'

'Do you indeed?' he said crossly. He braced himself, tense and irate.

'Perhaps she lives on the streets,' Mary suggested. 'I suspect she is poor.'

They turned again, now they could see her, a woman holding a child.

'I suppose I should see what she wants . . .' he said finally, straightening his frock coat. As the sunshine fell into shadow Mary saw that she stopped as he approached, and she could hear him protesting as the woman thrust the child, wrapped in a shawl, before him. He put out the flat of his hand and after several minutes the woman went off cursing. Shelley stood silent, his hands covering his face then slowly returned to Mary.

'I do not know her,' he said flatly, as they carried on walking. He glanced at Mary sideways. 'My dear, I don't like your look.' His tone was angry. 'These women, you know, think Englishmen can take their child on as easily as winking. In point of fact, I talked about it with Byron last time we met. What you say is probably right, she has followed us for quite some time. I sort of sensed she was about.'

'What – in Venice?'

'Yes, I sort of *felt* her. These things happen.' He pulled his frock coat closer about him.

'Well, she was very much there today.' Mary said firmly. 'I did not dream her and I did not dream her before. Neither did I sort of sense her, Percy. I saw her hanging about. I decided she wanted money but I had far too many cares of my own to give her much thought.'

Shelley continued talking. ' . . . A lot of children in Italy are abandoned by their fathers, you see, or their fathers don't know of their existence. The women wander with their babies, hoping that someone will take them away and raise them. It was a girl child, Mary. Would you have liked me to take her?'

Mary smiled. Shelley was indeed generous, even to the point of falling into serious debt for the sake of others. But he could not swallow up the cares of the world. And he did not have the wherewithal either. 'No, I would not,' she said finally, confused and frustrated. 'Why would you even think it? Anyway, she's gone.'

'I doubt we have seen the last of her,' he sighed. His eyes burned with anxiety. 'She was intent on me taking that baby.' He wrung his hands and stared stonily ahead.

'But she can't make you have it,' Mary said, glancing back and deeply concerned. The woman was nowhere in sight, but why had she chosen to follow them?

'She was trying to say the child was mine,' he said irritably. 'We've had a few young women help us out and . . .'

She turned to him quickly. 'And ...?'

'She doesn't say it's hers, either,' he added, dismissing her curt reply. 'She might be being paid by somebody's wealthy wife to dispense with a child. That sort of thing happens all the time in Italy. She might well have sent her to pursue me.'

She gave him a curious look. 'But she doesn't know who you are?'

He bit his lip and frowned. 'She could soon find out. I am Percy Bysshe Shelley, am I not, son of Sir Timothy Shelley, who was son of Sir Bysshe, 1st Baronet of Castle Goring . . . Word gets round. I really don't know what else I can say, my dear. But come now, let's enjoy our day.'

'What if she continues to follow us? What will you do? Will you talk to her again?'

Shelley watched his feet as they walked. 'What are you suggesting?'

Claire came hurrying with the child and they all walked on together, but Mary and Shelley were morose.

The new misfortune had put a stop to Shelley's work. Next day he sat pensive, grimacing to himself and staring about abstractedly. The least sound that morning made him start and Mary feared for his mood. He easily got lost in despair. And he feared it. It cut him off from the world, he said, from everything. Who was he; she asked herself, this brilliant man she loved, this man who felt like part of her very self. His thoughts were quick and colourful, more luminous than those of other men. His eyes were bright and questioning, his opinions forceful and firm. And she knew that he needed her just as she needed him.

Claire was busy, carrying out various tasks though her red rimmed eyes told of her state of mind. Mary still wondered about the stranger who had occupied her dreams through the night, dark, mysterious, and threatening, filling her mind with questions. Who was she? Who was the father of the child? Italy! Oh, Italy, what horrors it had brought her. And Claire wanted Allegra. She would not give up; she was a fighter and would always battle on.

'I've written to Byron in Venice, and I've asked him about Allegra,' said Shelley. 'I've told him we won't be in Naples very long and are set on returning to Rome. It will be better for William's health. I know of an excellent doctor there and I rather fear we might need him.'

Mary watched him biting his lip and staring about fearful. They all agreed that returning to Rome was the best course of action, Percy would get to see Byron, and Claire might get to see Allegra. They each rested in the hope of better things to come.

Mary gazed at her son. Each month he grew bigger and would soon need schooling. Boys always went to school. Everything about her was at one with her son's being; he was the very core of her existence. She had come to feel lost from Shelley. And they would soon have another child.

30

Back To Rome

'I thought it would take us much longer to get here,' said Claire, as they started unpacking their things. 'The weather was good and everything went well.'

Shelley looked hopeful and Mary was glad; Rome was fertile territory for his prolific imagination. Here he was, Shelley the crusader, the reformer, the lover. His mind flew in many directions and the old city excited him. The weather had been kind and he had found them a good place to stay. But neither Mary nor Claire felt calm enough to enjoy it. One place was much like another for them both just now. Mary had closed her eyes on her own existence, consumed as she was with preserving her son, whilst Claire still longed for Allegra.

Sir Timothy hadn't been well and it had given them food for thought. Shelley had accrued a multitude of debts, no doubt expecting to be rich as a Pharaoh soon, Claire had said wryly. Mary's main concern was to guard William carefully and see he wasn't chilled or overdressed. Shelley went out to find a nursemaid to assist them while she and Claire went about their tasks in a cloud of confused silence.

It was hard to get Mary out of doors and she watched the child keenly. He was used to his mother's constant attention, which itself seemed like a sickness for he now gave a heartfelt cry if she left him and could not settle. One day Shelley suggested Claire stay back to take care of him whilst he and Mary went into Rome together, for the Emperor of Austria was visiting the city for Holy Week. 'There will be music, singing and dancing!' he said, trying hard to sound cheerful. 'Mama is in need of amusement, is she not? How lovely it would be for her to see the celebrations. So much has been bad for us lately; I believe we are due a little respite.' He talked on quickly, the boy's eyes curious and dreamy. 'Claire will sit beside you and give you a lesson in drawing. You know how you like drawing.' He placed the flat of his hand on the child's forehead. 'Not too hot today,' he said cautiously. 'But best if you stay inside.'

The disappointed child looked tearful. Mary tried to console him. Shelley went out with Claire in the main; it would be good to spend time with him alone in the city, and she needed to exercise her limbs and allow her heart to experience a livelier rhythm. Claire had already brought her drawing things over to the bedside.

'Take care of Mama,' the boy said weakly to his father. 'And let me know what you see.'

'I'll make a list!' laughed Shelley. 'I shall be taking my notebook and pencil Wilmouse in case I'm inspired.'

'I doubt you'll be inspired,' said Claire, tossing her hair. 'You wouldn't get Byron within a million miles of all that. You'll be back before long.'

Mary felt tense wandering the sycophantic crowds. And Shelley was hardly inspired, with dogs barking round his feet and people shouting and laughing. And Claire would undoubtedly grow bored of amusing Wilmouse, thought Mary, for all her thoughts were of Allegra. The crowds were tiresome and loud and her concern for her son felt like a serpent winding itself about her trying to squeeze her to death.

'I need to return to Wilmouse,' she said defeated. 'You stay here if you like. I can make my own way.' There was noise and clatter all around her and she put her hands to her ears. 'I am rather dull nowadays,' she said loudly. 'But the sight of all these festivities is somehow offensive.' Children ran about between them, acting out the manners of the rich and poor respectively in the way that children did.

'I was wrong to bring you,' said Shelley annoyed with himself and irritable.

The strange high pitched sound of his voice rising above the crowds was thin and menacing. Whether he returned with her or not, she would hold with the mastery of her self. 'And I should never have let you persuade me,' she called. They turned and began to walk back.

They returned to find Claire seething with anger. A letter had arrived from Mrs Hoppner. Allegra was sick and Mrs Hoppner had taken to criticising Claire, accusing her of aberrant behaviour and calling her a bad mother. 'How dare she?' Claire pleaded. 'And what has happened to Allegra? It isn't enough to say she is ill, what is the matter?' Claire was practically a stranger, Mary protested, when had the Hoppners formed such terrible impressions? Had Byron been scheming to defile Claire's name? It was certainly possible. Claire maintained there was nothing the Hoppners could say that would justify such bitter words for she'd always been steady in character and not a single day passed by without she did not think of her daughter. Was it not true she pleaded, what was it they held against her? Nothing, it was all Byron! And what was wrong with Allegra …

Later that evening, Claire sat on a chair in the corner, her fists clenched in her lap. It was almost dusk. Percy sat silent his tall gaunt body bent to the table as he scratched away with his pen. The child lay on the chaise longue sleeping, Mary beside him. It was a still and intense atmosphere. Mary felt she was in a sort of waiting, seated by her son with a candle, waiting for a kind of safety when she might breathe more easily and relax. She was the carer, the organiser and felt somehow responsible for Claire and Percy for they were both wild spirits, though she felt she'd lost sight of the guiding star that was her mother and each day she sought to find her again through her writings. Her pregnancy was proceeding just as it should, but her son had weakened and she prayed some minis- tering spirit might somehow assist them. Fear crept through her as she gazed at his pale features. Oh, the loneliness of it, the sheer helpless loneliness she must yield to. 'Not again!' she murmured, fighting her desire to slumber as the candlelight flickered about him and Time took possession of her fear.

'I am here,' said Shelley, suddenly beside her. He kissed the top of her head. 'Do get some sleep, my love. It is well past midnight. Let me take over.' His words were slow and weary.

'He looks so pale,' she said, reluctant to leave him.

'I know,' Shelley said softly. 'But he lives. I can hear him breathing. Please go to bed.'

Mary got up and went to the bedroom where she found he'd been working on *Prometheus*. Pages of the play were scattered about his desk, the writing careless and scrawled. He'd been trying to write, but they both knew death was imminent for their son.

At the break of day there came a terror stricken cry. It was a cry Shelley had never made before and it pierced her. She rose fast and they both watched horrified as their boy convulsed again and again. The end came quickly. Shelley fell into a chair and wept. Mary entered the terrible silence trembling. Lifting her child she held his cheek against her own, her eyes streaming with tears. Claire slept on strangely unaware. Why should they wake her, what could she do? No one could help their beloved Wilmouse now. The doctor would come to certify another dead child; he could not make him live however fast he came to the villa. 'The marshes,' whispered Mary. 'It was the marshes.'

Dawn light flooded the room. The statues outside would soon claim the glowing morning, people would hold their normal excited conversations as they ventured about the city. It was June, 1819, early summer, but there would be no summer for their son. Only the cold dark earth awaited him. Malaria had claimed him for its own.

William Shelley, better known as Wilmouse, was buried at the Cimitero Degli Inglesi, the Protestant Cemetery. As the tiny coffin was lowered into the ground, his father murmured

> *'Where art thou, my gentle child?*
> *Let me think thy spirit feeds,*
> *With its life intense and mild,*
> *The love of living leaves and weeds . . .'*

262

Mary felt spirited away with her boy. The musty smell of the cemetery would not leave her. And she became very afraid, afraid of herself; afraid of her own thoughts and what was in them. But she would soon have another child, and she did not want bad feelings to pass into the foetus, for she had heard and read it could happen. 'I must rest,' she murmured to Shelley. 'I hate myself now. Could any mother be anything but despicable, having made such terrible choices?'

'Hush, hush, my love,' he said. 'What a monstrous idea. We've been most unfortunate. It is all too terrible to speak of.' He fed her eggs and bread, and she ate like a child as he took the food to her mouth. She seemed to have lost her will. Why was she living, what for? Would there be more of the same? In a fog of despair, they departed from Rome and moved to Liverno on the western coast of Tuscany, there the winters were mild and the summers had warm balmy days. But sadness did not leave them. And neither did Claire.

Time took hold of its own, and Mary's love for the child within her sustained her whilst her new surroundings in Tuscany provided respite. The blood rushed up into her features and new life flooded her being. As night followed day and day followed night, she felt better. She wanted to discover her old radiant self, for could she not restore it? She talked about happy times as a girl in Dundee, the mountains and the sea and she talked about her childhood with her father. But Claire stayed morose and silent for not a word had she heard about Allegra.

The people at Liverno gazed at them curiously. – The tall young man with the staring intense eyes, the fidgety woman who glanced at them nervously, and the heavily pregnant one with the auburn hair. They must have looked a strange trio thought Mary. People would wonder who they were and why they had come to Liverno. There was something the matter, for why did one of the women constantly fidget and the other always hide her face? Mary smiled to herself; they would think Percy a libertino, living a libertine lifestyle, but let them think what they liked, she felt victorious that happiness still came to find her, and she hoped for a better future.

But she still felt distanced from Shelley and wondered how to address it. That morning as he worked at the table, a page of his writing fell to the floor and she bent to retrieve it, catching her breath with surprise as she read through what he had written.

> *"My dearest Mary, wherefore hast thou gone,*
> *And left me in this dreary world alone?*
> *Thy form is here indeed—a lovely one—*
> *But thou art fled, gone down a dreary road*
> *That leads to Sorrow's most obscure abode.*
> *For thine own sake I cannot follow thee*
> *Do thou return for mine."*

She read it again, bruised and confused. Oh, such a sad poem. "Gone", what did he mean? Is that what he thought? He carried on writing absorbed and she made no sound as she replaced the writing on the floor where she had found it and returned to her chair. Had she really neglected him so badly? She sat for some minutes thinking. Perhaps she had. – But ah, did he know that *he* had failed *her*? Did he even consider it? He had failed Harriet and his children, he had failed her and theirs, did he care about that, about the vigorous ways of reality that twisted love into the ugliest of forms. Or were such issues concealed from him somehow, until they came of a sudden like a great storm of truth. Was that how it happened? She knew she was the mainstay in his life; she was there to support him, and would. She wanted to be with him always, to help him nurture his genius. – Oh yes, she had gone in a way, but had he not seen how she was trying so hard to return? It had hurt her to read his poem. He wrote such beautiful poetry, always such wonderful poetry, but whisperings about him had spread from England to the continent now. In Italy life was easier than in England and morals were less severe, but he had abandoned Harriet, his wife, he had left his children and run off with a girl of sixteen, and Harriet in her misery had killed herself. He could not get away from all that and people condemned him for it. But Mary reasoned Shelley had acted from the very best of his feelings, which he believed to be the true way of nature – poetry brought feelings to life, he said, poetry was their fruit, bitter or sweet as it was. Should that fruit be rotten to the core was it not the fault of life itself and the wanton chaos it delivered?

'My dear Mary,' he began, one wet afternoon finding her silent and pensive. 'That missive there on the table has numbed you out of your wits.' He glanced at the letter on a low table beside her.

'His heart has grown cold,' she said miserably. 'It means nothing to Papa that I have lost three children. I asked for a little sympathy, a few kind words that is all, but no, he sends me a sermon and he only talks about his debts.' She bent her head and sighed. 'He is afraid of the debtor's prison.'

Percy looked at her straight and sighed. 'He is indeed. And he thinks I will help keep him out of it.' He drew up a chair and braced himself, his eyes serious. 'I will, of course. Have I not always done so?' He clasped his hands in his lap. 'But dearest, why don't *you* help *me*?'

She was slow to reply.

'What do you mean?' she said finally. 'You have freedom Percy. You come and go as you wish. I ask no questions. I trust you. How can you say I don't help you?'

He answered quietly. 'You distance yourself like your father does. But your concerns are mine as well, are they not?'

She did not speak.

His features tightened. 'I have to say I shall withdraw from you though if you do not see that I too am affected by the deaths of our children and . . .'

She saw that he looked impatient. 'But wait . . .' she murmured. 'There are things you don't tell me.'

He looked at her again, waiting.

Her voice came in a whisper. 'I cannot forget her.'

'Forget who?' he faltered, turning away quickly.

'You know who I mean,' she said, watching his fingers working together nervously. 'The woman we left in Naples, the one with the baby. Perhaps there is something I should know?'

For a moment or two they were silent. 'Goodness,' he sighed. 'Why do you worry about a stranger?'

'That's if we *did* leave her . . .' she continued. 'I wonder if she still follows us. Perhaps she is close. – Oh, how she haunts us.'

'Why does she torment you,' he enquired sharply.

She drew herself up. 'We once had a maid who you talked with a lot. – I recall you sent her away.' She braced herself and pulled on her shawl. 'Why did you send her away?'

'She was troublesome.'

For several minutes they were silent. '"Troublesome", I see' she said quietly. 'You argued with the woman carrying the baby. Why did you argue, so passionately, out there in the open air? Did you know her?'

He rose and paced about the floor, wiping his brow with his handkerchief. 'Oh Mary, the maid I have found us here is excellent. And Claire agrees. You will like her. She has rooms of her own nearby. Surely you can see you are cared for.'

'No, I cannot,' she said firmly. 'You and Claire care only for yourselves. My father talks only of debt, not my needs. No-one considers my needs.' She picked up Godwin's letter and shook it in front of him. 'Read it, read it once more, then tell me if you think he loves me!'

He sighed and read it again.

"You were formed by nature to belong to the best of these classes, but you seem to be shrinking away, and voluntarily enrolling yourself among the worst.

Above all things, I entreat you, do not put the miserable delusion on yourself, to think, there is something fine, and beautiful, and delicate, in giving yourself up, and agreeing to be nothing.

Remember too that, at first, your nearest connections may pity you in this state, yet that when they see you fixed in selfishness and ill humour , and regardless of the happiness of every one else, they will finally cease to love you, and scarcely learn to endure you ..."

'So there you are,' she said irritably, as he placed it back on the table. 'He cannot endure me. No, he cannot bear the thought of me!' She covered her face with her hands. 'I won't go out this week. I shall take my food and rest, but I won't walk out. I am soon to have a child and I wish to feel calm.'

'You must do as you wish,' he sighed, straightening his clothes and reaching for his hat. 'If you want to be depressed, I cannot join you, my dear. I am all too easily affected. There is life to be lived and I intend to live it while I can.' With that, he left.

Alone in the lodgings, Mary made herself busy. She wrote in her journal and read from Richardson's *Clarissa*, the tale of a woman whose quest for virtue was constantly thwarted by her family, a nouveau riche set of people, preoccupied with trying to elevate themselves while obsessively trying to control her. The consequences of excessive aspirations had never been considered by the Harlowe's, and their daughter, Clarissa, had fallen victim to vice and finally committed suicide. '*Death, death!*' Mary whispered. 'Oh death, I know you well!' She had exposed herself to its terror so long it was like part of her living flesh. She read out loud from Clarissa;

> *"And what after all, is death?? 'Tis but a cessation from mortal life; 'tis but the finishing of an appointed course; the refreshing inn after a fatiguing journey; the end of a life of cares and troubles; and, if happy, the beginning of a life of immortal happiness."*

Clarissa's pain and depression had turned into self destruction. 'It is so soon done,' murmured Mary, closing the book. 'We are easily turned into victims of our own suffering.'

When Shelley and Claire returned, Claire went off to her room without speaking, her mind lost in abstraction.

'She complains she hasn't seen Allegra since April,' said Shelley, slumping into a chair. 'I thoroughly understand how she feels. She has a right to see her daughter. Byron should sort something out.' He rubbed his face wearily.

'And why doesn't he?' Mary said softly.

'Oh Mary, come, come. I think you know the answer. We are such a bad lot, you see, all of us.'

'Ah yes,' said Mary haughtily. 'And who is Lord Byron to judge?'

'I am far too tired to deal with it,' Shelley said at last. 'And Claire will not visit him herself, for she fears to leave you alone.'

Mary looked at him annoyed. 'Claire needn't worry about me,' she said curtly. 'I can manage quite well without her. In fact, I would like her to go away. I find her quite wearisome at times.' She shrugged at the thought.

'How cruel,' Shelley said quietly. 'Your tongue is becoming quite loose, my dear, it does not suit you. And I don't wish to argue. I am a little unwell at present, but I shall soon be better. Good fresh air and exercise will do it, always fresh air and exercise.'

For a moment or two they were silent. 'I saw some of your novel . . .' he said, changing his position in the chair.

She gazed at him curiously.

'"*Matilda,*"' he said, with emphasis. 'Yes, it was there on the chaise longue where you left it. I know you will send it to Godwin, and I know what he'll say. But I beg you not to let him see it. We have quite enough trouble with your father already. For goodness sake Mary, it tells of a mother who dies giving birth to a daughter. The daughter then goes to Scotland for a change. – How very inventive. – And what happens then when she returns, all grown up and beautiful? Well, she so resembles her mother the father falls in love with her.' He gave a strange little laugh. 'It's an incestuous story, my dear. And all that stuff about suicide . . . I ask you. Do you actually expect your father to like it? Your mother tried to kill herself twice, and you know too well what I suffer because of . . .' He stopped off quickly, then continued. 'He won't publish it I tell you. In fact, he'll be damned offended. Let it be!'

She turned from him angry. 'You ought never to have read it,' she said quietly. 'I did not give you permission.'

He leant forward and smiled. 'Do you not realise how your writing intrigues me? – You read *my* work and I allow it. I never complain. I like you reading my work. Our writing reveals our thinking in ways that talk never can. And in any case, Mary, you have often been silent when I've wanted to talk with you. – But I know you will try to get your father to publish that story and you shouldn't. You shouldn't even send it. Work on your dramas instead.'

'I shall do as I wish,' she said flatly. 'You mustn't dictate to me, Percy. I will not have it!'

He looked downwards, silent.

'It's best you don't talk to me Percy,' she sighed. 'You say you are ill, but all you want is attention. How you infuriate me sometimes. – So you've read my story. If the novel does well people will think it is Percy Bysshe Shelley who wrote it, not me, for that is the way it goes. And that would please you, wouldn't it?'

'You are being irrational,' he said straightening. 'Do stop it. It is most unfair. If I am questioned about *Frankenstein*, I say that I wrote the introduction, no more than that. I am fascinated by electricity of course, as you know. The thought of electricity excites me.' He gazed at the ceiling. 'Aurora borealis, for instance, those incredible shimmering colours that are sometimes seen in the sky in certain places, they are a sort of omen to many, they are God's wrath for our sins; to attempt to explain them through science – to suggest it is just *electricity*, a physical phenomenon, is seen as heresy.' He shook his head confounded.

Again they were silent, thoughtful.

'I have always wanted to see them,' Mary said abstractedly.

Shelley continued. 'Those glorious colours come into being when the wind and sun come together in very special ways; it is a sort of love. I do believe they crackle when they kiss.'

Mary smiled, amused.

He waved a finger in the air. 'Electricity you see has ardour and feeling. Those lights have been seen for ages, even by the ancient Greeks. How it happens is a mystery. But I suspect it will soon be discovered, there are scientists busy at work.'

'There are always scientists at work,' she sighed. 'But is it right to find everything out and use it for ourselves? Perhaps we shouldn't. Perhaps such inquiry has a price.'

'Perhaps it can bring the dead back to life,' he whispered, narrowing his eyes and giving her a knowing look.

'And then?' She frowned. 'You know what happens in my story. Doctor Frankenstein searches for the elixir of life and it does not matter what is sacrificed in the endeavour.'

'And your seaman, Robert Walton, your captain, the Arctic explorer, searches for "the region of beauty and delight." Shelley clapped his hands with approval. 'He wants to find a place that has never ever been visited before, to accomplish something new and marvellous, never mind that he risks his life and that of his crew. Yes, my dear, it is an interesting moral tale.'

'Folly, folly,' murmured Mary.

'Life is a game of exploration,' said Shelley with a shrug. 'Even the stories, the poems we write, are an exploration of feelings and possibilities, a quest for enlightenment . . .'

She sat stroking her heavily swollen middle. The child was well near due and eager for birth.

'There has been a massacre in England,' he said, drawing a breath. 'Hundreds of people have been injured; some have been trampled to death by sabre welding cavalry. Can you imagine?' He screwed up his face at the thought. 'I wasn't sure if I should tell you. It's a pretty stressful business.'

'Where was it?' she asked. The child moved strong within her.

'St Peters Fields in Manchester. People were killed. – Hunger, hunger, those people are giving their labour for nothing. It's wrong. They are demanding reforms and universal suffrage, arguing that if the vote included working men and not just those who owned property then the government would spend quite differently. I have talked with Byron about it. The people are livid with anger. When people are hungry they fight. The price of grain is kept high, which suits domestic producers, but those laws were made to protect the English farmers from cheap foreign imports now the cost of bread has risen so high the poor are starving.'

'But why did they bring in the cavalry?' She wondered about her father's thoughts back home. He hated riotous behaviour and claimed it negated reason.

Shelley talked on heatedly. 'The crowd had violent intentions.

And I'm not surprised – they should rise like lions! They can't just let the government starve them to death.'

'You are quite incensed,' she said, seeing he was white with fury.

'I am indeed, and I wish I was in England right now.' He spoke through his teeth angrily. 'I shall write to Byron. I suspect he will want to address it in the House of Lords.'

Flushed from the emotional exchanges, Mary went to the window and stared outside. 'And Claire?' she said quietly. 'What is to happen with Allegra?'

'The child's health worsens,' Shelley said gravely.

'Has Byron said so?' She turned to him surprised. She had scarcely spoken with Claire of late. She gazed at her husband sadly; the light of love had gone from his eyes, and she feared it had gone from her own.

Shelley nodded. 'Yes, I received a letter. But I don't fully know what is happening. I shall have to find out.'

'Have you told Claire?'

'Yes.' He breathed in deeply and continued. 'She would have gone to see her already, but you are quite weary of soul, my dear. Now be honest, how can she leave you?'

She looked at him sharply. 'Are you trying to blame me for keeping Claire from her duty?'

'I blame you for nothing. I am simply saying what is true.' Closing his eyes he pressed his hands on his chest. 'My dearest love, do not torture me so. My very heart complains.'

'What's wrong with me, Percy? Have I gone mad?' she said shakily.

He shook his head. 'No, my love, but you certainly might if you don't take heed. Madness sneaks up from behind; we don't know its face.' He thrust out his hands. 'My darling Mary, come back to me!'

She went to him and rested her head on his lap, wanting to say with strength that she would always love him, always support him whatever misfortunes befell them. She longed for those precious words but they would not come. But her spirits rose up; the move to Florence which they'd talked about revived her. The baby was due in November, Percy's friend, Dr Bell, lived in Florence. It gave her comfort to think he would be there for her confinement and Percy promised that tomorrow he would sort out the move.

31

Another Letter

Something scuffled beside him, some creature living by the water, but it was gone in seconds. Percy gazed at the bright afternoon sky, watching the rolling clouds, and contemplating the countless men who had died in war fighting for causes seemingly crucial because someone had said so. He could feel the march of history through the centuries, the mighty monuments built and smashed in the name of victory . . . He sighed then fell to thinking again about Claire's predicament, her pain, her anguish at the thought of losing Allegra to Byron. Perhaps he would go to see him. Perhaps he wouldn't. Just now he felt nauseas and his hands trembled so badly he could not write.

For the time being, however, matters went on as before, he and Claire went walking discussing her problems and hopes for the future, while Mary heavy with child stayed at the villa resting.

Earlier that day while the others were out, there'd been a loud rapping on the door and a youth had passed her a letter. Having discharged his duty he'd looked at her anxiously, then leapt on his horse and galloped off. There hadn't been time to ask who he was or where he had come from and soon he was out of sight.

Opening it quickly, she found it had come from one of their previous maids and her husband Paulo, a couple who had assisted them for a brief while in the past. It was a most unpleasant letter and she feared it. Were they trying to get money from Shelley through blackmail? She sat down shakily trying to remember . . . The dark figure of the stranger with the baby rose again in her mind. Had she given birth to a child by Shelley? The thought went through her like a knife. Was it possible? The letter certainly implied it. Their maids rarely stayed long and she tried to recall those who had come and gone during their various moves. She closed her eyes. 'Let it go away,' she murmured. 'Let it go away!' She sat down shakily. The letter contained such vitriol towards Shelley it was strange, for those who had aided them rarely got to speak with him and did not know him. Tears fell down her face. Shelley had been the most intimate being in her life, the one she'd confided in, even adored, he was almost her very self. The words were cruel, but she couldn't ignore them. Painful thoughts of betrayal flooded her mind. Might the child have been Claire's? For months she had worn loose clothing and at times had become nauseas, taking to her bed in the way of a woman with child. Had Shelley and Claire hidden the truth? She sat back in her chair, grimacing with pain. Perhaps Claire had given birth on one of the weeks she had claimed to be visiting Byron . . . though it hardly seemed likely, her feelings for Allegra were real and strong and she'd surely have wanted her baby. But Allegra was the daughter of George Gordon Byron, peer and politician, and a famous poet. How could she ever have confessed to being pregnant by Shelley with all his associated villainy? All their lives would be ruined. Mary went to lie on the chaise longue where she wept into the silent room. The baby was Shelley's whichever way she looked at it, either with the maid or with Claire. Or perhaps it was just a conspiracy. She breathed in deeply and sat up. Yes, that's what it was, a conspiracy! Shelley had enemies and people were out to destroy him.

After a couple of minutes she found she felt better. But Claire – Percy – did she *really* know them? Did anyone really know the true nature of another? In fact, did they know their own, or was it revealed to them slowly, act by act, decision by decision, over time.

The baby turned in her womb and she pressed her hands on her middle. Percy's baby. Percy, her husband. Feelings of fear and disappointment raced through her mind. The letter suggested talk about the stranger had now reached the ears of Byron, who'd become more intent than ever on keeping Allegra from Claire.

What did he know that she, Mary Wollstonecraft Shelley, hadn't been aware of?

But Byron distrusted Claire, asserting she could never raise Allegra in case she might morally corrupt her! The thought was absurd. Or was it? Claire had said it was Byron's intention to have Allegra placed in a convent, suggesting Italy could often be a dangerous place for children. Claire had protested and written back in a fury. Convents were cold and unhealthy, she'd argued, and the food was disgusting. Allegra would be neglected; she'd have little if any education and wouldn't be loved. – But Claire couldn't have her. Claire, terrible Claire, with oh such a bad reputation. Mary balked at that. – What of Byron's reputation, what of Shelley's reputation? Both men were heavily criticised, but no-one ever dared snub them, for was not Byron a peer of the realm, and wasn't Percy the son of Sir Timothy Shelley, 2nd Baronet of Castle Goring. Such men professed to have standards of ethics. But did they? Byron talked a lot about war. To fight for a cause was a great and potent thing to do, he'd said, but he did not seem to pursue any special purpose. And he was all too often drinking. She had thought her father a steady immovable man, but William Godwin clever and complex as he was had seriously let her down; she had reached for him in distress and found him wanting. She thought of Byron at Villa Diodati when the story of *Frankenstein* had first entered her mind. There had been much talk about women that night, about the way they trapped men into marriage, how they might lie about pregnancies . . . Mary knew women put their babies in convents when they didn't know what to do next . . .

Perhaps she would reply to the letter, and in no uncertain terms tell the cruel couple their accusations were misguided, even criminal. Or she might just throw it away and forget it! She did not want to discuss it with Shelley and Claire, for negative thoughts might interfere with the health of her baby. She rose stately from her chair; she was a mother, a wife, the sensible one who helped restore peace and order. She remembered the years of her childhood, when she'd comforted her father in his loneliness, she remembered how it had been after Mary Jane's arrival, when everything changed and she'd been sent to Dundee and had been forced to find hidden strengths to combat her sadness. Must there always be pain, she asked herself. Happiness, it seemed, was a thing apart, only occasionally bursting into her life like sunshine. She longed for the move to Florence.

Hoping to find some peace in her phantasmagoric life, Mary settled down in Florence, and Percy Florence Shelley entered the world with ease on 12th November, 1819. This was happiness indeed! His limbs were long and strong, and his nose, thought Mary, was decidedly like her father's. It gave her comfort to think he might be like her father, for Godwin was an acknowledged scholar and a man of substance on the whole, and she believed it was only lack of money that sometimes diminished him and the overbearing temperament of his wife, Mary Jane.

Now, with her new baby boy, Mary was all light and power. Curious tourists spied through the windows. Friends came to visit. She took to studying Greek in the evenings and worked on her writing. Shelley went wandering to seek inspiration, sometimes with Claire, sometimes alone. Reading his notes she saw that the statues in the Uffizi galleries had inflamed his sensualities for he wrote about eyes "swimming with pleasure", swollen lips and sensuous limbs, and had written down ideas for poems. But her soul was distanced from him now.

'It's not that I don't love you,' she faltered, when he came to embrace her. 'I shall always love you, but I feel we have changed . . . We have altered and grown apart.'

'But people must develop and grow,' he protested, confused and hurting. 'They must. We have been through much travail. We have dared unfamiliar territory, talked with people who speak in another language, their minds are different from ours, new experiences, new environments shape us in different ways.' He spoke earnestly. 'Mary, I need you.'

But she turned away from him fearful. She was not with him. She felt as if she were sleep walking, afraid to wake up. 'Let's not talk about it now,' she murmured. 'Not now Percy. You have your freedom, my dear, which is what you have most desired. You need not feel hard done by.'

Shelley gazed at her intently. And after a few more minutes staring around the room, he turned and went to the door.

'I must arrange for the maid to do various things for the baby,' Mary said one morning, as Shelley sat reading. She quickly found pencil and paper. 'You have chosen the maid carefully; she is capable as well as pretty. Well done, Percy, well done. And Claire will be away for a while so the girl is going to be busy.'

For a moment or two they were silent.

'I am not too happy about Claire going away,' he said quietly. He lifted his eyes from his reading.

'She will be gone but briefly, my dear. Have no fear,' said Mary with an air of nonchalance. 'She only told me yesterday. She wants to see Byron, and is intending to stay nearby.'

He spoke tiredly, as if in a trance of thought. 'I'm surprised she didn't let me know. She's been quite withdrawn of late, however. Yes, she must go to see Byron. I don't know what will come of it though. I doubt the Llewellyns will be allowed to let her inside.'

'There is bound to be a catastrophe,' Mary said sighing. 'Claire will make sure of that. But it's right to let Byron know her feelings in person rather than in a letter, which might be intercepted.'

'Exactly.' Shelley put down his book and stretched his arms above his head tiredly. 'I might have to join her later, of course, to ensure the best outcome. I will not let him upset her. He's done quite enough of that.'

'Byron will do as he wants,' Mary said, nonchalantly. 'But at least she might see what is happening rather more clearly.'

Shelley sat pondering, tapping his fingers on the wooden arm of the chair. 'He will probably put Allegra in a convent regardless.' He shook his head at the thought. 'Oh, he will, Mary, he will. I can tell he has it in mind. He likes the idea of convents.'

'I think you are right,' Mary said assuredly. 'That's what will happen. And Claire can do nothing to prevent it. But the child is quite ill at present. It will be good to know how she is faring.'

He turned to look at her straight. 'And will you be angry if Allegra is placed in a convent?'

'Allegra isn't my child,' she murmured, looking at him straight. She saw that Shelley looked perplexed. He had only turned one or two pages of his book that morning. She could feel his helplessness now and wondered how he would be if he had to replace her. *Really* replace her. She didn't think anyone could give him the freedom he needed as she did herself; freedom to talk, freedom to think, freedom to enter the future and past with equal vigour, and freedom to love . . . She drew herself up and straightened. She would not let herself ever fall apart in the way she had done before. She felt different now in both body and soul. The ghosts of her dead children were always beside her, along with the ghost of her mother, and she knew she had to stay strong for her new baby.

32

The Lonely Business Of Living

'Can unbelievers be pure in heart?' Gertrude Llewellyn asked her husband one morning, while peeling potatoes for dinner. 'I wonder about it, you see. I would like to be pure in heart.'

'And you are not?' said Frederick. He frowned and gazed at the beautifully beamed ceiling of Byron's kitchen. 'You say you are an unbeliever, but how do we know what to believe in? His lordship and Mr Shelley might argue all night but they never reach any conclusions.'

'Perhaps they can't,' Mrs Llewellyn said sagely, plunging the peeled potatoes into a bowl of glistening clean water. 'It's all about faith, you see, believing in something you don't understand and accepting it.'

'Ah that,' said Frederick, stroking his chin and frowning, 'the last refuge of the desperate.'

For a moment or two they were thoughtful. Frederick helped himself to another cup of tea. It was early morning. The sun shone through the windows in piercing swords of light, illuminating Fredrick's large proud nose beneath his grey mischievous eyes. 'Mr Shelley doesn't believe in God,' he said abstractedly. 'He wrote a pamphlet as a student once claiming he was an atheist and the university banished him.' Frederick grinned. 'Didn't put him off though, his own notions are all he cares for, just like his lordship.'

'It seems to me,' said Mrs Llewellyn, with a deep intake of breath, 'that some things matter to Mr Shelley more than we think.' She frowned. 'His lordship must hear all of Mr Shelley's troubles. And the man is always on the run. He's scared of his own shadow.'

'Oh he's a very live coal Mr Shelley, very excitable. His lordship tries to calm him down.' Frederick spoke with certainty. 'His lordship has an easier temperament though. That's when he's not having nightmares. Poets and nightmares, what can you do with them. – Shelley's wife wrote a story, you know, called *Frankenstein*, about putting together bits and pieces of corpses to make the body of a man.'

'But what is the use of that?' said Gertrude Llewellyn, wincing.

'Well, in this story, a spark of electricity brings him to life.'

'Never,' said Gertrude. She laughed at the thought.

'Well, it's only a story, my dear. It's a horror story, you see. I don't know what happens till I read it. His lordship is lending me a copy.'

'Ugh, what a horrible tale,' said Gertrude, suddenly thoughtful. 'I wonder what Mr Shelley is coming for today. His lordship won't budge an inch if it's about Allegra. And that poor little girl is so ill she can scarce take a breath. And what a to-do there has been about that woman who kept coming with the baby, hanging around the villa like a ghost. It makes you shiver. And now I am told her baby is dead. I'm not surprised though, she carried it hither and thither like a bundle of rags. I'll bet it was left to freeze all night in the cold.'

'So sad,' sighed Frederick. He bit his lip thoughtful. 'And the mother has now disappeared. Very mysterious. But I see there's a sort of tranquillity between his lordship and Mr Shelley now. Last time he came they went sailing.'

'But Mr Shelley can't swim,' said Gertrude, dropping a potato on the floor as she said it. 'It's easy to drown in Venice, especially if you drink that laudanum.'

'How do you know he drinks laudanum?' Frederick Llewellyn looked at her surprised.

'I've seen him. He has it in a bottle in his pocket.'

'And how do you know he can't swim?' her husband persisted.

'I heard him telling his lordship. It shocked me. I wonder that he never learned. I heard he did a lot of rowing as a boy and he's plenty of brains.'

Frederick shook his head at the thought. 'He's plenty of brains for writing poetry, but he looks so pale and unwell. I doubt he's very strong in body.' Frederick Llewellyn stood up, all six feet of him above her. 'I was swimming at three years of age.'

Gertrude Llewellyn laughed. 'Oh you swim like a fish. And so does his lordship. His lame foot never holds him back. You have to admire him.'

'Oh, his lordship's a man amongst men.'

For a moment or two only the sound of Frederick pouring out tea entered the silence.

'But I so want to be blessed,' said Gertrude, sighing heavily.

'I'm sure you do, my dear.' Her husband sighed and faced her. 'And I expect you are. That's another curious word isn't it, what does it mean to be "blessed?"'

Gertrude stared at the floor. 'I suppose it means gaining mercy or something. But you have to go through the narrow gate to get it.'

'What?' said Frederick gazing at the white potatoes sparkling in the morning sunlight. His wife murmured words from the bible

'"Enter through the narrow gate; for the gate is wide and the way is broad that leads to destruction, and there are many who enter through it. For the gate is small and the way is narrow that leads to life, and there are few who find it"'

'Aye, little gates and narrow pathways are the scourge of my existence,' sighed Frederick. 'Oh, the lonely business of living. We are born alone, and we die alone. We are just the dream of the elements.'

'Now you're talking like his lordship,' Gertrude said with a laugh.

'Oh, you're probably right,' said Frederick. 'He's an excellent thinker and he never keeps me outside, he makes me take part, and once he's excited my brain my thoughts go full speed ahead. The man is a true genius.'

'And you think it rubs off?'

Frederick straightened. 'I daresay it does. In a certain sense, that is, as far as a man of my station is allowed. I mustn't get too clever for me station Gertrude.'

'So there are times when you pretend not to think?'

'That's it. But it isn't much to ask if that's how his lordship wants it. I'm sensible and that's how it is.'

'And you never want to change how it is?'

'Not as he'd notice, my dear.' He kissed her cheek tenderly. 'But don't you worry about that. I've got Lord Byron right where I want him and he knows I'm his man.'

'You mightn't be his man much longer,' said Gertrude, frowning. 'He's getting very serious with the countess. He might take off with her. She'll not be in need of any servants in that palace.'

'Aye and her married an' all. Her husband knows the whole of the story, but he doesn't bat an eyelid.'

'He's twice her age, that's why,' Gertrude said with disgust.

Frederick Llewellyn shrugged and smiled wryly.

'So she married the count for his money did she,' said his wife, 'and his lordship is just for entertainment.'

'Oh, he's more than just entertainment, there's a lot of silences between them, long sighs and such. And she likes Allegra.' Frederick spoke with satisfaction. He loved Allegra, and Gertrude had made her a very pretty doll which she carried everywhere she went.

'Yes, she's kind to her,' said Gertrude, smiling at the thought. And the countess talks to his lordship in ways that delight him, and she isn't afraid to argue with him either. She knows a lot about Napoleon and his conquests. – They talk about the Carbonari, who are still in mind of the French revolution and want to defend the rights of ordinary people. They talk so earnestly.'

'Ah the Carbonari!' Frederick pointed a finger in the air as if to mark the well known name. 'The Italian revolution against Austrian rule. The Italians round here often speak of them.' He shook his head concernedly. 'Revolution, revolution everywhere. Be careful what you say though. There's a lot of babble about revolts. I have heard his lordship deliver some powerful speeches to the countess.

There is fierce fight in his blood. The countess listens and claps. But you're right, dear wife, if he goes to live with the countess he won't have any need of us and we'll have to return to England.'

Gertrude stopped her work for a moment, listening for more, but Frederick had done with words for a while that morning.

It was now 1821 and little Percy Florence, so called because of his birthplace, was an energetic and lively child approaching two years of age. He stood to attention when his father required him to listen, and hung on his every word. He was very much loved and it seemed highly intelligent. Mary had learned that the child rumoured as her husband's had perished and that the woman in pursuit of him had gone, no-one knew where, or indeed who she was, nor was it known how the innocent baby had died. Mary however, could not deny the relief she felt as she cast the weight from her soul.

But there was still the problem of Allegra. Must the child sever connections with everyone who loved her all because of her father was stubborn? Byron made lots of decisions without their knowledge and usually carried them through, while Claire went away on her own to stay with people she knew who would listen to her miseries. It had come to pass that Allegra had been living in the convent of Bagnacavallo, a most unsuitable, secluded and lonely place for a child's essential development according to Claire. She had hoped her daughter would live in a place she might visit, she said, without Byron's interference, and had spoken to Mary of a family she knew who would very much like to take her. But the idea had passed and Claire had fallen into a state of abject despair. She did not beg of Byron now to think of her as mother and protector of their four year old daughter, in fact her appeals were exhausted, and Byron acted as if Claire no longer existed. But exist she did, and intensely! Anger raged in her blood and she gave vent to it constantly. Her daughter living in a convent! It would not do! And it had happened surreptitiously.

And something else had happened behind her back. During the last few years Byron had taken several mistresses, his latest being the married Countess Teresa Guiccioli, who he had now gone to live with in the Guiccioli palace along with her husband, who was very much older than Teresa and had taken warm heartedly, it seemed, to the handsome young Lord Byron, him being English aristocracy and all. In a letter to Mary, Frederick Llewellyn had said he'd expected it would happen, and that the countess was good to Allegra. Allegra had been taken from the convent and had now been moved into the palace to live with her father and the Guicciolis, and Lord Byron had taken Llewellyn and his wife to assist them. Gertrude Llewellyn understood his tastes in food and Frederick understood his animals.

Claire despaired even further when she heard that Allegra had grown deeply attached to her "Mammina", meaning, of course, the countess, and that Frederick Llewellyn's wife, was making rag dolls for Allegra, which the child "utterly adored". Claire wept and moaned while Mary tried to console her, suggesting it was all for the best, though she had no idea what the best might be for the situation was impossible. According to Frederick Llewellyn, the countess was happy for Allegra to live with them, but only on a temporary basis; in time she must return to the convent. She herself had had a convent education, she said, and claimed to have benefitted by it. His lordship had written to the Hoppners, who had agreed that the convent would be a safe haven for Allegra, given the difficulties faced by children in Italy. Claire however, had protested and complained that her daughter's little bruised heart had been battered. It was all too much! Surely she would die of heartbreak!

'Claire can do nothing to influence Byron's intentions,' Mary said to Shelley, one morning. 'And Allegra is taken from pillar to post. Claire is constantly tormented. She has a rich and engaging mind that could be put to far better use.'

'And what do you suggest?' murmured Shelley. He did not raise his eyes from his work, and continued to write on quickly.

'I think she should find employment,' Mary answered flatly. 'Her choice, of course. It is only an idea.'

'Have you thought what leaving us might do to her?' he said, over his shoulder. 'Should she find this "employment"?'

Mary persisted. 'She needs to have a change of environment, talk with other people, do something useful like . . .'

'Like what?' He turned to her slowly. There was a silence.

He had an air of resentment about him and she knew she would have to argue. Would Claire live with them for ever?

'You never said this before,' he said frowning.

'Before what?' She saw she had touched a nerve.

'Before Allegra was living with the countess. It isn't too bad, you know. The child will be clothed and fed to the highest standard. It is bound to be better than living in the convent, surely. Claire would be wise to stay silent.'

'You mean she should just let Byron do as he wants?' said Mary, looking surprised. 'Allegra is Claire's child, too.'

'I know these things, my dear. But Claire can't keep on fighting for the child, for Allegra will be torn apart by it all. Don't you see?' His pen trembled in his hand. Their days together of late were often a misery, he was tightly knit with Claire and Mary believed his most fervent feelings were all for her stepsister now. Tired from her pregnancy and highly sensitive, it was irksome to hear Claire's high pitched grievances echoing around the villa, and little Percy's pale blue eyes looking sad. "Bring her to live with us Mama," he would say. "If only it were possible, my love," she would tell him perplexed. "I have told you before; Lord Byron will not send her." But she was half glad of the fact and couldn't imagine them all living together. Seeing Shelley was waiting, she wiped her eyes with her handkerchief and braced herself. 'You have done all you can,' she said softly. 'I don't know what else you can do.'

Shelley turned away and wrote on.

'She enjoys reading and instructing,' said Mary, irritated looking at his back. How often he turned from her now. 'Perhaps she would like to be a governess.'

Shelley put down his pen and turned again slowly. 'A governess? You want Claire to be a governess? But when would she see us if she had to live away?' He clasped his hands and looked downwards, hiding his expression. 'And I rather doubt she would *like* it.'

'On the contrary Percy,' Mary said, determined. 'She would, I'm sure. And she could visit us just as she wanted. A governess isn't a prisoner.'

He shrugged. 'Oh, I don't know about that.' He breathed in deeply, frowning and vexed. 'Do you have something in mind?'

Her soul lit up at the thought that he might agree. He was hardly likely to accept her idea, but once she had started it was easier to unfold her plan. She had been making a few enquiries. – Claire could live with the Boiti family, who were good and caring people. Doctor Antonio Boiti was physician to the Grand-Duke Ferdinand III of Lorena. His wife was German and Claire might learn another language while teaching English to the children. Mary's tone was emotional and she faltered slightly as she spoke.

'I can see all this upsets you, my dear,' said Shelley. He spoke more calmly now. 'It isn't good for the baby. You haven't to let things disturb you – or you know what might happen. He gazed at their son, playing with his toys on the floor.

'We are always discussing Allegra,' Mary said uneasily, 'where she is to live, who she will live with, how her mother must be supported and cared for, but . . .'

He searched her eyes quickly. 'I know, I know. The bother is driving our poor dear Claire insane, but I'm not sure working as a governess would suit her.' He got down playing with his son. 'My boy, my boy, you look so well!' he said, brushing back the child's hair. 'And your eyes sparkle with the future. I'm so glad. Oh, how I love little Percy. I won't have you injured, not for anything, neither in body nor mind!'

'Will Claire go away?' asked the boy.

'Perhaps,' said his father, his eyes darkening as he spoke.

'Allegra doesn't come to see us,' the boy said plaintively.

'No,' said Shelley. 'She doesn't. And I doubt she ever will.'

Mary looked down at them, watching her husband's long white fingers winding through their child's hair, noting her son's great blue eyes searching his father's and her heart filled up with thoughts of the children she'd lost. Shelley grew serious. He stood and took hold of her hand, kissing her palm tenderly. 'All will be well, my beloved. 'Trust me,' he murmured.

There was a silence, till the boy said softly. 'Mama, the sleeves of my coat are too short. I shall need you to buy me another.'

'You grow so fast,' laughed Mary. 'I believe you will be tall like your father.'

'And perhaps he'll write poetry,' said Shelley, smiling at the boy. 'It had better be good if he does!'

'He will be just like his father,' smiled Mary. 'Your equal in all things.'

Shelley looked away, murmuring. 'I hope he will be more than my equal, for I believe I have fallen short.'

33

The Call Of The Water

The idea had overwhelmed her at first, but after they had all talked it over, Claire decided that becoming a governess to the Botie children in Florence, it was in her nature to teach and she'd been successful with her small brother. Mary and Shelley reassured her it would all work out, what's more if it didn't, she could always return, said Shelley, and need not yield herself to a cruel uncaring world; it would be but sacrilege to do so for life battered and broke people half a chance. Shelley sat frowning with displeasure, then lapsed into silence. Now though, Claire had changed and was in need of a new direction, said Mary, and teaching the Botie children English could be quite an uplifting experience. After much deliberation, Claire accepted the idea and made it her own. It would help her cope with her concerns over Allegra, she said. And she needed to be more independent. The kind and courteous letter she'd received from the Boties had helped her decide. She brewed a pot of tea which they all three drank together in a sort of ceremonial manner. There was nothing else for it, she would leave. What she really wanted however was Allegra, Byron and love, but it seemed she'd been robbed of all three. And so she packed her belongings and was very soon away. It had been a long five years.

'One thing I wonder,' Mary said later to Shelley, 'is whether she will settle . . . Oh, the uncertainty of it all! The countess has said

Allegra must return to the convent eventually, she has no intention of keeping her.'

'Claire will not settle anywhere until she hears what is happening with Allegra,' said Shelley flatly. 'How is she to teach the Botie children, when her own daughter is ill and she cannot see her.' For a moment he sat thoughtful. 'Some words speak to us in poetry,' others speak in prose,' he said gravely, 'and there are words that cannot speak to us at all for they are locked in the darkness of our souls.'

'All is not darkness, Percy,' she said brightly. 'The light floods in when we least expect it. That's how it is for me. I wait for the light and joy.'

'Not so for me,' he said grimly.

'You are Prometheus bound, my love, the lone genius,' she murmured.

'Ah yes, heaven's winged hound, constantly tears at my flesh,' he said, closing his eyes and wincing. 'Damned Jupiter and his tyrannical kingship! – Damn the lot of them!'

'Byron included, no doubt,' she said softly.

'I want so much to understand him,' Shelley said, letting his shoulders rise and fall in confusion. 'But how . . .'

'He is being difficult on purpose,' said Mary, sharply. 'I fear he enjoys his awkwardness. He thinks it makes him unfathomable. It doesn't, of course, it rather makes him intolerable. The countess won't care a bit about Allegra. She will humour Byron a while and pretend, but she won't keep Allegra there long. I wonder if the child likes her, she has her own little foibles, you know. She hides things, even hides herself sometimes. She won't be easy to manage.'

'I believe the Llewellyn's are there,' Shelley said, looking relieved. 'He relies on them a lot. They are quite familiar with Allegra and love her. But Claire has never heard a word from Augusta. Nor does she hear from Skinner Street. People are full of surprises.'

'Indeed,' Mary said softly. 'I suspect Augusta is jealous of the countess. I wonder how she feels now her brother is living with such a wealthy, beautiful woman. I expect she is a little put down.' A flood of unpleasant emotions came to her as Shelley referred to her home, and she imagined her father talking with Mary Jane, and that awful look of I told you so spreading across Mary Jane's face.

Next day, seated by the water, Mary heaved a sigh of relief. But her mind swirled with speculations. She was now in a sort of limbo. Claire had gone, but it was she who had made it happen, not Shelley. Perhaps he would hate her for that. She tried to relax. She had nothing to reproach herself for; she had done her best for her stepsister, if anything she had probably been over solicitous about her for Claire would take care of Claire, come what may. Shelley however, was hers, not Claire's, though Mary had built up stories about Shelley in her mind, tortured herself with thoughts about the stranger with the child, created mythologies about Shelley and Claire and the secret life they might have led. But were they not simply imaginative musings created by fear. In a crude exchange of letters, she had insisted to the Hoppners that "Claire had no child", they had lived in lodgings, she'd said, and she knew all the entrances and exits. The very idea was absurd. But however she tried to stop them, the thoughts continued to torment her.

She shivered, the afternoon sun had gone and she gazed at the cold white sky. *The child, the child* . . . She'd had such bad feelings about Claire and Shelley there were days she could scarcely breathe, and she knew that Claire wouldn't stay long with the Boitis. Wasn't it the whole problem of life; emotions having their way, flying wherever they would, uncaring for the mind they inhabited. Feelings made people bold, jealous and destructive. Were they not the ruling force in life all told?

Letters went back and forth, to and from Claire. She wrote to Mary, and she wrote to Shelley separately. Occasionally Mary found a letter on his desk and would cast her eyes across the words. There was a youthfulness in his exchanges with Claire, something he had lost with her. She didn't want to share him like that with Claire. Not now, not ever. She covered her face with her hands, as if the feel of her cool palms might soothe away her fears. Everything seemed worse than before.

Time passed by slowly. She wondered how it was with Allegra and Byron and the countess, how it was with Claire and the Boitis. She went out walking with her son. It was good to be out with the boy, holding his small hand. They did not talk, he was a quiet and contemplative child and she hoped he wouldn't be capricious like his father or need to take laudanum. She had noticed Percy's bottle would be half empty then full by turns though how the tincture was acquired she did not know, and neither did she ask, the heaviness in his eyes and the weariness of his sighs rendered her silent. The boy grew strong and with his thick glossy hair brushed back, looked very much like his father and gazed about everywhere with the observant eyes of an artist.

It was a quiet still afternoon when Shelley rushed into the villa his voice loud and tremulous. 'Come to me, my love,' he pleaded, falling into a chair. 'Give me your hand. I have terrible news.'

She dropped down by his side. He was cold and trembling. 'What is it?' she gasped. Her thoughts moved quickly to her son out with the maid. Was he safe?

'Allegra has died,' he cried. 'Ah! – Claire has been inconsolable. The child died in the convent.'

Mary's heart beat fast. It was so unexpected. 'But how?' she asked, trying to keep her composure.

'They think it was malaria,' Shelley pressed Mary's hand to his lips.

'"Malaria"?' she whispered. 'Oh, my love.' Terror came up in her again. 'Poor Allegra. Poor Claire. – 'And Byron?' she sobbed.

'He is lost in sorrow and guilt, he scarcely saw her after she'd returned to the convent. I believe she wrote letters, but he left them unanswered. She had begged him to visit . . .'

Mary lowered her voice. 'They sent her back to the convent and the child's letters were unanswered. I can hardly bear it. Did she . . . Did she die quickly?'

'I don't know. I called on Byron and heard the story from Llewellyn. After that, I went to see Claire. Llewellyn had written her a letter.'

'So you didn't see Byron at all?'

'No, he'd confined himself to his room and Llewellyn said it was best to leave him alone.'

'You would like to have seen him, of course?'

'Of course!' cried Shelley. 'There is much to be done, and I suspect he will need my support.' He spoke wearily, exhausted with grief.

She held her husband tightly, as if he were a weeping child. It was mid afternoon. 'I must go to see Claire,' she said softly. And she thought again of little William, her son, dead and buried in Rome, a child so eager for life. Where did such energies go? But at least he had lived beside her; no-one had taken him away.

Shelley was shuddering. 'I couldn't make Claire feel better,' he said miserably. 'She begged me to leave her.'

'And you did.'

'Yes, I came here, straight to you.'

For a few moments they were silent.

She clung to him and looked in his face. She needed so much to belong to him again.

'Oh, my treasure, my dear,' he said shakily. 'I'm so sorry.' He glanced about urgently. 'Little Percy is well, I take it?'

She nodded. 'He is out walking with the maid. We shall have to decide when to tell him.'

She gazed all about her. Shadows were forming in the room, stealing the light. Percy didn't believe in God, so could take no strength from the thought of a divine being. Byron in his grief might pray. Claire would probably crash her fists against the wall or even blaspheme. Just then she would like to have embraced her stepsister, oh how she felt for her loss! Doctor Frankenstein had shown it was folly to try to outwit the Almighty. She drew her husband close and kissed his soft blond curls, so warm with the scent of life. Allegra had lived five years. She'd been a strong and wilful child, earnest and bold like her mother and clever like her father.

"Her father" . . . She trembled at the thought. The worst of her fears rose in her mind. Was Byron really Allegra's father . . . or might it be Percy . . . And was the baby in the stranger's arms

Percy's also? She closed her eyes and tried not to think. She was used to pain, both physical and mental; it had become a part of her existence. Frankenstein's monster had seen life as cruel and unforgiving. She wasn't afraid or cowed by life herself, but how hard it had been to grapple with her losses. At least Allegra would now be spared further torment, for the child must surely have known much sadness and pain. Mary wished she'd tried harder. If only she'd joined with Claire and demanded the child's return! But what was done was done, and nothing could bring her back to life.

At length Percy got up. 'I need to go out,' he said, reaching for his coat and hat.

'Where are you going?' she asked him.

He stood for a moment motionless before her. 'I'm not sure. I shall take a boat ride I think.'

She saw that his eyes were afraid. 'Alone?' she asked weakly.

'No, no,' he said in a cold and distant voice. 'I'll call on our friends and see if I can find a companion.'

Mary sat silent. He was detached and withdrawn as he went to the door and opened it. She heard his footsteps by the window and listened until they had gone.

That night he didn't return.

It was a full six weeks before she heard about the storm, and all became clear when it was learned that his boat had been engulfed by gigantic waves and had sunk in ten fathoms of water. Three men were discovered dead on the beach off Viareggio, halfway between Lerici and Livorno, only identifiable by their clothing – that was apart from Shelley whose pocket held a copy of Keats' poems. The letter sent to Mary said the sea had devoured a lot of his face and hands and in order to conform to the Italian government's quarantine directives the men were buried in the sand. Later, his body was exhumed and cremated in a pyre. Those who attended included Byron and one or two others. She herself was absent for English customs ruled women should distance themselves from funerals in case of disease.

Shelley had gone to ashes, only his heart had outlasted the flames as if it might be saved for her. Mary told herself their love lived on

like a phoenix, a child of the sun. It could not and would not die.
When the heart was sent to her, she wrapped it in silk and kept it in
her writing case always beside her. His ashes were buried in the
Protestant Cemetery at Rome whilst a tablet above them held
words from Shakespeare's *The Tempest;*

> " . . . *Nothing of him that doth fade,*
> *But doth suffer a sea-change,*
> *into something rich and strange."*

Some days she went to the sea, her eyes searching the horizon.
A wild instinct said she might see him. The thought of seeing him
again in the flesh dominated her mind for months. People were
uneasy before her. She wept from shock and suffering. Then she
would watch her son, seeing her husband in his features and
movements. Yes, she told herself, in some magnanimous way the
dead lived on.